PLACE OF DRY WATER

BY

CHARLES WALKER

Published 2006 by arima publishing

www.arimapublishing.com

ISBN 1 84549 109 2

© Charles Walker 2006

Printed and bound in the United Kingdom

Typeset in Garamond 11/16

Swirl is an imprint of arima publishing.

arima publishing
ASK House, Northgate Avenue
Bury St Edmunds, Suffolk IP32 6BB
t: (+44) 01284 700321

www.arimapublishing.com

For Maz

PROLOGUE

The girl reined in hard and the bay stallion dropped from a racing gallop to a standstill in seconds, creating furious clouds of swirling sand and dust from the thorny scrub beneath his hooves. He stood excitedly, pawing the ground and blowing hard through his nostrils which glowed red inside, through the dilated membranes. Small flecks of foam marked the hard, bunched muscle on his shoulders and he glistened with sweat from the early morning exertion.

The first rays of the African sun caught the slowly settling particles, holding them in suspension, making them pulsate with all colours of the rainbow before finally releasing them to settle back to the ground.

The girl stood up in the saddle to drink in the raw glory of the sunrise. Ash blond hair cascaded onto her shoulders and a shake of her head placed it in order. She inhaled deeply, letting the still cool, crisp air invigorate her.

She sank to the leather of the saddle, letting it mould to her body again. The Kalahari desert beckoned her onwards and she gazed into its hearth. A herd of zebra started to cross her field of vision and she focused on them with a grin. Dancer saw them too and he readied himself for what she would certainly do.

Jade held him steady, like a jet fighter on the brakes with engines screaming, then she leant forward down his neck and whispered in his ear.

" Let's go wake them up "

She released the pressure on the reins and just brushed his flanks with her booted heels. Dancer rocketed forward with Jade pressed down onto the smooth mane which she brushed and combed each day.

Within seconds they were amongst the startled zebra. The herd responded as she knew they would - by panicking and stampeding. She guided Dancer into the middle of the herd and let him run with them. The pair jinked and swerved with the animals as the herd changed shape and speed like a flock of birds. They came up close and bumped into her legs, sandwiching Dancer so that he couldn't turn, and then melted back to either side. Clouds of dust and noise enveloped them and it didn't matter. They were in another world. She had done this before, loved it and was pretty sure Dancer did too, but she also knew when to stop. Zebra running like this have an explosive energy, but not as much stamina as her mount. They would soon be blown, stop and confront whatever it was that had spooked them. Her grandfather had once terrified her with a tale of exactly this situation happening to him as a youth, when he and others had dismounted to get closer to a small number of completely exhausted zebra. A male had lunged forward and bitten one of them south of the equator. They had thought it uproariously funny until the victim collapsed with blood pouring out.

Oupa, thought Jade, you only made me want the thrill more. But nevertheless, there's no way I'm getting off.

Jade eased the stallion back a little, intending to take him out through the side of the herd now. Without warning she was suddenly catapulted forward over Dancer's neck which had collapsed under her. She somersaulted in slow motion, seeing every animal and grain of swirling dust suspended around her. Then she hit the earth desperately hard, and with the help of a zebra hoof on her skull, the sun went out.

*****

The mid morning heat was taking its toll on the girl - only she didn't know it yet. She was still unconscious and had an impressive lump on the side of her head. If she could have wished unconsciousness to descend on Dancer, then she undoubtedly would have done so. If she could have wished death on him then she would have done that as well. For the horse was lying on the ground with his broken foreleg still down the hole which had caused their fall. He had been stunned for a short while as well, but the pain from the first hyena bite had brought him round.

Now the scavengers were circling warily, waiting for their chance. One of them had already been hit by a flailing hoof and had retired screaming. They knew they would win. It was just a matter of when. The horse knew it as well. He thrashed his head around, trying to keep them in sight all the time. Big brown eyes wide with fear and alarm.

They worried him in pairs. One ran forward to rip at his underbelly while another got his attention by pretending to go for his throat. Dancer soon grew weary, concentrating his reserve of strength on the creature that was actually trying to bite him. Then of course, the tactics changed. Jaws gripped his throat while he was unsighted and a cascade of blood soaked the coarse haired hyena. She hung on grimly until all movement stopped, until after the last pathetic beating of hooves on the ground was over, until the prize was certain.

CHAPTER

ONE

A blow on the head is never a good way to start the day and the small leopard cub with the torn ear was not about to disagree with that statement. She sat up swiftly, or as swiftly as the weight of her bloated and tightly stretched belly would allow, finishing up with both hind legs pushed out past the front ones, looking like a naughty and indignant kitten.

The immediate object of her fury was several feet away and would have been regarded with instant respect and fear by most other creatures, be they two or four legged. Indeed, most would proceed to put a healthy distance between themselves by the quickest available method. Torn Ear inclined her head slightly and stared across the floor of the den, considering her position.

Her gaze was returned by a pair of clear glittering eyes with that characteristic slight squint, and the head inclined very slightly to match that of the cub. It challenged the offspring to respond to the parental justice that had just been meted out.

The decision was reached, and to the accompaniment of cracked and treble growls of wrath, the cub launched a further assault on the front paw of the mother leopard, which had been the original target. She leapt at the offending paw but was surprised, when reaching the spot where it had been, to find it had been removed and was now descending on her, pinning her small wriggling form to the ground. Torn Ear struggled against the weight, pedalling frantically through thin air with all available legs until she was exhausted and ceased the fight.

Mother removed the huge paw and bent down to lick the little form back into life with short strokes of a rasping tongue. The desired effect was achieved and Mother picked the cub up by the scruff of the neck, carried her to the back of the cave where two others lay sleeping soundly, and gently put Torn Ear in amongst the bundle of fur, where she too fell asleep immediately.

The big leopard padded slowly away and then turned to look at her cubs. One was snoring quietly, although precisely which one was impossible to tell, and once in a while a cub twitched in its sleep. Her eyes wandered and rested on Torn Ear, quite literally, the black sheep of the family, for the cub was jet black from head to tip of constantly twitching tail. She was naturally puzzled as to the arrival of one black offspring but if she had to declare a favourite then she knew which it would be. If there was adventure to be had or trouble to be caused, then the little black cub was never far away. She disappeared on numerous occasions, to return bedraggled and exhausted from unknown adventures, and once had to be rescued from an acacia tree after trying to chase a baboon up it. As soon as the embarrassed primate realised the size of his would-be attacker he rapidly turned the tables. Only the timely intervention of her searching parent saved Torn Ear.

Ironically, the only injury the cub had ever sustained had been in play with her two brothers. A mock fight had got out of hand and a set of razor sharp milk teeth had pierced her left ear. She had jerked her head back to escape, hence the neat tear down nearly the whole length of the ear. Even at this early stage of her life it gave her a somewhat piratical appearance, the two parts never quite managing to act in unison, one being forward when the other was back.

Mother turned back and continued on to the mouth of the den. As far as she was concerned, this was the ideal home. The cave was about half way up a steep rocky slope; the path up to it being narrow, with a considerable drop off one side down to the dry and sandy river bed below. The entrance was just big enough to admit the full-grown leopard and was in fact a good foot off the ground, which necessitated an amount of undignified scrambling to gain entry. This also acted as a natural barrier, preventing the cubs from exploring outside when she was away. Inside, the cave stretched back for several yards and the roof rose steeply to give more than ample headroom. At one point in the roof the stone had split and fallen away to give a hole which allowed a through draught of air to ventilate the den and also provided a certain amount of light. It might also allow the rain in, but seeing as it was October, and the beginning of the Kalahari summer, that was the least of her worries.

The leopard left the cave and jumped softly down onto the patch of worn ground that constituted her balcony. From here she had a fine view of the river bed below her, and even in the diminishing early evening light she could still make out the acacia tree some distance away which was her larder at the moment.

The previous evening Mother had come across an injured springbok which had broken a foreleg. The creature was in agony and frightened to the point of insanity. When it sensed the leopard it was almost relieved that the end was in sight and made the killing stroke easy. Mother had straddled the carcass and dragged it several hundred yards to the old acacia tree where, after some effort, she had succeeded in lodging it on one of the higher branches.

She had already taken the cubs to feed just before dawn and now intended to repeat the performance, despite the fact that they were probably not yet hungry again. The uncertainty of a predator's life, especially where cubs are concerned, made it necessary to feed whenever possible. The next meal might be days away.

Mother turned back to the den entrance and slowly put her head inside, bringing it down softly so that her chin eventually rested on the hard rocky lip. This part she enjoyed best. Without making a sound she could virtually guarantee that within a few minutes the cubs would wake and stare at her questioningly with owlish eyes, full of sleep.

Then, when they became aware that food was on offer, all three would bound for the exit. At first Mother had found she needed to issue a few short peremptory grunts to call the cubs to eat, but as the days and weeks progressed, the need for sound decreased. So now she just watched the still sleeping bundle.

Sure enough, within a minute, a small black head appeared like a worm emerging from its burrow. This time there was no need for questioning looks, and all three raced the length of the den, only to get stuck together in the entrance.

Mother, having seen this show before, withdrew a little way to watch the bodies forcing an exit. For once, Torn Ear was last out. A slight confusion over limb ownership at the outset had left her with a fractional disadvantage which had been exploited to the full by her brothers.

The cubs knew where they were going, so Mother let them go ahead, in single file, while she brought up the rear with an eye open for hazards, of which the bush had plenty.

The family trotted along happily until a short way from the larder, when a familiar scent assaulted the adult. She sank to her belly to survey the ground ahead. So too did the cubs in front of her.

The big leopard was now fully alert and fighting anger was coursing through her veins. Food was to be protected if at all possible. It could mean life or death for her cubs. She was not about to give it up without a fight.

Slowly she crept past the inert cubs, giving them a low growl of warning in passing. Her eyes were now half closed, with hard, pin-sized pupils and her ears were flattened back against the short roundish head. As she crept forward, head close to the sandy parched earth, the muscles in her haunches alternately bunched and extended, creating the familiar fearsome profile of a hunting cat. Cautiously she moved through the dried yellow grass and scrub, skirting gradually to her right to ensure the acacia tree was upwind of her.

Eventually she rested behind a small thorn bush and was able to see, through the lengthening shadows, what she had guessed at earlier.

An old dog jackal was sitting at the bottom of the tree, gazing skywards, and wondering how he was going to persuade that feast of drying, now slightly putrified, collection of flesh and bones to join him at ground level.

He was a veteran of many confrontations and his reddish flanks were scarred in numerous places, with dry scabs formed over recent wounds on the nape of his neck. Every few seconds he dropped his head to allow the muscle to rest before turning his gaze upwards once more. So engrossed was he that he had failed to sense the return of the owner.

However, that fact was brought to his attention some ten seconds later when a bolt of black lightning streaked across the gap and succeeded in planting a set of deciduous incisors in the left cheek of his rump. The scarred warrior let out a howl of surprise and pain and jumped a good distance into the air.

By the time he returned to earth Mother was charging to the aid of her offspring. A formidable array of gleaming white teeth and the promise of a speedy demise eased the jackal's hunger pangs for the present. The small scavenger scrabbled around wildly in the loose dirt, seemingly uncertain of which way to go. He made his decision just as he could feel hot breath at his shoulder and darted off into the shadows. Mother came to a halt beside her daughter in a cloud of dust and blood red sand, relieved that she had seen the attack in time to prevent the jackal from retaliating. Brave the cub may be, but she was also foolhardy, inexperienced and easy prey for this would-be adversary.

Mother turned to face the cub and, by way of relieved parental retribution, issued a solid wall of snarling sound directed straight at the miscreant.

Torn Ear, basking in the glory of a successful attack, was almost blown over by the fury of the blast and stepped back a few feet. Never had she seen so much anger in her mother. For one usually without fear, she felt the slightest trepidation as Mother came closer to her and brought her head down to look straight into the eyes of the juvenile. Mother snarled once again, quickly and harshly, and snapped a pair of monstrous jaws in front of the cub.

Torn Ear jumped visibly and Mother promptly forgot the incident. The lesson had been learnt - it was time to concentrate on the original object of the foray again before other night scavengers made an appearance.

During the day, a hind leg of the carcass had shifted and now hung down from the branch where Mother had left it. The leopard looked up at the dangling limb and then launched herself at it, front legs and claws fully extended.

The big cat seemed to twist in mid-air like a gymnast and then both sets of claws found a hold on their target. For a moment both bodies hung in space as one and then, to the accompaniment of much snapping of dry branches they plummeted earthwards and landed in a heap.

At this point Dune brought his head up from the dry baked earth, where it had been firmly placed at Mother's order, to get a better view. The eldest of the leopard cubs, by a full five minutes, was never happier than when he was burrowing and playing in the vast sandy dunes which stretched out as far as the eye could see, above their den.

Mother had by this time managed to extricate herself from the tangle of bones and all three cubs trotted over to dinner. They were, however, still having a little trouble with their vastly oversized feet and every once in a while one would trip and collapse in a little cloud of dust, only to recover just as quickly and jockey for position again.

In actual fact there was not much edible material left on the carcass and the cubs found that with their small mouths and teeth, even that eluded them.

The meal soon degenerated into a game of hide and seek with the unfortunate springbok as the main cover. The adult leopard settled down some way from the tree with a large bone, broke it in two with a single movement of her jaws and began to gently remove the marrow from it. She would have preferred it to have been zebra, but it had been some months since she had tasted zebra marrow and was likely to be some time before she did so again.

While they relaxed, the last light from the sun finally disappeared and the African night arrived, with its customary speed. As it did, the orchestra of the night could be heard. Crickets began to zing and whirr and in the distance zebra could be heard giving their characteristic harsh sawing call. Mother knew it was time to head for home.

Although she was, if anything, a nocturnal creature, the night held more dangers for her cubs than the day. In a few months they would be strong enough and knowledgeable enough to accompany her during the hours of darkness, but for the time being they were still vulnerable.

Mother got up slowly and stretched out to her full length, arching her back in ecstasy as she did so. Then she led her family in single file back across the scrubland, which was now bathed in moonlight. There was a full moon just beginning to show and it turned the landscape into crisp images of intense black and white, with huge areas of inky dark shadows. The familiar features of their home territory were changed beyond recognition.

The female leopard, with her tail held high to expose the white fur at the tip to guide her cubs, led the family home without incident and deposited them at the front of the den.

Getting them in however, was more of a problem than getting them out. To make an exit, they simply fell out of the entrance and landed rather unceremoniously on the ground some fourteen inches below. To get them back in, Mother had to take hold of the scruff of their necks and lift them in. This was no problem in the early months, but as they grew they were obviously heavier to lift and Mother found it increasingly difficult. The operation was not helped by the fact that the offspring were beginning to develop a sense of dignity and were showing some objections to continuous manhandling. However, a couple of nights spent on the balcony in the surprisingly cool temperatures helped to dissipate the sense of dignity for the time being, and the cries of protest were small ones.

The exception to the rule was provided by the younger of the male cubs. From the age of six weeks he had developed the ability to jump with considerable ease and agility. By the time he was two months old he could enter the den by himself with the grace of a klipspringer. He revelled in this attribute and watched the antics of his brother and younger sister with glee as they tried unsuccessfully to emulate him and had to be lifted in. Quite naturally he was christened Spring.

It was some time before the cubs settled down in the den but Mother was eventually able to leave them. She took up her favourite position on the balcony.

She felt naturally at ease during the night, as if released from her responsibilities by the curtain of darkness, and stretched out, resting her head on giant paws.

The atmosphere of the night gently washed over her as waves lapping up on a deserted shore. The many different sounds were occasionally punctuated by the familiar call of the jackal, a long drawn out wail followed by a staccato ya ya ya. This addition to the orchestra passed unnoticed as the big cat relaxed.

As the night progressed so the moon rose higher and lit the landscape with its eerie brilliance. The intense velvety black of the sky was covered with sharp pinpricks of glowing light. Being in a tropical region, the stars burned with a brighter ferocity than their insipid colleagues in the distant hemispheres, and almost touched the ground where darkness met desert.

After a couple of hours Mother had recovered from the mental exhaustion of the day. She rose in one lithe movement and padded silently past the den entrance, climbed the rocky scree beyond and finally bounded over the ridge into the open desert. Here, vegetation was sparse, with only one or two thorn bushes visible from time to time. There was no underlying water to provide life for searching roots, as was the case in the fossil river valley, and as a consequence the desert was master.

Huge walls of sand were shifted and shaped by the wind - the landscape could change overnight. The cat climbed quickly to the high ridge of the nearest dune, her size and power suddenly dwarfed by the immense creations surrounding her. She looked around. The desert stretched to eternity in all directions ; the emptiness and vastness were overwhelming.

The big cat was a kitten again. She cast a glance behind at the deserted playground and then launched herself down the long sandy slope in an uncontrolled careering slide. Footing was soon lost in the treacle like sand and the leopard rolled over and over down to the base of the dune, landing on her back. She jumped up, shook off her new gritty coat and clambered up the opposite slope to repeat the procedure.

Time after time she made use of nature's slides, sometimes jumping straight off the ridge into the slope, or sliding down from the start, gently at first, then picking up speed to land in the inevitable sandy tangle at the end.

During one traverse she disturbed a scrub hare who had also ventured into the dunes. It careered off ahead of her and Mother chased it playfully along the side of a dune, throwing up clouds of sand as she made impotent swipes at it with her front paws. Eventually, exhausted, the pursuit was abandoned and she allowed herself to roll down to the bottom.

All the cares and worries of the day had been erased by this frenzy of playful activity and she lay there while her breathing returned to normal.

Mother had slipped into a shallow sleep when suddenly she woke with a start. She tried to work out what had woken her but could detect no danger, only a vague sense of uncertainty, on a level which she had never experienced before. Her mind filled with thoughts of infant anxiety and nervousness. She had been away too long.

The familiar shock of adrenalin bunched her heart muscles as it had done so many times before and the killer animal was galloping back to the only home she knew, to face a danger she did not.

Experience guided her feet along the dune valleys, picking out the line where the ground was firm and true. Not once did she falter, nor was there any residue of fatigue from her exhausting leisure activities in the dunes. Although her belly still flapped with the last of her milk, she had returned to a peak of fitness and could sustain this pace as long as necessary.

Distance melted swiftly in front of the bounding leopard, eaten up by a determination second to none. As the first grey light of dawn lit the horizon, the ridge above the den swam into view.

*****

It would be overstating the case to say that Torn Ear's assault on the old jackal had actually done him permanent damage. The lean wizened frame had suffered, and survived, a lot worse. However, it had made an impact on two other counts.

Firstly, his pride had suffered a severe dent. It was not often that another creature managed to get within striking distance without him knowing about it, least of all a stumbling immature cub, leopard or not.

Secondly, and far more importantly, he now knew that there were cubs in the vicinity, and cubs of whatever variety were potential food.

There was only one obstacle, which weighed approximately one hundred and forty pounds, and from the end of its nose to the tip of its tail measured nearly seven feet. Life expectancy in the immediate neighbourhood of the adult leopard would be very short indeed, as he had nearly discovered.

However, he was not going to let one little obstacle stand in the way of a good meal, so when the family finally left the remains of the springbok carcass he had followed at a discreet distance and was able to discover the remote track up to the den.

There his courage had failed him for a while and it was some hours before desperate hunger forced him to tread slowly and warily towards the cave. He could hardly believe his luck when, on rounding the final bend, he saw Mother's tail disappearing in the opposite direction.

After a few more minutes he edged towards the lip of the entrance. His long mouth was slightly open and he was almost panting with combined fright and anticipation. The short yellow teeth were exposed just enough to gleam dully in the moonlight and as he breathed, the stench of stale carrion spread like a fine invisible mist.

Dune couldn't have chosen a better moment to exercise his vocal chords if he had tried. Some future vision of adulthood had temporarily descended on him, and for no better reason than he felt like it, the cub let rip with his best imitation of Mother's growl.

The actual noise he succeeded in producing crackled and jumped from bass to treble and back again. The effect, however, was out of all proportion to the sound produced. The old jackal suddenly realised that he had totally discounted the possibility of there being an adult male in the family as well. This lone thought, combined with the sudden growl which had made him jump good and high, was enough excuse to send him scuttling back down the track. There he stayed all night long, while the cubs slept and Mother played.

By the time the false dawn showed itself he knew he had to try again, if only to satisfy himself that there was another adult leopard in the den, and that the cubs were definitely beyond reach.

Having steeled himself for the purpose, the scavenger crept slowly but surely up the track again, keeping to exactly the same path he had used before.

It was three days since he had eaten, not counting the few bitter acacia leaves which had caused almost instant vomiting, and fear of counter attack was receding. Purposely trying to make contact with an adult leopard was tantamount to attempting suicide, but unless he had proof he would always regret a lost opportunity. It was kill or be killed, he was that desperate. The jackal reached the lip of the den and stopped.

A moment of final hesitation and then he jumped silently inside and to the right of the entrance, pressing himself against the smooth, still warm rock, and waited until his eyes adjusted to the gloom.

Gradually, vision extended further and further back into the cave and he could easily make out the sleeping shapes, all small and huddled together. There was no other creature there at all. His heart leapt with pleasure. The killer picked a target and stepped forward.

Mother could smell the evil of the jackal as she slithered down the rocks and landed perfectly on the balcony.

Without checking her stride she entered the den in a rush of hate and strength, making no sound at all except the rustling of leaves caused by her passage.

The interloper was still near the entrance and as she entered he crouched down and let her go to the cubs.

As she did so he made a bolt for the exit behind her back. Mother spun round instantly at the sound and lashed out with a front paw, razor sharp claws fully extended.

One of them caught a glancing blow across a grey haired rump and raked a line down it, catching some matted hair from the bushy black tail as the terrified creature managed to escape its clutches, like a fish freeing itself from the angler's hook.

For an instant the injury stood out clear and proud, as if it were the first incision of the surgeon's scalpel. Then bright red arterial blood welled up along the entire length and began making its way into the forest of hair that surrounded it.

By the time Mother had checked the cubs and scrambled down onto the balcony the enemy had vanished.

She stood there for a few minutes in the first rays of sunlight, considering the situation, tail lashing furiously from side to side. She was angry and alert, the adrenalin that had kept her pounding back through the arid sandveldt during the night was still in her veins. It enhanced her body colours and stature, showing her at her best, an awesome feline specimen.

She had a short roundish head, ears nearly always pricked up straight and angled forwards. The deep chested body was lithe and muscular, now fully recovered after maternal confinement and inactivity. With constant grooming and a relatively abundant supply of food her coat had become magnificent again, a veritable treasure for any human hunter.

Her back and flanks bore rosette shaped spots which were almost black, with a lighter central area. The rest of her body hair glowed a yellowish red with the exception of her underbelly where it was a very light grey.

Along the length of her spine, from shoulder to tail root, was a parallel line of eleven rosettes, which in turn gave way to the powerful tail. As is characteristic with all leopards, the fifth limb moves constantly unless a conscious effort is made to still it. This Judas of tails is often the only way of locating the hidden leopard, as their markings break up all body contours and allow the hunter to blend into the background with the ease of a chameleon.

Her strong, relatively short, legs ended in broad round paws, which were well haired, except for the naked rubbery pads on the underside which allowed soft and noiseless tread. Each paw was well equipped with offensive weapons in the shape of fearsomely sharp curved claws. These she kept sheathed until required, and like all other leopards therefore, left no claw marks in her tracks.

She turned to look back at the den entrance and was not entirely surprised to see a small black furry face returning her gaze with smiling eyes.

Mother brought her instincts back to focus sharply on the present.

The safety of the den had been compromised, its location could now be passed on by the jackal and it might return. She could not allow that to happen.

Before she set out, the cubs needed to drink to ensure they survived the dessicating heat of the day. It could easily take her that long to track and kill the prey.

Quickly she mustered her family on the balcony and led them down to the nearby water hole. She had wandered for months looking for such a good site for a den and had no intention of being forced to do so again.

The water hole was the largest for some miles and nearly always had visitors. She unceremoniously scattered a small herd of zebra and springbok and led the cubs down.

Normally they would have watched from a distance for a while, giving the cubs a chance to observe the animals, learn their habits and weaknesses. Today, time was their enemy and they drank quickly, not taking the usual trouble to find an area clear from cloudy sediments stirred up by the hooves of the recently ejected customers.

Every few seconds Mother would look up from her squatting position and scan the environs to ensure their safety. For her own part, lion was the only real threat, but cubs attracted the attentions of many a would-be predator.

As she brought her head up from the water, huge glistening drops leapt down from one long whisker to the next, catching the still cool rays of sunlight and glittering like molten diamonds.

Dune and Spring were puzzled by this change in their daily pattern and were even more bewildered to be placed back in the den when the heat of the day did not yet demand it. Only the female cub seemed to grasp the importance of the matter and did not protest.

If Mother had qualms about leaving the cubs alone again she did not let them surface in her mind. Every time she hunted they had to be left and their safety was mainly provided for by the seclusion of the den. If a potential enemy discovered their cave, the scent of leopard would, hopefully, persuade them that an easier meal could be had elsewhere.

She left the balcony without further thought and concentrated on crossing the spoor of the jackal, which was by now nearly an hour old.

By the time she reached the bottom of the track there was still no sign of it, although she knew he must have fled this way.

As a final precaution she lifted her tail high and jetted a milky liquid around the thorn bushes where she stood. Mother usually reserved this behaviour for marking the boundaries of her hunting territory, but it might help to dissuade other predators from getting too close to the hidden track.

She turned and began to search in slow semi-circles, constantly moving outwards, minutely examining the sand and scrub for tell tale signs.

The black backed jackal leaves almost dog-like pug marks, the front paws having pads bunched closer together than the hind ones. A uniformly small claw mark is left by all four toes on each foot, thus distinguishing itself from the bat eared fox which has long digging claws, and the side striped jackal which has altogether larger paws.

After only a few minutes the leopard simultaneously cut the spoor and caught the last vestiges of scent. Her prey had gone straight out across the river bed. The tracks were clearly visible once she had grown accustomed to picking them out from the myriad of marks left by other desert creatures and she began to follow them at a fast walk.

From time to time she discovered a speck of blood to the right of the spoor and recalled the wound she must have given his flank.

In this particular area of the Kalahari the fossil river bed acts as a huge divide.

On one side of it lie the sandy dunes, mile after mile of unending desert, incomprehensibly vast, even to a bird in flight. A more inhospitable place it would be hard to find.

On the opposite side from the leopard den the desert relents somewhat. There are still some dunes, but of a less formidable variety. The ground still burns with the heat of the early afternoon sun and the stagnant air still seems to sing and crackle, as though in an oven. However there is some life.

Acacia and wild fig trees give some limited shade, their presence pointing to moisture deep below the surface sands. Even the occasional mopane tree puts in an appearance, the bright green making a welcome splash of colour against the dull and parched surroundings. Areas of low scrub and tussocky yellow-green grasses cover the ground, with small fresh shoots sprinkled amongst them.

Mother usually hunted on this side of the divide and knew it better than the far recesses of her own den. If there was prey to be had nearer home then she would take it if possible, but there was more often a good chance of a kill on this side.

At a fast walk the leopard covers about four miles an hour. By the time that hour had elapsed she had left the hard crystalline surface of the pan and was threading her way through thorn bushes up to the relatively lush pastures.

Her speed hardly ever faltered, even though she constantly checked the ground, following the enemy spoor. Pug marks in the sand, a strand of hair left impaled on a thorn, blades of grass bent a different way, all pointed out the jackal's passage.

Mother's speed was masked by her soft and resilient steps, almost as if she were trying to avoid damaging the earth. She carried her head low, with the jaw often hanging slightly relaxed, allowing air access to the blood vessels in her tongue. In the swiftly growing heat of the day it was her only way of cooling. Normally she would lie in the shade, and allow heat to be lost also from the soft spongy pads of her feet, but that would have to wait.

The trail seemed to last forever and Mother sensed that the jackal knew he was running for his life. She was fighting for the future of her cubs and as far as she was concerned there was only one possible outcome. It was simply a matter of when and where.

This sense of absolute purpose filled her senses and dissolved the feelings of heat and exhaustion in her body. It was like raw energy to her muscles.

The leopard powered on through the scrub.

******

Gradually, she became aware of a group of animals in the distance.

As she grew closer the shapes materialised into a small herd of zebra. They were grazing near the shade of an acacia tree.

Every few seconds the nervous animals brought their heads up from feeding to search the horizon for a predator, and to sample the air for the smell of danger. Occasionally a hoof could be seen gently scraping the ground to expose fresh grazing, and tails were constantly whisking and flicking back and forth, keeping the assaulting mosquitoes at bay.

They were a hindrance to Mother and she wanted them out of the way.

Quickly she circumnavigated the animals so that her pungent scent would carry downwind to them, hopefully scattering them back the way she had come, thus avoiding damage to the jackal's trail, which continued on the other side of the group.

No sooner had Mother settled into her new position than a striped head twisted, staring long and hard in her direction. She was concealed behind a clump of taller grasses and shrubs, hidden from view, but when the zebra's ears pricked forward at her she knew her presence was about to become common knowledge.

The young mare issued a short series of excited barks and stamped a hoof, hard, several times.

The prospect of becoming lunch held little appeal for the herd and they made good their escape at a flat out gallop, the largest stallion taking up his usual defensive position at the rear.

Unfortunately for Mother the herd panicked in exactly the wrong direction, at some considerable speed. She watched with mounting despair as they headed towards several distant thorn bushes and the wilderness beyond.

What was bad luck for a leopard was total unmitigated disaster for an old dog jackal, taking his first rest in the relative safety of a large thorn bush.

The oncoming rush of hooves brought him rapidly out of a semi-comatose state and he jumped up suddenly, only to be reminded precisely where he was when two thorns stabbed him just below the left shoulder blade.

He yelped with pain, scrambled clear of the bush and then jumped out of the path of the zebra.

Still half asleep, he stood in the searing dry heat of the sun, staring after the diminishing cloud of dust. His long bushy tail hung down low in dejection between his legs, and the bright sunlight reflecting off the ground made him screw up his eyes and squint into the distance. The wound in his flank had stopped bleeding but now throbbed fiercely, the torn muscle jarring with pain at every step.

He had never felt so utterly exhausted, he simply wanted to lie and sleep. Even the ever present gnawing hunger pangs had disappeared, a sure sign of defeat.

Mother sat up on her haunches to watch the dust settle and try to plan the next move.

It took her a few seconds to realise that the creature which had bolted from the thorn bush like a scalded cat was in fact her quarry. She sank back behind the inadequate screen of vegetation and then began to make a slow but steady advance.

The zebra had stopped some distance beyond the jackal but were still skittish. The smell of leopard - never one of their favourites - was lingering in their nostrils and they trotted round in small circles, blowing hard, kicking up a lot of dust and generally panicking the remainder of the desert fauna in the immediate vicinity.

The jackal was still standing watching the commotion. Had he been even half mentally awake it might have crossed his mind to wonder what had caused the sudden exodus. He might even have sought to hide himself again, and then wonder about it. He did neither.

The leopard swiftly realised that the noise of the zebra was excellent cover. She advanced quickly, even daring a few yards at a loping canter, before slipping deftly into a natural hollow formed by a small crescent shaped dune which was liberally sprinkled with flourishing tufts of grass.

With ears flattened back against the side of her head she raised herself so she could just see over the lip of the dune.

The scavenger had roused himself and was now walking off to the right with a leaden step. She could see how he limped and favoured the injured side with every pace. He would pass directly in front of her, albeit at a distance, in a few moments. The leopard sank back and tried to estimate when the jackal should have passed her position, enabling her to follow and pick the killing time.

Mother waited an eternity, keeping her breathing shallow and quiet, pulse racing. Finally she raised her head and looked straight into the enemy's eyes. He had stopped to rest and had picked the worst possible site.

Instantly the leopard launched herself forward. She cleared the crest of the sand without leaving a mark on it and landed at the gallop, pursuing the fleeing jackal.

He twisted and dived, knowing that the leopard could not keep up a sprinting gallop for long. It was his only slender chance.

The huge cat soon came up behind her prey, matching his movements. She too knew her limitations. Long distance stamina was possessed in ample quantities, but sprints could not last long.

In a fleeting instant of movement she detected the beginnings of a turn by the jackal. He was going to dive off to the right, propelled by the last strength in his healthy left flank and at the same time giving momentary respite to his injured side.

Without conscious thought the leopard bunched her hind muscles and lifted into the air.

The jackal turned.

Mother had judged the leap perfectly and landed astride her prey, crushing him to the ground.

Swiftly she searched for the neck, grasped firmly and broke it with one powerful move. Gristle tore, bone splintered and disintegrated with the killing stroke and she felt hot blood spurting into her mouth from the torn carotid artery.

There was no pleasure. Only completion of what had to be done. She left the still twitching body and went in search of water to rid herself of the taste.

******

Golden rays from the dying embers of an early evening sun lit the balcony like soft spotlights on a theatre stage. Trees, rocks and animals were bathed in a halcyon sheen.

The cutting edge of the midday heat had gone and it was now pleasantly warm, with a slight breeze ruffling leaves and fur alike.

A general air of peace and tranquility had spread throughout the desert, as it did every day about this time, for early evening was when hunter and hunted could afford to relax under the auspices of an ancient unwritten law which decreed a period of relative calm. Nocturnal creatures were still waking up, preparing for their activities. Those who had been active during the day were making arrangements for a safe night of sleep, and those who were able, were relaxing, enjoying the jewel that the desert presents to those who have faced and survived another day.

Three diminutive faces filled the entrance to the den, eyes blinking against the low level assault of sunlight.

They had been there for about half an hour, in the certain knowledge that Mother was nearing the end of her return journey.

When she finally appeared on the balcony all three tumbled out as one and swamped her in a deluge of affection. As with most infant enthusiasm, the display was soon over and the cubs fought playfully amongst themselves, trying to use a days' worth of pent up energy all at once.

Thankful for the respite from their attentions, Mother lay down on the balcony directly under the den entrance. The smooth rock was warm and acted like a poultice on her tired muscles, soothing and relaxing them.

Gradually her fatigue faded into a memory. The leopard had long since discovered that sleep itself was a luxury and not a necessity. Provided she could rest herself in a state of relative peace, her body usually recovered, and she could do without actual periods of sleep for several days.

Fortunately, her offspring slept all night and part of the day - nature still had a sense of responsibility.

Mother opened one eye to watch the cubs at play.

As usual, Dune and Spring had joined forces and were matched against Torn Ear. As usual, Torn Ear was winning handsomely and enjoying every minute of it. She had developed the ability to stand, for a few seconds anyway, on her hind legs and deliver devastating right hooks, until gravity took hold and forced her down to ground level, usually ending up in the horizontal position.

In this activity the claws were always kept sheathed. Indeed, none of the cubs had discovered the destructive ability of their paws and could not yet extend their weaponry at will.

At first her opponents were literally floored by this new tactic but then learned to duck and make a rush for her legs, bringing the black cub crashing down.

The adult watched with a detached sense of pride. Already she could see that Torn Ear was the master of the situation, both physically and mentally. The cub was bigger and heavier than her brothers and Mother could see muscles forming under the sleek black coat. Her paws were also proportionately much bigger than her brothers'.

The tussle was brought to a close when Torn Ear decided she had had enough. She rolled onto her back in the characteristic gesture of surrender. The others stalked off in disgust, convinced they had been cheated out of a memorable victory.

Shadows were lengthening now and the clear blue of the Kalahari sky was darkening into hues of reds and ambers with the setting sun. Soon it would dissolve into inky darkness with patterns of diamond bright stars.

Mother was of the opinion that it was now about time to hoist the family back into their home. The cubs were quite willing to obey, however their method of entry proved to be unorthodox, to say the least.

Led by the usual ringleader, the cubs used the well muscled flank of the adult leopard as a springboard and bounced quickly in.

Mother raised herself from under the den entrance and growled in mock anger at the cheeky faces which now peered at her from inside the darkened cave.

The faces instantly retreated to the sleeping area at the back of the den in a happy confusion of sound.

Mother settled back on the balcony to spend the night buried in blissful ignorance of everything in the world.

CHAPTER

TWO

"I'm fourteen years old and I'll damn well do as I like ".

Jade Viljoen twitched the left rein and pressed her right leg hard against Dancer's flank. He twisted round in continuous circles, throwing up clouds of dust into the early morning rays of the African sun.

"I'm fourteen years old. I'll damn well do as I like and you can't stop me."

She pulled the bay stallion to a halt and leant over his shoulder, challenging the man to deny her.

Molo groaned inwardly and sighed the world weary sigh that fathers round the world have perfected to an art. The only difference being that he wasn't her father, or anybody's father for that matter. He was a worker in a huge stock ranch in South West Africa, on the very threshold of the Kalahari Desert. However, for the past fourteen years, and two weeks, he had been guardian, mentor, confidante and most everything else to the teenager who faced him now.

Sun bleached hair cascaded in front of her face briefly before she angrily pushed it off. Jade was fourteen going on twenty five and she knew it. She was also fourteen going on four most of the time and didn't know it.

She swung her right leg over the pommel and slid easily to the ground.

I'm sure they taught you the right way to dismount, thought Molo, in those expensive riding lessons that the boss got for you, and it sure wasn't like that. But he didn't bother reminding her. He'd kicked over the hornets' nest before and still had the scars.

"I always take Dancer out first thing while it's cool. You know I do." She spat the words out like bullets. "I know the rides backwards, frontwards, upside down and to the moon and back, so I'm taking him into the bush a way for a change. What's wrong with that, eh ?"

Jade leant forward, pivoting on her slim muscular hips to try and intimidate him. It had never worked before and today was not destined to be a first.

"What's wrong with it, young lady, is that I have forbidden it and you have conveniently forgotten it."

Molo inclined his head to one side, raised a single eyebrow and grinned. For the words of authority came not from him, but from the towering figure of Tony van Niekerk, grandfather of the fourteen year old horsewoman and owner of the farm.

Jade squinted up into the sunlight to try and gauge his mood but could only see shadow beneath the old Stetson hat he wore. Even as she vented her spleen on him, she knew it was a fatal mistake. Still, common sense never had got in the way of a good fight before.

"I can't do anything round here AT ALL. There is nothing in this godforsaken hole to do except ride and you damn well won't let me do that. I have to stick my nose in books all week so the only thing I get to look forward to ......" Her words tailed off as she realised she was addressing them to the disappearing rump of the stallion. His tail twitched expertly up to dislodge a horsefly as she looked on in frustration.

Molokoane, Molo for short, had vanished, as had all the other onlookers who had gathered. It seemed that work was now infinitely more preferable to being the target for any remaining thunderbolts of wrath.

Jade let out a long growl of anger. A single tear of impotent rage slid unchecked down her bronzed cheek. She pulled off both her calf length boots, slammed them heel first into the dust and stalked back off to the house. The only problem with that was that she couldn't kick the door open very satisfactorily.

Tony handed Dancer's reins over to Molo in the blessed cool of the stable block. Already the fierce African sun was sending people and animals alike for shelter. The two men looked at each other in silence. The girl needed more than was here, but neither knew really what it was or how to go about looking for it. Molo lifted up a leather flap on the saddle and started to unfasten the girth. It was a bit too loose, as usual, as Dancer had the habit of pushing out his belly when the saddle went on, thus ensuring that the rider couldn't fasten the strap uncomfortably tight on him. Tony walked back to the house, picking up the discarded boots on the way and shaking the sand out.

Fifteen years ago, Marie van Niekerk had married a strikingly handsome man in a cool dark church in Windhoek. She fell pregnant almost immediately and shortly afterwards he was called up for National Service. They were together for two weeks during the entire confinement and never saw each other alive again. Marie died giving birth to her daughter, so it was Tony who held the angry infant while doctors tried in vain to save the mother. He waited in a small tarnished back room while one life was exchanged for another and his life was turned on its head.

He took the new born baby girl to the farm four days later because it was the only home there was. The father had been told of his new daughter hours after the birth and had been ecstatic. He had managed to scrounge a few days leave from his company, and transport to get back with. He was so preoccupied with his thoughts that he had forgotten the primary rule of driving in the notorious Caprivi Strip, just this side of the Angolan border - drive fast or not at all. That way if you triggered a land mine you were past it before it exploded. He drove too slowly round a bend in the sandy desert track and the baby girl was an orphan. Tony hadn't had the heart to break the news of Marie's death to him at the same time, so he died knowing he had a daughter but without knowing he had lost a wife.

Plunged back into childcare for the second time in his life Tony set about engaging a series of live-in nannies while he tried to keep the farm going as well. Over the following years difficulties and problems rained down on him like hailstones, while all the time he dealt with the grief and the joy that the situation brought each day.

The easiest part was naming his granddaughter. She had striking blue / green eyes which sparkled as an infant and never faded. The choice was natural.

Right from the word go Jade was attitude with a capital A. She was into everything that was dangerous and ignored the rest. Tutors came to teach in the early years and invariably went away disappointed. As she grew older Tony sent her to a weekly boarding school in Windhoek, which seemed to make some progress, primarily because she was on her own and trusted to do things for herself to a certain degree.

Jade herself lived for weekends, holidays, horses and of course for the vast wide expanse of the Kalahari. When all three were combined she was in heaven. When she had to be inside, the girl could always be found sketching and drawing in her room. The walls were covered with impressions of views, animals and sometimes people although she found that particular animal very hard to capture and consequently they turned out as caricatures - unintentionally. She only liked pencils and crayons to work with, watercolours reminded her too much of tutors and school and you couldn't rub oils with your finger to give a gorgeous blending of colours on the paper.

The results went on her walls - until she was either fed up of them or there was no space left. Then they were unceremoniously ripped off and binned to leave the way clear for more.

The magic of art was being demonstrated now, for Jade sat cross-legged on the floor creating a meerkat out of paper and pencils. Sometimes she would just sketch in shades of grey and this cheeky looking animal was just right for it. She had seen him a few days ago from a shady spot underneath an acacia tree with Dancer asleep on his feet next to her. Her blast of temper was gone and forgotten, but out of it had come an idea, and as most teenagers' ideas are, it would not have been approved of by the management. So she didn't bother them with it.

The day droned slowly by and the meerkat assumed his position between two portraits of Dancer. Jade wandered back down to the stables in the late afternoon, just before general activity started again after the enforced midday siesta. Even so, she still kept to the shady sides of buildings, which was just as well because she narrowly missed bumping into her least favourite person, who was coming out of a shed and didn't see her at all in the shadows. Harry de Beer was a surly Afrikaner who worked the outlying and remote areas. Normally he would ignore her completely, but had taken to giving her funny looks of late. She didn't know what they meant at all and just kept out of his way.

Oupa would be in his study now, resting and trying to forestall the next bout of malaria which was about due to make a hit again. Molo would be still in siesta mode in his pit - you could run a herd of elephant past his room right now and not have him stir at all. Great, stables to herself.

Dancer whickered a gentle greeting as she walked into his stall, rustling the straw on the concrete floor. Jade took up the currycomb and brushes and lovingly started her daily routine of grooming. She hated being at school and having to leave the care of her horse to others. Really hated it.

Stroke after stroke she put into the already glossy coat and mane while Dancer nuzzled her gently. Eventually even she was satisfied and sat down on a pile of clean straw in the corner. After a quick glance round to make sure there was no one about she dug down into the pile of straw with one hand. Carefully she felt round the bundle. Siesta time was really useful - she hadn't met anyone at all earlier when she had hidden her treasure.

The next day was Sunday and after that was a week's holiday from school. Just perfect. As usual Jade was up with the sunrise, or just before. Actually she hadn't really gone to sleep at all for fear of getting up too late. Quietly she crept down the back stairs from her bedroom - the main ones creaked like a timber ship on the ocean swell - and made her way across to the stables. Dancer was still standing there like she had left him. Did they ever sleep at all, she wondered. She tacked him up in a jiffy and then muffled his hooves by tying old sacking round them. The stallion looked at her with what she took to be mild amusement. She wished he could talk. Then she tied her small bundle onto the back of the saddle and led him quietly out of the stable, through the yard and off the farm.

There was no real boundary that marked where the farmland ended and the desert proper began. It just seemed to drift. Jade twisted round in the saddle and could still see the outline of the buildings against the dawn sky. This must be about it she thought. She jumped off, untied the muffles and vaulted back on. Then she urged Dancer into a quick walk and they were off.

Two days away would be enough. Enough to slake her thirst for empty space and freedom, for crystal blue skies and shooting stars at night, for the chance to show them she was not a child and didn't have to be treated as one. Anyway, they'd have to lump it. She'd left a note and made sure that she would be far enough away for them not to bother tracking her by the time they read it.

In fact, the fourteen year old girl was no stranger to this part of the desert. A year or so ago she'd been allowed to go out for a week with Sam, on his stock duties. Sam was an old farmhand with more than a touch of Bushman in him and a soft spot for the girl with a small birthmark on the side of her neck which she grew her hair to hide. He had taken her into the desert and given her the best week of education that money couldn't buy. He had shown her how to find food beneath the surface of the rough sand, how and when to shelter from the sun, and even where a water hole was - that could satisfy a thirsty horse miles from his stable. She took it all in and stored it. Now she would use it.

****

Molo was the first to raise the alarm. Or rather he wasn't. It was no surprise to find Dancer missing first thing in the morning. But when the pace of life slackened off around midday, and the stable was still empty, a worry surfaced in his mind and refused to vanish when ordered. Jade always had him back much sooner than this, normally to show off a sketch or relate some tale of adventure, but somehow today felt different. He didn't like to bother Tony with it at the moment, but even if he had wanted to it would have been impossible. The owner of the farm was sweating through a fully fledged bout of malaria in his bedroom. It was a bad one this time - listening at the door Molo could hear the mumblings of delirium. He was out of it. Any decisions on Jade were down to him. The farm worked under the much disliked foreman when Tony was not around, but Jade was his responsibility.

Molo scuffed his way across the wide yard, head down and slightly more concerned than before, if only because the weight of any decision was now his alone.

" Molokoane, you asleep on your feet there ? You so caught up in that head of yours that you can't see I'm lookin' at you boy ? "

Siesta time approached, and by the look on Emmy's cute face she wanted to spend it with him. Well that was just fine by him. Molo perked up and his mind suddenly dumped Jade onto the back burner. She'd most likely be back in a couple of hours anyway. The line of footprints in the dust altered by ninety degrees and headed purposefully for a small doorway to living quarters.

It was a very mellow, and rather exhausted Molo who wandered back into the stables later that afternoon. He checked Dancer's stall and found it still empty. Not good. Then he noticed a torn piece of adhesive tape on the wall in the stall. It looked new, as if there should be something attached to it. There was, but it was mixed up in the straw now. Jade had stuck the note on the wall and then reversed Dancer out of his home. He had brushed past it and torn the note off.

Molo fished around in the straw. Good job Jade kept everything clean here. He pulled the paper out and quickly read the contents. She had really done it now, he thought, the boss will go crazy. Well, he would if he wasn't already half way there. Nevertheless, Molo ran upstairs with the note to see if Tony was back in the land of the lucid yet. No joy, he was out cold in a drugged sleep now. Molo sat down on the top stair outside Tony's room. There was nothing he could do - she had a full day's start and presumably had some sort of plan, which didn't include suicide by heatstroke. Tracking her was pointless because she would be back tomorrow. He silently wished her well, because he knew she could cope, and decided to do nothing. He hoped he would still have a job if Tony discovered where she had gone. He wondered if Emmy would come with him when he was sacked.

****

Jade and Dancer watched the sun go down at the end of their first day of freedom. Well, Jade actually watched while Dancer hid his nose in the bag of pellets that had been brought for feed. She thought they had had a fabulous day. The pair of them had trekked and explored the fringes of the desert, watched two scorpions fight to the death - Jade had wanted to separate them before one succumbed but couldn't work out how to do it quickly enough - and generally reveled in their adventure. They had eventually found the water hole, which had been quite usable for the stallion, and were now camped by the side of a huge rock while the end of the day crept up on them. The rock was warm and would radiate heat during the chilly night which was ahead. Funny place, the desert, thought Jade, baking hot all day but by the end of the night you could be shivering with cold.

Tomorrow, she decided, would be another gorgeous day. They would be up before dawn to enjoy the sunrise, and then start for home by a different route. Coping with Oupa would be a problem, but at least she would have shown them that she could do it. She would weather the storm and then later she would be able to repeat the holiday with their blessing. Jade took a long draught from her canteen, which was still over half full, and chewed on a strip of biltong as the last heat went from the sun. Life was OK really.

CHAPTER

THREE

The jackals had finished. The vultures were bloated and waddled into the shade. They had to digest some of their food before they could even think about attempting a take-off.

Even the hyena were no longer interested in the few remaining bones which were scattered at random. They wandered away from the churned up area of dull red sand, some clutching small morsels of flesh which they intended to devour at leisure. All had blood stained muzzles and heads where they had dived into their victim to feed. As they walked slowly back into the scrub they looked like creatures who had been caught at some dreadful act, and, knowing their guilt, had blushed furiously before slinking away.

The unforgiving desert sun was now high in the Kalahari sky, whose flawless blue rivaled that of a heron's egg.

All morning it had watched over the carnage and its rays had begun to make their presence felt on the unconscious figure which lay hidden from view behind a wedge of sand and thin wispy grass. Around Jade lay the few scattered items which her pack had contained - a canteen, still half full, with a long canvas strap, a wickedly sharp five inch knife in its leather sheath, an old camouflage cap as a concession to the midday sun, and two strips of hard biltong. Not much, but all she really needed for one night in the bush.

Tiny rivulets of salty moisture had run tracks down her forehead and then dripped off onto the sand where they quickly dried. A gentle zephyr of a breeze ruffled the blonde hairs on the girl's head, pushing them gradually over her forehead and in front of her eyes. It also took an edge off the dry heat, masking its ability to burn and desiccate. In her unconsciousness she sweated profusely into her clothes which then dried out quickly. Then she lost more fluid which soaked her clothes again. She was wearing a slightly oversize checked shirt which had been liberated from a bottom drawer in Oupa's room, a pair of comfortably fitting cream jodhpurs and her favourite leather riding boots. Inside the boots her feet swelled with the heat and her calves filled out to stretch the leather taut.

Midday passed in sweltering calm and near silence. The scene of the carnage was now strangely peaceful and settled. The already tanned face of the girl showed signs of sun damage, turning more red than tan. The rays sought out gaps through the hair to her scalp. Greedily turned them red as well.

An eager head appeared at the crest of the sand wedge, looked down at the figure, and then further on at the last of the dispersing diners. Too late, as usual. Nowadays he was always too late.

The head had a muzzle which was liberally sprinkled with short silver hairs and belonged to a black backed jackal. He let his head drop down for a minute to try and ease the nagging pain from a neck wound. He knew it would soon dry and heal. All the others had.

The old dog jackal disappeared from view and trotted round the wedge of sand to reappear a few feet from Jade.

The easy meat had all gone, but perhaps this one was actually dead as well. He moved a little closer and stretched out his neck to sniff cautiously at the nearest arm. A new smell certainly, but it was a definite possibility. He might even have been successful. He might have been successful if he hadn't had to avoid a laden vulture having trouble gaining height after a laborious takeoff. The ungainly aircraft forced him to dodge left and stumble into Jade's head. He bumped heavily into the egg shaped lump caused by the zebra and a searing pain lanced deep into her subconscious. She groaned, flapped an arm across in a purely reflex action and hit the jaw of the retreating scavenger.

His whole head swimming from the impact, the jackal lurched away like a drunk from a party and staggered back into the desert.

His day was destined to get a whole lot worse.

Jade however, knew nothing of this encounter and concentrated her entire effort on trying to return to normality. She drifted in and out of reality for the next twenty minutes or so until she felt able to move her arms and legs. Then she sat up.

If I can sit up then I'm OK. If I'm OK then I can stand. Jade stood up, facing away from the wrecked carcass that was once the only thing she lived for.

A wave of nausea billowed up in her and she vomited swiftly and suddenly, then collapsed onto the ground. Smaller waves washed over her so she stayed where she was until they subsided.

She tried again, and had the same result.

All right, all right. I'll stay down here if that makes it easier. Jade crawled slowly around on all fours gathering up her few possessions. She kept her eyes screwed up against the reflected glare of the sun. Somehow keeping them like this made the prospect of sickness recede, well a bit anyway. She eventually made a little pile of them in front of her as she sat cross-legged and then put them into the bush hat. Then she noticed the pain from the side of her head. Gingerly she felt round until her fingers encountered the result of her attempt to head butt a zebra's hoof. It felt massive, like a hard boiled egg ready to burst. She explored its properties a little by means of gentle pressure. The egg didn't budge but a finger of pain ran round in front of her eyes and gave a very creditable low budget firework display for her. She winced and shut her eyes fully for a few moments.

Her mind was in a complete daze. She remembered only sketchy details of how she came to be here. *Where was Dancer ?* She looked round through squinting eyes, shielded against the sun by her hand. Still sitting down she turned her head painfully through a full circle. Somewhere in that turn she expected to see four legs. She didn't, and the scene of the horse's death was hidden, at her level, by the same sandy wedge which had saved her life.

Thank God. He's gone home by himself. All I have to do is follow him. Completely disorientated and thoroughly confused by heatstroke and the loss of body fluids she tried to work out which way to go from the position of the sun. Hopeless. Then she looked for his tracks. A set of hoof prints could just be seen heading out from beside her. She looked closely at the first few prints as they swam in and out of focus. They were the right shape, weren't they ? As she concentrated, tunnel like, on the prints, the rest of the world on the edges acquired a fuzzy grey mist which whirled around.

Jade pulled her shirt out of the jodhpurs at the front and stuffed the bush hat and contents up it, and tucked it back in. Then she started to follow the prints. On her hands and knees. Away from Dancer's death, unaware of it, and straight towards the interior of the Kalahari desert. The zebra had done more than kick her. It had also left a rogue trail for her confused mind to follow. Instead of heading shakily in the general direction of rescue, she headed shakily away from it.

In the distance an acacia tree could be seen, with most of its leaves still intact. It promised shade and protection from the desert. When Jade looked up, the zebra prints seemed to lead straight towards it. They did, but then so did the rest of the herd's prints. Down at sand level, Jade was following one single print after another - it was all she could concentrate on. Concussion, heat and dehydration had sapped her thought processes and energy and was gradually whittling away at her very chance of hanging onto life. The herd had galloped this way en masse. Jade was merely following individual prints in the melee of all the rest, and she had no idea that it wasn't a continuous spoor left by Dancer to lead her to safety.

Her concentration was intense and all consuming. She lived for each hoof print which formed up in front of her, and then the next, and the next. The sun lashed her head and she bowed it closer to the scorched ground. With each pace she crawled forward her head lolled a little further from side to side but she kept the snail's pace going. The routine was killing her and to stop would kill her quicker. In the space of a few short hours the Kalahari had taken a healthy vibrant girl, exposed her fragility and waved death in her face. She could sense the closeness, feel the hot breath of it on her shoulder and knew it might yet claim her. *I am alive if I move. I ....will....keep....moving....*

The crawl for life continued slowly and relentlessly. Her tongue grew and longed for moisture inside a parched mouth. The top of her head cried out for shelter. She ignored them both because she couldn't register the sensations. Inside her shirt the water bottle sloshed and the bush hat rubbed against her skin. Gradually the goal came closer.

When the tree was finally reached, its properties proved to be as substantial as a mirage of shimmering water. They were non-existent. The sunlight simply blasted its way through the leaves to give a slightly blurred, speckled effect on the ground. Nevertheless, Jade collapsed gratefully onto her belly.

Everything around her was dry. She grasped handfuls of sand and let them fall back down to the ground. The airborne streams made peculiar patterns in front of eyes that she couldn't really focus now. The sand was coarse and gritty, bleached pale by centuries of sun and wind, the ultimate levelers. There were fragments of dried bark and twigs around the base of the tree. They crumbled into dust when she reached out for them, and a burst of hot air threw them into her face. She didn't have the energy to brush the detritus off. There was nothing left in reserve now. The journey across to this place of sanctuary had sapped her beyond belief, in her body there was emptiness. In her mind however, was a feeling of definite strange discomfort. *What is it ?*

She tried to marshal thoughts and instincts, get her memory to recognise the feeling. Gradually the tentacles in her mind reached out to each other. *What is it ? Where is it ? It's important and it makes me hurt - or does it ?*

She focused with all her might. It was coming from her chest, no from the ground under her chest. It wasn't pain but a bulk. A cumbersome object between her chest and the ground. She rolled exhaustedly to one side. Several shirt buttons had ripped off and the water bottle slipped out and rolled down beside her. It was the sound of water that woke her mind. In a dream she forced her fingers to unscrew the stopper and administer a tiny sip to her burnt and bone dry lips. The liquid rolled over her parched and swollen tongue with seemingly no effect. She couldn't feel it. Tried again. More precious water this time. Like oiling an unused and neglected machine, her tongue and mouth came to life and she was alive again.

Despite her raging thirst and the need for the comfort and reassurance, Jade rationed the water so that there was at least a quarter left in the canteen. The effect had been remarkable. Her body was still exhausted, burnt and lethargic but her mind was back working for her again - at least for the moment.

She sat herself up against the rough trunk of the acacia tree. Her legs and feet were literally boiling up inside the leather boots and after the water she could feel the pain from them. She used recently found, and very transient, strength to haul them both off. For glorious seconds her feet felt cool as air circulated round them. Then the feeling evaporated like a morning mist and they were as hot as the rest of her.

God, I hope Dancer made it back OK. Oupa will be out of his tree....

Jade looked down at the hoof prints around the tree. She could focus properly and saw the myriad of prints from a spooked herd. The tracks headed off into the distance, continuing into the desert. She realised that Dancer's tracks were now hopelessly entangled and impossible to detect. *Anyway,* she thought, *I followed them OK up to here, and they don't go off anywhere else. He must've kept on this way and I just can't see them in amongst the rest.*

So she got up gingerly, testing her head for altitude sickness. A little dizzy perhaps but fine to walk now. Jade slowly picked up the canteen and hung it over her shoulder on its strap, pushed the sheath knife behind the elasticated waist of her jodhpurs in the small of her back, rested the bush hat carefully on her head, and slotted the biltong into a pocket.

Although following what she believed to be the way home after Dancer, Jade was still mature enough to recognise the near hopelessness of the task. She could either sit under the tree and wait to become a victim, or follow the tentative hope that she had created for herself, in error.

Water. She would need more water and there was none here. The canteen would be empty soon. Then she would die, and that would happen long before she ever managed to walk home. *I rode hard for a whole day.......I must have gone miles.......this could take forever.*

Water. She needed water and there was none here. Jade made her decision. The decision of a girl who wanted to survive, and if the desert wanted her it would have to fight for her. She would head in the same direction as Dancer, and find water on the way. Jade picked up her boots and walked carefully away from the friendly tree and its desperately small shade, her first ally in the desert.

There was no goal within reach and no certain prize at the end. She soon began to tire again as the zebra tracks vanished before her eyes. Nevertheless, she kept going in the same direction. It was the only hope she had. Ridges and dunes appeared on her route and each one was harder to scale than the last. Her feet sank into the treacle-like sand and could only just be dragged out.

Still she carried on, for no better reason than to stop admitted defeat. With every passing minute Jade's thirst grew stronger until it occupied her every thought. She imagined long glasses of ice-cold liquid with condensation running freely down the outside. She pictured the rolling waves of the Atlantic breaking on the rocks of Cape Cross, dousing all and sundry with their icy spray. The girl was a seal, diving sleekly and engulfing herself in the breathtakingly cold waters.

Finally she stopped and sat. With every breath hot air passed through dry cracked lips, over a tongue beginning to swell again and furred with thick saliva, past an aching throat and into burning lungs. She was desperate to drain the canteen of its blood warm contents, but knew that it was her last reserve. Using it meant admitting defeat to her, a totally alien concept to the fourteen year old, and signified that the end was near. *No way, no how.*

She was beginning to feel confused and a little disorientated. Jade pinched her arm hard to try and clear her senses, and noticed that the small mountain of flesh stayed where it had been pinched. Only very gradually did the blood flow back in and reduce it.

Perhaps, she thought, things might have been different if she had gone the other way from the acacia tree.

In the distance she could see a slight change in the contours. The scrubland had a definite sharp edge to it, as if it fell away somehow. She would aim for that simply because it was different.

Jade scrambled to her feet quickly. Too quickly, because the sudden exertion made her exhausted body rebel. She stumbled back into a thorn bush which then punctured her leg in several places, drawing out bright red beads as the needles retreated. The pain merely acted as a stimulus and she stood up again, though more slowly, and hung her head down until it felt safe to face the world once more. Then she started forward. The boots were forgotten - left by one who had lost the need for them, or the strength to carry them.

Her goal extracted the last reserves of strength, and as she lay looking over the edge of the ridge it didn't seem to warrant the effort.

Below her, the ground fell away for several feet and then flattened out into a small pan, perhaps some hundred yards in diameter, before rising up again to a corresponding level on the opposite side. There were several dead trees and bushes in the middle, where there was also a more pronounced depression. The surface was hard with caked sand which glittered as the sunlight caught grains of quartz. It seemed barren and lifeless.

Jade crawled to the edge and let herself roll over and down to the pan. She came to rest on soft warm sand at the verge where it changed to hard uncompromising earth.

Without conscious thought a foot dug itself painstakingly into the sand. It was cooler below the surface. Jade pulled the limb free and peeled her jodhpurs off. Then she pushed the foot back in and dug deeper. Blessed relief was found in the cool depth and she summoned up untapped willpower to aid in the digging. The sand was easily moved and the human mole was soon buried up to her chest in a miraculously chilled environment.

Relieved of the constant burning heat, Jade laid her head, egg side up, on a hastily shaped sand pillow and pulled the shirt up over her shoulder length blonde hair.

Secure at last in her cocoon, and protected from the sun, she fell instantly into a deep dreamless sleep.

Gradually the searing rays lengthened and disappeared. Darkness filled the long abandoned watering hole and the gentle night breeze made the dried leaves rustle on the ground. Many years ago the underground stream had changed its course and forsaken the surface creatures. They had moved on and left the trampled oasis to recover.

Now the only reminder of the past was the slight ammoniacal smell of elephant urine which had lingered on, trapped in the caked layers of sand.

Jade slept on, mercifully oblivious to everything. Morning would arrive all too quickly.

The night was soon in full command and the air temperature dropped like a stone, having no clouds for insulation. The ground however, retained some heat and held the fragile human safely in its grasp.

Down at eye level a night visitor appeared on the scene. A large female scorpion moved noiselessly forward to investigate the intrusion into her territory.

The insect stopped an inch or so from Jade's face and stared into the unseeing eyes. Slowly she raised a clawed limb and pulled, with the minutest strength imaginable, at the cotton shirt which had been thrown back in the movements of sleep. Satisfied, the grip was released but the animal continued to stare at the unfamiliar object. Above its back the curved tail and deadly sting swayed from side to side.

Minutes passed in silent curiosity before the scorpion grew restless and decided to continue her journey over the new hill and back home to her lair.

Jade continued in unconscious slumber, unaware of her encounter with a member of the Kalahari fauna.

Cold and cramp finally acted as an alarm clock and she woke just before dawn. It took some seconds for her dulled brain to remember where she was, but when she did, the sledgehammer blow completely knocked out her usual impatience to greet the day. She lay, still half in her cocoon, staring at the sky, her mind a thoughtless blank.

Above her, the first tentative rays of gold dust were striking the thin retreating layers of grey night cloud. They turned the soft underbelly a mellow peach red for a while before banishing the cloud completely. Fingerlike shafts of light grasped the still cold blue of the sky and warmed it to a rich deep colour as the sun rose to its daily task.

The majesty of the changing sky reached into the mind of the girl far below. As the scene slowly changed she watched and allowed the peace and tranquility of it to permeate her thoughts. Such was the calming effect of it that her troubled mind gained more rest in that hour of dawn than it had during the previous night.

Almost as the show ended she decided it was about time to do something. She became aware that the cooling sand was now cold and clammy, sticking to her legs and restricting the blood flow. Her stomach felt tight and painfully empty and her tongue was dry and swollen, as if it were a foreign body. She felt weak and anaemic even before she had extricated herself from the ground.

When she finally became mobile sand still stuck to much of her body, giving a second skin. It was hardly noticed, and even if it had been, it would have stayed there. Energy was precious and could not be spared for mere cleaning. However, this unsolicited clothing did provide some protection against sunburn and perhaps saved her from very severe burns during this critical stage. Her arms, face and lower legs were conditioned to the African sun to a large extent. The rest of her body was not. Jade had no time or inclination for sun bathing, so the rest of her was lean and supple but dangerously pale.

Jade stood in the glittering heat without a direction. She only wore the big shirt now, which hung down just enough to cover her underwear. Those few items she had were stuffed down a trouser leg, which was crudely tied in a knot to keep them in. She had allowed herself two swallows of water - one to wake her mouth up and the second to be pure gluttony. Her throat was so dry that she coughed and choked on the second one, retching and blowing most of it up her nose. Shock waves bounded round her head and the pain seemed to last forever until it finally dissolved into the centre of her head. The egg felt just as big and permanent. *It'll never go and I can be the egg-woman at the circus with the clowns and jugglers and tight something walkers and horses. Dancer where is he I miss him terribly.*

Despite this, the stopper stayed firmly on the canteen

Her head was bowed, without the bush hat which was down the trouser leg, like a child waiting sullenly for its punishment. Already she could feel the rays warming the top of it through her blonde hair, which offered only limited protection. Staring at the hated, inevitable sand by her feet, her eyes slipped in and out of focus, tinging the world with a fuzzy edge. She was tired again and the creeping lethargy of drowsiness gradually enfolded her in a python like grip. Her legs buckled and she collapsed into a kneeling position, swaying back and forth.

Voices filled her head with strange hurried talking, always getting faster. The words seemed to be going round in ever decreasing circles, but never disappearing. They were as clear and crisp as ice but she could not understand them.

Jade felt herself slipping away and there was nothing she could do about it. The welcome release from her torture was near, its warm grey oblivion drawing ever closer.

A new voice overpowered the others. It sang sweetly inside her mind and seemed to banish the demons.

Such was the sound that Jade eventually realised it could not be imagined, it must be real. She dragged herself back from the brink and the sound took shape inside her confused mind.

" Honey, honey, quick quick, honey " it sang, again and again. The voice was sweet as honey itself, with lilting insistent tones that repeated the summons.

" Quick, quick, honey !"

The very thought of food brought the last drops of moisture jetting out under her tongue and she gingerly tried to lick the swelled and cracked lips. What little fluid she managed to transfer was instantly evaporated by the burning sun and she grimaced in anger. At this movement the cracks parted and small globules of bright red blood escaped to the sand below, causing an intense smarting pain to the girl.

Needled back into the land of the living by this discomfort, she lifted her head and looked for the singer.

There was nothing except a little brown and white bird staring curiously at her with its head cocked to one side. It was on the crest of a dune a few yards from Jade.

As she watched, the bird hopped away several feet and turned round to look at her. Getting a somewhat limited response, the bird returned and repeated the performance.

Jade watched the second show with interest as the bird returned to its original perch. A shower of delightful sound filled the air.

" Quick, quick, honey, honey ! " it sang.

" Honey, honey, quick " and hopped away and back.

It had an enticing manner and Jade wondered vaguely how it could speak English.

Again the sweet singing. The bird increased its effort, ruffling up brown and white feathers and giving a masterful performance.

How could the human refuse ? The temptation was always too much. They were not allowed to ignore it.

Jade took a kneeling pace towards the singer. At once she was rewarded with an ecstasy of sound and the little bird hopped a corresponding distance away. The message was beginning to form - she was supposed to follow the bird. Why, was a mystery, but where else did she have to go ?

She had stopped and the guide was impatient again. Jade struggled to move, eventually settling into a slow painful crawl which would just have outpaced a tortoise.

The ground bit into her knees every tortuous step and her flesh soon bore the white imprints of each piece of quartz, stone and dead vegetation it encountered. Still the bird beckoned and sang encouragement when she faltered, fluttering around her. Occasionally she stumbled and pitched head first into the sandy scrub. She wanted so much to stay on the harsh carpet and rest. The temptation was almost insurmountable.

Hot sand and dirt caked her hair and face, fastened to it like concrete with the help of tiny beads of sweat which had been perched on her forehead. Particles crept into ears and nose, and her mouth was never free from the crunch of grit between her teeth.

Jade no longer had any awareness of the pain and discomfort which assaulted her from all angles. She had only enough mental energy to concentrate on following the winged guide. Nothing else mattered. She crawled until her body told her she could crawl no more. Then she crawled again, and, with the single mindedness of an automaton, kept going forward. Her mind was doing all the work, the body had collapsed long ago.

The goal was reached and the honey bird settled carefully on a thorn bush. Below, the human was curled up in the foetal position where it had been for a few minutes since collapsing for the last time. The bird could do no more. It had fulfilled its part of the bargain and could only wait. There was one more partner to arrive and the guide anxiously searched the horizons, sure that its incessant calling would have summoned him.

Gradually Jade became aware that the guide was no longer beckoning her forward to further exertion. The gentle song had been replaced by an intermittent harsh buzzing and she opened her eyes to see a huge termite hill directly in front of her.

The buzzing seemed to emanate from this mountain. Jade uncurled her legs. The skin felt like paper. It crackled and tore with every movement. Amazingly she still had her few worldly goods with her. So, she remembered was her water bottle. She allowed herself one complete mouthful and then screwed the top back on with a resolve she never knew she had.

Jade pulled herself back a few yards to get a better view. The high rise insect block had long since been abandoned by its original occupants. There was now a constant traffic of bees through the entrance which was a little way above ground level. The network of passages and catacombs left by the termites was ideal for storing the precious nectar and the colony had flourished.

Hunger and thirst had honed her senses to a razor's edge, so the faint sweet odour which she could now smell was tantalising beyond belief. It promised life, pure and simple. In years to come, the unexpected aroma of honey would instantly transport her back to this moment in time.

A sudden burst of excited sound from the direction of the thorn bush made her look up. The little brown and white bird was hopping around in agitation and looking past Jade, along the route which it had led her.

She drew back a couple more yards and listened to the strange call which she could now hear getting closer. An urgent whistling filled the air, followed by a distant chuckling sound. This was soon accompanied by the noise of scurrying feet and an eager, hurrying animal came into view.

The honey badger was a robust, dark grey creature trotting fast on sturdy, slightly curved legs. It was the desert equivalent of the city gent on business and it ignored the girl, heading purposefully for the termite hill.

An audience of two watched him with rapt concentration. One knew all. The other knew nothing. The master of his art sat back on thick grey haunches for a couple of seconds to survey the problem. Coarse wiry hair rippled up in waves along his quarters.

Thinking time was over, the honey badger had work to do. He trotted over to the hive entrance and examined it. A few careful scrapes with the digging claws on a powerful front foot and the preparation was done.

The badger then slowly backed up to the entrance and gently lifted his hind quarters so that they fitted the opening. His balance was assured by solid planting of the forelimbs.

The animal then gave release to one of the most natural of bodily urges. The end effect was akin to the use of smoke by the bee keeper, and the occupants of the hive were temporarily subdued. Tough badger hide can easily weather the onslaught of an enraged African bee, but when the sting is delivered in an enclosed hive the sickly sweet odour of venom will madden the rest of the swarm to attack.

His role completed, the badger left his perch and stood a short distance away.

Incredibly, the eyes of both animals turned to Jade. Inspiration and intuition guided her hand. Still on her knees, she crawled to the entrance and reached in for the trophy. It came away easily and she brought out a long comb of dark purple honey. The sweet smell permeated the depths of her parched body, bringing saliva jetting out under her tongue.

She removed several combs, and the most natural thing in the world was to place one in front of the bird and one in front of the honey badger. They expected nothing else and did not flinch when she approached close enough to touch them.

In giving part of the sweet prize to both animals, Jade continued the pact of mutual assistance that had existed between them since that first occasion, timeless centuries ago, when the honey bird recognised the abilities of the diminutive humans called Bushmen and, in a gigantic leap forward, used and helped them. Indeed, such is the bond between them that even to this day, the code of the Kalahari Bushman compels him to follow and assist a honey bird whenever its demands are broadcast. Failure to do so is almost unheard of.

Exhilarating energy spread throughout her body as the honey worked its magic. Jade blessed her foresight in saving some of the water until now, for the new food would have been almost impossible to swallow without its assistance. At the end of the feast her canteen was empty. She could feel her limbs being rejuvenated and at last, her painfully empty belly had fire in it once more. Luckily, the supply was exhausted before the gorging teenager made herself sick.

Once returned to the world of the living, her pain and discomfort reappeared, seemingly a hundred times worse. Her re-awakened nerves delighted in their ability to send messages of anguish to the brain. The thirst quickly returned and her tongue seemed to fill the whole of her head.

Although the sun was now on its downward path in the sky, Jade knew that to journey further would be a mistake. She needed to rest and try to mend herself before going on.

Quickly she searched around for a suitable place to be a mole and found it in a sand dune which had a steeply walled crescent shape and already gave some limited shade. It lay about a hundred yards from her, across a flat plain of tussocky grasses and scrub.

Before leaving the hive to recover from the plunderings, Jade removed three more combs and put them at the base of a mopane tree some distance from the termite hill. There she carefully packed them with fresh green leaves, laboriously plucked from branches as high as she could reach, and placed them in a little dug out pit, piling stones around the sides and top to complete the construction.

Unsure as to whether her fortifications would keep out any determined creature, Jade started out for the crescent shaped dune. She was well aware that despite her efforts, she would probably not be able to use the stored food. It would more than likely be stolen or melt into oblivion as the sun warmed it. Still, if left with the original owners it would be firmly beyond reach and taking it with her was impractical.

Jade stopped after a few minutes walking to look back at the hive. Both her new found allies had disappeared and the bees were going about their daily business as usual. Already it was only a memory.

The new found energy stayed with her about as long as the mist on a midsummer's morning. Her legs ached and trembled visibly with fatigue and as she slumped into the relative shade of the dune, minute explosions of colour filled her vision. The whole inner core of her body seemed to be tingling with cramp - like pains.

Her sight recovered somewhat after she had been lying down a while, allowing her to focus on a puny three leafed green shoot which appeared close to her face at ground level. It was the same as others she had seen, but this one was particularly vivid and almost inviting. Why was it familiar ? What had Sam shown her during their week all that time ago ?

You look on the outside of the desert girl, you see nuthin. You ain't never gonna catch no food on the run. Sit and be a part of it - be a part of where you are. Look down. You standing on it girl. The words of the old farmhand floated out of her memory.

Jade reached out to pluck it. She expected it to come away from the earth with ease, exposing a tiny root system. This it steadfastly refused to do, so she tugged harder but still it remained attached.

Finally, the stem parted in the middle, leaving a small green stump protruding from the sand. Curiosity aroused, Jade dug around the stump, eventually revealing a large potato sized tuber, dirty dark brown in colour. It needed not a second glance. Juices dribbled down her chin as her teeth sank into the crisp young flesh. She ate it in its entirety and it was possibly the best food she had ever tasted.

The same treatment was rapidly delivered to two others nearby, their presence shown by the tell tale green shoots.

The transformation was miraculous, if not physically then certainly mentally. The prospect of starvation and death receded swiftly. Blinkers fell from her eyes and she saw the desert in a new light. It was still a living world with creatures flourishing on what nature provided.

Armed with a fresh enthusiasm for living, the girl went in search of survival in the days that followed.

She found food at the foot of dunes and sheltered levels where huge Tsama melons sat in groups. They were nourished by supplies of water hidden deep within the dunes, stored since the last rains and therefore preserved from evaporation by the sub-tropical sun.

Desert cucumbers, with their spiked armour, were temporarily beyond reach until she discovered that, when twisted, the spikes left their charges quite easily, leaving them to her mercy.

Jade soon learned that a twist and curl of a tiny leaf above the sand was a sure sign of a great bulb concealed beneath. In the course of time she would learn to recognise and differentiate between the tubers, but right now they were food, plain and simple.

Once discovered, the desert seemed to have endless varieties - desert potatoes, artichokes, parsnips, onions and even truffles could be found. These were supplemented by supplies of triangular wild figs, raisins and berries, all provided courtesy of the Kalahari flora and yielded with varying degrees of reluctance.

The new diet required a certain amount of readjustment. Flavours and textures were totally alien, as were the rejections by her internal processes, which thankfully ceased after registering the initial discomfort. Melon juice was the most unpalatable to start with, having a very bitter taste. However, once she grew accustomed to it, the shock was quite stimulating and refreshing. As a parting gift, the juice left an aftertaste of sweetness. It soon became a firm favourite.

In order to help her obtain the buried foods, Jade acquired a digging stick for herself. This was a suitably shaped branch of an acacia tree which she managed to break off by swinging on it for several minutes. It was a close run thing as to whether her arms or the branch gave out first, but the tree tired of the struggle and gave the girl her first aid to desert survival.

She was triumphant, launching the stick high in the air in celebration. It promptly lodged itself in one of the middle order branches on the way down. Jade looked at it in disbelief and disgust, but she had no choice. She climbed gingerly out onto one of the sturdy lower branches, stood up on it even more gingerly and reached up to shake the offending part of the tree. The digging stick obligingly returned to earth.

The implement was worth rescuing. In the not too distant future it would save her life, and change it forever.

She found a roughly surfaced flat stone and set about sharpening one end to a point. Her knife sliced easily through the bark and brought the stick to a fine point very quickly, but she realised that it was too sharp and fine - it snapped under any sort of digging pressure. So she cut off the end square and started again, with the aim of getting not such a good point. As she bent forward, the ever present blistering sunlight cut through tousled blonde hair which hung like a curtain in front of her. The light caught the tiny glistening beads of facial sweat, making them into diamond droplets.

The last effort made and she was finally satisfied with the result. Around her waist she wore the belt from her jodhpurs, over the outsize shirt, and she thrust the stick between body and belt, then stood up to stretch her aching back.

Burning heat on her legs was signal enough that the day was getting older. Shade was needed so Jade returned to the base of the recently climbed acacia tree. She sat with her back against the rough scaly trunk, knees pulled up to her chest. Thoughts and ideas washed over her mind like waves lapping up to a shoreline. For the first time she almost felt at peace with the world she had been given. She was mature enough to realise that she was utterly and completely lost. She blamed herself for not being able to follow Dancer's tracks well enough and the ensuing results. Nevertheless, she hoped she was reasonably near to the edge of the desert and determined to survive as best she could until any search party happened across her. That was her mental survival strategy and was just as important as the physical one. Without hope she would have given up and been claimed by the desert. With hope anything was possible. In fact she was further into the interior than most men ever ventured. It was years since any other human had looked on this part of the desert, and still would be.

She had found her way over the first hurdle with the help of a small brown and white bird, and was now able to appreciate and begin to understand the harsh beauty of the desert. So, when the sun started to climb, hibernation was normally the order of the day. Jade would burrow her way into cool sand or seek whatever shade the desert condescended to provide and ride out the heat as best she could. Activity during this period was strictly emergencies only. Fruit was always to hand to provide protection against thirst, and there she stayed.

Miraculous relief came towards the end of the afternoons when the great yellow orb started to sink and the rays of scorching heat hit the earth at an ever decreasing angle. Animals emerged to forage. So did the girl. Relentlessly she searched for, and found, enough food to live on. When that was done Jade occupied her time gathering every variety of leaf and plant she could find. Her lust for knowledge combined with a natural inquisitiveness developed her into a lethal young botanist. Every specimen was minutely examined. Texture, colour, size and appearance were all noted in her memory.

So passed most days, and as they drifted together Jade settled into a routine, hanging her very cloak of existence on its fragile shoulders. For each month she survived in this barren wilderness she matured a year. Constantly roaming the desert, and probing deeper and deeper into its interior, helped shed the puppy fat from her. She became lean and mean. Muscles developed, strengthened and were toned to a fine pitch. Her already blonde hair bleached rapidly to the colour of chalk, contrasting starkly with her skin which was now a mahogany bronze and effectively repelled the sun's rays.

The oversized shirt had been removed and tied round her waist. This position it shared with the belt and digging stick, only coming into its own at night when she curled up beneath it like a cat. The jodhpurs served as carrying pouches during the day and were rolled up for a pillow at night. Her exposed chest, tanned to the same dark golden brown, became as well muscled as any boy's. In short, she flourished. Every day saw her growing closer and closer to her new surroundings and becoming more at peace with them. They were home to her now.

Memories of life before the desert faded a little, but never disappeared. Some days were better than others. Some days she ached and longed for life to be as it was. On these days she could cry for hours and sometimes stayed buried like a mole. She called these her scrambled egg head days and knew that nothing would be done until the mood lifted. Deep in her mind she knew that the only way to recover what she had was to survive until someone found her. So survive she would. She had always been a solitary animal, preferring her own company above that of others. Nothing was more acceptable than to be allowed complete freedom, which was what she had yearned for in her previous life. Now she had it, but the price was the responsibility for keeping herself alive.

******

The juvenile blue wildebeest pulled himself to a halt and clouds of swirling dust gradually settled, glistening in the early morning light. Flecks of clotted white foam were scattered about his neck and flanks, thrown there from a mouth already drooling again with long ropes of thick saliva. The lean, sparsely muscled body heaved with the pressures of frantic exertion, which had also bathed his coat in a sheen of moisture, bubbling up into thin lines of a pale soapy mixture where the rough hide formed natural creases. His breathing was loud and rasping, being drawn swiftly through dilated nostrils. Constantly moving and sweeping the horizons with quick, agitated movements of his head, the animal was close to panic and utter exhaustion.

Down his left flank were three long raking claw marks through which the clean white bone of a rib could easily be seen. As the chest heaved, these long wounds opened and closed like a gasping fish out of water.

The frantic commotion woke Jade who was curled up in a teenager-sized hollow some little way from a mopane tree. She had decided against spending the night at the base of the tree on the grounds that several weaver birds had made it their stop over point. Bitter experience had taught her that the calls of nature also apply to feathered species, and when they were roosted above you, the outcome was less than pleasant. What annoyed her most was that the miscreants seemed to show little or no remorse when confronted by the angry victim.

The daylight was already good enough to see by, the wildebeest coming into view as Jade stood up. He was obviously still a youngster, small and runt like. The body was a dark grey colour, tinged with a silvery sheen. On the neck and shoulders were a series of darkly pigmented bars which extended back to the mid-body, giving a brindled appearance.

Drooping over the shoulders was a long dark mane, the same shade as the whisk of hair which hung from his tail and nearly touched the ground. A fringe of identical growth hung from his throat, stretching out along the entire underside of the neck.

Jade moved slightly and caught the very extreme of his field of vision. The head swung round instantly and lowered slightly to take in this new threat.

The sides of his face were grey, and the russet coloured hair on his forehead was still present in juvenile abundance. Glittering black eyes stared out from beneath immature horns.

As is the practice amongst the huge gregarious herds of wildebeest, the young male had been unceremoniously evicted from the female herd where he had been born and raised, and was now searching for other adult males and juveniles to join up with. To date he had been remarkably unsuccessful, failing to make even one contact.

A sixth sense made the hair stand up on the back of the girl's neck. She suddenly noticed and read urgent danger signs. The animal was in fear of its life, but for no apparent reason that she could immediately discern. No matter that her human mind told her it was safe, the developing animal instincts told her it was not. She was an interloper in the animal world and would obey animal instincts. Carefully, Jade walked to the mopane tree, her every movement being followed by the maned black head.

She took hold of a branch above head height and, with strength that surprised her, hauled her lean teak body up onto it.

Safely established astride her perch she had a much better view and set about deliberately quartering the surrounding landscape to pinpoint the threat.

Sparse dry grass waved forward, imperceptibly, but not quite properly. It grabbed her attention like a sudden hand round the throat. Eagerly she strained her eyes, only to feel a zephyr like breeze touch her forearms, pass by, and move the grass again in exactly the same way.

The breeze passed, the swaying dried stalks ceased to gyrate and the moment dissolved into a shimmering of white heat, sand reflecting the burning rays.

" Something's there " she whispered to absolutely no-one, and was instantly shocked at the sound of human words in the echoing silence.

So she watched the spot for a full long ten minutes. With rapt concentration her vision blurred, swimming in and out of focus as the light, indistinguishable colours of the vegetation merged with the rippling waters of heat. Rough bark and spiny edges bit into her bare legs, begging for movement to release pain and nagging cramp, but Jade waited and watched.

The wildebeest waited and watched too. He was calm now, breathing regularly, sweat drying on his flanks. Blood dripped systematically and monotonously from the wound, staining the desert scrub pink in a slowly expanding circle.

He shifted his weight anxiously and let one hind hoof hang relaxed, just touching the ground with its tip. The diminutive body felt as weak and underdeveloped as it was. Even without any more outside interference he would last no more than a day.

High above their heads in the lower levels of the atmosphere, a distant relative of the grass twitching breeze was at work.

For several days the wind had relentlessly pushed a large domed cumulus cloud across the featureless desert, seemingly trying to unite it with others of the same family. It was destined not to succeed, for at this time of year the nearest to be found would be gently rolling off Table Mountain, some seven hundred miles to the south. The whole of West Africa was scorched with continuous heat.

Still the rogue cloud wandered on, casting its single lonely shadow. Gradually it approached a mopane tree in the Kalahari, insignificant almost to the point of invisibility. For a moment it masked the spot in comparative gloom, relief from constant light. Then it passed, roaming westwards, until eventually the tenuous collection of gases would abandon their collective shape and scatter into billions of molecules.

The sudden, if momentary, relief from blinding sunlight took all concerned by surprise. Jade felt her eyes relax noticeably as the iris muscles allowed more light in to compensate.

The reflected glare from the scrub and sand vanished to reveal a pair of light brown rounded ears, attached to a head with smouldering yellow eyes. The wildebeest saw the crouching young lioness at the same time as Jade. Frantically he scrabbled at the ground with panic stricken legs, already convinced of the inevitability of the situation.

Hardly had he gone two paces before the golden thunderbolt struck him, pulling hind quarters down and ripping open his belly with terrifying ease. An experienced hunter would have ended the matter then and there with a bite to the throat or nape of the neck, usually waiting for the unfortunate victim to bleed to death.

However, the lioness was young and inexperienced, testified to by the fact that the quarry had already escaped her claws once.

She had never actually made a kill before and now the huntress lingered an instant too long, pinning his hind legs down, with the still intact intestines spilling out over the sand. Grotesquely, the gut continued to pulsate.

In a last desperate move the wildebeest pivoted his upper body round on shattered quarters, angled his head down and lunged once at the golden killer. Both horns found their mark in the neck, either side of the windpipe. They stabbed through hide and flesh with the ease of a stiletto, bringing fountains of arterial blood.

An outpouring of enraged sound filled the still air. Such was the physical force of the bellow that Jade could feel tremors through her branch as the creature vented its surprise and anger. The lioness went again for his neck and swiftly finished the matter. Then she jumped away from her prey. It was forgotten now as she tried in vain to lick her wounds and stem the steady flow which was already starting to form sticky pads in her fur.

She bellowed again with frustration and panic when it was apparent that no amount of frantic head twisting would improve the situation. Indeed every neck movement pulled at torn muscle, punching white hot agony into her. A vicious circle of effort and pain quickly drove the creature to distraction. She became oblivious to everything except a respite from her wounds and half cantered away into the scrub of knee high thorn bushes and grass tufts to seek some form of relief.

Roars could clearly be heard retreating into the distance, growing ever more plaintive until they finally disappeared.

Jade scrambled down from her perch to survey the carnage and suffering. She looked around quickly, to satisfy herself that there were no other animals which could harm her.

She knew that she would soon have to learn to hunt in order to survive. Her supplies of fruit and berries, although still sufficient, were becoming more scarce and she had to search long and hard, using all her acquired skill, to locate them.

There was also the competition to be considered. Nocturnal foragers were now much in evidence, destroying food before she even found it. She had watched the long haired brown hyena rolling tsama melons away like a natural ball player and had often been forced to eat the husks left by small rodents after they had had their fill. She was not yet confident enough to compete with them in their world, during the night.

She looked at the dead wildebeest and forced herself to realise that whatever it might have been ten minutes ago, it was now a source of food and material. Or at least it would be if she knew what she wanted and how to extract it.

A flapping of huge ungainly wings brought the first vulture down and it hopped aggressively forward, staking its claim alongside this unexpected scavenger.

Jade drew her sharpened digging stick, a tiny seed of anger germinating in her belly. Any prize was hers and a carrion eating crow would certainly not be getting any if she could help it. Jade lunged swiftly with the stick and the vulture withdrew to a respectful distance, but she knew that her time was limited now. Soon there would be ten where there was one, and she would be overwhelmed.

Straddling the carcass, she gripped the leathery hide where it had been sliced open at the ribcage. It pulled back surprisingly easily, exposing bloody flesh and bone. Steeling herself, she brought a stone down time after time on the naked ribs, breaking most of them eventually. Then she sliced around the edges of the broken bones with her knife and was able to prise a section out. It immediately slipped from her hands to receive an instant coating of sand and dust.

Airborne reinforcements were arriving rapidly now. Jade racked her brains for anything else which might be of use. Inspiration came and she jumped back astride the body, scattering the braver of the new arrivals. The hide of the wildebeest was covered with thick coarse hair. It would keep her warm during the chilly nights.

Swiftly she pulled hard at the section that was already parted from the owner. Using her knife as a dissecting scalpel she was able free a large section with little effort. Then she sliced round the back of it with a sawing motion and it was free.

As she leapt off the carcass, clutching one prize wrapped in the other, it was engulfed in a sea of fighting grey wings and hooked beaks. The body seemed to come alive as it was jerked and pummeled, performing a last ritual death dance.

Jade hurried away to more than a respectable distance. A kill attracted all kinds of animals and anything in the vicinity was likely to become the second course if it became too curious. She was also well aware that the flesh she was carrying acted as a powerful magnet in that respect, and distance was the only safety.

The girl trotted off into the bush at a steady pace which she could keep up for quite a considerable time. She used it for long distances and had discovered that it was actually less tiring and dehydrating than walking. The fierce sun had less time to act on her and if she cleared her mind to a blank, concentrating on a rhythm, her legs could almost go on forever as long as the pace remained the same. A far cry from the girl who used to be exhausted by a hundred yard walk in the desert. *Wish I was back at the school now......I'd run those two smart arses into the dirt......and have steam left to go round again.....God I'd give anything to be back there and suffering German again.....guten Tag, Fraulein....wie geht's ? Jade.....kannst du lesen bitte ?*

She had no idea of the actual distance she covered, it was simply a matter of reaching her goal, whether it was a water hole, shelter or food supply. In fact, in the searing temperatures, few athletes could have matched her stamina.

The majestic old camel thorn acacia tree was about half a mile from the killing ground, a distance judged by her to be quite safe. The tree itself was a landmark and could be seen when you were still a day's steady journey away.

Rough scaly bark bound the massive trunk together and it was crowned with a wide umbrella of silvery green foliage. A thick horizontal branch had been taken over by a colony of weaver birds who had constructed their communal home on it. A marvelously engineered structure, it was shaped like a nightmarishly huge bees nest laid flat, and skewered by the branch. More than fifty individual nests were now contained within it, housing some three hundred birds.

Every so often a new pair would build their dwelling, adding a minimal weight to the nest, and the struggling branch would sag imperceptibly. In the fullness of slow desert time it would lose the battle, splintering off at the trunk with a tremendous slow cracking and deposit the whole colony firmly on the ground, crushing eggs and fledglings. Survivors would grieve over the loss for a day or so and then go their separate ways to become founder members of new settlements.

Jade slowed to an easy walk some way from the tree, so that by the time she reached it she wasn't even out of breath. Observing the weaver bird colony, there was a choice to be made. Sit in the relative shade under the nest, or settle by the other side of the tree with its limited protection from the early afternoon sun.

Experience told her it was much pleasanter to be out of the killing heat, so she had to suffer the weaver birds.

The flesh was laid out on several flat stones to keep it relatively clear of sand, but as she wasn't prepared to even contemplate eating it raw, cooking it posed a problem. Fires and barbecues were started with matches, paraffin and the like. Without them, making a fire would be hard work. Raw meat stayed on the stones while Jade went foraging for some food that she knew what to do with.

Her skill had her back under the tree within minutes, pondering further on the problem as she absent mindedly scuffed earth and sand off a bulbous tuber. Its white flesh was crisp and dripping with juice, giving her mouth a fresh clean taste.

A combination of relative shade, fatigue and a full stomach was too much for even the hardiest of spirits to resist. Eyelids drooped and Jade fell into a deep slumber.

Succulent new grass, however limited, is a highly sought after commodity in such an arid and harsh environment. As well as food it provides precious moisture, freeing animals from the hazardous visit to scarce water holes. It is well worth a small risk to obtain.

Two young springbok were currently taking that small risk. Green shoots were prising their way through dried vegetation and scrub all around the camel thorn acacia, making rich pickings for the pair.

They gradually edged closer to the tree, as the grass around them disappeared and their courage increased. Of course they had long ago seen the strange recumbent creature in the shade and had observed it for a considerable time before deciding that it was of no danger, for the moment anyway.

Every so often there was a natural pause in the search for food and, in a gesture of courtship, the female would nuzzle the face of the male and be rewarded by her partner rubbing his facial scent gland against her flank. There was no urgency in their ritual. In due course they would undoubtedly mate, and twenty four weeks later bring a leggy bundle of wet fur into the world. However right now food came first, and was worth at least ninety eight per cent concentration.

Observation can also be a two way process. From beneath half shuttered eyes Jade delighted in this opportunity to observe wildlife at close quarters. To all intents and purposes she was lifeless, the only movement being a slow closing of her eyelids about every thirty seconds.

Long hours were often passed in this, her favourite of pastimes, and being practiced in the art of playing dead was better than having a photographic hide.

Fascination and curiosity filled her mind, along with a longing for her sketch block. *No point though...... I don't have a wall to stick them on.* There was also an imp of a mischievous thought.

The animals approached closer, so that she could even clearly see how their long pointed ears curved round like new leaves waiting to mature into their full broad shape. A bright cinnamon brown colour adorned the upper body of the springbok, with the characteristic dark reddish brown horizontal band along the flanks, separating it from the snowy white underbelly. The white fur extended back, under the hind legs, up to colour the centre of the rump and along the lower back, tailing out into a dorsal crest of long erectile hair.

The observer held her breath as a chalky face stared directly at her, lower jaw moving steadily from side to side, chewing the freshly severed shoots. The springbok disposed of the mouthful and allowed its head to sink lazily back to the ground where it nosed about in the scrub, selecting only the Kalahari's finest.

The moment was right. Jade pushed herself quickly upright into a sitting position, at the same time brushing both hands forward in the loose sand, making two clouds of a swirling mass which flew out beyond her outstretched feet.

Two more startled creatures it would have been hard to imagine. They were still for the best part of a heartbeat, then in unison they bounced high into the air with backs arched, their legs stiff and a fan of white back hairs proclaiming alarm. On landing, the bouncing movement or pronking was repeated, sending them another five feet up and an impressive distance away. They merged rapidly into the heat haze and arid bushveldt, looking for all the world like children on pogo sticks.

This classic springbok response was exactly what Jade was looking for. Deep down inside a stirring of mirth arose and slowly forced its way out, as a volcano has to give way to the inevitable. Corners of her mouth twitched, edging upwards and tiny laughter lines appeared by sparkling blue-green eyes.

Finally a rich infectious chuckle bubbled up from the depths, heralding peals of laughter which seemed to echo and ring out, announcing happiness to the whole world. Indeed as the final chortles died a natural death and re-emerged as a healthy sigh, Jade suddenly realised that she couldn't actually remember when she had laughed last.

She roused herself and stood up to stare at the dying embers of the sun. Golden shades of reds, purples and ambers were reflected by high cloud into a vast fan of darkening colour in the sky.

As the huge glowing sun fell steadily below the horizon it silhouetted a distant tree with a small herd of zebra grazing contentedly around it. A single barking gecko called out into the dusk, announcing nightfall to all his subjects. Her world was at peace. Her world was beautiful.

Bending down again to retrieve the long forgotten flesh, she discovered it grilled to perfection. The flat stones had combined with the sun to provide her with a cooker. Breakfast would be a luxury.

Tomorrow, she decided, would be a day for traveling. She knew of a fossil river valley at the edge of her explored territory which was bigger by far than any other she had seen. Tomorrow she would go there. Yes, tomorrow she would definitely go there.

******

The open topped Land Rover finally reached its limit. The front wheels were digging themselves into the sand and the driver knew he could go no further. As it was, the only way out was mats under the tyres and a lot of spadework.

He cursed softly under his breath and shrugged a pair of wide shoulders in resignation. Looking at it realistically, he hadn't expected to be able to coax the old workhorse this far.

Tony van Niekerk climbed out over the welded door and luxuriously stretched the six foot three inch frame that made a mockery of his sixty eight years. He could have been a classic white hunter, put out to grass in his declining years. He could have been, had he not possessed an abhorrence for the sport of hunting for its own sake. He knew several 'sporting guides' and despised them bitterly as they kowtowed to the whims of fat sweating Europeans or Americans who blasted away their frustration with modern day life from the safety of an armoured truck, sometimes leaving the guide to risk his life rushing to perform the coup de grace before a gutshot beast disappeared into the bush to die in prolonged agony. God, how he hated that carnage and suffering.

Over the years the sun had burnished his skin to a freckled leathery consistency, but had left him the tell tale laughter lines etched into his face. He was still a powerful man. Running a huge farm on the edge of the unforgiving desert left no time for a rocking chair on the stoep, putting on fat.

He pushed back the wide brimmed hat, revealing the long dried in sweat marks from years of toil. A new one might have been more pleasing to the eye, but this had seen him through thick and thin. He could see no reason to change it. He wiped away the current moisture with a red necktie.

A strange shape hanging onto a half grown thorn bush caught his eye. The persistent breeze was filling it and trying to move it on, like it had done before. Tony took three strides to it and caught it just as it was about to be carried off.

He looked at it and turned it over in his hands. It was barely recognisable but he knew what he saw. The feed bag was torn and faded, but the strap was still attached at one end. Trembling slightly, he looked for writing on the underside of the strap. Just visible were the words " STOLEN FROM DANCER " in a girlish hand.

He cradled the material next to his chest and a single unashamed tear rolled unchecked down three days growth of beard as he stared out into the shifting heat images of the sands.

"After all these months ", he whispered. " I have to go now, but I will come back. I promise. Please wait a little longer."

The grandfather stooped down to the thorn bush and fastened a metal tag to its main trunk with a length of wire.

Without looking back into the desert he returned to the Land Rover and slowly reached for the shovel.

CHAPTER

FOUR

The Kalahari is the largest continuous stretch of sand in the world. It is bounded by the headwaters of the Zambezi River to the north, plateaus of the Transvaal and Zimbabwe to the east, the Orange River to the south and the highlands of South West Africa to the west. It is possible to travel for some two and a half thousand miles in a straight line without crossing its boundaries. Within the vast expanse of its arid wilderness live creatures which vary from the tiniest red spider mite to the majesty and power of the herd bull elephant.

From an aerial point of view, the martial eagle, recently the proud father of three, regarded a two hundred square kilometer patch of this sandy ocean as his own, to hunt over as he saw fit. Soaring high into the sky on thermal air currents born from the intense ground heat, he surveyed his territory with a keenness added to by hunger and new found responsibility.

Keeping his slate grey wings almost motionless, the hunter allowed himself to be carried along by the steady breeze, all the time cris-crossing the ground below with superb vision for any tell tale movement that might herald the closing moments for a small creature.

A sun baked mound, no bigger than a pimple on the horizon at this distance, caught his eye. There was movement.

He was, however, going to be unlucky, for the occupant of this undesirable residence, now visible to the eagle, was an alert meerkat.

The suricate was acting as lookout for the other foraging members of his clan and had spent the last hour in the blistering heat diligently searching the skies for just such an enemy.

Standing upright at his post, with forelegs dangling limp in front of his slender grey body, he was dedication itself. The safety of his colleagues depended on his ability to spot an aggressor, for as they searched 'heads down' for food, they were open to attack. Eventually another team member would take over, but until then the responsibility was his alone.

A speck moved in the sky, just within the watcher's sight line. Concentration was total. The body stiffened like a flagpole and his head craned forward. A mere suspicion to this experienced meerkat was quite enough, and the speck looked very familiar.

He was not about to be denied his moment of glory and changed the reassuring vocal "peeps" to a short cry of alarm. This was rapidly followed by the scurrying and skidding of hind quarters in the sand as a dozen furry bodies disappeared down a well placed bolt hole, as easily as rainwater down a drain.

Part of the art of desert survival is to be able to read the reactions of other creatures and act accordingly, in your own best interests.

The ground squirrel, sitting on his haunches, was dozing upright in the shade of a blackthorn acacia bush when the sudden flurry of movement by the meerkats brought it into the present with a start. It hurried out from cover to see what had happened and promptly came across an eerie lack of fellow creatures.

High above, the predator was wheeling around in a long circle and was about to search elsewhere when a meal appeared from under a bush.

In a reflex action the eagle began to parachute steeply earthwards, shooting out razor sharp talons at the end of his long muscular legs. It struck seconds later in complete silence, the impact killing the ground squirrel instantly.

As the bird ascended again, somewhat weighed down by the additional burden, a pair of cautious grey heads appeared in tandem at the top of a hole in the ground and anxiously scanned the horizon. Soon they would forage. The system had worked again.

A mildly interested observer of these events was lounging languidly on the branch of a mopane tree. It was hot and the jet black leopard cub with the torn ear closed both eyes again to resume a long overdue siesta. She was lying along the branch with legs draped over each side, chin resting on the bark.

Dune and Spring were stretched out in the shade of a gigantic granite kopje, whilst the leader of this first fully fledged safari into the wilderness had all three charges in sight from her vantage point at the base of a spreading leadwood tree. These light grey hardwoods, as Mother had quickly found out, provide much better shade than the mopane as the latter's leaves, paired in the shape of butterfly wings, fold up in hot dry weather, allowing sunlight through.

Mother had decided that it was about time the cubs began to learn how to fend for themselves. They were big enough to tackle small prey and the sooner they developed a killer instinct the better.

Her decision was mainly prompted by Torn Ear, who was growing and maturing by leaps and bounds. Her brothers were a little way behind in the physical stakes but matched her spirit in full. However, at the back of the parent's mind was always the nagging thought that an accident or attack would befall her, leaving the cubs to starve. Once they were equipped with survival skills she would rest easier.

Today was lesson one and had been notable so far for its remarkable lack of success.

The adult had taken them further down the fossil river valley than she had ever gone before, to search out new environments and challenges, with, hopefully, some suitable subjects for teaching hunting skills.

So far they had encountered only a solitary francolin among a pile of loose rocks. At their approach, the bird had risen up to the accompaniment of hysterical cries and had made them all jump as one.

The safari continued into the mid-morning when conditions, as usual, forced abandonment until the afternoon and its relative cool. Each found his or her resting place and waited for the zenith of heat to pass.

Normally, the hours of darkness are preferred by leopards for hunting. However, they are also daylight opportunists and Mother had decided to conduct an initiation where she could keep the pupils in view.

Time wore on and still the family slumbered, with only Mother stirring occasionally to check on the cubs. The air hung motionless and heavy and the temperature continued to rise.

Despite its meagre shade, the mopane tree was better than nothing. Or so a group of zebra thought. They inched their way laboriously through shimmering heatwaves, and on reaching it allowed a nursing mare and foal the prime position, directly under the largest branch. The infant was some weeks old, and as such was well able to keep up with its elders, but it was still very small. It stood in the combined shadow of its mother and the tree and flapped its wispy tail in a vain attempt to defeat the ever present vicious mosquitoes.

It might have served the zebra well to be a little more choosy about their lunch stop, and a glance upwards would have saved a lot of trouble.

A solitary black eyelid flicked up to survey the nature of this new disturbance of the peace. Torn Ear had been oblivious to the zebras approach but had been wakened by the occasional whinney and stamping of hooves as another mosquito struck home.

The second eyelid opened more rapidly as the possibilities became apparent to even this embryo hunter. The leopard cub manoeuvred silently into a better position, bringing a pair of limbs back onto the branch. Beneath, the animals were blissfully unaware of the impending hazard.

Across the scrub Mother watched with eager anticipation, holding herself rock steady lest she alarm the zebra.

Torn Ear lay poised. She knew what had to be done, but exactly how to do it was largely a mystery.

Minutes passed in concentration.

The desert heat continued to sing in silence while the zebra rested and absent mindedly shifted their weight between alternate sets of hooves. Their only concern was surviving the dry suffocating air.

The infant zebra coughed, racking its whole ribcage forward in a single movement, and then was still.

Around the other side of the trunk the lead animal spotted a shadier tree and made to escort the others to the better position. That the other tree possessed even greater danger, they were never to know.

The foal started to walk and in an instant the black leopard conceived her first hunting strategy, the simplest possible. She dropped from the branch straight onto the back of the foal.

It's one thing to conceive a brilliant idea but it's quite another to execute it with the desired result. Torn Ear omitted to hold onto the flanks of the foal and, before her weight pulled it over, she slipped neatly off it like a saddle with the girth suddenly cut.

The cub picked herself up out of the dirt in the middle of a global conflict.

A trembling infant stood still under the branch, but the air was full of dust and flying hooves as the frantic mother bolstered the foal into action and endeavored to do permanent harm to the leopard at the same time.

As luck would have it, the parting and only blow to establish contact merely glanced off Torn Ear's shoulder and floored her again.

By the time she recovered, her very first quarry was making good speed into the hinterland together with its relatives. Torn Ear stared ruefully after them for a while and then sat back down to make a start on cleaning her coat, which had turned from black to a dusty grey.

Mother closed her eyes and slowly rested her head on the ground again.

Mid-afternoon found the leopards threading a path through arid thornveldt. The flora here had been deprived of water for too long and the thornbushes were dead or dying. The protruding thorns were brittle but still as sharp as needles and prone to breaking off if they punctured the skin. Easy for a human to remove, but they would find a secure home in a leopard's hide, encouraging infection and disease. The cats trod carefully, nose to tail, Mother in the lead.

Eventually the fossil river valley widened further and the terrain merged into sparse grassland with sand a deep ochre red. The sides of the valley were mere sandy bars at this distance, speckled intermittently with dark green.

Occasionally the family would pass herds of springbok, zebra or wildebeest, grazing on what vegetation could be found. Despite the fact that the hunters came fairly close to these herds, the herbivores paid them scant attention. They sensed that they were in no danger, as the leopards were clearly visible in the open and carrying their tails high, their universal sign that hunting was not on the agenda.

A deserted antbear hole prompted a change in Mother's attitude. She issued a short grunt and crouched down directly above the hole, but in such a manner as to be almost invisible to any small homecoming creature. The cubs positioned themselves in supporting pitches, a little way from the entrance.

They did not have to wait long, for the occupant was already on his way home.

Since the other two members of his sounder, or family, had been taken by hyena, the male warthog was the sole inhabitant of the hole. He stopped just short of the entrance to sniff the afternoon air before retiring, thin tail still held stiffly up and slightly curved.

His body was grey and sparsely covered with coarse bristles. The mid-back had a crest of brown and yellowish erectile hair running from the ears to the base of the tail, at which point there was a tuft of blackish hair. It seemed impossible that his slender legs could support the chunky body and elongated head with its curved canine teeth protruding several inches out of the mouth. With huge warts on each side of the face, and a pig like snout, he would be regarded as quite ugly - by everything except a female warthog.

This time it was Dune's turn to steal the show. Unable to contain his enthusiasm any further, and mindful of the expedition's purpose, he launched a full frontal assault on the target.

The warthog, although taken by surprise, refused to panic. He waited until Dune was uncomfortably close and then stepped neatly back into his cosy dwelling.

A leopard cub, travelling at full tilt, needs a certain stopping distance. As this was now not available, Dune proceeded to cannon into the hole like a tube train into a siding. Or at least his head and neck did. The shoulders didn't quite fit in. Hardly surprising, since the dwelling was designed for a totally different type of occupant. In consequence he found himself to be firmly stuck, staring at the disappearing rear end of the warthog.

It took an amount of backpedaling to extricate himself, and showers of sand descended on the others in the process.

When recovery was complete, Mother was no longer looking over the top of the hole. She had gone to cover the back door and had captured the animal making his escape. The leopard disabled the squealing animal with a vice like bite to the base of the spine and waited for her cubs.

The leopard is not, by nature, a cruel animal. Cubs needed to be taught how to kill, and to introduce them to this necessary skill Mother was now giving them a crippled animal to practice on.

The warthog could still drag himself along with his forelegs but his hindquarters were useless. He had no hope of escape and he knew it. He also knew what he was to be used for.

The pupils quickly gathered round the warthog. Spring pawed at it tentatively and jumped back startled when the animal tried to attack in return. This was not expected.

Mother withdrew to watch from a distance. Warthogs are renowned for their bravery and spirit, especially when cornered. A lesson was about to be learnt.

Dune approached from the other side, making a half-hearted side swipe. The warthog twisted quickly and was in time to deliver a short stab with one of his canines. It reached its mark and drew blood from the retreating paw. In the same movement he twisted back again and stabbed Torn Ear's front leg.

The smarting pain goaded the cubs into more concerted action, wanting revenge. They crowded round, concentrating on anticipating and avoiding the attentions of the teeth. Torn Ear grabbed out with a paw, vicious intent in her mind, and unconsciously revealed her claws for the first time. They raked furious red lines along his already paralysed hind quarters.

The screaming warthog descended into a frenzy of pitiful crawling and snapping at the closest limb. In his maddened state he bit his own useless quarters several times as he had twisted round so far.

In a final effort the creature managed a semi-leap at Torn Ear, biting and holding onto the flesh of her haunches.

She saw the light at last, lunged at the source of pain and gripped the neck of the warthog, closing powerful jaws as she did. The movement brought flesh and bone together as life was extinguished with a rush of stinking body fluids into her mouth.

The breakthrough had been made. Mother allowed them to devour the carcass as they saw fit, without a share for herself. Dune and Spring had seen what was required. A lot was learnt and changed in a few minutes.

When they had finished, shade was sought and was provided nearby by a pair of respectably sized granite kopjes. Over the years a Namaqua fig tree had become established on the rocks, a seed germinating in a crevice where it had been blown by chance. The pale cascading roots now squeezed into fissures as they explored their territory and split the rock as they grew. Colour and precious shelter would abound when the tree flowered, but now the bleached trunk and branches reached towards the heavens like an old witches' hand.

Torn Ear sat up and yawned, long and hard. Then she walked over to a nearby termite mound, anchored her front paws on it and stretched luxuriously, pulling her body to its limits. The occupants of the mound were much in evidence so she was careful to avoid their stinging bites as she leisurely jumped onto the top to gain a better view of the surroundings.

The clear blue dome above was streaked with wisps of high white cloud, as if done with a fleeting stroke of an artist's brush. An easy breeze wafted past her erect ears, gently moving the soft downey hair. Peace and tranquility reigned, and her belly was full.

The cub moved her gaze from left to right across the panorama of the landscape. Most things she saw she could now assess as either food or enemy, shelter or danger. The beauty and majesty of the untouched land, with its rugged African harshness, was beyond her capacity to appreciate. To her, it was a territory to master and survive in.

Sitting at the base of a mopane tree was a shape she could not recognise. Being almost in the middle of the dry sandy river bed, it was distant enough to be oblique in her vision.

The shape moved. Torn Ear cocked her head to one side to try and get a better view. The object remained tantalisingly mysterious.

Inquisitive as always, the cub jumped down and trotted off to investigate.

Mother stood up, out of her shade. She too had caught sight of the new shape, but her natural curiosity was tempered by caution. A sixth sense signalled danger and she moved off slowly after her youngest cub, padding soundlessly through the scrub with tail held in a long low loop. An inkling of a hazard warranted full self preservation measures. The leopard lowered her sleek body into a semi crawl so that the shoulder blades rose high and proud with every step.

*****

To stop so late in the day for a rest, without having found a suitable site for the night, was unusual for Jade. Most days that was the first decision to be made, whilst cleaning her teeth with the chewed and frayed ends of a freshly bared twig, or scrubbing herself with the pith and juice of a bi tuber. The juice from this particular vegetable was so bitter and foul it was horrible to drink, but was really refreshing and cleansing to rub on. If possible, she carried one on her travels to cool her through the hottest hours in the middle of the day.

Whilst musing over her minor problems, Jade finished the last of the truffles that she had discovered earlier in the day. They had a salty fungus taste which unfortunately made her more thirsty than usual. As luck would have it, buried in the same area as the truffles was a collection of young Morama bulbs. Aided by the loose structure of the desert sands, these tubers could, individually, grow to weigh 200 kilogrammes. However, Jade made sure that two of them would not get the chance and they quenched her thirst quite adequately. She had grown used to controlling her thirst and satisfying it with the juices of these desert vegetables. Occasionally there was the luxury of drinking from a water hole, when the contents seemed clean, but these were very few and far between. When that happened she would fill her water bottle and carry it strapped round her waist, as were most of her possessions, to see her through the rest of that day. She had found that if she kept any water longer than a day or so in the canteen it would smell decidedly off and be undrinkable.

She made her decision. She would simply stay where she was. It was new territory certainly, but equally, she was too far from her home ground to return there tonight. Besides, today was supposed to be for exploring, she reminded herself. Jade began to clear a suitable area of debris and a primitive campsite took shape.

Nowadays, her bed consisted of a hollow dug in the sand, with as much soft dry grass as she could find to line it, together with the patch of wildebeest hide. The grass was definitely an optional luxury, depending on what the desert condescended to provide. Once in, she covered herself with the shirt, by way of a sheet, and piled leaves or whatever other vegetation she could find, on top. It wasn't perfect by any stretch, but at this time of year it just about managed to keep her warm.

She generally marked out a small area as her own with branches from dead thornbushes. These served as a protective stockade, more for peace of mind than anything else. The fencing wouldn't have denied access to a determined springhare and in consequence she quite often didn't bother with it.

Preparations finished, minus the fence, Jade sat down again at the base of the tree to wait for the afternoon to drift into evening. Something which she always did, and which she did now, was to strap her knife onto the sharp end of her digging stick. She used the belt from her jodhpurs and managed to twist it round to hold the knife there. The idea was that if she was woken by an animal at night, she could use it instantly to give herself a bit of distance and keep it at arm's length. *Knife'll probably drop off, pin my foot down and I'll get eaten quicker. Not much meat though, and I stink so badly that it'll give them the runs.* Nevertheless she fastened it rock steady and laid it down beside her.

In the sand in front of her she noticed a modest sized spider making similar domestic arrangements. She had encountered a backflip spider before and had been intrigued by its activities. As she watched, it laboriously dug itself a minute hollow in the sand and then spun a web, into which it incorporated grains of sand, disguising it. The spider then flipped onto its back in the hollow and pulled the sandy web over itself. To a careless insect the trap would be invisible, until it landed there.

Jade was jerked back into reality from her observations by the silence of the desert. She tried to analyse why the lack of noise should mean anything and almost at once she had the answer. Above her head, perched in the mopane tree, a Namaqua dove had been quietly cooing. Now there was silence. A silent warning without a specific message.

She sat up. Her searching eyes were instantly drawn to the jet black leopard trotting unconcernedly straight towards her.

Jade had never actually seen a leopard in the flesh before, and certainly not a black one. She thought it looked magnificent. About half adult size, she supposed, but still with the innocence and curiosity of a cub. She knew, of course, that leopards were dangerous - the same as lions - but somehow this one wasn't hunting at all. *I think it's coming to say hello. Stay put. Hell I can't outrun it anyway and I don't want to. What did Sam say......be a part of where you are. Unbelievable. See its whiskers.*

Filled with nothing but curiosity for each other, both examined their counterpart as the gap closed.

Having just eaten, the thought of hunting was the last thing on Torn Ear's mind. There was a whole range of scents and sights to be had here. They just needed investigating.

For some reason, Jade felt no fear at the approach of the leopard. Rather, she was desperate to meet this beautiful cat. As a consequence there were no hints of fear or aggression transmitted out for Torn Ear to find. Excitement welled up like a physical being inside her. She squatted down into a crouching position to lessen her height, and stretched out a hand.

Two worlds met when Torn Ear planted a cold nose firmly against the back of Jade's hand. Both held their positions, a little unsure of the next move, the leopard's tail waving peacefully from side to side.

Very steadily, so as not to create the illusion of an attacking move, Jade slid her hand down to stroke the velvet fur on the leopard's throat. She was rewarded with an almost undetectable purring and ventured on to a gentle rubbing.

Several minutes of contact eased away any trepidations on either side. Torn Ear moved nearer Jade, intentionally brushing against her still crouching form.

The only spectator to this unique meeting stood her ground at a respectable distance, unsure for the first time in her life of what to do. The now recognisable form of the human had filled her with fear for her cub. She had only ever seen them once before and had witnessed the resultant slaughter of game with awe. Instinct had set her racing to the cub's aid, only to be halted by an inner sense. If Torn Ear was attacked now, she was too far away to make any difference.

A strange mellow feeling, which she could not quantify or recognise, was however, a more powerful force in stilling her feet. To interfere seemed unwarranted and out of place.

Mother watched intently.

A new experience attracts attention and concentration. The more unusual or sensational it is, the more it occupies the minds of those concerned. The encounter of a lifetime had the total thoughts of child and leopards.

For a few minutes their environment was forgotten. The environment brimming with unexpected danger which they have to be alert to and survive in.

Had Jade taken the trouble to observe the dove perched above her, she might have wondered why it had become alarmed, for it could not possibly have seen or sensed the approaching leopard cub. The bird was facing completely the opposite direction, aware of a greater danger. Satisfied that now was an appropriate time to leave the neighbourhood, the dove flapped noisily upwards and then sliced effortlessly through the air into the wilderness.

Both Torn Ear and Jade looked up at the sudden departure, the latter with the first twinge of concern. The desert was still deathly silent. Not a sound of living could be heard. No distant barking of zebra, no springbok moving through the bush, grazing at leisure. Not so much as a falling leaf.

Some twenty yards in front of the mopane tree the desert plain rose quite substantially to form a ridge, behind which, years of erosion had carved out a hollow the size of a large maned Kalahari male.

The lion shifted his weight slightly, bunching immensely powerful limbs under his body, ready to spring out from the niche. A fluttering bird warranted not a glance, he knew exactly what it was. Smouldering yellow eyes gleamed with anticipation. He was a young male on his own, very nearly full grown, but lacking in weight due to a series of unsuccessful hunts. His belly groaned and contracted painfully as if to remind him.

Carefully, he risked one last look over the edge to ensure his prey was still in situ, and was surprised to find it had doubled, giving a choice of two. He would take both, human and cub. The monstrous cat pushed hard against the smooth rock of the hollow and propelled himself over the edge.

Below, in the peaceful shade of the mopane tree, everything happened in terrible slow motion.

Jade twisted round on hearing a scrabbling sound to face a huge maned head and body filling the entire horizon, blocking out daylight like a sudden storm. It's ears were laid straight back, making the forehead flat and broad, with evil intent. A solid blast of sound echoed out from a gaping jaw, lined with yellow fangs. It rang off her eardrums, threatening to burst them with its ferocity.

Her first conscious move was for Torn Ear. She lifted the cub bodily with both arms and almost threw her up into the tree, hoping she would land on a branch. The cub struggled in alarm at this unexpected move, subconsciously unleashing her claws and drawing blood from Jade's forearm as she lifted. The cut went unnoticed.

Mother bore down on the scene. She was always going to be too late. She knew it, and moved with an ever deepening pit of dread in her stomach.

Jade faced her attacker, gripping the digging stick with attached knife which was lying close. It seemed a hopeless gesture of defiance.

In the last seconds, the calmness of inevitability descended. The panic in her vanished, to be replaced with an inner anger and rod of steel. She had held onto life here and would keep it now. Nothing had the right to deprive her. Aggression seethed up within her along with a fighting spirit that rose like a mist in her mind. She could not recognise this courage and strength as it took her over.

The lion rose into the air in a final lunge, intending to land on her. Jade could smell the foetid stench belching from its huge lungs, could feel the body heat coming from the beast in that drawn out microsecond of time as it towered over her.

Above the scene Torn Ear spat and hissed, lashing out as far as she could with a set of claws, firmly anchored to the rough bark with the others.

The attacker momentarily diverted his attention in mid-flight to this distraction, lifting his head.

Jade crouched down, holding the stick in both hands down to the right of her body. *Wait, wait, wait.........now !* The lion was above her, looking at the leopard. She swept the stick from right to left in front of her, in an upward arc, with all the strength that was possible. The razor sharp blade scythed through thin air, almost too quickly because of the effort behind it. Her one and only chance. On and on it went. Then it met an exposed throat and cut viciously in at the very top of the arc. The five inch blade buried itself in fur, muscle and windpipe as it cut in. The stroke faltered and Jade felt her swinging motion stop cruelly as the knife twisted in and broke free of the stick which snapped at the top.

Cascades of warm blood fountained from the severed jugular vein, covering the girl as the dying animal crushed her to the ground. The lion fought for breath with horrible gasping grunts while his own blood drowned him.

Jade struggled frantically underneath the foul weight and terror, expecting, almost experiencing the lion's killing stroke. As if in a dream world, it never came. She pulled herself free, his blood in her hair, dripping down her face, hands and trickling into her mouth as she panted and sucked air in. Still she believed nothing in case her mind was taunting her with a last cruel trick. The lion juddered beside her, trembled uncontrollably and was quiet.

Final realisation dawned. The inner steel melted, her courage vanished and her legs collapsed, pitching her into the lion's soft warm flank. Acid bile welled up furiously within her. Jade was sick until there was nothing left for her stomach to retch on and then she lay on the body, breathing heavily, smelling her own vomit and not caring.

Minutes passed until Jade regained some sort of composure. Still feeling weak and shaking, she rose to her feet to the realisation that she had been unable to control either end of her intestines. Dignity was restored as swiftly as possible.

Examined at leisure, the lion was a magnificent specimen, she thought. She was sad that the natural chain of events had brought about its death and fervently wished it could have been otherwise. However, the deed was done, but the fact that she had actually killed this great cat had yet to sink in. To come closer to death, and survive, would be practically impossible.

Jade retrieved her knife first and then the majority of the digging stick that had saved her life. She cleaned the knife as far as possible, but the stick was beyond repair. It was blunt and scarred, stained a dull red and was attracting several tiny insects as she held it up.

A solitary vulture circled overhead, trying to establish if it was worth the trouble to land. Jade saw it on the first circuit.

A lion such as this, she thought, did not deserve to be hacked to pieces by scavengers. She would bury him, the only fitting alternative she could think of.

Quickly, she set about the task and had soon excavated a grave in the sand behind the body with the help of a manageable flat stone. Despite the ease of digging it was exhausting work, requiring a couple of stops to stretch aching back muscles.

Once it was complete she stood in the hole for a while, recovering her strength. It said much for her stamina that in spite of the ordeal and the forced labour afterwards, her muscles returned to their peak in a matter of minutes, with the rhythm of breathing hardly disturbed.

She then went to the end of the grave closest to the body and grasped the thick hard tail. Persistent pulling, combined with the sand acting as rollers, finally deposited the lion unceremoniously in his resting place. Jade jumped with shock as the last air in his lungs forced its way out in a deep rumbling grunt. She grinned sheepishly at her own alarm, only feeling half certain that she knew what it was.

Moving round to clamber out of the hole, she stubbed her toe on a stone. By second nature, she bent down to rub it without even a glance. Not having any footwear meant that minor injuries were a frequent occurrence. Her fingers touched the stone in passing. It felt cool and smooth, unlike any other stone she had encountered. She pulled it out to get a better look.

It was a chunky stone, fitting nicely into the palm of her hand. Although it was cloudy and opaque, in a milky white sort of way, it still reflected the sunlight a little in a pleasantly relaxing manner and simply felt comforting to hold.

Jade slid it into the top pocket of her shirt, buttoning it down afterwards. She would call it Lion Stone.

Being forced now to look closely at her only garment, in daylight, she had to admit that it was finally showing signs of collapse. Months of constant use, both as clothing and bedding, left it ragged and torn with patches wearing through. Besides which, it was positively filthy. However, this time there was no real way of using the lion's hide as she had done with the wildebeest. Jade had some rough idea of how long she had been in the desert but she had been unable to keep an accurate calendar and things had sort of blended into one another. Today was in fact August 2nd, which made her fifteen years old.

Jade scrambled out and quickly shovelled the sand and earth back into the grave. That task at an end, she placed as many stones as she could find on top of the mound, flattening them by jumping on them. As a final act, she hammered the digging stick into the ground at the head of the grave until only a hand's width was visible. *You don't get the knife coz after all you did try to make me into dinner.......and I think I'll need it again.*

Now she was tired. Dragging her weary feet to the makeshift campsite and sliding into her own pit was to have been the last conscious act before letting sleep take over. She remembered the black cub just in time and returned to the mopane tree to see what had happened to it.

Torn Ear was exactly where she had been thrown, perched on a branch. Crouched down, her sparkling eyes watched all with rapt attention, ears pricked straight forward. The cat was alert and, thought Jade, very beautiful. She reached up, and with the confidence that eludes even the most experienced of game wardens, lifted Torn Ear down. The thought of danger or attack from the leopard never entered her head. Her honest no fear attitude and a firm grasp were her insurance policies.

Half asleep, Jade affectionately scratched the top of the leopard's head and then began to weave a path the few yards to her bed where she collapsed in exhaustion.

Mother watched the drama from where she had skidded to a halt after seeing her offspring thrown up to safety. Whatever else the human might be, it was apparently not a threat to the cub. Without doubt, Torn Ear's life had been saved and the lion had been killed, a remarkable feat which even Mother would probably not have been able to manage. A fully grown lion weighed more and was more powerful.

The adult was confused by the early evening events. Humans were supposed to be avoided as they had a habit of unnecessarily killing everything they came across. By the same token they should not have bothered to save Torn Ear before themselves, and most of all, they should not be able to kill a charging lion. It was too complex an issue for her limited logic to work out.

Torn Ear sat, occasionally licking her front paw. She had not recognised the threat of the lion as quickly as Jade and was aware that her life had been preserved by this hitherto unknown creature.

Standards in the world of this immature leopard usually dictated that the bigger and more powerful overcame those lesser than themselves. Those standards had just been turned upside down. The cub looked curiously at the departing child with what amounted to the beginnings of a sense of respect.

Mother called to her offspring with a short bark. It was time to return life to a semblance of normality, for the moment anyway.

At the third time of asking Torn Ear returned. The cub was obviously still affected by the experience but greeted her brothers with the usual gusto, rolling over and over in mock battles.

Impatient to be off, Mother curtailed activities and led her family into the gathering dusk to continue the teaching session. The cub at the rear of the file shot a last swift glance at the mopane tree; any more risked incurring parental displeasure.

Morning brought domestic activities for Jade. Along with the usual chores, such as foraging for food and the ever present battle with personal hygiene, a digging stick was required. Now that she had come to terms with surviving in the desert, there was one luxury that she dreamt of and that was simply to have a normal toilet. She hated scooping out a little hollow, squatting and filling it in. She still felt embarrassed and always made sure no-one was looking. *Like who the hell is going to be looking !! Same thing as putting frosted glass in aircraft loo windows......I wish someone was there to look. Mean I would be rescued.* That thought stopped her dead. Life was, well, it was life. She always loved her independence and the harsh, unforgiving desert which she had looked upon since her earliest memories. She was torn with guilt for even allowing herself to consider she might be happy here. Oupa would be racked with loss and Dancer.......*who has him now. Does he miss me ? Does he even remember me ?*

Jade forced herself out of her reverie. Whatever happens will happen, she thought. She had slept deeply, allowing herself to recover, both physically and mentally, from the stresses of the day. Her body was still tinged with remnants of fatigue but it was the sort that would soon burn off as she got going, pumping fresh energy into her mind and muscles.

She jumped out of her pit. In the cool light of dawn there was a blueness to the air, making it new and refreshing. Jade took several deep breaths, letting the cold air work its way down as far as it could. Memories of these moments, and the knowledge that they would return, helped to see her through the appalling midday heat. As she revelled in it, the first rays of the sun started to work on the atmosphere, but for the moment the forces of night held them off.

She wandered away in search of a suitable tree which was willing to donate a small branch. This time she picked a long straight branch which had a fork at the end. It yielded without a struggle and she carried it back.

The branch was shaped in such a manner that she could snap off the fork at the end by standing on it, and be left with two decent sized digging sticks and a much longer one. Following a deal of close examination she discarded one of the small ones and set about sharpening the other. As before, the knife came into its own, but it was still slow work. Apart from being useful in excavating tubers, the stick was her only defence, as had been proved all too clearly. It was the first priority.

With her task half completed, Jade stopped to make inroads into an intact Tsama melon which she had found nearby. The juice was luscious and still cool from refrigeration during the night. She ate slowly, savouring each mouthful. The fruit would have to be finished or abandoned today. She had no way of storing it once it was begun and it attracted a multitude of tiny and not so tiny creatures should she leave it unattended..

Jade sat back. The stick would be ready in about half an hour or so she imagined, depending on how soon she stopped taking it easy and got back to work.

A miniature visitor appeared on the scene, ready to investigate the sounds of eating. Jade watched it with interest and the Kalahari sand lizard returned the compliment. It was a yellow and brown creature with a pale orange tail and when it walked, its body undulated from side to side in the normal fashion of its species.

The lizard trotted cheekily back and forth in front of her a few times, always ending up within striking distance of the food supply. Finally she succumbed and tossed a minute piece of the fruit towards the beggar.

At the approach of the missile the lizard darted speedily off, only to return an instant later and devour the huge chunk with relish.

As the system seemed to work, he bobbed a bit closer and waited for the next morsel, which was thrown just in front of him. The lizard stepped up, grabbed the titbit and again waited in expectation.

Gradually, Jade persuaded the reluctant reptile to approach ever closer until he actually snatched a fragment from her fingers. Either this pressure was too much, or the stuffed belly could not accept any more gifts, for the lizard then scuttled off to a nearby rock to sun himself. She watched him for a few moments, admiring every detail of his colour and skin texture.

Jade then returned to her task with renewed vigour, born of a guilty conscience. When she looked up after some minutes of work the lizard had vanished.

She continued on, youthful muscle and sinew standing out in effort from her deeply tanned back as she reduced one end of the stick to a point.

Long days in the desert sun were now changing her golden tan to a darker, more permanent, ebony shade. The pigment change was apparent on her shoulders to start with and, with time, spread down like a dark stain on a cloth, eventually covering her entire exposed body. Quite often she spent periods of the day entirely naked, but for the rest of the time dignity was preserved by tying the long suffering shirt round her waist. Her small amount of possessions still lived in the left leg of the jodhpurs, which she carried like a sack. The right leg had long ago been cut into strips of cloth to tie round her forehead to keep sweat and hair out of her eyes.

Her body hair was by now bleached almost white, providing a startling contrast with the body colour. Tiny silver hairs on her forearms vied for position when disturbed by the breeze and even eyebrows took on the snowy appearance of elderly wisdom.

The weapon was finished. She felt secure again. Thoughts of what might have happened without it still crowded into her mind and it needed some effort to banish them.

Morning passed into afternoon, unnoticed by Jade, who spent it foraging for food Prolonged exertion combined with delayed mental fatigue from the previous day made for a good sleeping draught. She saw nothing of the remaining daylight hours and curled up into the night.

Far into the small hours she woke abruptly with a start, muscles twitching in a spasm. She felt confused and drained, as if from a nightmare which she could not remember. A shiver of gooseflesh burred up her naked back and down her arms. The cold must have woken her, she thought, and pulled the wildebeest hide closer over herself. To a girl at low ebb the night was suddenly alien, unfriendly in its silver blackness. She fell back into uneasy slumber with a disquieting sense that something else besides the temperature had disturbed her.

Daybreak, with its promise of cloudless skies and heralded by the arrival of soft glowing light, failed to arouse the sleeper. Neither was she unduly disturbed by the padding of uncertain feet and associated rustling in the bush.

However, a cold wet nose pressed tentatively against her warm exposed thigh had the desired effect. Unaccustomed to being woken in this manner, she jerked rapidly upright to come face to face with a large dusky leopard, whose left ear seemed to be flicking in opposite directions at once.

Jade woke up properly and instantly recognised Torn Ear. She sank back onto her elbows, breathing a sigh of relief. The cub withdrew to a respectable distance, sitting now on her haunches and trying to take up as little space as possible.

Whilst walking through the thornveldt she had brushed past spiders webs, dripping with early morning dew, which had coated her head and shoulders. Such was the preoccupation of the leopard that it had gone unnoticed until now. Torn Ear nervously cleaned herself.

Puzzled, the girl watched and waited. There was something bothering the leopard whose life she had saved. If she had returned simply to renew an acquaintance Jade would have expected some greeting. There was none, or at least none that she could recognise. As she watched, Torn Ear shifted her weight and held one paw uneasily, just off the ground.

Jade scrambled up and squatted on the balls of her feet facing the cat. Torn Ear raised herself immediately and padded away, tail at half mast and oscillating slowly from side to side. Quickly, she gathered her meagre possessions together to follow the animal. Torn Ear turned her head just once, saw the girl behind her, and accelerated to a fast walk. Her tail rose to the characteristic "follow me" level and the leopard weaved a path away into the low dunes and scrub.

For a good hour Jade stumbled along behind as the grey dawn turned to day. After a while her muscles began to warm and wake up, encouraging her to break into a steady jog. In the cool this was infinitely easier for her to maintain and she barely had to change the rhythm of breathing. Torn Ear sensed the increase in pace as Jade closed up the gap, herself moving up to a slow loping canter.

Leopard and young woman travelled in unison and all the while Jade wondered at this turn of events. She wished she could communicate with the cub, but then that wasn't the first time she had wanted to communicate with an animal. *Funny, I feel as close to this wild leopard as I felt to you Dancer.* Her thoughts slipped back for seconds. *Come on scrambled egg head. Think now, not then. Stay awake.* She banished the thoughts and brought herself back. Without thinking, her free hand strayed to touch the part of her head which had indeed resembled an egg for a long while. There was still a small residual bump as she ran her hand over the area. There always would be.

Three yards ahead, Torn Ear was experiencing the self same abstract desire to impart knowledge. A sense of frustration at not being able to convey the urgency of the situation surfaced in her mind. She could at least do that with her own kind.

She was unable to tell of a night time encounter and the devastating results. Of the lashing hooves belonging to an outraged zebra stallion, previously unseen by any of them, who had interrupted a hunt. Of a full vicious kick knocking down an adult leopard mid-leap. Of the concern and uncertainty of three inexperienced cubs, nosing and whimpering around the still form. Of a sudden intuitive mental connection, to the only concept of help the cub knew of, and a journey through the night. None of these could be told.

Dune and Spring were sitting bolt upright in front of Mother. They knew of their younger sister's return long before the unlikely duo appeared amid swathes of early morning sunshine.

Mother lay on her side, giving an impression of almost total normality, apart from the fact that she now breathed in short panic stricken gasps which rasped through a constantly open mouth. Jade stopped short, not wanting to encroach into sensitive territory and stood wondering what she should or indeed could do.

It was patently obvious that she had been summoned to render assistance. She had been brought by the black cub, that was also clear, for the adult had already assumed the classic mental attitude of death. She had sustained an injury which, although not in itself fatal, rendered her unable to fend for herself, and thus promised eventual death. Mental submission usually quickened the end.

Jade moved closer. The fact that Mother showed no objection to her approach confirmed her state of mind. Dune and Spring grudgingly moved apart to allow visual access.

The injured flank had been struck a powerful blow, breaking the surface in a rounded pattern. Around that semi-circle, ribs had been neatly severed. Jade watched the broken ends moving around, as if in liquid, as Mother fought the fiery ring of pain with each breath.

She sat back on her heels, rocking slowly and feeling a rising panic of helplessness. There was certainly nothing she could do for the wound itself. Given time, it would either heal itself, or not. The problem was to provide for the other needs of the leopard during the recovery period. Jade withdrew to give herself time to think and get a detached view of the whole situation.

The leopard lay in the middle of a flat sandy plain, quite typical of this part of the Kalahari, with occasional thornbushes and baobab trees. In the middle distance, flaming red dunes rose to meet the eternal sapphire blue of the sky in a crisp confrontation. To either side the desert continued unabated for as far as the eye could see, the only substantial shade or shelter being provided by several gigantic granite kopjes which sat some fifty or sixty yards to the left, as if dropped there from on high.

A day in the unrelenting heat would be the end. The leopard needed shade to survive, first and foremost.

While Jade puzzled over the seemingly insurmountable obstacle, the three cubs paced around constantly. Increasing daylight and its accompanying desert activity worried them. Mother was vulnerable in the open, they were all vulnerable. Although now quite substantial creatures in their own right, they were still prey to lion. Anxiously, all alien movements were observed.

It was impossible, mused Jade, to move the leopard on her own, even if she was prepared to let her try, which she doubted. Encouragement was needed from her friend, the black one with the funny ear. *What happened to you I wonder. Gives me something to call you though.*

Jade got up out of her contemplation and approached Torn Ear who looked at her expectantly through crystal clear eyes, shaded with the slightest touch of an emerald green.

Very gently, she took hold of a front leg and pulled it towards her. The owner, of course, was none the wiser when the pressure was released, and looked on blankly. The young woman repeated the movement several times, pulling just that bit harder and walking away afterwards.

Patience was called for, big time. Finally, Jade released the limb for the last time and walked backwards towards the shade of the rocks, constantly keeping eye contact with the leopard. On reaching them she lay down in the relative cool and dark, and waited.

Torn Ear stared after her, seeing her in the shade now. Then the black leopard sat down by Mother. She would not leave her alone out here.

Jade saw the impasse and ran back to them. There was no other way round it. She gingerly grasped Mother's paw and pulled towards the rocks. Torn Ear saw the light at once, willing Mother into action as she had never tried before.

Long minutes elapsed before Mother's head came up from the sand. She gazed past Jade to the rocks. Her fur was already hot from the sun. Cool was preferable.

A combination of all these forces raised the adult to her feet where she stood, swaying, and trying not to breathe in order to lessen the agony in her chest. Taking steps was an abomination of torture. Red hot lances danced round the grinding ends of bone, stabbing home at every chance. Surrounded by the cubs, Mother made her way across the scrub and tried, in vain, to control her collapse under the kopje. She knew she would live or die on this spot. The leopard was weak from lack of food, she had let the cubs eat first. Now she could hunt no more. That would be the death of her.

First battle won, thought Jade. Watching Mother gasping for breath in small weak movements, it dawned on her that she had just assumed responsibility for the family of leopards. The more she thought about it, the more complex and impossible it seemed. To start with, she had to try and nurse the adult, keeping her alive while she healed, hopefully. That required food, and therefore hunting. Not only did Mother need catering for, but she doubted whether any of the cubs were capable of catching prey yet, so she had to act as provider to them as well. To cap it all, the invalid and her charges needed protection against attack. She had no illusions as to the luck which had been involved in killing the lion. In future the odds would be very much stacked against her.

Mother's breathing was steadier now. In the cool she had calmed down and relaxed somewhat. Jade looked up at the angle of the sun and then again at the huge boulder, for the moment providing shade. Towards early afternoon, she estimated, the shade would evaporate, bathing the area in waves of stifling heat. Mother was in no fit state to change position again so she needed to construct some form of sunscreen to cope with the problem.

Approach it one step at a time, she told herself. Take it bit by bit and it will all fall into place. To make a screen she needed foliage and branches. To get branches she needed to cut them off whatever trees she could find in the vicinity. To do that she needed a sharp instrument, better than her knife which she really didn't want to ruin on branches.

Jade wandered around the rock, looking for a form of stone she recognised. A quick forage at a suitable site and she had it. Long ago she had discovered that certain types of stone, when cracked sharply against a much harder rock, tended to split lengthways. If she was lucky, she ended up with a long cutting edge, not unlike a modest axe blade. Luck was on her side today - she had success at the first attempt. Mildly surprised, Jade set about the next stage of the operation.

Trailing her throughout, and watching intently, was her feline black shadow. Torn Ear's initial observations were tentatively made from afar to begin with, but when no discouraging signs were received she trotted up and sat quite close, looking and learning. Jade was amused and then flattered by the attentions, both other cubs remaining in the shade with Mother. Jade decided that to show any interest in Torn Ear's presence, either way, might put her off, so she simply got on with the task in hand. However, when Jade went a little distance away, to savage the local tree population, the cub returned to the front of the rock and sat stoically with the rest of the family.

The axe was a roaring success and Jade determined to keep it for future use. Previous ones had chipped and flaked away after a short time.

Construction of the shelter started by placing a long bough against the rock, thus forming a triangle with Mother lying in the middle of it. This branch had a distinct bend towards one end and Jade pushed this end deep into the sand. This resulted in a lot more space inside the shelter at ground level. The upper end of the branch was firmly wedged into a cleft in the granite, making this primary support quite robust.

In this fashion Jade built a framework of branches, big and small, up against the side of the rock. She gave it a certain amount of internal strength by twining and linking branches and, where possible, using long spiny thorns as makeshift nails to hold things together.

One end of this strange tent was left open as the entrance, the other being brought to a sharp pointed conclusion as she rapidly ran out of building materials. Around the base she planted barricades of dead thorn bushes, piling them up the sides and pushing them firmly into the ground. The lethal spikes were the only form of defence she could think of to give the vulnerable shelter.

At last the skeleton was finished. The only task now was to add more leaves and other vegetation to it, to block out the light. This she painstakingly did.

When she had finished it was noticeably pleasanter inside the construction, as the sun had now robbed the last of the shade from the kopje and was baking it in the mid-afternoon heatwave. Jade lay down inside to rest an aching body and was soon asleep. Her strange bedfellows, four leopards, stretched out beside and around the human. There was just enough floor space for all.

Unlikely companions, but circumstances had welded them together, for the time being anyway.

Sweltering afternoon beyond the makeshift shelter passed into a cooler evening bliss.

******

Although normally a nocturnal forager, the porcupine had decided on an earlier expedition to supplement supplies for her three youngsters still bound by age in the resting hole.

Gradually, she snuffled along the desert floor looking for tubers and roots which were her normal food, although wild fruit or carrion would be taken if necessary. Coming across the barricade of thorn bushes presented her with the combined scent of leopard and man, and it was not a welcome surprise.

The creature froze motionless, erecting her quills in the standard response to danger, real or imagined. With the armoury of long black and white pliable spines and stout sharp quills raised, the porcupine stood nearly three feet high.

Sounds of an intruder in the vicinity woke Jade and alerted Torn Ear, who had never been asleep. The black leopard swept past her, heading for the exit, and in doing so gave Jade a fleeting impression of weight and strength. She followed quickly.

Torn Ear may still have looked a juvenile in some respects, but she had outstripped her brothers in size and showed no signs of slowing down. Muscles showed themselves under a sleek coat, promising to blossom further. The playful, sometimes innocent, twinkle in those eyes could now be replaced at will by a speculative gleam, clearly indicating a change of intention.

For a couple of seconds both of them faced the porcupine head on. Without warning the creature then did a rapid about turn, exposing the business end. Jade had seen a porcupine in action once before and wondered if Torn Ear knew what might come next. She decided to be safe and gently but firmly pushed the standing leopard out of the line of fire, in itself something of a task.

If cornered, a porcupine has the unnerving habit of rushing backwards to plant sharp quills into an adversary. The quills themselves are not poisonous, but if they break off in the flesh the wound can become infected.

With a cracking of dry twigs and branches, reinforcements arrived on the scene. Dune had glimpsed the impending conflict and had decided to dispense with the formality of the provided exit, breaking his way out through a sparse patch in the defences instead.

Jade groaned out loud and shouted a rebuke at the cub who thankfully stood still, more in astonishment at the new sound than anything else. He left a gaping breach in the wooden wall behind, but that seemed to concern him little.

Meanwhile the porcupine was trotting off into the distance, apparently of the opinion that a conflict here was not worth the trouble.

Crisis over with, Jade immediately set about repairing the damage. Luckily, the damage was only partial and could be remedied by resetting the original branches back into position.

Dune watched the reconstruction from close quarters, sitting very prim and properly like an oversize house cat. At the end Jade sat down and looked him square in the face.

" You are a stupid young cat ", she breathed at him in mock scolding. Dune pulled his head back a fraction at this, for the human was still very much an unknown quantity.

Jade stood up and went back inside to look at the patient. Torn Ear was already there, licking the side of Mother's face with a pink rasping tongue. The adult leopard had not changed position, only the laboured breathing showed she was still alive. Jade squatted to examine the injury, gently blowing and then brushing away some sand which had found its way into the fur during the recent commotion.

She was pleased with what she saw. The site looked clean and uninfected. Gingerly she systematically worked her way round the wound, pressing the body to determine the extent of the damage. Going by the response of Mother to the gentle pressure, there was only the one injury, whose effect seemed to be contained within a small area. More than that was mere guesswork.

The big leopard continued to lie with her chin on the sand, gazing dejectedly at the ground. It was apparent that she was weakening by the hour. Nourishment was needed and from the attitude of the cubs, they were expecting Jade to supply it.

That should be easy enough, she thought, and ran out quickly to dig for her usual supply.

With the second stroke of her new digging stick a terrible realisation struck. When had she last seen a hunting cat eating fruit or roots ? Never. Food to them was meat, ripped off the bones of a creature which had been hunted and killed.

Nevertheless, Jade pulled out the tuber and took it back.

The next ten minutes were spent vainly trying to convince Mother to eat some of the flesh which had been extracted from it for her. To no avail.

In the end, Jade settled for dribbling squeezed out juice into her mouth, hoping for some sort of benefit. The liquid was tart and bitter, but the leopard just coughed once in response to some going down the wrong way, and showed no other reaction.

Torn Ear sat up after having finished washing her parent. The cub stared long and hard at Mother, occasionally chuffling to her to try and illicit some positive response. This form of communication takes the form of blowing sharply through the nostrils two or three times. Roughly, it conveys the sentiments, " I am here, all is well ".

It had no effect, other than to bring Dune and Spring round Mother to add their collective voices to the appeal. As a final gesture Spring pawed gently at the lowered head. In days long gone by this would have been the prelude to playful fighting and rolling in the dunes, culminating in exhausted sleep by all four participants.

Now there was nothing. Jade felt deeply for them in their anguish, but she could only watch. Torn Ear was alarmed and for the first time in her short life she felt alone, even rejected.

Outside in the gathering dusk a lone hyena uttered a series of mournful whoops. Crickets could be heard tuning up for their deafening night long performance. It was time for hunters to begin roaming.

With silent accord both Jade and Torn Ear left the shelter and started out into the gloom. Neither could communicate with the other, in the normal sense of the word, but each recognised the inevitability of the situation.

As they were gradually enveloped by the darkness, the leopard leading, neither found it strange to have the other's company. Every assistance was welcome, as this hunt had to be for real. Second place is no good when there is a family depending on your, as yet unproven, abilities. Game time was over.

Torn Ear lengthened her stride, breaking into a slow lolloping trot. Some yards behind, Jade kept pace with ease. In the blessed cool of evening this speed was almost pleasant to maintain. Quickly she settled into her rhythm, bare feet picking out the best route and avoiding obstacles. She had no plan of her own. She had only her knife and digging stick and a determination to do whatever she could.

*****

During the dry season in this part of the Kalahari the only permanent springs of water can sometimes be found around the edge of salt pans, where water flows between the surface limestone and the underlying layers of clay. Undulations in the strata push the flow upwards, and a water hole is born.

They were now heading towards one such place. The leopard knew that she could wander all night without so much as seeing a suitable prey, let alone killing it. Many animals used the cover of darkness to stop and drink and they all had to come to this watering hole, the only one for miles in any direction. Tonight, the leopard and the young woman would also drink.

Light over the chosen watering hole was provided courtesy of a waxing gibbous moon. In a few days it would mature into a full moon but nevertheless gave almost as much light at the moment.

From her position of concealment on the crest of an elevated ridge Jade marvelled at the eerie silvered world which she gazed upon. Prolonged periods of activity at night had previously been taboo due to the increased danger of attack. When she had ventured abroad at such times it was for a specific purpose, which was conducted as speedily as possible. Sightseeing was not on the approved list.

So she lay still, absorbing every detail, effect and contour of the moonscape. Beside her crouched an inky black shadow, ears flattened back to disguise her profile. She too watched and waited, mentally quartering the killing ground below, spotting and noting shadows, false and firm earth, escape routes and points of ambush. The skills and experiences of countless generations of spotted hunters were ingrained into her subconscious.

Torn Ear possessed one additional advantage over her feline compatriots. Genetic mutation had changed her coat to the darkest ebony, rendering her virtually invisible in the shadow of night. Only when direct moonlight passed through icy green eyes, and was reflected back, was her presence betrayed as they shone briefly like headlamps.

The hunters crouched and the night progressed. Stalking requires infinite patience and a disdainful regard for the passage of time. A careless move or sound can destroy hours of painstaking effort, and once undone, when the would-be meal is made aware, there is no alternative but to start the whole laborious process again elsewhere. Jade knew this and so did the leopard.

Both lay motionless, watching a moonlit circus parade that a wildlife photographer would have traded his soul for.

At night, the drinking patterns seemed to Jade to be different from those which she had observed during daylight. In the early morning and late afternoon all types of animals congregated at water holes. Zebra rubbed shoulders with gazelles and the stately eland. Kudu, the male resplendent with his long corkscrew horns, vied for position with the equally magnificent gemsbok. Even the cheeky warthog could be seen scuttling to the waters edge, dodging in and out of long giraffe legs.

During the hours of darkness, behaviour was much modified. It appeared to Jade that each individual species had its own allotted time slot for drinking.

When they had finished, they left the stage vacant for the next group, who were waiting patiently in the wings. Quite often, animals who had drunk earlier in the night would later on for a second session. Nevertheless, there still appeared to be a pecking order and it was rare for two groups to be present at the same time.

To watch the long parade was no hardship for the young woman lying beside the leopard. Despite the hour, slumber was the last thing on her mind and she never lost sight of their objective.

Throughout the vigil they watched numerous animals pass before them without any real possibilities presenting themselves. With their inexperience the only hope was for one to stray off from its fellows.

Almost the last to attend the water hole was a herd of springbok. They had been there before and both watchers recognised the young male who had tried to attach himself to the group as they drank the last time. He had been driven off fiercely by several in the band and reluctantly disappeared. Now he was back with them, hovering around, obviously trying again for acceptance.

Torn Ear scrabbled forward slightly to get a better look. It was going to be their only opportunity and it was essential to take food back for Mother. This had to be the one.

The leopard had decided. She crawled stealthily back from the ridge, giving herself a couple of minutes to stretch and flex leg muscles which were cramped and cold from the wait. Jade turned round, watching for her cue. Torn Ear however, trotted off to her right, executing a flanking manoeuvre to get on the other side of the quarry.

It was apparent to Jade that she was to stay put. This she did, continuing the observations. In front of her the springbok drank sporadically, glancing nervously round every few seconds. The male was preoccupied with his acceptance into the herd, to the exclusion of all else. He constantly approached animals, tail pumping furiously from side to side in submissive gestures, and was always rejected, sometimes with a violent scuffle and short chase.

A quirk of nature had over the years shaped this water hole into a thin elongated reservoir, some twenty or thirty yards long. One side allowed an easy approach to the water, with a gentle slope down to the edge. It was at this side that the animals drank, for the other was too steep to allow access.

Looking beyond, far beyond, the end of the watery strip, Jade made out a swift shadow flitting between points of cover. If she hadn't known what to watch for she would have missed it. Torn Ear crept gradually forward in the classic style, trunk of the body as close to the ground as possible and shoulder blades coming up alternately, like an engine camshaft. Her ears were back against the skull, making her head appear as flat and menacing as a snake's and she inhaled through a slightly open mouth, letting airborne scents wash over her tongue.

A crude pincer movement was forming around the herd. Escape to one side was blocked by the water, Torn Ear approached from another and Jade now realised that she was to bar their passage going the other way. There would be only one exit. Jade readied herself for action.

Despite her victory over the lion, the prospect of a scrambling conflict here started small waves of anxiety in her belly. She tried to conjure up the anger and ice cold nerve which had previously turned fear to strength and courage. After some effort she decided it was beyond her control and simply steeled herself as best she could.

In the middle distance Torn Ear was getting closer. The herd was still unaware, drinking and moving around, relatively unconcerned. The leopard did not have any one individual as a target. She intended to panic the herd and take whatever opening presented itself.

Silently, Torn Ear rose up to a half crouch and began a gentle canter forward. To the herd she was virtually invisible. The first thing they would be aware of would be an indistinguishable rustling and scuffing of sand.

A mature female springbok threw up her head in concern. Acute hearing had saved her many times before, but for a vital split second she could not identify the source. Peering intently into the dark the heartstopping silhouette was suddenly recognisable, bearing down with menacing ferocity.

Panic froze her momentarily, as a rabbit caught in the beams of a truck. Then she snorted in alarm, stampeding the herd in the opposite direction, along the edge of the water and away from danger. The unwanted male was caught up in the frenzied rush and even in the panic found himself pushed out to the fringes of the herd by the water.

Now at three quarter speed, the leopard harried and chased the fleeing herd, although she was still not within striking of it.

Recognising her moment, Jade revealed herself and leapt out into the path of the springbok, shouting and windmilling her arms to present as big a threat as possible.

The herd was thrown into turmoil. Front runners did a rapid about turn, ploughing their way into the others who kept on doggedly trying to go forward, being only aware of the menace behind. Almost instantly the area was a seething mass of confused animals, thrashing about, seeking a way out.

They were only used to running from a single enemy, using their weight of numbers as a shield. A two pronged attack threw the strategy out totally.

Being so close to the water in such confusion, the inevitable was bound to happen. It happened to the male who didn't belong and it happened as the rest of the herd found the funnel of an escape route back into the scrub. Suddenly he was floundering on his own, up to his knees in foaming muddy water. Panic stricken, he fought for a foothold in the shifting silt of the water hole.

A fluid arrangement of loosely articulated flesh and bone, capable of compression and rippling, allows the leopard a fast forward charge second to none. Seeing the obvious target separated from the herd, Torn Ear altered her direction and accelerated to full pace.

Some yards from the springbok she leapt viciously to the attack, coughing explosively in anger, hard muscle and sinew fully extended. She struck just as the victim thought he might be able to make it out of the water, hooking outstretched claws into the sodden tan fur of his rump and dragging him down.

Both predator and prey collapsed back into the shallow water, sending up a wall of spray. Torn Ear knew in an instant that she needed to make the killing stroke at the base of the neck, and make it quickly. She released her claws from their vice like hold of the rump and in a single blur sprang for the neck.

Continuous wild kicking of his legs then gave the victim a chance at freedom, for as Torn Ear let go of his quarters, two hooves found purchase and pushed him half upright. In consequence the leopard only managed a partial grip of his neck and the situation was far from resolved.

Sprinting towards the struggle took Jade about five or six seconds. It seemed like a lifetime. Closing on it, she saw what was necessary and splashed noisily into the fray, throwing herself bodily at the hind quarters of the springbok.

The animal crumpled again under the momentum of this human projectile, crashing over into the muddy broth.

With the back end pinned, however temporarily, Torn Ear could concentrate on finishing the job. The matter was soon beyond question. Both the bedraggled hunters stood up, tepid water dripping off them in streams.

After a short rest Torn Ear bent back down into the water, gripped the lifeless neck again and dragged it onto the churned up area of sand.

For the leopard, the first priority now was to groom herself to get rid of the recently acquired watery grime. There was no apparently no immediate danger of losing the prize to other carnivores, and the scent of human acting in concert with leopard was enough to make all have second thoughts.

Methodically, she licked her entire body area clean, using her rough tongue to draw water from her sodden coat until the fur bristled like freshly towelled hair. Those parts that to the onlooker seemed inaccessible were reached by feats of twisting and suppleness. When even that failed, the required part was dragged into order by the application of a carefully hooked claw.

Besides cleaning, this interlude provided a well deserved rest, prior to the labours which lay before them in transporting the capture.

Dawn had already been threatening for some time, and the crescendo of warm colours appearing in the heavens warned them that this blissful cool would vanish with the speed of morning mist, and they had better commence their task.

From their nest at the top of a Tamboti tree, a breeding pair of secretary birds watched the jet black leopard grasp the neck of the springbok, the girl lift the hind quarters and the pair of them half carry and half drag the carcass away.

The long legged birds stood as still as statues on their nest, unblinking shiny black eyes taking in the performance below.

Many exhausting miles later two ravenous cubs fell upon the meal and were quickly repulsed by a tired and angry sister. Thinking it another game, the brothers returned, only to be cuffed and bitten with such ferocity that they retreated squealing. The meal was for Mother. Torn Ear was annoyed that the others had thought of themselves first. With a final warning growl she left the carcass at the entrance to the shelter and went inside, closely followed by Jade.

An unmistakable pungent odour greeted the pair. It was, thought Jade, unavoidable, since the leopard couldn't move, but it emphasised the impression of sickness and infirmity.

Otherwise, Mother appeared to be in much the same state as when they left. Jade cleaned the wound of some sand which had probably been kicked up by the cubs as they passed her to leave the shelter. A dry scab was forming and looked healthy, but she knew that the greater damage lay beneath and would take weeks to heal.

All the time in the background was the rasping noise of Mother painfully drawing breath. It was constant effort.

Torn Ear went back outside to begin on the carcass. Typically, the contents of the body cavity were extracted first. These, she carried in to Mother.

Both Jade and the cub were intensely gratified to see the leopard eat a considerable quantity, and look better for it afterwards. Mother brought her head up and took an interest in the surroundings for the first time.

Jade, however, was worried that Mother had had nothing to drink for a long time. She stared hard at the adult, trying to see signs of distress. Apart from the injury, she could detect none and decided there was nothing she could do about it anyway. In fact, if heat stress is avoided, the body fluids of a kill can satisfy the liquid requirements of a leopard, which Jade would guess over the next few days.

While the adult ate, Jade cleaned and replaced the soiled sand.

Only when Torn Ear was convinced that Mother had had her fill did she allow Dune and Spring to feed, along with herself. Jade watched the routine as they disposed of the remainder of the internal organs and rump, followed by the limbs. They tore hungrily at the tender flesh, pulling out pieces of meat with their incisors and using cheek teeth to break up small bones and shear off rib ends. Rough tongues were used to remove awkward and inaccessible fragments of meat from the bone.

When feeding was completed the leopards groomed themselves meticulously, removing all traces of blood and viscera.

Suddenly Jade realised that she had been running on pure adrenalin and, for the first time in her life, had gone a full night without sleep. Everything developed a hollow, unreal sensation and slumber descended on her like an irresistible physical force. In the last moments of consciousness she crawled in beside Mother, curling up against the soft warmth.

Having worked a full night shift, her body didn't feel inclined to wake her until fully refreshed. Both Jade and Mother slept solidly, completely missing the heat of the day.

The cubs spent the day resting in the shadow of the rock and taking turns at sentry duty, with the entrance of the shelter in sight. They were all approaching adult size now, Torn Ear even more so, and the presence of one of them would be quite sufficient to discourage curious visitors. Despite their outward appearance the two male cubs were still immature, often playfully fighting each other and chasing their tails. They lacked a certain inner core and strength which had developed in their younger sister.

Torn Ear withdrew from antics more often than not, preferring to stay alert and watchful. Her favourite place for guard duty was the shady branch of a nearby tree. It was high enough to give her a good view of the shelter and all the surrounding territory, and yet near enough the ground for her to leap down in one bound and be running to help if the need arose.

Towards the end of the afternoon hunger pangs growling in her belly dragged Jade back into the land of the living. Feeling refreshed, but still a little fuzzy headed, she crawled out of the shelter into brilliant sunlight.

The carcass was slightly to the left of the entrance and still had an intact hind leg. If she could only make a fire, here was dinner. Had she been awake earlier she would have known that it was no accident that the leg had been left. Torn Ear had made it quite clear to the others what would befall them if they ate it. Dune and Spring abandoned the carcass in disgust - their sister was definitely no fun any more.

A black shadow streaked across the sand to greet Jade with tentative rubbing against her leg. She stroked the cat gently, after which Torn Ear immediately returned to the Guard Tree. Formalities were complete and work must be resumed.

Jade sat and puzzled over her problem, absentmindedly fingering and scratching around with a nodule of rock which her straying hand had picked up.

She could find no solution and was resigned to the usual menu for dinner. Raw meat had no appeal whatsoever. With a sigh she lofted the stone high into the air, watching for it to come down and strike the granite kopje.

Strike it it certainly did, with the accompaniment of a bright spark which caught her eye just as she was turning her head away. Sudden realisation awakened an idea. Jade scrambled up, ran the few steps to the huge boulder and retrieved the grey nodule of flint.

Eagerly she struck it against the side of the granite and was rewarded by a large spark falling at her feet. Time after time she repeated the performance, discovering that at some angles nothing happened and yet at others, large sparks could be created by no more than coaxing the stones together.

She took a flaked off piece of granite and her flint back to where the carcass lay.

Preparations for harnessing her discovery were quickly made. After a few minutes thought, Jade dug a pit in the sandy scrub and half filled it with the lightest dry grass she could find. Then she prepared a stockpile of modest twigs and leaves and finally, a supply of larger branches, broken into manageable pieces.

Now for the moment of truth. To start with, her stones refused to spark until she examined them and found she was striking smooth edges together and there was no friction.

Changing over sides gave her a spark of varying size every two or three strikes. Patiently she continued, trying to direct the tumbling flares to the dry grass. Most simply fell through to the earth.

Jade rearranged the grass and tried again, and again. Eventually, two sparks, created in quick succession fell on the same spot. Their combined energies caused the piece of grass to glow briefly. Jade spotted the success immediately, dropping both stones and tenderly feeding the embryo with more food.

Fire was born. It grew slowly and delicately at first, smouldering with an almost invisible flame in the sunlight. Jade blew softly on it, then presenting more substantial offerings as she saw fit. Gradually it began to crackle and spit most satisfyingly. Finally she added the larger chunks of wood, watching them being engulfed and the fire burn steadily on its own.

With a further supply of fuel to hand, Jade quickly skinned the leg and lay it across the top of the fire, each end being supported by opposite sides of the pit. Then she left it to roast on its own. Judging by the heat of the fire that could take some time. *Three hours at Gas Mark 1, but who cares ? I did it.....what a buzz !*

Now she turned her attentions to what remained of the carcass. Having dragged it across a considerable part of the desert, she felt she had to use whatever part of it she could. Although the cubs had devoured a part of the hide, the vast majority was left intact. Jade set about removing it with her knife.

Then began the process of softening the hide. To help with this she kneaded and rubbed in the subcutaneous fat which was next to the hide.

The whole thing was back breaking and tedious, but if the end result was to be anything like useful there was no way around it. To speed her endeavours Jade positioned the skin in direct sunlight. It made the job hotter and more uncomfortable for her but the rays seemed to act as a catalyst.

Within minutes of starting droplets of sweat rolled down her forehead and off the end of her nose. They bounced down into the melee of fat and skin, and were ignored by the craftswoman at work. There wasn't a spare hand to wipe them away.

Every so often Jade took a break and went to examine her fire. Unbelievable aromas wafting over her were proof enough that the meat was actually cooking, so she simply needed to turn it over and restore flagging embers. The greatest will power of all was required to leave it there and return to the hide. The slim deciding factor in the end was that the longer she left it, the more tender it would be. However, it was a close run thing.

The springbok hide was utilised in total. Jade fashioned a rough skirt from part of it, simply tying both ends round her waist. The remainder she hung onto the makeshift wall of the shelter, covering some of the surface and making the inside a little darker and cooler.

Strangely enough, the process left her with a single strip of hide, about two feet long. A gleam of an idea wrestled its way up from her subconscious, but before it could surface properly Jade was drawn back to the fire where a sudden flurry of sparks showed that part of the pit had collapsed and was about to plunge the roast into sandy oblivion.

She rescued it just in time and then examined it thoroughly, making deep incisions with her knife to see if it was done. Clear juice sprang out from beside the blade. *Finished. Fab. Time to pig out.*

Only as she sat down by the glowing embers did she notice that she had an enraptured audience. Dune and Spring were sitting bolt upright, bright eager eyes following her every move. Torn Ear had descended from the Guard Tree, joining her brothers. Even Mother was watching with interest from within the shelter.

Jade smiled broadly at her companions, raised the meat a little in salutation and proceeded to clean it to the bone. It was delicious.

Followed by a palate cleansing tuber, which she dug up nearby, it made a perfect meal.

She added more wood to the fire, letting her eyes drift out of focus into a pleasant blur as she watched the flames licking skywards.

As usual Torn Ear was the one who could contain her curiosity no longer. She approached the fire cautiously, slowing as she felt the heat emanating from it. Eventually there was reached a point when uncertainty balanced curiosity and the cat halted.

Observing the cub's mental battles, Jade realised that it was highly possible none of them had ever seen fire before and that it was an entirely alien experience.

Although the desert was bone dry for much of the year there was sparse concentration of combustible vegetation. Any spontaneous bush fires would tend to be small and short lived, confined to the immediate area and petering out when the fuel was exhausted.

The cubs, thought Jade, could treat this most basic element as a plaything if she were not careful. It was essential that they learn to respect it and learn its dangers. No time like the present. They could start now.

She took a small twig from her stockpile, one with a few dried leaves still attached, and made a specific point of showing it to Torn Ear so that the cub noted, she hoped, its present state. Then, with exaggerated movements, she slowly lowered it to the glowing embers.

For a couple of seconds nothing happened. Then it burst into a flower of red and amber. While it was still burning Jade withdrew it and showed it to Torn Ear.

Initially the cub baulked at the heat and the unknown and pulled her head back. Not wanting to alarm the cat too much, Jade took the twig away and held the palm of her other hand to it at the safest distance. The she pulled that hand right away from the flames and then took it back up close.

Having demolished several twigs in repeating this performance she tried a different tack. All the time the black leopard watched her intently, learning with every minute, storing every movement.

Jade lit a rather larger branch, placing it on the ground in front of Torn Ear. She let it burn for a few minutes while the cub contemplated the dancing flames.

The she sprinkled some sand on it, partially dousing the flames and let them stutter and spit their way back to life. She repeated this several times.

Finally Jade fully extinguished the branch, letting Torn Ear sniff at it and turn it over with her paw. The next step was to relight the branch and do exactly the same to it. Several times she lit and snuffed out the flames, showing, she hoped, complete mastery over the element.

Dune and Spring were now in close attendance as well, watching the last part of the lesson. Jade patiently repeated the first part for them. All the leopards were thoroughly engrossed and fascinated. The experiments continued long after dusk.

When they had finished Jade added a pile of thick branches to the glowing remnants. That would see it through the night she thought to herself. Then, on hands and knees she crawled drowsily into the shelter, snuggling up beside Mother.

As sleep descended, her body curled up into the foetal position. Imperceptibly, the adult moved her hind legs as far round Jade as she could, cocooning the sleeper in warmth and protection.

Outside, three adolescent leopards kept a silent vigil until the moon was high in the starry velvet darkness. Leaving one of their number always on guard, the cats then passed the night exploring and hunting.

They watched, the young woman slept, and the fire flickered.

CHAPTER

FIVE

Hours formed themselves into days and days fused into weeks. Gradually the unlikely companions bonded themselves into an effective unit, their main purpose to care for Mother until she was fit again.

Provision of food was almost exclusively the province of Torn Ear and Jade. They had developed a joint strategy which had been half tried by accident at the water hole on their first foray.

Jade would circumvent the victim or victims, placing them unknowingly between the leopard and herself. When the time was right she would show herself or allow the animals to get her scent. The creatures would invariably bolt off in the opposite direction, straight into the claws of the concealed leopard. Out of a fleeing herd, Torn Ear could easily select and capture her prey.

The meal would be carried back to the shelter and Mother given the choicest cuts.

If there was any left after all had finished, one of the cubs usually dragged it up into the Guard Tree for storage.

Any carcass was certainly safe enough in that larder but Jade drew the line at eating the remaining meat after it had gently stewed all day and been visited by numerous flying insects. One fairly explosive bout of illness convinced her that even cooking could not eradicate some bugs once they had been allowed to ferment.

So when the meal came back for a second time, Jade returned to her diet of fruit and tubers. The leopards never suffered from her ailment and gave her quizzical looks when she left them to it. She was convinced they had old cast iron boilers instead of stomachs.

Security was left to Dune and Spring. One of them was always in the Guard Tree or on top of the kopje, with a good view of the surroundings.

While one watched, the other rested or tried solo hunting. Occasionally a spring hare or rabbit was caught and displayed with great pride to the family, but the hunter never strayed far from his companion and since small fauna had long ago departed from this suddenly undesirable area, successes were rare indeed.

By virtue of manual dexterity, and some modest knowledge, Jade found herself in the role of nurse as well.

It was a delicate task for both parties. Jade had to clean the shelter to ensure that hygiene was maintained and yet try to leave the adult some dignity as well. Mother still constantly tried to scratch earth over the droppings, as she would in the normal course of events. This was, of course, quite impossible to begin with for any movement caused intense pain and undoubtedly retarded the healing process. Still she persisted.

After Mother got used to her nurse, Jade tried tentative steps at massage to at least keep her limbs supple while confined.

To start with Jade simply stroked the leopard, getting her used to being touched and building a bond of trust. Several days passed before she judged it right to progress on to a firmer pressure and gentle manipulation. Eventually she graduated to extending and flexing the dormant legs, stimulating and keeping the muscle in tone.

Mother soon began to look forward to these sessions which relieved her boredom at the confinement and gave her pleasant new sensations to experience. She particularly enjoyed it when her skin was scratched softly under the fur, purring and wriggling with contentment. These small expressions of pleasure gave Jade a marvellous sense of communication and achievement, and she warmed to her task.

So instead of vegetating, the leopard managed to keep a little of her condition, boredom and frustration being the main enemies. Jade looked forward to the day when she could see Mother running and jumping like her cubs.

As the unspoken ties between the companions grew stronger, Jade found she was developing a sense of purpose to her existence. No longer was it simply a question of feeding herself and surviving, just for the sake of it. There were living creatures who depended on her, to a greater or lesser degree. This responsibility sharpened her resolve and attitude to life in all aspects.

She ran faster to keep up with Torn Ear on their hunting forays, she concentrated more on her stealth and cunning, she forced herself into more hazardous situations in support of the leopard, finding her senses and reactions acute enough now to extricate herself when necessary.

Just as the cubs learned from her, so Jade acquired new skills and awareness from them. Simply by watching their reaction to everyday events she learned to read her surroundings in much greater depth, recognising danger signals, locations of prey, competition from other predators.

Gradually she learned their moods and behaviour. When a waving tail meant an invitation to a playful romp, when it was the final signal before an attacking leap. She recognised their need for solitude and their need for each other. She laughed at their astonished expressions when dust caused an unexpected sneeze, and she suffered with them while removing a thorn from a paw held high in the air.

Spending the majority of her time with, or near, the black leopard, Jade quite naturally found herself developing a greater affinity for Torn Ear. Most of her new found knowledge came from this source as they worked together.

After a while, each developed an understanding of the other's strengths and limitations, and they compensated and took account of them. As a consequence they hunted better as a team and were successful more often.

Torn Ear still hunted by herself on occasion, often at night when she felt more comfortable and more invisible, and Jade still foraged on her own. Nevertheless, as time progressed a partnership was forged. The leopard still had her independence, as she would always have, but as she grew accustomed to having a partner it seemed slightly strange when that team mate was absent.

However, the leopard realised, there was a distinct lack of enthusiasm from Jade when she was woken in the small hours to take a trip into the scrub. Torn Ear really could not understand it. Was it not surely the best time to hunt ? It was at these times that the black leopard with the torn ear could be found alone.

After several successful hunts Jade began to feel slightly superfluous. It was after all the leopard who made the kills, actually obtaining food for them all. Certainly Jade played her part and without her Torn Ear would have had a much harder time of it, but that was meagre compensation.

Long hours were spent in idle and passing contemplation of this predicament. There seemed absolutely no way round it. She had tried fashioning her long stick into a spear, burning a hard point onto it in the fire, but she didn't possess the strength to hurl it with sufficient force. It merely limped a few yards before skidding to a premature landing. No use to her at all.

In the outside world people used guns. *Oupa's beloved Purdy shotgun hanging on the study wall. Hardly ever used it.......didn't like to get it dirty......hated hunting. What would he think of me now ? What's Dancer doing ? I know I've got a friend here now, but nothing will replace you and sooner or later I'll be back with you. Promise.*

She needed something to hurl a projectile, like a catapult, except that elastic was a little hard to come by right now.

Sitting outside the tent, Mother keeping her company from inside as usual, Jade's eyes fell on a strip of animal hide almost hidden from view at the base of the kopje. On closer examination she found it to be that long piece of the springbok hide that was left over after the rest of it had been used.

Jade picked it up and moulded the leathery skin in her fingers while extracting the seed of an idea that had germinated a little while ago.

She looped the strip and tentatively placed a stone in the pocket formed at the base of the loop.

A sling, she thought, did the same as a catapult. A sling looked basically like this, so with a bit of luck it should work.

Even as she thought, the stone rolled over of its own volition and dropped at her feet. A frown creased her brow as she replaced it, only to find it disappearing off the other side.

This would require some work. Jade picked a stone as smooth and round as she could find. Kneeling on the ground with the leather in front of her, she gently rubbed and twisted the stone in the middle of the strip, ever so gradually flattening out a suitably sized pouch within it.

Standing up, her back muscles creaked in protest and went unheard, but the stone stayed put.

Now she had a strip of leather, both ends held in one hand, with a stone in the pocket at the bottom. One full swing of her arm convinced her that throwing it was not going to be easy either. The stone dropped out at the top of the swing, bounced on her head and hit the ground.

Rubbing her tousled mass of bleached hair, she came to the conclusion that the faster she swung the sling, the more chance there was of the stone staying put. She reloaded and set her right arm twisting like a propeller.

When she had it going as fast as she could, Jade let go of the sling. The whole strip fell to the ground and the stone rocketed past the left ear of a dozing Spring who ducked with a muted squeak of alarm.

Undeterred, her second shot cracked into the granite kopje above their heads. Four furry faces watched from the entrance to the shelter where they had congregated. It seemed like the safest place right now.

Jade practised and experimented long past dusk. She tried different methods of holding and releasing the sling, quickly establishing that by releasing only one end the stone flew more or less where she was looking and had the added advantage of keeping the sling in her hand for a quick reload.

She walked off to the Guard Tree to use its ample trunk as the first intended target. The cubs made to follow but were counselled against it by Mother. Even in her still tender state, she now took an active interest in events, the first sure sign of recovery.

It was sound advice for the first few shots bounced considerably wide of the target, in both forward and reverse directions.

Limited success failed to staunch her youthful enthusiasm and as the practise continued shots came nearer and nearer until with a resounding thunk one hit the trunk fair and square. Although it was somewhat of a fluke, Jade was overjoyed and let out a howl of excitement.

A combination of no light and no remaining stones closed the day's play on a high note.

In her sleep that night she clutched the sling close to her chest and dreamt of flying stones.

First light of day was heralded by the same sounds that had seen the departure of the previous one. Leather cutting savage swathes through the air, occasionally ending in the smack of stone on wood. There would be short intervals as the armoury was replenished, and then it would begin again.

For the moment this was the all enveloping passion. Even food came a poor second. The leopards settled into their daytime positions unnoticed.

Had Jade not been so engrossed, she might have seen Mother gingerly push herself up into a sitting position inside the shelter. It felt strange to have some height in the world after such a long enforced stay in the horizontal. The adult soon noticed a giddy feeling so let herself slowly slide back down. The pain in her side was no longer an icy stab, just a dull tired ache, and it was almost possible for her to take a full deep breath. She could feel herself improving rapidly and was all the more impatient with her body now that it was on the road to recovery.

Mother looked on while a tall figure of burnished teak wearing a roughly tied animal skin round the waist eagerly flung stones at a tree trunk. Needless to say, the Guard Tree had been abandoned by the guards.

All three cubs sat on top of the kopje observing activities keenly, with a sense of self preservation uppermost. If any more missiles went astray they could take swift evasive action.

Perched a perilously close distance behind the trio sat a young rock hyrax, the size of a rabbit. Being fairly early for him still, he was only half awake, basking in the warming rays. In actual fact the cubs hadn't moved since he arrived, so engrossed were they in the show, and therefore the hyrax had not taken the trouble to consult his memory as to the silhouetted shapes in front of him.

An ear twitched and a paw moved up to swat an irritating mosquito.

The rock hyrax started in alarm then instantly propelled himself outwards from his sunbed, landing with a soft but bone jarring thump some feet below. That had been too close for his liking.

Torn Ear twisted her head round at the muffled sound and saw nothing but smooth rock curving away in brilliant sunlight. She squinted into it for a while and then decided it was time to find shade. The lithe form descended in one flowing leap, long tail curved up elegantly and seeming to balance the downward movement.

Even Jade needed a respite from practice. In the shelter she used siesta time to make a pouch out of the side of her garment in which to store stones.

As soon as the heat was bearable she was out again and as afternoon progressed the sounds of contact on wood became more constant. She found she could aim to a certain extent, placing stones to a particular area on the trunk.

Torn Ear came to Jade shortly after dark. The leopards had not eaten for nearly a day and a half. Bellies were beginning to flap against backbones.

Jade was eager to accompany the huntress. It might be possible to test the sling, even in the dark.

The pair were soon ready, striding away from the shelter into the moonlight. For some reason, while they were still in view, Jade stopped and turned to look at Mother, Dune and Spring. As usual all three were watching them disappear, one cub each side of the recumbent Mother.

Jade shook her head briefly and trotted after the vanishing Torn Ear, leaving her family behind.

They jogged steadily into the sandveldt, heading for an area not visited for many days.

Without warning the leopard disturbed a bushveld gerbil which bounded off in front of them. Torn Ear caught it quickly in a mini sandstorm of flailing feet. She ate it on the move, nothing more than a quick snack and only just worth bothering with.

An hour or so into the trek the pair came across a small mixed herd of zebra and wildebeest. Both sets of animals had juveniles and young ones in amongst them and were too good to pass by.

The two hunters split and with infinite patience began to outflank and stalk.

*****

Imperceptible, yet it was there. On one side and then on the other. But so quiet that Mother could hardly call it a noise.

Then it was there again. From both sides at the same time, the signals came. It was dead leaves being rustled and hurried along by a zephyr of a warm night breeze. It could be nothing else.

Fur prickled up along her spine. There was nothing there, and now she wasn't sure any more.

Her children were outside, dozing by still warm embers that were made by the strange creature who was their friend and supporter.

Her children were outside, and from where she lay she couldn't see them.

If only Torn Ear were there, her favourite. The one for whom she suddenly felt a gigantic surge of impending loss.

At that moment her world exploded.

The side of the shelter folded under the impact of two heavy golden bodies, reeking the rank smell of lion.

Mother rose swiftly to try and meet the challenge. She twisted round and in doing so severed the rib which had only just managed to tentatively heal. Forced inward by the unnatural turn, the razor sharp point pierced the left ventricle of her heart. Mother was dead before the stinking breath and yellow teeth closed around her neck.

The remainder of the pride pounced simultaneously on the awakening cubs.

Fighting valiantly, they inflicted horrific injuries on several of their attackers and might possibly have persuaded them to retreat had they not been separated.

Both bodies were rapidly engulfed in separate mountains of tearing, heaving flesh. Not for them the easy route of a swift killing stroke. Claws and teeth sliced through groin and underbelly, working their way up to the internal organs in a collective frenzy of attack.

Long minutes of searing agony and panic passed before unconsciousness dragged them free into oblivion.

The attackers left as they had arrived, in silence. The mutilated corpses lay untouched. Predator kills predator out of hate. They had no use for the flesh of an enemy as food.

*****

Unease crept through the minds of Jade and Torn Ear. It sniffed at the edge of their thoughts and feelings and yet when challenged as to its presence, it retreated as a misty shadow into the wilderness.

Jade could tell that the leopard felt anxious too, even across the divide of peaceful animals that separated them. She constantly looked around herself, trying to fathom a cause for this sixth sense of alarm. A danger perhaps so blatant and obvious that they had missed it, and that her recently acquired survival instincts had sensed.

There was nothing she could see, nothing she could smell, nothing she could hear.

Zebra and wildebeest munched quietly on the few worthwhile stalks they could find, scuffing hooves in the sand and dirt as they shuffled around. What little wind there was, was blowing directly across the herd, from left to right, taking the scents of the hunters away from the prey as it did. They were totally unaware.

Perhaps hyena were stalking the stalkers. Jade took time out to squat down and painstakingly quarter her whole field of vision. Turning a full circle, she examined every contour and shape in turn, not passing them by until she had established their identity, which was not always easy in the shallow moonlight.

Still nothing. She could do no more than place a preparatory stone in her sling and carry on.

Travelling at a speed in excess of fourteen miles per second, a solid mass of nickel and iron entered the upper atmosphere at a slight, grazing angle of incidence.

It rapidly acquired a nose cap of ionized air, increasing with every fraction of time that passed, and became brilliantly luminous.

The forward surface of the meteorite began to melt with the intense heat, fine droplets of the molten mass being swept off and then condensing almost instantaneously into a resplendent trail that blazed behind it.

At a height of seventy five miles the fireball effect became visible from the earth.

A dazzling white head, shaped like a teardrop, was followed by a scintillating wake, exhibiting all the colours of the rainbow, while shedding sparks that faded from bright orange to a dull red.

The meteorite streaked down and across the atmosphere at supersonic speed.

An instant later the whole landscape was bathed in a light more intense and revealing than the noonday sun.

The shooting star seemed to hang in the sky for whole seconds, like the brightest of flares on a parachute. It banished night, exposing a naked and vulnerable desert with its searchlight beam of white. The scene was caught as if by the flashgun of a camera.

It was gone in an instant, continuing its journey into oblivion, etching a fiery trail over the hemisphere and away.

In the seconds of life over the Kalahari the meteorite had lost much of its kinetic energy, burnt off in brilliant incandescence. Twelve miles above the dunes, and far away, its light finally faded and it fell to earth as a dull spent body.

For a moment all was eerie and quiet, while creatures viewed the single still frame picture that had been left imprinted in their eyes. Even before discovery, Torn Ear knew she was found out and sat bolt upright in the classic gesture of defeat in the hunt, so that all could see her.

Bedlam arrived shortly afterwards in the form of a snorting, barking stampede of hooves and bodies. They disappeared into the darkness in a flurry of relieved activity.

A thought, an image, a picture, forced itself into the mind of the cub. So severe and violent and full of a cry for help that Torn Ear couldn't comprehend it for a second. Then it was gone and replaced by acres of emptiness and a sudden rising tide of her own panic and anxiety.

Why did it stop ? Why could she sense nothing else ?

The leopard responded by throwing herself into forward motion across the ground, where dust from fleeing hooves was still settling. Stride lengthened and body hugged the contours as she moved like never before.

As Torn Ear had received clarity and a specific appeal, so Jade, at the same instant, experienced a stab of fear in the base of her gut. It was heartstopping in its ferocity and she knew of only one thing that might justify it. The sight of Torn Ear passing in front of her confirmed her worst suspicions.

With a silent prayer that somehow she might be wrong, and the deepening pit in her stomach telling her she was right, Jade set off after the leopard.

Jade knew she could never keep up. Torn Ear was travelling faster than Jade had ever seen her before. If she went flat out then she would be able to keep the leopard in sight for a short while. To do that would burn her out and she wouldn't make it back before the grey dawn arrived.

So, against the instinct and pleading of her heart she settled unwillingly into her normal gait and began the most tortuous journey of her life so far.

Moving with the speed and confidence of one who is totally at home and familiar with her environment, the jet black leopard was destined to arrive a good half hour before her companion.

Deep inside, she soon knew what had happened. Where there had always been communication and a presence in her mind, was a void, aching and painfully empty.

Torn Ear was sitting upright at the top of a mound when Jade saw her. She had her back to the approaching runner, and the tail, for once, was curled tightly round the side of the haunches. In silhouette Jade could even make out the split ear.

Exhausted to the point of sickness, chest heaving and belly wanting to retch, she watched the unmoving shape until her breathing returned to normal. There was no hurry now. The daughter of the family would not be sitting there if there was. Jade would need as steady a nerve as she could muster to face the horrors she knew must lie on the other side.

Incongruous beauty sprang out of the heavens as if unaware of the agony below. Dawn spread its message quickly to the desert. Sudden light hurt tired eyes, galvanizing Jade into movement.

It was easier than expected. This was no longer her home. It was unrecognisable.

It was unrecognisable if she chose to overlook the warm embers of the fire she had made last night, if she missed the half chewed bone which Spring always left for the morning, if she scuffed sand over the distinctive pawprint with a crooked third clawmark, if she avoided touching her long spear which still stood where she had planted it like a flagpole. Yes, it was unrecognisable, she told herself.

Gently, oh so gently, in an unreal nightmare, she pulled the unreal corpses together without looking into the bloody scarred faces. She placed the bodies on the ground where the shelter had been, on the ground which had cared for their mother and almost healed her. On branches which had sheltered them.

The lone shadow of a watcher remained where it was. Torn Ear would never set foot on the site again.

At the base of the granite kopje Jade laboured in silent grief and kindled fire there for the last time.

She set sparks to each corner and the sides of a funeral pyre. Flames soon crackled and burst evenly around that which had been home and companionship.

Jade retreated, climbing the mound to sit close to the leopard. Close, but not quite touching. Each with her thoughts watching the smoke rise steadily. Watching as fire ate, destroyed, cleansed and purified. The flames blackened the side of the rock, leaving the only clue as to its history.

Through the life of the fire the two sat and watched. Long after it had died, they sat in silence. Both apart and yet both together, sharing feelings.

Sun rose high in the sky, burning onto exposed bodies. It went unnoticed. It really didn't matter.

Lengthening shadows saw no change. Through the rest of the day and into a starry night, each came to terms with the situation, dealing with the mourning.

With the first light of a new day, Jade moved a stiff arm across and gently touched the top of a velvet head, cool and moist with a minute amount of dew. The leopard started suddenly and then relaxed.

The pair got up and descended from the mound, walking slowly away. In this cruel desert, what is gone is gone. They had a life to lead.

CHAPTER

SIX

The miniature jaws of a cone headed katydid snapped together with a soft click, cracking open another seed. The grasshopper stood for a minute, dealing with its latest acquisition and surveying the landscape for further supplies.

It had already decided that the grass seeds were greener on the other side of the fence and had thus hopped purposefully under the three strand wire barricade, which had impeded its progress about as much as a few grains of sand.

Entering the outermost area of the Niekerk farm meant nothing to the small insect. To Harry de Beer it was now fair game, in his territory, to do with as he pleased.

The remains of a Namaqua dove testified to that. Plucked feathers around his stretched out legs and congealed grease on a chin thick with stubble.

The bird was a real conquest. He had shot it with the ancient Winchester provided for his protection out in the bush. It had made a welcome addition to the meagre provisions sitting in the back of the open topped Land Rover.

Of course, cooking it had been a problem. It would require effort and work to make a fire. In consequence Harry didn't bother with such niceties.

Entertainment was on the menu now. Anything to beak the monotony of driving along the endless kilometres of barren scorched earth, checking the eternal fence for damage. For God's sake, he hadn't even seen a single animal that this wire was supposed to keep in.

The grasshopper jumped forward to investigate some blackthorn acacia seeds.

Behind the creature, a heavy boot, pivoting on the heel, descended slowly. Quickly enough to pin the insect to the ground by its oversized hind legs, but slowly enough to ensure that it had an idea of what was happening before its brittle outer skeleton was crushed, and brown liquid oozed out from under the foot.

A brief grin hung on the bullet head for a few seconds. Then the victory paled and he was bored again.

Somewhere in a mirky past the Afrikaaner had a touch of Kalahari Bushman in him, the result of a brief but enforced liaison with a characteristically diminutive woman captured during a raid on the hated people. The unfortunate victim had survived confinement in captivity and virtual slavery, but had died giving birth to Harry's distant relative.

Nevertheless he found himself gifted with some of the skill and craft of that race of people, and used it to his advantage whenever the occasion arose. Hence the demise of the normally alert insect.

It was getting hot. The head of closely cropped fair hair glanced skywards to confirm what he already knew. Blue heavens burning to a white disc around the sun and not a cloud in sight.

He climbed back into the truck and manoeuvred it to the side of an ancient baobab tree. Then he pulled a tarpaulin out and rigged it up between the vehicle and tree. It was now the best shade for miles around. It was the only shade.

The big man eased his frame down into the darkened area, coming to rest against the dry gnarled trunk. He reached out and captured a stray bottle of beer which had been rolling about in the front of the Land Rover and was now by his feet. Putting the neck into his mouth to release the ill fitting cap, he suddenly halted, holding the bottle in mid-air.

There were stirrings within. With care, he cultivated and gently nurtured them until he knew he had been successful. Belching satisfyingly, Harry rolled the taste around his mouth before exhaling. It was the dove of course. It had been a while since he had eaten raw meat.

The bottle continued its journey, spilling a small froth of warm sweet liquid out of the corner of his mouth as it was opened.

He didn't pause for breath until the entire contents had been dealt with. Throwing the empty container to one side, he waited patiently for the inevitable consequence, and was not disappointed.

Harry nestled down into a more comfortable position. He would pass the heat of the day here, dozing in a shallow alcohol induced sleep. Why should today be any different to the others ?

The danger of being caught idling was so small that it didn't even warrant consideration. The old boss man was in bed, wrestling in a delirious sweating fever with another attack of malaria. The only other Boer on the farm was the hated foreman, and he was away in Windhoek for several days. It was almost bearable.

Eyes closed and breathing became steady and deep. With time, there could be heard a slight rasping sound from within the slack jaws

Nothing stirred in the breathless solid heat. Had the sleeper not been so engaged he would have found the wire too hot to work with anyway.

Harry arrived back at the main farm buildings shortly before dusk, throwing the old vehicle into a sideways skid in the ample yard, sending up clouds of dust in the process. More by luck than judgement it ended up adjacent to the side of a shed and he leapt out, grinning from ear to ear.

Well over six feet tall, he was endowed with more than his fair share of weight. This cunning disguise of nature had led prospective opponents to believe him to be slow and clumsy. A supposition not borne out by the results of bar room brawls. Word soon travelled around the locals and Harry found a severe lack of competition. A fact which never ceased to disappoint him.

With the exception of the stubble on his face, shortly to be removed, his head was close cropped and kept that way deliberately. Hair could be pulled and held, and where the hair went, so did the head.

He brushed a hand over his darkly tanned face, wiping off the ever present sheen of perspiration and in turn smearing streaks of dirt across his features. The man sweated constantly. His clothing was never free from stains and spreading patches of darkness were invariably present. He couldn't have cared less. It mattered not to him what impression other people got and besides, that certain aroma did tend to keep them at a distance and that was just fine by him.

Standing in the early evening sun, Harry absentmindedly ran a finger down the length of an old scar which stretched from the eye to just below the cheek bone on the left side of his face. It had been a constant companion for years, ever since his first serious fight, over the favours of a lady of the night.

He had won it and the resulting prize. However, the loser had returned later with reinforcements and Harry had nearly paid the ultimate price.

Two lessons were learnt. One, pleasures of the flesh can be obtained with little effort and are not worth fighting over. Two, knives cut.

Lesson one was usually recalled directly after each relevant encounter and as such was virtually useless. Lesson two resulted in the acquisition of a wickedly sharp blade of Sheffield steel which he strapped to his ankle under the clothing.

Depressing a button on the side of the case caused the blade to spring out, ready for use.

After healing, the scar remained obstinately white, contrasting with its sun-drenched surround.

" Aitch, aitch " called a voice heavily accented with Afrikaans. " Boss wants to see you."

H, as he had forcefully insisted that the other farm workers call him, coughed deeply and spat into the dust at his feet.

" What the hell does the old bastard want now ?" he grunted none too softly. Despite the expressed sentiments the Boer roused himself and started to walk across the yard.

Sitting behind the massive stinkwood desk in the study was an effort of Tony van Niekerk. During the ever increasing bouts of malaria everything became an effort and he knew that to get up out of bed did nothing to aid recovery.

Still, he needed to speak to one of his employees and he could hardly maintain a position of authority and respect lying on his back in a pool of sweat, watching the room go round.

Slowly he reached for the bottle of tablets standing on the leather bound blotter and swallowed one with a mouthful of warm water from the desktop carafe. The chloroquine treatment usually took three days to see off an attack, but nowadays it seemed to be increasingly difficult to defeat the disease.

He had caught a glimpse of himself in the mirror on the way down. Flesh had melted off him, leaving a tall gaunt frame without any padding. Eyes had sunk back into their sockets, looking bloodshot and raw. The loss of red blood cells made him appear anaemic and jaundiced, and to accompany the hectic fever his intestines were suffering the delights of gastro enteritis. His only consolation was that, like the other times, this attack would eventually pass.

However, an admission of the effect of the disease was the abandonment of the search.

Countless months, and then years, of scouring the accessible areas of the Kalahari sands had produced nothing except the canvas feed bag. Even that small token of hope would have been enough to keep him searching, had successive attacks not weakened him to such an extent that he was now incapable of crossing his own yard without stopping for a rest. The token police force had done no more than create a record and a file which had gathered dust a long time ago, if it was still even in existence. There was no crime and she had obviously gone of her own free will, according to the note. The consequences were unfortunate, but everyone living here knows the risks of desert travel. We'll call you if we hear anything.

To continue the quest for the granddaughter he had raised, the old man had then hired light aircraft and pilots from Gobabis and Kalkfontein over the border in Botswana. Their brief, to look for the upturned white faces of people in the desert, which from the air, seem to shine out of the sands and demand attention.

Sinking deep into debt, even the most unscrupulous charter company finally refused his hirings, recognising that the likelihood of payment was small and that of success in the mission even smaller.

There was but one string left to his bow. He had to send a tracker into the desert after her, to do his job for him.

Deep inside there was the almost certain knowledge that all this effort was in vain. The girl and her horse would undoubtedly have succumbed after only a couple of days in the wilderness, but she was the only family he had. The search was the only real interest he had in life now. It had become an obsession and to give up on her was to give up on himself.

The farmer's mind drifted and swam back to a glittering wedding, well over seventeen years ago now. The radiant woman who was his daughter and the fine young man by her side. Time changes everything.

The old man's head had fallen to stare at the top of his desk, supported on each side by a huge weatherbeaten hand. The mind drifted further. Back in his life before the farm to his first day as a detective in the Rhodesian police. A murder and two rapes and he was all there was.

He looked up gradually, to see the almost menacing figure of the arrogant worker swim into focus.

H was grinning, he had the old man off balance, whatever it was he wanted with him.

"Don't you ever knock ?" rasped the farmer, struggling to grip his mind and force it into order.

"You wanted to see me " slouched the reply, matter of factly.

"I have a proposition for you, " started Tony, straightening himself up. He would have made it an order, but this man had a dislike for orders and would probably have disobeyed him for the sake of it.

"Simply put, it is this. I want my granddaughter back, if she is still alive. I can no longer manage the physical effort of the search and I need someone to carry on for me. I want you to do it."

The big Afrikaaner let loose several guffaws of laughter, mocking laughter.

" You're mad, " he scorned. " If you think that after all this time..........."

" Listen to me, damn your hide, " whispered the old man so fiercely that it stopped H in mid-sentence. " Then give me your thoughts, if you can manage any."

He paused, to marshal his breath and the sentence.

" While you are away I will double your wages and have them placed in whatever establishment you wish. " The attention was back with him and Harry was silent.

" I have instructed stores in Windhoek to provide you with whatever you deem necessary and debit my account. Initially, you may take a vehicle, a horse, or both. I imagine however, you will then track on foot.

Find her and return her to me, unharmed, and I will pay you five thousand rand, in cash. If she is dead, provide the location of the body and suitable evidence as to identity and I will give you a cash bonus. It will, needless to say, be considerably less than if she were alive. You may start immediately."

The Boer was silent. He had decided to take the offer as soon as the higher wages were mentioned. Everything else was a plus. Still, it wouldn't do to appear too keen.

"The bonus is ten thousand, " gambled H. " The desert is dangerous."

"And you lived in and on it for over a year. You could have been a Bushman. Seven thousand, not a cent more."

Harry was scheming already. If he found Jade, seven thousand rand was more than he could earn in a long time. But even the doubled wages could provide him with more delights of the flesh than ever before. Enough for two, at the same time. His breathing quickened at the very thought.

In seconds, standing in the inner sanctum before the desk, his animal mind weighed up the consequences of acceptance.

Succeed or fail, he would be richer. The longer he could string it out the more he would get, although he had no illusions as to the time it might take.

A return to a basic subsistence lifestyle, even for a while, appealed to his survivalist instincts.

He was sick of the routines, day after day, and of the boredom of it all. Despite his inherent laziness he needed a challenge every now and again to keep the adrenalin ticking over.

There should be no problem surviving in the desert if he remembered the old skills learnt at the hands of the experts. The old man was right, he had almost been a Bushman. Not out of choice, at any rate not to begin with.

Killing an officer during a bar room argument meant he had to leave his National Service Unit a lot sooner than anticipated. The only place to hide was in the desert. It was either that or face a court martial and certain firing squad.

It had worked out fine, until his gently cultivated friends eventually decided that all was not well. Over the course of several weeks they headed towards a little used rutted track on the edge of civilisation, where they intended to leave him for his own kind to discover.

That family of trusting desert folk now had an unmarked communal grave near the track.

Only after he could take the desert no longer did he return to face the consequences. To learn that his whole unit had been wiped out by a terrorist attack hours after he left. Buildings razed to the ground and all records destroyed. He had been presumed dead along with the rest.

In view of that and of the story of courageous fighting with which H rapidly endowed himself, he was granted an honourable discharge. The man came out smelling like a rose garden.

H was about to speak when a realisation of profound significance struck him fair and square just below his ample belly.

In the unlikely event of the old man's granddaughter being alive out there, she would be alone with him. His memory recalled long flowing hair and a firm supple body. Doubtless she would have developed in the intervening years, although he really couldn't remember at all how long she had been missing.

If he found her he would have her and the vultures could finish the job. Somehow the attractiveness of the extra bonus seemed to pale into insignificance.

" You just bought yourself a bloodhound." He turned and strode out of the study, leaving the door open behind him.

Tony stared after the disappearing figure. It was like setting a pack of wolves after a blind rabbit.

Logically, he told himself, the Afrikaaner was the only one to send. He was the only one with enough knowledge of the Kalahari to be able to survive and also track. Anything he came back with would be a bonus, but Tony held out little hope of anything positive. It also meant that the troublesome worker would be out of circulation for some considerable time.

If it was the right thing to do, then why did the lump in his gut refuse to go away ?

The old farmer exhaled deeply and signalled for the maid to help him back to his room.

*****

It was almost ten days later before H finally arrived at the tagged thorn bush where the canvas feed bag had been found, the only clue as to where the girl and the horse might have entered the interior. The trunk of the bush had grown round the wire and incorporated the foreign body into itself, making it difficult to unwind.

Old tyre tracks still led to the spot and Harry thought he could even see where Tony had dug the vehicle out, over a year ago, or was it two ?

Expense accounts were something new to Harry, so he made the most of them before settling down to the business of actually acquiring that which he needed on his mission. He didn't intend to be as ill equipped as he was on his last foray into the desert.

The specially designed back pack had detailed maps, compass and a compact powerful torch. Emergency food rations came in the shape of high protein bars, but he did not intend to use them unless absolutely necessary. He would live off the desert as before.

As far as weaponry was concerned, he had thought long and hard about taking a hunting rifle. Certainly it would ensure that he never ran short of meat, and he would feel that much safer. With these considerations in mind, H had almost fallen for a Remington 7.62 which beckoned to him through the gun dealer's window, from behind steel bars.

Sense finally overcame greed, just. However much it might provide in the way of food, carrying a cumbersome rifle around on foot in the desert heat was just not on. He needed to have as little with him as possible.

Instead, the ultimate safeguard was provided by a Browning self loading pistol strapped to his waist. The back pack contained six extra magazines for the weapon, each with ten rounds of ammunition. All purchased on the Van

Niekerk firearms permit. The pistol was balanced by an evil looking hunting knife hanging on the other side of the belt.

H ripped the rusty tag off the bush, throwing it into the back of the Land Rover. Then he pulled out a ten gallon drum of drinking water. The surface of the heavy duty plastic scored slightly on jagged metal as it came out.

The hunter, for he was surely no rescuer, bent down and held his head under the simple tap. As the cool water gushed out he gulped and swallowed mouthfuls, letting the excess flow over his neck and chest.

Twice he stopped and came up for air. H knew that if he carried on drinking after the initial thirst had been satisfied, the extra water in his belly would keep him going longer still. He stooped again.

Despite his efforts the container still looked remarkably full when he finally replaced it in the vehicle and fastened the tarpaulin over it.

The Land Rover was staying here. It was to be a sort of base, with some supplies, to give him a friendly point to aim for if he needed to make an unscheduled exit from the sandveldt. He had already buried a water tight canvas sack nearby. In it were tins of food, rudimentary medical supplies and, of course, two extra bottles of water. The morphine ampoules he placed in the first aid kit that was going with him.

In the back pack were thin hollow tubes for extracting, Bushman style, the foul tasting grimy liquid from beneath the arid surface which would be his water for however long he was out there.

The time for putting off the inevitable was over. H took out the detailed map and, for the hundredth time, wondered at the huge uncharted spaces which were still shown on it. He marked the position of the Land Rover, folded up the map and shouldered the pack. Then he walked back to the tagged thorn bush.

Whatever prevailing wind there was here, he mused to himself, came from the north east, and as such might have blown the canvas bag to its resting place.

From where he stood, the compass showed that north east was directly on his right. It was as good a direction as any to start in. Once he could pick up a definite place of entry into the desert then he could try and track his quarry. Finding that place was guesswork and luck.

Above him, the sun was well into its downward track. Lengthening rays struck the shallow dunes, throwing slight shadows in front of them and mellowing the appearance of stark bushes, their slender bodies bleached by the elements.

High in the sky a tawny eagle wheeled and circled in the constant quest for food. The human profile he could easily recognise. Indeed, spotting the movement of the tiniest mouse at over a hundred yards presented no problem. As long as the man was there, other creatures would keep away. The poor man's golden eagle would search elsewhere.

For a few minutes Harry stood and mentally attuned himself to the desert again. He had to be part of it if he was to survive in it.

He saw the same objects, colours and outlines, but he could see no beauty. It was merely an environment in which he happened to feel at home, comfortable and in command.

The big Afrikaaner strode off to his right, the sand grinding softly under his boots.

******

The passage of time had bleached the ancient wildebeest skull to the colour of chalk. It was the remains of an old lion kill and had lain in the same place since the demise of its owner.

A desert creature crouched down on its knees, craning forward to inspect the object in every detail.

The skin of the observer was darkened to an almost impossible degree by the sun and in places appeared that it might even be leathery to the touch. The hair was bleached to a shocking white and tied back in a crude ponytail. The fringe had been hacked short but the rest was thick and dirty. She had long ago stopped worrying about the constant itching - she would rather not know and couldn't do anything about it anyway. The body was naked save for a well used and familiar animal skin which was around the waist. Hanging from this garment were two slings, one obviously new, along with a modest pouch that held specially selected stones. Thrust through a hole in the other side of the skirt was a sharpened digging stick.

As Jade leant forward it was obvious it was obvious that nature had at last taken an interest in her development. Her tanned chest, previously flat and muscular, had thickened substantially to give her an athletic female shape. She had also had two or three periods now, which she dealt with using cut strips of absorbent animal hide. Not ideal by any stretch but the periods were light and short. She was careful to bury these strips deep in the sand when they were finished with. *Emmy, you lied to me girl........there's no pain and I don't feel like throwing cooking pots at any man I see before it happens.......OK so there isn't a man within a hundred miles........did Molo give you a baby yet........thought I didn't know ha ha......blind man in a sandstorm saw what you were doin'........*

The object of Jade's intense observations were the twin horns which stood out proud on the skull. On the dry surface of these horns was a multitude of tube like projections which had apparently grown up like stalagmites on a cave floor.

Jade had been watching these structures on and off for a couple of hours and curiosity had now got the better of her. Cracking open one of the miniature towers revealed an elfin sized caterpillar cocooned inside.

The incentive behind her interest was now pure and simple. Food. Long ago she had discovered that the full grown caterpillars of mopane emperor moths provided a tasty snack. At nearly two and a half inches long, the hairless black and green animals could make a substantial meal if there were enough of them.

However, these were destined to be a disappointment. A tentative sample showed them to be definitely worth leaving exactly where they were.

Stretching back to an upright position, Jade brushed off the sand which had stuck to her knees. In front of her the huge orange sun was sinking slowly below the horizon, silhouetting an old baobab tree. Nearby, the sharp barks of a territorial male gecko could be heard announcing the onset of night.

From her position in the fossil river valley, Jade could see a fluid black shadow exit from a cave and make its way down a path, of sorts, almost hidden by vegetation.

The leopard came at her out of the gathering gloom, running forward in a swaggering trot, almost side on, making her appear bigger than real life.

Jade quickly removed her digging stick, planting it upright in the ground beside her longer spear. Then she took off the slings and bag of smooth round stones, throwing them down near the other weapons.

Running to meet the challenge, Jade suddenly dropped to the sand and curled up into a ball, tucking her head in as far as she could.

A short distance from the crouching shape the leopard launched herself softly into the air, claws sheathed within huge cushioned paws.

Timed to perfection, the shape exploded into action as Torn Ear was overhead, leaping up to grab the mass of fur and muscle as it descended.

They landed as one in a forgiving sand dune and the two companions rolled over and over, playfully fighting and wrestling until Jade was finally exhausted.

She called a truce and they lay on the ground panting, bodies covered with debris from the desert floor, until the strength to move returned to them.

Torn Ear stirred first. She got up and wandered lazily to the acacia tree which she regarded as her own.

Standing on her hind legs she raked the bark of the tree with exposed foreclaws, ripping the material in long jagged wounds. There were many other such marks on this tree, for this was the nearest one to where they spent most of their leisure time.

Moving back to the figure on the ground, Torn Ear watched the almost imperceptible rise and fall of the girl's back as the latter tried to keep perfectly still. The leopard however, knew just how to provoke action.

Before too long, whiskers came alongside her face and a chunky rasping tongue swiped her exposed cheek, just once. Jade knew when she was beaten. If she stayed put, the barrage of assaults would continue until her face was red raw. A tongue that can remove meat from the bones of prey by itself is not to be trifled with.

Jade leapt up, laughing and wiping her face at the same time. Torn Ear had won and she knew it. After a minute of gloating the leopard made to walk off and Jade ran after her, gently grabbing hold of the cat's long black tail and swaying from side to side with it in exaggerated movements as the pair walked up the hidden path to the cave.

The days and weeks after the lion attack had seen them take up a nomadic existence. They never stayed longer than a day in the same place, sleeping in whatever shade could be found, and on the move again come nightfall.

When they made a kill, they ate what they wanted then and there. Seldom did Jade have the time or inclination to allow herself the luxury of a cooking fire. Torn Ear showed no interest in storing the carcass. It was as if she cared little for the future. It could do with her as it wished.

Whether it was fate or conscious intent on the part of the leopard, Jade never knew, but one early morning found them looking down on a huge fossil river valley which it was apparent Torn Ear found very familiar.

For a day and a night Torn Ear steadfastly refused to go any further. Jade guessed they had come to a watershed for some reason or other and left the leopard to reach her own decision.

With the next sunrise the choice was made. Jade followed as the leopard weaved her way down into the river bed and started out across it with definite purpose.

About an hour passed before Torn Ear led the way up a path Jade would never have found on her own.

When they reached the balcony Jade knew instantly what this cave had been. She knew that by returning, the leopard was conquering, or at least coming to terms with, the death of her family.

Torn Ear sat on the balcony staring into the gloomy depths of the cave. Memories flooded her mind. She could almost sense the physical presence of Mother, Dune and Spring. Even now, to see the others come tumbling out of the entrance would have been no great surprise to her.

The leopard jumped in, filling the entrance as she passed. No more the growing cub who needed a springboard to enter her home.

Jade waited patiently for the moment when she would remind the leopard of her presence.

From inside came the sounds of a short but violent scuffle, and an evicted young mongoose landed unceremoniously on the balcony. Taking one look at Jade on the pathway and remembering the nightmare which he had woken up to inside, he decided to take his chances with the direct route down and promptly vanished over the edge, as the lemming takes to a cliff.

After a few minutes silence, while Torn Ear searched the darker corners for remaining intruders, the leopard reappeared at the entrance. Making an exit in one fluid movement, she landed deftly on the balcony and it was time for Jade to view the property.

She scrambled through the hole head first, like a torpedo being manoeuvred into the firing tube and was pleasantly surprised to find she could actually stand up, which she did.

Waiting for her eyes to get accustomed to the light she sensed the presence of the whole family inside the den. It was almost as if part of them had remained there and that they were really still with her, the only difference being she couldn't actually see them. The pain of death was still sharp but somehow being in their home eased it, blunted the edge. She was still sharing part of their lives and Jade felt instantly comfortable in the cave.

She explored minutely, discovering everything from the lip of rough and uneven rock just behind the entrance, to the size and height of the hole in the roof at the back where light was allowed to filter in.

More than anything it felt cool. The bare rock inside was actually pleasant to touch, even the air felt fresh and clean. To have a blessed escape from the eternal scorching heat was a long forgotten dream from those first nightmarish weeks on her own.

The layers of soil and rock on all sides of the cave insulated it from the attack of the sun, absorbing the heat from the rays beating down. Inside, it remained wonderfully dim and cool.

At night, the insulation would reverse its role. Releasing the heat which it had stored during the day, it kept the temperature a few degrees above that of the outside world, which sometimes dipped to freezing.

Torn Ear joined Jade inside the cave and lay down in the darkest corner to wait out the hottest hours in a coolness she had not known for weeks. The leopard was at peace and Jade was happy to know it.

*****

The first few days of acclimatisation are always the worst. Trying to mentally adjust to the survival attitude, searching for sustenance buried by the desert and more often than not, missing it.

Travelling during the easy hours of darkness and checking bearings in the first light of day.

Slowly, skills returned. Harry remembered that when a long journey had been required they always pushed hard at night, hardly stopping and using every minute of darkness. It had seemed unnecessary and pointless. He learned otherwise on the first day. Had he not been totally exhausted it would have been nigh on impossible to rest, let alone sleep, during the day. Fatigue, the body's need to recover, overcame the uncomfortable heat, for a while at any rate.

He remembered that every resource was vital. To control natural urges and to end each night with a full bladder. Mixing the urine with sand, he made a paste which could be spread over exposed areas of his skin. As the sunlight and heat increased so the liquid evaporated from the sand and took heat from his body.

Every morning H dug a hole in the ground, in an area he was certain would be bathed in sunlight all day. Into it he put any vegetation he could find. Living grasses and leaves were best, but if there were none then anything else would have to do. On top of the pile he placed a beaker, open end facing upwards and then put a roof on his construction, a thin plastic sheet held down at the corners with stones. This sheet should not touch the beaker.

The final step was to place a very light stone in the middle of the plastic, so that it sagged slightly. Then he would find shade and pass the day dozing.

While he slept, the vegetation would heat up and the moisture given off would collect as condensation on the underside of the plastic sheet. When sufficient had accumulated, the tiny droplets ran down to the middle and dripped into the beaker. Hardly a waterfall but every little helped.

On the third dawn, lady luck dealt a cruel blow to a five hour old springbok fawn sprawling awkwardly at the feet of its mother.

The buck sensed him approaching long before the hunter got close, indeed, he never noticed her at all.

She left her infant concealed in the long grasses where it had been led immediately it could walk, for the smell of the afterbirth would attract predators to the original site. Wildebeest young can stand when three minutes old and walk when less than ten minutes have elapsed. Those of the springbok do not lag far behind, their very survival depends on it.

Lying hidden from view is the best defence a springbok infant can have in its early days. It knows to stay perfectly still and has no scent whatsoever. It should remain undiscovered, for the parent to retrieve once the danger has passed.

H stumbled across the pitifully small creature totally by chance, and for a second looked into the innocent liquid brown eyes before blooding the knife and accepting the gift with thanks.

It was some hours before a confused and worried mother stopped nosing the slightly flattened grass in an effort to discover her infant and rejoined the herd.

The meal was cooked quickly while H performed his routines for survival during the day. He found a clump of bushes nestling beside an outcrop of rock, shadows already betraying the fact that most of it would soon be in shade. That would do as his resting place.

Despite being in shade, the brain numbing heat would descend as usual. Lack of direct sunlight merely dulled the cutting edge.

Harry had learnt from his tutors that the key to beating it was in the mind. Stay calm and rational, take fluid whenever possible, and although uncomfortable, you will survive. Panic, get flustered and confused, and you start on the slippery slope.

The Afrikaaner brushed sand over the thin blue flames and then ate the flesh while it still ran with blood and juices. The unfortunate fawn had consumed its first and only meal before death. Warm milk from its belly now filled the stomach of the hunter. Water comes in many forms and is precious in all of them.

Red droplets glistened like tiny rubies on his short stubble when he had finished. They were carefully licked away.

Then he gathered up the infant carcass, carried it some distance away and buried it deep in the warming sands. Concern for the spirit of the creature was not his motive. Bodies attract scavengers like flies round a jam pot and he had no wish to fight off a pack of hyena.

While the sun was gathering up energy to climb aloft into a pure blue sky, H was asleep in the shade, oblivious to everything.

*****

Deprived of the need to care and cope with a family and an invalid, the leopard and the young woman settled into the typical semi-nomadic existence of that feline species.

The pair roamed over the twenty square miles or so that Torn Ear had declared her home range, returning to the cave every three or four days and staying until hunger or boredom spurred them into travel again.

Whilst out collecting food for herself, Jade began to notice that certain types of stone were to be seen in certain similar places down the fossil river valley. She was always on the lookout for sling ammunition and in consequence made a point to notice all the stones and rocks along the way.

The ones she liked had the same cool sensation about them as the Lion Stone had, when she first picked it up. They were all different shapes but none were bigger than her first, and most prized, one.

As she acquired them on her travels, Jade held each one up to the sun and examined it minutely. Although roughly the same size and weight, they were all individuals.

Some were so opaque that they looked almost boring, until sunlight was applied. Then a surprising display of rotating colours would appear in the heart of the stone, as if by magic. They sparkled and shone with a beauty Jade had never seen before. And with each stone the pattern and diversity of colours and shades was different.

Others seemed simply to glow with a single yellow, blue or green flame. Hold these up and the fire roared inside, flames licking and growing as the stone was turned. The rough edges of all these stones tended to dull and cloud the inner display, as if holding in their power and beauty like a caged animal.

For some reason which Jade could not logically determine, she felt the desire to take each of these stones back to the cave and keep them there.

They were entirely the wrong shape and weight for the sling and there was no other practical use for them at all. And yet, held up to the last shaft of dying sunlight that penetrated the cave, they exuded splendour and mystique, tinging with richness an otherwise harsh and barren life.

These nodules of pure carbon, that are the birthstones for April, were lovingly stored in a roughly hewn bowl.

Above the cave, across the bare dunes interspersed with featureless scrub through which the valley cut a swathe, thermal air currents had begun to boil, whipping up dust devils which careered around like mini tornados. Snake like bodies writhed and gyrated in the air, rising up to heights and then collapsing back to earth in a little cloud.

Before their dust had settled, another rose up like a phoenix from the ashes, to take its place.

Fuelled by the hot wind of change, the dust spirals continued their rampage.

Noses held high, eyes slitted and facing into the wind, a pair of jackals sniffed the passing air, ignoring the flurries of sand that occasionally whipped round them. The ice blue sky lied to them. They knew what was coming.

Morning found Jade curled up at the foot of an ancient baobab tree. Above her, on one of the lower branches, Torn Ear yawned cavernously, stretching her open jaws towards the sky.

Straddling the branch in front of her was the carcass of an old wildebeest who just hadn't been quick enough.

Torn Ear returned her attentions to it. She drew back her lips in a distasteful grimace and, using her incisors, continued to pluck out small bunches of hair which were stuck together with saliva and blood. These she dropped carefully from the branch to form a growing accumulation on the ground. She had already fed quite well and was merely being ultra selective about the final few mouthfuls.

Oblivious to the tiny mountain that grew at her feet, Jade slept on through the dawn and early morning.

When she eventually woke, she lay with closed eyes, savouring the remnants of sleep before the inevitable sunlight pierced its way through and forced her eyelids open.

Sure enough, she could detect the light of morning but this time there was no blinding sharpness about it, merely an awareness of a dull daybreak.

Something was not as usual. Jade sat up and looked out onto a different world.

Clear blue sky and shafts of brilliance had been banished by a solid blanket of grey. No longer was the landscape divided up into areas of sharp black shadow and blazing reflected light. Everything was bathed in the same cool opaque grey. Searching the sky, Jade could find no hint at all of where the sun might be hidden. It had vanished without trace.

She stood up to get a better look at this different country. Despite the cloud, the heat was still there, building up gradually as the day progressed. However, its power was muted and its strength disguised. No longer did she continually have to screw up her eyes against the glare, always using one hand as a sunshade.

The unthinkable was going to happen. After years, it was going to rain in the desert. She didn't know exactly when but the certainty of change was there. A sense of excitement slowly began to build within her.

Relieved of the need to shelter from the sun, Torn Ear and Jade went about their business throughout the day, all the time gradually heading back towards the fossil river valley and their home. Jade was constantly aware of the low leaden sky above her now and looked up at least every ten minutes throughout the day.

Morning moved through noon and on into heavy oppressive mid-afternoon heat. Waves of sultry air swept upwards to ferment in the clouds and change their mood.

Jade watched as the formations above her changed. Beneath the grey blanket small dark shadows appeared and grew. They joined with others moving around the sky, propelled by an ever strengthening wind, blowing in anger now.

Soon the shadows matured into flocks of heavy black bottomed clouds, hanging so low that they almost seemed to touch areas of high ground and dunes. As they grew in size and numbers they formed a menacing presence over the whole desert.

Torn Ear dropped silently down the last few feet onto the floor of the river valley, followed equally silently by her companion.

To their left, perhaps a mile away, clouds joined with the ground in a continuous stream of darkness. Directly above them kites swooped and plunged, the birds harvesting swarms of termites flushed out by the turmoil.

Trotting across the darkening valley the pair passed close to a herd of springbok with a few interloping wildebeest. The animals cavorted around, bucking and snorting, anticipating the rain and playing as if they were infants again. They completely ignored the dangerous strangers.

Without warning, a fork of lightning flared against the bruised velvet sky and came to ground courtesy of a wizened old acacia tree standing alone ahead of them. Almost instantaneously thunder crashed overhead, deafening Jade and sending the kites from their hunting to seek shelter.

Two further thunderbolts followed close on the heels of the first, both striking targets so near to Jade that she could smell the ignited air before it was blown away.

Thunder rolled above them again and then the desert was quiet. Jade shivered involuntarily, noticing that the air around her was cooling quickly, aided by the stiff breeze. She opened her mouth and tasted moisture on the wind. A little distance in front of her the springbok had ceased their antics. They stood still now, all facing into the oncoming cool moist air, welcoming the inevitable.

A splash of dark appeared on the packed sand as Jade watched. It arrived with such force that the nearest ewe jumped with shock, even though it was exactly what she had been expecting.

Seconds later another struck Jade on her warm naked shoulder. The rain drop was cold beyond belief. She had forgotten that anything could be that cold, and she jumped as well.

Another landed squarely on top of her head and she could feel it dispersing amongst her thick bleached hair.

At her feet huge drops began to smack steadily onto the ground, each one sending up a spray of minute droplets as it made contact, such was the force behind it.

Before the last of these drops had made it to earth flood gates were opened and the full force of the rainstorm was unleashed.

Rain like Jade had never seen before fell around her in torrential solid sheets. Continuous beautiful cool rain. She stood with her head arched back, letting the drops sting and pound against her body, raising excited goosebumps.

Cool water flowed in abundance over her throat and she drank. This was the first time in her desert existence that her thirst could be entirely satisfied, and there was more to spare.

Still the unbelievable bounty fell around her. It quickly formed pools on the surface and ran off the newly waterlogged earth in swiftly moving streams, now carrying a cargo of churned up sand and mud.

Torn Ear didn't revel in this rarely experienced element. Already her sleek black fur was matting together and holding the water, making her look, and feel, distinctly wet and miserable.

One look at Jade told the leopard that it would be some time before this strange new game was finished. With tail swishing behind her at low level, she continued her journey at a streaking pace, reaching the den in a few tortured minutes.

In an ecstasy of pleasure Jade ripped off her only garment. Delightful rivulets of cleansing liquid ran the entire length of her body. Vigorously she scrubbed away the layers of grime and accumulated filth that coated her from tousled hair to cut and leathery feet.

Gradually the dirt fell away, lightening her mahogany tan several shades. She teased the knots and tangles from her coarse hair, almost managing to get a lather from the pulp of a fruit which was exposed by the rain and then snatched off the ground.

As clean as she had ever been before, Jade stood in the raging torrents, head turned up to the thunderously black skies with her eyes shut against the onslaught. She let the constant sound and body massage wipe the cares of life from her mind.

*****

Days stretched into weeks, and weeks lasted an eternity. Sleeping in whatever shade could be found in the flaming sands and trekking on by moonlight.

Such is the mental concentration required, that the actual goal of the hunter slipped unnoticed to the back of his mind. This element was his and he lived the existence totally, each setback hardening his resolve and sharpening his awareness. No mistake was made twice.

Some days there was no shelter from the blistering rays and solid heat which deadened the senses. Those days it was impossible to sleep or rest. They passed in a daze of fatigue, H covering his head and curling up on the desert floor, unable to make use of the daylight hours because of his tiredness and the stifling conditions.

During one of these days he used up the last of the good water that he had brought with him from the outside world. It had been eked out as long as possible, but now it was gone. He was totally dependent on the desert and his own abilities.

Although H usually found enough to eat, either fruit, or meat if he was lucky, the demands on his body caused him to shed a considerable amount of his excess weight. His frame became leaner and hair began to grow past its normal cropped length. Had it not been a light colour then his age might have been betrayed by a generous sprinkling of silver amongst the growth.

It was nearly dawn. A soft orange glow showed over the horizon and there were no stars left in the panoply above.

H decided to wait where he was now, until the light showed him a suitable place to endure the interminable hell of another day. He lay back carefully, eyes closed to the daily miracle unfolding in the sky - it held no interest for him.

He did not sleep but merely waited and rested until the shadows disappeared.

His experienced eye ran over the surroundings and selected the place to shelter. Returning to closer territory, his gaze stopped at a mound which was somehow alien to others around it. The shape was out of place, not recognisable as anything definite, just out of place.

H squinted at it in the gathering sunlight, trying to figure out why it had aroused his curiosity. He always trusted his senses and instincts. With him, first impressions counted.

He rose up effortlessly and moved to investigate. Carefully he brushed several years of accumulated sand off the mound and his heart jumped with excitement as he realised the value of his find. He pushed his calloused hand down and dug into the dry earth. He found the gap, the gap under the pommel of a buried saddle. He pulled hard and Dancer's saddle erupted from beneath Harry's feet.

He lofted it high above his head and laughed out loud as the sand and debris rained on him. He shook it and laughed more, a harsh triumphant sound. This was the starting point. If the girl was alive then he would find her now. By God he would find her. He *would* succeed.

Harry unwrapped a celebratory protein bar. This sudden windfall after all his searching had banished his fatigue entirely and the heat of the early morning went unnoticed. H knew that vital clues must be hidden here somewhere and he had to find them before knowing which way, if any, to proceed.

Methodically, the hunter began to quarter and search. Moving outwards from the spot where the saddle had been he searched like a detective at a murder scene. Eyes first and foremost, hands kept in pockets and only moving forward when certain that his feet would not be disturbing anything of importance.

Minutes progressed towards the first hour. H encountered a large flat rock and investigated it meticulously. Nothing.

Getting a sudden brainwave, he climbed ontop of the stone, raising his height almost three feet. From here he could survey the entire area from a different point of view, and was rewarded immediately.

There were signs of many animals moving together towards the saddle site, then the tracks swerved as one and headed......H turned on the stone......towards that acacia tree. The impressions in the crusted sand and dirt were vague of course, he could have come across them at ground level and completely missed them, but when viewed from above the pattern emerged.

All around the saddle there were no real prints or patterns, as if it had all been wiped or scoured. The saddle was here, but why would she have taken the saddle off ? Especially in the middle of a herd of zebra, for that was what the prints were.

If she didn't take it off.......then the horse had it on him......and if the saddle was under the sands, then so was the horse and he was dead. Scavengers at the site would have obliterated all the tracks as they fed on the body. So, he mused, the horse died or fell in the middle of a herd of zebra, but why ? Not important. It was dead, which meant that she went from here on foot, or didn't go anywhere and died here as well. Which was it to be ?

H knew what he had to do next and that he needed to wait until the relative cool of late afternoon to do it, for it involved careful examination of a large area surrounding the saddle site to see if any human had left the scene of the disaster alive. Or if they were both buried here.

The only shade in the region was provided by a solitary acacia tree about a hundred yards away. H shouldered his pack and headed for it.

*****

The desert was quiet and empty when he woke. In the middle distance a modest heat haze shimmered and shook, evaporating into nothing as the hunter gazed into it.

Lengthening rays allowed the oven to cool to a mere blistering heat. H looked forward to the chill and darkness of that night with real uninterrupted sleep. He had already promised himself at least one nights rest here, whatever clues he found.

The big figure jogged steadily back to the site, his eagerness to get started overcoming the cardinal rule of minimum exertion in the heat.

Standing on the rock for a few minutes he mapped out his strategy. Sunlight glistened on his tanned arms and their tiny globules of sweat. Somewhere in this area were clues that would tell him if she survived or not. He was already certain that Dancer had perished.

While his mind was in efficiency mode Harry realised that he hadn't marked this discovery on the map. He jumped down, took several compass bearings and remedied the fault. Service in the South African Defence Force had given him some skills after all. He had been taught how to search for clues after terrorist bomb blasts. At least here there shouldn't be secondaries for a second bite at the cherry.

Then he started. Marking out a part of the ground with sticks, H examined the surface, quartering it with wide awake eyes. When that was done, with no success, the hunter delved below the surface. Gently at first, blowing and teasing away layers of desert. Then he dug down with hands as big as trowels.

The next section was marked out and treated in the same way, and the next, and the next.

By the time night fell he had recovered the bit which had once been attached to a set of well worn reins. H fingered the cylindrical piece of metal, feeling slight grooves where the horse's teeth had gripped, time after time.

The searcher curled up and slept by the large flat rock. It was a deep dreamless sleep, untroubled by nagging doubts, although once in a while a foot might twitch in spasm, sending a mini shower of sand a few inches into the night air.

Waking well before dawn, H felt more refreshed than he had done in a long while. Breakfast was dug up and eaten while squatting on the rock.

Early morning rolled past and the backbreaking search yielded nothing but a crop of frustration. H stood up from his labours for the last time. The marked out area was well and truly demolished, looking like a freshly ploughed field. He had found only the saddle, bit and part of a long bone which was obviously horse sized. All of which told him that they had been here. He already knew that.

The hunter arched his upper body backwards, both hands supporting the lower reaches of his spine, like a pregnant woman easing the weight of an unborn child. Taut muscles creaked and complained.

For the first time in this trek he was almost at a loss for what to do. Sure, he could take the name plate off the saddle and the bit to van Niekerk, claim the meagre reward and go back to a life of mending fences. Like hell he would. He could almost feel her presence here and to go back now would mean the end of his freedom, crawling to the boss man again, admitting to all intents and purposes that he had failed.

A careful decision was called for here and that was the hardest thing for the Boer to make. H walked over to the acacia tree to catch some shade and sort things out.

For some reason he circled the tree from the opposite direction and as good as tripped over a single human footprint encrusted in the floor of the Kalahari. It was the right size for a fourteen year old girl and led away from the tree. It was the first step Jade had taken when she left the friendly tree, and it had betrayed her. Near to shelter, it had survived intact somehow and might as well have been a flashing neon arrow with attached foghorn.

H dropped to his knees in unbelieving adulation. He examined it carefully, quickly discounting the possibility that it belonged to a Bushman.

There was no doubt in his mind. It was exactly what he was looking for. It charged his evil veins with electricity.

" You beautiful bitch " he breathed slowly, still gazing into the indentation left by the bare heel. " The horse is jackal meat so you've gone to be Tarzan. Great. Find what's left of you in a day or so - if there's anything."

He would dearly have loved to follow the spoor now, but a cruel and unyielding sun was already high above him. He would have to begin in the late afternoon, utilising the few hours of daylight left to him then. He could only watch the single print and wait.

In the course of her travels in the desert Jade had in fact ended up relatively close to the area where she originally started. The fossil river valley was only a few days journey from that first acacia tree, but her initial wanderings had taken her off at an angle and so the first weeks and months had been spent almost parallel to the valley, but some considerable distance from it.

Eventually, circumstances had conspired to bring her nearly a full circle, to the valley she called home, with a leopard she called friend.

So as the hunter set out to follow the spoor in the comfortable lengthening rays, he was closer to his goal than he could ever have imagined.

To an experienced tracker, the trail was as easy to follow as any this old is. H was now forced to travel in daylight in order to follow the tell tail signs. His day altered. From being a totally nocturnal creature, he changed to a lover of the twilight hours. He tracked the spoor in the cool of morning and evening.

Progress was quite naturally slower than before. He had a definite trail to follow and had to be sure that he stuck to it. He also had less time in which to be active.

The fact that there was a spoor to be followed at all gave him cause for some thought. He fully expected to find evidence of a quick demise. Instead, the spoor progressed and he soon found himself several days into the journey.

Every so often there was a little shred of evidence along the way, often a small triumph. A pair of boots, just recognisable as worn by Jade, now weatherbeaten and full of sand. Then he found a burrowed hole in hard sand at the edge of a long abandoned water hole. Although occupied by a number of creatures during its existence, it was moulded to the size of a teenage girl.

Next to an old termite hill, which had probably been used by a colony of bees, he found a strange construction. The swarm had moved on, leaving a derelict tenement block behind. For all the world it looked as if an attempt had been made to hide something of importance in this little dug out pit, piled high with stones. It was of human construction, but no Bushman ever built anything such as this.

As the trail progressed Harry grudgingly acknowledged that a modicom of respect was due to his quarry. She was surviving. She was surviving on her own. It crossed his mind that if he ever found her she might be more trouble than he had imagined. Many was the time that he had enacted the sequence of events in his mind's eye, should he be lucky enough to find her alive.

Over the next few days H found himself preoccupied with the weather. Heat and drought possessed only one advantage - they preserved the spoor. Now for the first time in at least two or three years, he couldn't remember exactly, rain was on the cards and rain would completely obliterate any chance he had of finding her.

Desperate to try and beat the elements, the hunter increased his pace, forcing himself through midday heat in an effort to increase the distance covered. Shady rest was suddenly a thing of the past.

When leaden clouds appeared in the sky it was a blessing and a terror. They meant cooler days and the chance to follow the trail all day. They also meant eventual rain and the dashing of his wafer thin chances. They spurred on his frenzied activity.

Two days later and not a single encouraging sign. Since entering the old river valley there had not been one single indication that he was still on the right line. H knew the matter was due to be decided one way or another very soon. He had no option but to keep going the way he thought she might have gone. To scour around in a circle to see if she had changed direction would waste time, and time was one thing not on his side.

It had now become appreciably cooler. H heaved the pack off and let the soiled and weary canvas bag slide to the ground. H sighed heavily, blowing the breath out like a snorting stallion.

A fat drop of cold rain hit the back of his hand and made his spirits drop like a runaway elevator. Time was gone. The sands had run out on his expedition.

Seized by desperation and a madness born of frustration, H grabbed a strap of the pack and started to jog, and then to run. Almost laughing in the steadily falling moisture he tried to outpace the storm. Tried to beat it to the dry ground ahead where he might still find a track.

The last of his strength was gone. He tripped and fell into a sodden dune. Crawling to the top of it, he realised soberly that he was beaten and that the storm was raging over his head. Solid walls of water crashed down about him. He lay face down on top of the small ridge.

Lashing torrents served to revive the exhausted man. He cupped both hands together and drank several long draughts. It was cold and sweet. Swiftly flowing rivulets ran a multitude of paths down his face, some being channelled by the scar and raced straight into the corner of his open mouth. Others headed into the excesses of a newly grown and untrimmed beard.

H sat and stared disconsolately into the middle distance. As he looked, a sight materialised that brought his vision sharply back into focus and made his jaw drop open in disbelief.

He could see a human figure standing in the fierce rain. Without doubt it was a girl. Cascades of long bleached hair fell down her back as she arched her head skywards.

She pulled an odd shaped cloth from around her waist, throwing it to one side. H caught his breath and his pulse quickened. The pressure of adrenalin on his heart was matched only by that in the loins. She had to be the end of his road.

Feasting his eyes, H unhooked the backpack and scrambled higher on his ridge.

It was Jade. She might have left a girl, but she was a young woman now. The breasts were small and firm, stimulated to points by the stinging drops. The voyeur watched with mounting excitement as an unashamed Jade cleansed herself under the torrential shower, her femininity kept tantalisingly out of sight as muscular long brown legs swayed from side to side.

H slithered down the other side of the small ridge. Now standing thirty yards or so from Jade he could observe her movements clearly through a hazy curtain of falling rain. Had Jade opened her eyes she would no doubt have seen him too. She did not and the drumming of the landing drops completely drowned out any sounds of approach.

Nearer still he moved. Slowly, step by step, savouring every moment and at the same time half expecting the mirage to vanish before his eyes.

Now he was near enough to touch the brown skin on a bare back, muscles moving beneath the surface as she still caressed and cleaned. He saw that the cold water had raised tiny white goosebumps on her buttocks. A dribble of saliva escaped unchecked from the side of his gaping mouth.

Prepared for the unexpected, H called out softly. Too softly. There was no response. He spoke out again.

" Jade "

The word was a thunderbolt from the storm above. Jade froze and an instant later spun round on her heel to confront a voice from the past.

Looking at H, remembering him and everything else from before, the safe walls of her world began to crumble. He spoke the single word for a third time and demolition was ensured.

Shock hit her like a sledgehammer. Nothing was real any more. She was totally numbed, unable to move. Unable to resist calloused fingers stroking a line down her chest.

H reached round the back of her neck, taking firm hold of the strong hair, wrapping it round his hand. She was going nowhere. The free hand fumbled with the wet leather of a belt that held filthy stained denims.

He forced the unresisting and dazed young woman down on her back. He was the master now.

No sooner had incredulity and terror been struck into Jade's mind, than the same emotions hit a powerfully built young leopardess, drying herself in the mouth of a cave which was home to them both.

Torn Ear could see nothing of the drama below. The curtain of rain prevented that, but it could do nothing about the special bond of communication which had been forged between the two companions. The picture of desperation painted by the message which forced itself into the leopard's mind was so real and vital that the big cat was moving before she realised it.

Instinct told her that seconds were precious. To take the winding path down to the valley might lose her the battle before she had started. Without conscious thought, Torn Ear launched herself over the edge and down the steep rocky scree for the first time in her life.

Padded feet touched the side of the slope only two or three times during the descent, then the impact of landing was borne by her muscular shoulders, stretching their powers of elasticity to the limit.

Not pausing to regain the wind knocked out of her, Torn Ear set off at the fastest speed she could muster. Her body was slung close to the wet ground, limbs pumping in unison and muscles working flat out under shiny black velvet. It was the speed she normally reserved for an attacking charge whilst hunting.

She could see virtually nothing through the rain, and the drops were now hitting her face and eyes with such force that she closed the lids to narrow slits to protect her vision for what was sure to come. Memory reminded her of where the obstacles were in this, her most familiar territory, and confident feet overcame minor variations in the terrain caused by the storm.

The leopard struck like an express train hitting a vehicle in its path. Forward motion pushed the monstrous figure from on top of Jade. Two sets of claws embedded themselves in his rib cage, acting like hooks for the momentum of the charging attacker to pull him off completely.

As both man and beast rolled over, the razor like talons released their grip and raked lines across the darkened flesh. The incisions stood out as if made with a scalpel, the falling rain washing out slowly welling blood.

H screamed once, the sound a man makes when he knows he is about to die.

The anguish was well founded for Torn Ear had turned swiftly and in one leap was astride her victim, searching for the throat and the rush of hot blood into her mouth.

Jade moved her head, and saved the life of the farm worker who had violated her. Not intentionally it must be added, but her small movement caught Torn Ear's eye and suddenly priorities changed. Her concern was for Jade, her friend who long ago had saved her life. The thought of killing vanished from her mind. The leopard had removed the source of danger and now she left it, to pay attention instead to Jade.

Staring blankly into space, Jade was vaguely aware of the leopard nuzzling up to her. She draped an arm around the neck of her friend and leaned her weight on the shoulder.

At last the rain eased from its torrential flow. As it did, mists seemed to lift from her mind and reality took over. Anger surfaced as it dawned on her what had happened here in this storm. Confirmation came by way of self examination. There was nothing she could do about it. Nothing could change what had been done to her.

Unbelieving, in the midst of her emotions, Jade watched the man in front of her reach down to a belt that was around his knees. Almost in slow motion, a gun came into view, the dazed man fumbling with the mechanism. He intended to kill her.

Instinct sent her right hand for the sling, which of course was not there. By way of a substitute, her groping hand found a fist sized rock. Freeing it from the sucking surrounds of mud, she drew her arm back and threw it.

At a range of about three yards the stone was never destined to miss. It cracked sharply on his temple and H fell back with a grunt. Small splashes of watery mud jumped up as the body hit the earth.

Jade stood up and looked down at him, as he moaned softly. Now she remembered him fully. Those funny long looks years ago and the shivers down her spine. In the space of minutes he had turned her settled life on its head again. She felt utterly violated, in body and in spirit. Injustice and bitter anger welled up.

*How did they fight......I remember now......sort of ....like this.......*the young woman balled her right fist and swept a haymaker down that landed squarely on the side of his stubbled jaw. The moaning stopped.

" Bastard, bastard, bastard. Die here and now ! " she screamed. She hoped with all her heart that he would obey. Then she turned to walk to walk for the cave, and home.

Before leaving she retrieved the gun from where it had fallen and threw it away with all the strength she could muster. It landed just the other side of a permanent ridge in the valley floor.

By the time they reached the den it had stopped raining entirely. A slight glimmer of evening sunlight could be seen through a chink in the armour of the heavy cloud.

Jade collapsed into her sleeping pit inside the cave, pulling a fur over herself up to the neck. Never had any other bed felt so comfortable and secure. She fell at once into a deep, and thankfully dreamless, sleep.

Torn Ear slipped noiselessly into the cave a few minutes later and regarded the comatose form with a glittering gaze. Then she lay down, facing the entrance, with her head just inside the lip of rock. The chunky, powerfully set head rested on a massive paw stretched out in front of her.

Torn Ear remained on station all night while Jade slept. Though hungry, the thought of going hunting and leaving her charge alone was repugnant to her. The instincts were those of a mother with cubs.

Jade woke to the usual bright sunlight. She felt raw and tender in the body, abused and defiled in the mind. A concoction of fat, applied gently, served to soothe the former. Only time would heal the rest.

Clothing herself with a hastily prepared skirt, she wandered to the entrance and clambered out, joining Torn Ear who was cleaning herself on the balcony.

Having spent all her life in the climes of Southern Africa, Jade had never experienced the thrill of pulling back bedroom curtains to see the whole landscape covered in a thick layer of freshly fallen snow.

This was the best the Kalahari could do, but the impact was a thousand fold better.

Everywhere she looked, green life was sprouting from the barren desert. Tiny infant shoots poked up through the earth, forming a carpet on the valley floor. Desperate to flower and complete their life cycles before the precious moisture was lost, the dormant vegetation was working overtime and giving one of the best shows on earth in the process. The spark of rain had lit their fuses and each one was now determined to outdo the other in the race for maturity.

Jade sat on the balcony for nearly half an hour, drinking in the beauty and freshness which was her desert now. Warm sunshine glowed pleasantly on her naked back.

Feeling mentally able to cope with the nightmare of reality that she knew lay down in the valley, Jade got up and stretched long and hard.

" Come on " she said softly to her alert companion, " let's go and see if there's anything to see."

Properly equipped with sling, digging stick and knife this time, she set off down the familiar track with the leopard at her heels. The ground felt strangely damp and almost cold. For the first time, Jade had an urge for a pair of shoes.

It was only a few minutes before she could see the hunched up shape in the distance, exactly where she had left it. A knot of cold anxiety grew in the pit of her stomach, for she had no idea how to deal with the man, alive or dead. Silent steps faltered and shortened in their approach.

A little way off, Torn Ear pulled sharply in front of Jade making the latter stop in her tracks.

Yes.......you're right.......it's a dangerous creature.......watch and listen first ....as we always do......what would life be without you now.......

So they stopped and waited and watched.

The man was alive. Lying face down, sprawled at an awkward angle, but still breathing regularly and obviously alive. *Skull as thick as an elephant........pity....* The shirt on his back was ripped open, as if with a knife, long shallow wounds visible on the flesh. Consciousness had yet to be regained however, judging from the state of undress. The first act of a male in such a predicament would undoubtedly be to cover his dignity.

It was all she could do to stop herself being physically sick at the sight of him. What was she supposed to do with him now ? Much though she hated the big Afrikaaner, and she had always disliked him anyway, she couldn't bring herself to abandon the ingrained habits of civilisation and kill him here in cold blood. She could have done it yesterday and was honest enough to admit that thought to herself. A life of kill or be killed had moulded certain aspects of her. They were there for good now. *Pandora's box, but I'll open it if I have to......I know that now.....*

Abandoning him here was the alternative, but that was tantamount to murder in any event. Indeed she supposed that it was only the aftermath of the rain that had kept predators elsewhere last night. However, if he survived being left where he was, he would get off scot free, and that was unthinkable.

Gradually, she was coming round to the only acceptable alternative. She turned to look down the valley and think.

A hand reaching for an ankle was unseen. It gripped the polished wooden handle of the flick knife strapped there. A thumb pushed the serrated metal switch forward and the blade revealed itself with a sound like a gunshot.

Jade and Torn Ear turned as one to respond to the sound and it was already almost too late.

Silver flashed through the air in terrible slow motion. Jade drew herself backwards from the source of evil, but at full arm stretch the knife was able to score a faint line across her deeply tanned belly. A line of ice along her stomach.

Even in retreat Jade was arming the sling with one hand. The shot was enough to stun, through the thick skull of the Boer, and struck at the same time as the leopard.

Torn Ear landed at the limit of her jumping ability, actually astride H's left leg. Without thought for further upward progress, she sank her teeth into the naked thigh, tearing muscle and grating on bone. Dark venous blood crept out from the side of a velvet black jawline.

Incredulous at her own injury, and her own escape, Jade saw that the man who had tried to kill her twice had only seconds left if she did nothing.

In a slowly passing second she decided the fate of the semi-conscious man and in doing so set the course of her life for years ahead.

" Torn Ear, no ".

The command was out before she realised it, surprising herself with the gentleness of her own voice.

The leopard looked up from her nightmare task. A globule of foul blood dropped from a glistening white tooth.

Jade had never before interrupted the predator when she had a kill, let alone try to dissuade her from continuing.

Trust between them was complete, for Torn Ear left the man without a murmur and padded over to sit with her companion.

Jade glanced at her own wound, shivering a little. It was seeping a little blood, but was quite miniscule by comparison to H's.

The young woman pulled herself together. She had stopped the attack, however unless there was some action on her part he would undoubtedly die anyway. She jumped up and started to gather suitable leaves and vegetation to stem the bleeding. Luckily Torn Ear hadn't found an artery, so she stood some chance of stopping it.

A couple of minutes searching gave her the rudiments of a field dressing.

Approaching H again, she had Torn Ear by her side. Third time lucky it certainly would not be for her assailant. Another attack and the leopard could have him, principles or not.

Jade looked down at the man. H was only partly conscious and moaning softly from time to time. In the melee with the leopard he had been turned onto his back, exposing his genitalia. Jade avoided looking directly at it, grimacing as she covered it with a large leaf. Then she concentrated on the leg while Torn Ear stood guard at the other end. The leopard was, quite literally, breathing down his neck.

Eventually she managed to stop the flow, binding the dressing into place using two lengths of animal sinew, laboriously prepared some weeks ago for any such eventuality. It was her most precious commodity and only after a great deal of soul searching was it wasted on him.

Jade sat back when she had finished, wiping the sweat from her brow. The bleeding had almost stopped, but there was no more she could do anyway. As for infection, well he would just have to take his chances. It was probably about fifty fifty, she reckoned.

Leaning over her handiwork to check it for the last time, the usual mass of long bleached hair fell forward like a stage curtain, cutting out most of the direct light. She took the remaining piece of sinew and tied her hair back in a crude ponytail. The bit at the front, ...*fringe......ha ha........more like a wildlife preserve.....,* she would have to hack at again soon with the knife. She pulled her fingers harshly through it and quickly squashed an indeterminate bug which dropped out. If you didn't catch them first time they bounced off and were lost.

The immediate problem was now dealt with as best she could. Those that remained to keep her company were thorny and difficult.

She moved into the shade of a camelthorn acacia tree to plan her next move. The round bright yellow flowers on its branches bobbed about gently in the godsend of a breeze that still wafted up the valley. As she settled against the trunk there was a rustle of sound and the leopard jumped effortlessly onto the lowest of branches, and then on up to one which apparently suited her better. Torn Ear adopted the classic position, all four limbs hanging over the side of the branch and chin on the scaly bark as well.

Jade knew already that by saving the life of her aggressor she had burnt her bridges. Somehow she was going to have to find her way out of the desert, and eventually into a courtroom. He was her ticket out of the Kalahari and now she wasn't really sure she wanted to go.

Still, there was time enough yet, she kidded herself. She looked across at H. Remembering him well now, her thoughts drifted back to life before the desert. She guessed that Oupa had sent him out here in desperation. The last straw to clutch at while really believing in his heart of hearts that she had perished in the first few days. She had no real concept of how long ago it was, but guessed it was years and not months. In fact, the zebra had kicked her on the head exactly two years seven months and four days ago.

Surely he couldn't have come this far without provisions she mused. He had a gun of course, where was it now ? She searched her memory to try and recall where she had last seen it.

Jade moved her head a little as concentration furrowed her deeply tanned brow. Rays of sunlight caught her blue green eyes, bringing out their sparkling life which had inspired her grandfather to name her after the translucent gemstone, the colour of which her eyes so accurately reflected.

She had thrown the gun away. *Over that ridge there.* Jade scrambled to her feet.

A soft thump by her side brought the leopard to her heels. The young woman motioned for her companion to stay and guard the semi-conscious form on the sand.

Mounting the ridge, Jade found the gun immediately, although it had skidded along for a while and in the process had covered itself with a heavy sprinkling of sand. She picked it up and blew the coating off it. She knew little about guns in general, so she held it by the butt, pointed the barrel sandwards, turned to retrace her steps and walked into the rucksack. It was so out of place here in her desert that a couple of seconds passed before she knelt to examine it.

Getting close to the tired canvas material she knew how it had got where it was. The stink was unmistakable, pungent and rancid. Scent brings back memories more powerfully than any other sense and as she pulled at the straps of H's backpack she shuddered.

Inside was a treasure trove to the girl who had lived off the desert for longer than she could remember.

Despite the impression given by the outer cover, inside the pack was surprisingly ordered and clean, especially considering the arduous nature of the journey it had been required to provide support for. Jade delved into it.

First to come out was a long curved hunting knife, polished and gleaming. It was slightly oiled and slippery to touch. Jade treated this with even more respect than she had accorded the pistol, laying it down slowly on the sand. Now she had three knives, instead of the faithful old one which was a sight less sharp than it had been at the beginning. She made a mental note to retrieve the other one from where it had fallen.

That thought made her look up to check that everything was in order elsewhere.

The sleek black leopard was sitting upright, quite close to H, gaze never straying from her charge. The long tail stretched out at right angles from her haunched quarters, the end twitching and turning as if it were a separate entity. H lay quite still, chest rising almost imperceptibly in a steady rhythm.

Next out was a first aid kit in a soft plastic container, with a strange airtight zip, again made of plastic. Inside was the usual variety of tubes and pills, and also some phials of a clear liquid and a syringe equipped with needle and cover.

The only one who, she imagined, could need these, was lying under guard and threat of death. She had managed to exist without them. It would give her great satisfaction to launch the pack into orbit and never see it again.

However, common sense prevailed. Nothing should be wasted and certainly nothing discarded. The pack was placed to one side.

Rooting about further yielded a small powerful torch, which still worked, maps which she would study in detail later, a compass and what looked like a miniature sun dial. There was also food, in the form of wrapped bars of a rather indeterminate chewy looking substance. The coverings had become torn and filthy, and the bars smelt like the canvas material of the pack. The rule of the first aid kit didn't apply here - she removed the wax paper and threw the bars away.

A side pocket revealed a set of shiny metal handcuffs, complete with keys, neatly preserved in a leather pouch. Jade knew exactly what these were intended for. They were to ensure cooperation. She grinned. They would ensure cooperation all right.

There was very little left inside now. Jade up ended the pack and shook it gently.

Out rolled a chunky piece of smooth metal and a worn metal name tag from a horse's saddle.

She knew one instantly and the identity of the other sprang to her mind a heartbeat later.

These simple inanimate objects with their store of nightmares were too much to bear. Dancer was dead. He had been dead from the very first day and she had walked away from him. Left him alone.

Jade toppled from the knife edge of calm which she had struggled to maintain and fell gratefully into the release of grief.

Huge sobs racked their way through her body, salty tears mingling freely with the desert sands. The child who had carved her way into premature adulthood under the unforgiving sun of one of the harshest environments in Africa, cried herself into a sleep of mental exhaustion.

CHAPTER

SEVEN

From the bottom of the hidden path that leads to the home of the leopard and the young woman, it is possible to see a Shepherds tree that usually provides a nesting site for a pair of Namaqua doves.

The tree has flowers rich in honey, and summer berries, at this all too brief time of year. It is also seven minutes flying time from the nearest reliable water hole, a fact of paramount importance for the doves as they are seed eaters and must drink regularly.

If the tree is still there in thirty or forty years, future generations of doves may have a shorter journey for the wizened trunks of older specimens collect and store precious rainwater.

Viewed from the path, the tree is also an accurate indicator of the whereabouts of a small cave, as it stands some ten yards from the entrance.

This cave was at the base of the same steep rocky sides of the valley wall, but apart from that, was very different from the den up the hidden path.

The entrance was as big and wide as the inside itself and as there was no other opening to admit light, it tended to be dank and dismal. The floor sloped upwards slightly, towards the back wall and consisted of layers of compacted sand which had been laid down by storms over the years, there being nothing to bar the sand from entering.

At one side of the cave the sand layer was much thinner and in some places rock hard earth showed through. It was in this part of the floor that Jade found what she had been looking for. It was why she had had to reject two others closer to home.

Growing up through the floor of the cave was a tree root. Initially it had only shown itself as a bump, so Jade had dug around it with a flint tool until a semi circle of root appeared. The ground was so hard that without the tool the task would have been virtually impossible.

The root itself was obviously dead but had the strength and consistency of ivory. At the height of its arc it was about two inches clear of the ground.

Hammering on it with the flint made little impression. That was exactly what she wanted. Not for herself though. The small cave possessed qualities that wouldn't have been out of place in a prison. Still, as the occupant was a prisoner anyway, it seemed quite fitting.

Above tousled blond hair, tied back in a ponytail still, a soft orange sun diffused its first rays onto the desert. There would be no clouds today, no short heavy showers of warm rain to darken the sand and make it stick between your toes as you walked. No cool ground at all, by mid-morning the Kalahari would again be painfully hot to linger on in bare feet. The desert had been given her meagre supplies and there was no more on the way.

Jade stood at the mouth of the prison, watching her charge.

H lay on his back, in an exhausted sleep brought on by blood loss. Around his right wrist was a stainless steel cuff, the other in the pair was closed to its maximum extent around the tree root. He probably didn't know how much a captive he was now. Last night he had been barely conscious when the pair of them had pulled, pushed, cajoled and threatened him into hobbling the hundred yards or so to the new cave with the aid of a makeshift crutch.

As he moved in sleep, the manacles chinked from time to time.

There was freshly dried blood around the dressing. The wound had obviously opened up during the brief walk, but that was only to be expected. Jade thought that she might change the collection of vegetation for a proper field dressing out of the back pack later that day.

She walked on past the cave, further up the valley. The misty grey dawn was tinged with a delightful fuzzy shade of tangerine. The sky too had a reddish glow to it, as if a coloured mist was diffusing through it.

She watched a couple of young springbok bouncing on stiff little legs, happy at the prospect of fresh succulent grass, and water to drink. The sand they kicked up was held in suspension by that first light and the whole atmosphere turned into a gorgeous sleepy red haze as the grains drifted slowly to the ground.

Jade filled her lungs several times with the crisp air. Everything seemed quiet and at peace. The day always started with a clean slate. She looked, really seeing for the first time the multitude and colour of flora which moisture brought about.

At this point in the expansive valley, which Jade had not actually visited before, water was collecting in natural drainage lines, creating sweet water pools out of dry pans. Hordes of wild fowl now came into the area to take advantage of this new habitat, no matter how short lived it may prove to be.

In her travels Jade found that red billed teal proved to be the most numerous but there appeared to be endless varieties searching for food, dipping and upending in the modest lakes.

Her sense of survival was not outweighed by the occasion, and she soon had two of the birds at her feet, courtesy of the ever present sling.

The child of the desert sat for a long hour and watched the habits of the new, unfamiliar creatures as they dived and splashed in the water. She knew the liquid would not last. Already there was a faint tide mark where the level had been yesterday. As soon as it dwindled into nothingness the birds would leave. It would be a very short time of plenty.

Jade got up. Brilliant warmth burst on her back in a solid blow and she knew the sun had risen into another cloudless sky. It was time to return. She needed to prepare a meal and if there was an audience, there was a speech that had to be made.

The big Afrikaaner was awake when she got to the cave entrance. He was propped up on both elbows and watched her in silence. She could see that his right wrist was raw and a little bloody, but the handcuffs were still intact.

Torn Ear lay in the crook of a tree branch. Even in the bright sunshine the branch was in near perfect shade. One powerful leap would land her at the mouth of the cave.

" There are certain things you have to know. When that's done I don't want to talk to you again." Jade's voice cracked and wavered in spite of herself. Even lying down and cuffed, H maintained a frightening presence. He had violated her and she couldn't get that out of her mind. He scared her - more than she was prepared to admit.

" You will stay here until your leg has healed and you can walk. Then we will go back to the farm and I will give you to the police. While you are here you will be handcuffed - like I was supposed to be. I will unlock them to let you......." she gestured to a hole she had carved with the hunting knife, which had a pile of earth next to it in lieu of a flush.

" I will give you food and water, but " she threw the canvas bag down beside him, " you will clean the wound yourself."

Jade had removed all the items of value from the backpack. It only contained first aid dressings now.

" The last thing." She was almost enjoying herself now. Speaking so many words all at once, out loud, was quite a novelty.

" Outside, on the branch of that tree, you can see a leopard. The leopard is with me. And I think you've already met. She will kill you if you so much as bring one finger too close to me. She will always be here when I am, and quite often when I am not. You only get this warning. Make my year and ignore it."

Outside, Torn Ear looked impassively on with eyes of glittering ice. Her jaw was slightly open as she panted slowly to dissipate some body heat, clearly showing the points of two long canines. The end of her long black tail hung down from the branch, twitching from side to side, and every once in a while she gently raked a set of foreclaws along the underside of the branch.

H looked at the leopard and then at Jade.

" Be sure and keep your pussy with you then girl, " hissed the voice, " coz the first hope I get, you'll be fucked, sliced and fed."

Jade left without another glance in his direction. She heard the sound of material ripping, interspersed with stifled moans of pain. Must be changing the dressing, she thought.

In her mind she had the clearest of premonitions that the man needed to be out of her life now. She should bury him here.

But it was too late for that. The heat of the moment was gone and she would have to live with the decision. Killing a fellow human, no matter how repulsive or dangerous he may be, in cold blood, was beyond her.

She wandered back up the path to her home. Torn Ear remained in the tree, the shade there was quite adequate for her.

Once again, the girl and the leopard had an injured party to take care of. Only this time it wasn't a labour of love but of necessity.

Jade left food twice a day. Melon, or some other fruit if she could find it for herself, in the morning, and meat of some description in the relative cool of evening. Water she collected in the canteen, but left for him in one of her roughly hewn wooden bowls.

As luck would have it, there was an adequate supply from small surface lakes which had been filled to overflowing by the torrential rains. However, she knew what a short life they would have in the blistering heat. Even now, animals were stumbling and fighting over muddy pools, churning up what remained of the sweet liquid into an undrinkable sludge. When the mud dried out again, and cracks like earthquake faults appeared in it, they would reluctantly leave, or die.

Whenever Jade went into the dark cave Torn Ear would be there. Padding around H, sometimes so close that long whiskers brushed his skin, making him recoil. He never spoke to his jailer, let alone risked any movement. He could see desire in the eyes of the leopard.

Nevertheless, Jade disliked unlocking the handcuffs. It meant she had to get close to the loathsome rubbery hide and taste the foul body odour in her mouth. Sometimes skin touched skin, causing a shudder to run down her spine.

For the first few days she simply opened the cuff which was fastened to the tree root, examining the tough wood for any sign of damage which might weaken it, and let him go. Then she realised that with half a set of steel handcuffs dangling from his wrist, she had unwittingly provided him with a weapon. Should he decide to attack her, or the leopard, a blow swung with those on the end of his arm could spell disaster.

From then on she removed the cuff from his wrist and left the other one round the root.

As days passed she let him have half an hour or so of relative freedom to exercise and perform bodily functions, as opposed to continually using the hole in the cave. Thunder box Oupa used to call it......well, I got the thunder but without the box.....

Jade allowed him to hobble off to a discreet distance for this, under Torn Ear's close supervision. Even from day one he had used the improvised crutch to walk with and help maintain some degree of privacy.

The fact that his most private of affairs was now timed and regulated, and even watched, frustrated and annoyed him out of all proportion. He thrust a solid barrier of hatred in front of himself to try and create some distance.

Every day the humiliation mounted in his mind. Every day the hate grew larger like a cancer in his belly.

The wound which Torn Ear had inflicted seemed to be getting better faster than Jade had planned for. She left the dressing and care of it entirely to H, but could see from his movements and lack of blood seeping through the material that things were mending. The weeks of desert life on his own had toughened the flabby, beer drinking physique. The pounds of spare flesh had deserted him. As a consequence, the body was recovering well.

As for the state of mind it was hard to tell, for no words had been exchanged since Jade had spoken, several weeks ago.

Each passing day saw him obviously getting fitter and he could manage his exercise without the aid of the crutch now. She watched him stretch and manipulate the new, relatively pale flesh, and saw the rents left by teeth and claws. There was still a pronounced limp, and the trouser legs of vastly different lengths made it almost a humerous sight.

Jade felt now that events were overtaking her. Each day gone was one closer to her departure from the place which she had grown to love as home.

During this time she appreciated her life here more. She drank in and stored every aspect of beauty that was provided, to tide her through the inevitable change that could be seen looming in the distance like a bank of thunderheads.

Everything seemed to have a special quality about it, from the crisp light of early dawn, through the timeless burning heat of day which cleansed to a harsh purity, to the soft easy hours of multi-coloured sunsets.

So engrossed was she in her own thoughts and problems, that she was unaware of the leopard's presence until a nose and set of whiskers pushed their way under her arm in an uncharacteristic gesture of affection. Jade was sitting right on the edge of the balcony and the sudden shock nearly sent her over the top of it. She scrabbled about for a few seconds, her feet despatching several loose stones to the depths below, until she regained the safety of the ledge.

When challenged, the big cat's head tilted slightly to one side, the classic mischievous stance.

Jade gave the leopard one of her stares, which had about as much effect as a good sneeze. She had to remind herself that despite Torn Ear's adult status, she was still prone to the odd prank or two. Jade looked critically at her companion.

The sleek jet black coat covered layers of hard bunched muscle which rippled like an ocean when the cat moved. Huge paws held the killing machine to the ground at each corner, claws sheathed in the velvet glove. The chunky head, set on a thick muscular neck, followed Jade's gaze with clear but curious eyes.

" Time to take you for a bit of exercise I think, " murmured Jade. " You've obviously got too much energy to spare, lying around all day. Let's go check on the man and then we'll disappear."

Torn Ear was already half way down the path. Her antics had had the desired result.

H was lying on his back, staring blankly at the roof of the prison.

Jade placed half a melon within reach and refilled the bowl with precious water. Then she threw in a sharpened stick, hardened to a black point with the aid of fire. It was her only concession to his safety while both of them were gone, for their presence served to protect as well as imprison him.

She always retrieved the stick on return and it was always in exactly the same spot where she had thrown it.

He didn't acknowledge her at all and continued to gaze upwards with clouded sleepy eyes, but Jade knew that he was well aware of every little movement around him. She shivered suddenly in the solid heat of the afternoon. Quickly she checked that the tree root and handcuffs were intact and then hurried out into safe bright sunshine.

As soon as the pair set off across the valley floor Jade was aware how much she valued the sense of dependence and companionship she felt with Torn Ear when they went to hunt together. It was just the two of them against the world and they usually won.

Winning didn't necessarily mean making a kill, but rather being able to make the most of the opportunities that came their way and staying out of danger themselves.

A sinking feeling in her stomach told Jade that this could easily be the last time they hunted together.

Within half an hour they were out of sight of the den and about to make the ascent up the other side of the valley. Once on the ridge, hunting country was upon them.

Torn Ear cantered slowly to an acacia and bounded onto the lowest branch. Jade moved off in the other direction twenty yards or so and climbed onto a boulder. There she sat for a good ten minutes, legs crossed underneath her, simply drinking in the atmosphere. She listened to the sounds of the desert, sucked the air and its scents through her nostrils and watched the stage for any clues as to how the performance was due to run.

Torn Ear stiffened suddenly and then moved cautiously down from the branch. Then she dropped into a crouch so that her distinctive colour was more hidden against the background of tussocky dry grass and dark crumbling soil. Trusting implicitly in the keen senses of the born hunter, Jade followed suit by rolling off the boulder and walking carefully and slowly to a skeleton of cover given by a long dead bush.

There they waited with infinite patience for events to unfold. Jade had no idea what the leopard had sensed, but had it been danger she would undoubtedly have been made aware of it. She settled down to watch and wait.

Long minutes passed. With limited vision forward, Jade found that hearing and smell became more acute and she could gauge what was going on in front of her without needing to see it.

Above her head a crowned plover swooped and dived with effortless grace. Only the sound of warm air rushing over feathers gave its presence away. The bird was gone and Jade hadn't turned a hair to look at it. She didn't have to. The sound told her what it was and an unnecessary move could easily betray her cover and waste an advantage. Out of the corner of her eye Jade watched Torn Ear. Watched where the leopard concentrated her vision.

The jet black shape in the long grass bunched up, drawing her limbs closer. Jade recognised the signs and listened intently.

For an age, nothing. Then a rustling and cracking of dry stalks, and then silence again. In her mind's eye she could see the nervous creature edging forward out of it hiding place and stopping to scan the horizon for danger. Still unsure of its safety it would nevertheless venture a few steps further before courage deserted it and it stopped again. Sounds of movement and silence, repeated again and again. Jade could even tell the position of the timid creature.

Torn Ear stayed as still as death, not even allowing her ribcage to betray breathing.

Slowly the animal passed in front of Jade, putting itself between the two hunters.

The young kudu bull eased its weight nervously from foot to foot. He was desperate to get back to the herd. His first foray on his own had been disastrous and to cap it all, two hyena had decided to rest up on the very route he needed to take to get back. For nearly three hours he had stood hidden in the undergrowth while they rested. Now that the chance had come, he had lost the scent of his mother and was anxiously looking for her.

Although only four months old, the young antelope was already developing horns which would eventually mature into the spiralling weapons of a bull in its prime. He had large rounded ears which appeared to be stuck onto the sides of a handsome inquisitive face. His body was grey-brown with seven or eight vertical white stripes down each side. The bushy tail, with its white underside, hung uncertainly down.

On the far side of the bull a tremendous commotion suddenly broke out. The nervous animal jumped and then sagged as if all four knees had been turned to jelly for an instant. Jade risked a look and saw that the cause of all the fuss was a mongoose who had found the well hidden nest of the crowned plover that had been flying above her head just a few minutes earlier.

The mongoose is an inveterate egg stealer and devourer of fledglings. It is invariably mobbed by small birds whenever it is seen, especially when trying to attack a nest. Jade watched it darting forward time after time, to a crescendo of noise and dive bombing attacks, to get at the eggs. The brave creature was almost the same shape and size as a meerkat, except that the head and mouth were more wolf-like and thinner, and it was a chestnut red colour.

The kudu was absorbed by the fight and the noise covered Jade as she crept further to her right to get behind the young bull.

A pair of pied crows, usually seen as scavengers at kills, had now joined in the defence of the nest and the mongoose found himself outgunned in all directions. He used his discretion and scuttled off into the scrub. The noise ceased, and Jade was in position.

She jumped up, waving her arms above her head and shouting at the top of her voice. The young bull sprang forward and all the leopard had to do was leap up as he passed her, and it was all over.

Although Jade knew the urgency of hiding the kill now, or at least removing parts of it to take away, she let Torn Ear have her fill. The leopard hadn't eaten properly for several days and as long as she kept watch they were relatively safe.

So keep watch she did. Watching a hyena pack congregate on top of a low ridge. Soon they would have the courage of numbers to come down and challenge for the prize.

Jade knew that they would have to relinquish the kill when the hyena came, for carrying it away was impractical. The only solution was to make the most of it while they could.

Torn Ear was well aware that the hated scavengers were around but didn't waste time gawping at them. Eating as much as possible was now a priority and the leopard concentrated on shearing warm flesh from the bone. Dark liquid congealed quickly on her black fur, giving a sticky death mask.

Jade spent several very successful moments removing a hind limb with the new hunting knife. The implement was honed to perfection and sliced through with blissful ease. At least she could take this part of the meal with them. She sprinted away with it to a nearby tree, jamming it firmly in the crook of an upper branch.

Now the challenge was to keep the hyena at bay for as long as possible to let the leopard gorge herself before the kill was lost. Quickly Jade looked around to make sure she wasn't being outflanked herself. Nothing behind or to either side and nothing which could conceal a hiding animal. Good, she could concentrate her efforts in one direction only.

There were about ten of them, all adult and well built. Jade dropped into a crouch beside the eating leopard, fitting the first stone in her sling and swiftly surveying their mood. Torn Ear didn't even look up.

Jade was ready. She was facing the hyena from behind the carcass, and had stones laid out on her left hand side ready to fit to the sling without the necessity for her to look down. A fierce spark of spirit glowed in her blue-green eyes.

She sprang up and sent the first missile. It fell slightly short, spitting a shower of sand into the eyes of the intended victim.

The second shot had the range and hit the side of its chest. Jade waited to see the effect.

The hyena retreated to the rear of the pack. For a while they stopped their tentative advance. Then, as no further attacks were forthcoming, they came on again. This time spread out into a thin line and not bunched up as a pack.

The sling flashed twice, hitting animals at the extreme ends of the approaching crescent. They were the danger points. If the hyena managed to get around her, she would have to direct her energies two ways, and their escape route would also be in jeopardy. One leopard and one frail human were no match for ten killers with jaws like heavy metal vices. She had no doubt that to delay too long was certain death for both of them.

Torn Ear knew that too, but with the confidence of utter trust she continued to eat from the carcass. Not once did the leopard feel the need to check around her.

Jade squatted behind her cover. Eight stones left. She had maybe three minutes before retreat was essential. Quickly she thrust five back into the pouch on her hip. Now she had the three heaviest ones left.

She eyed the nearest hyena. It was a particularly ugly animal, with several naked scars on its flanks which hair had refused to cover up again. He was well ahead of the rest.

Suddenly she was up, twisting the sling deftly in small circles around her head.

The hyena stopped. He was caught in the open and he knew it. There was nowhere to go except forwards. The creature leapt towards her in a desperate attempt to frighten her into retreat.

Jade waited. The sling scythed through the air with an audible hiss.

She had so much time. The hyena appeared to be galloping through invisible treacle. Still she watched, pumping pure adrenaline through her veins.

He was almost ontop of her now. The thrill of judging the closest she could let him come suddenly vanished. It was right. She loosed the stone, giving the last twist an ounce more effort.

Bone cracked in an evil skull, and then there were nine.

Before the limbs had finished twitching in their last efforts to hang onto life, Jade had sent the last two stones on their way.

She didn't stay to see where they hit. It was time to go. She pivoted on a heel, driving it into the warm sand and touched Torn Ear lightly on the shoulder. The two of them raced for the tree and joined the stored meal in an uppermost branch.

Panting with exertion, eyes wide with the sheer high of combat, Jade watched the hyena consume the remainder of their prize.

Afternoon passed languidly into early evening, and evening found the pair of them wedged into the fork of a tree branch. Both were slumbering in the shady heat, the only way to get through some parts of the day.

The leopard lay belly down on the lower branch, with her quarters pushed right into the V shaped crook with another bough. She had begun with all four legs neatly positioned under the mass of silky fur, but during the period of unconsciousness a rogue forelimb had escaped and now dangled from the branch on its own. Every so often it would twitch and jump around like a flag in front of the breeze. Torn Ear was oblivious to this, and anything else, except danger signals passed to her resting brain by the nose or ears.

Half curled up on top of the leopard, and propped up from behind by the second branch, slept her companion. Most of her weight was actually taken by that branch, and her feet rested securely in holds either side of the huge cat.

Jade's head lay on the leopard's back, in the dip between massive shoulder blades, the shock of white blonde hair making a startling contrast with the fur beneath it. As she breathed rhythmically , the silky black hairs near the draught moved back and forth, keeping time perfectly. The little sunlight that was admitted by the leaves above made a diffuse speckled pattern on her broad naked back.

A drowsy right eye opened to survey the landscape, and Torn Ear wiggled her long whiskers to get rid of a fly which had decided to make a stop there.

The slight movement woke the other sleeper, who knew from past experience that once the leopard was awake there was no chance of being allowed to snooze a while longer. She grabbed hold of the meat and vaulted to the ground. The impact dislodged the makeshift bra she had taken to wearing on account of H, and she readjusted it. She was quite proud of her achievement in this realm and was now well aware of the effect on him.

Suddenly thinking of him made her realise that they had been away quite long enough. The couple set off on the return journey at a steady trot. As was their usual practice when travelling through relatively unknown territory, one partner kept well behind and to the left of the other, a flanking movement designed to spot and guard against unwelcome visitors before they got too close.

Dusk came upon them with the usual African speed, bringing with it welcome coolness. The leopard and the young woman kept up the pace, eating mile after mile.

It was dark when familiar landmarks came into view. A full moon cast its false light, allowing an eerie recognition. Because of the return route, they came to the small cave first.

Jade stopped outside for a couple of minutes to regain her composure and then went in to retrieve the sharpened stick.

A deep ice cold chill settled in the pit of her stomach as she realised the cave was empty. The old tree root had been dug out at one end, a feat which she had thought was impossible, and the handcuff slid over it. The stick was standing upright directly in front of her, stabbed into the sand in the middle of the floor space, its frayed and tattered ends showing exactly how the escape had been made.

Jade ripped it out of the ground and cracked it hard against the rocky wall in frustration. The stick snapped neatly in two, the smaller portion cartwheeling away to the back of the cave and landing silently.

At her feet, where the stick had been, the letter " H " was etched in the sand.

Icy limbs of fear spread their tendrils out from her belly and the seeds of panic began to germinate. She forced them away with a conscious physical effort but her feet wouldn't move yet. The enormity of the empty cave was just dawning on her. The brush of velvet fur on her calves went unnoticed.

Only after looking at the scene for long minutes did Jade begin to think logically.

H had escaped. He had either gone back the way he had come, or he had decided to wait and take his chances on ambushing the two of them when they returned. Hairs on the back of her neck stood up at the remote possibility of the latter. The darkness suddenly became an enemy.

Jade turned and left. She sat down at the base of the Shepherds tree, the place where decisions usually came to her.

Forget who it is......forget how much you hate him.......think it through......... knowing where he is now would be a good start........look for tracks...... he's still a crip after all

By the light of the moon it was easy to see the scuffed and heavily trodden area around the mouth of the cave. She could make out the many large prints heading away in a similar direction, where he had taken exercise every day. With an uneasy premonition, Jade cast around elsewhere, in areas where he had never been taken.

They were there. A single line of unmistakable heavy footprints, with no attempt to cover the spoor. They stood out like a cool blue river carving a swathe through the wilderness. She followed cautiously, Torn Ear stalking the other side of the tracks.

Within seconds she knew where they were heading. Although H had never been to their home up the hidden track, it would have been obvious to him that the pair needed a base not far from where they were holding him, and once free it was an easy matter for him to follow the worn path to it.

With the possibility of a trap firmly in mind, they took their time and made an utterly silent and stealthy approach up the track to the balcony. They were good. Hunting had made it an essential skill.

Once at the top, Torn Ear slid noiselessly under the lip of the entrance like a snake and took up position opposite Jade. The woman allowed herself several long deep breaths of the cool night air.

She would rather have faced any creature in there except this particular human. Everything was in there, a knife, the gun and the map. She had hidden the pistol in her special place but harboured no illusions about the ability of the man to find it. He could have had hours to look round inside.

Jade wiped her palms down the back of her legs as she stood flattened against the rock. They were sweating more than usual. The moisture seemed to have migrated there from her mouth, for it was dry as a bone and her tongue seemed like an intruder.

She fingered the big hunting knife in her belt and drew it gingerly. There was only one way to solve this situation and sitting here thinking about the consequences would ensure they lost heart. With a rush of adrenalin, she motioned to the leopard and they went in like a whirling tornado.

Torn Ear went right and Jade went left. Both lashed out violently in the dark with their respective weapons, but they only cut through thin air. Almost desperate to find him, they stormed feverishly into every inky black corner. Jade expecting at every turn to see the blinding flash and hear the thunderous crack of a bullet dispatched. Her skin crawled and physically itched with fear of the unknown.

It took desperately long seconds for the pair of them to establish that their home was empty. Jade was panting with exertion and tension. Big sucked in gasps of air. She sat down on her familiar bed space and found that her hands trembled uncontrollably as she picked an animal skin up. Trying to control one hand with the other was no use either, each was just as bad.

She clutched the home made blanket in her lap and waited for recovery. In all the time on her own, she had probably just experienced the worst few seconds then and there.

The back pack was gone. So were the maps and other oddments that she had briefly glanced over and then crammed back into the disgusting canvas all those weeks ago. On an impulse, she had however removed the pistol and magazines, putting them in her safest place.

She walked to the back of the den and groped around on the smooth rock floor for the key to her safe. It was a fist sized chunk of stone which she always kept at the back of the cave. Knocked with a certain amount of force against a particular part of the cave wall, it caused a circular crack to appear, slightly bigger than the span of her hand. Manipulate the crust of loosening rock carefully and it would come away in one piece, revealing a long narrow passage, the end of which she could just reach with her fingertips. When the 'door' was replaced, it was as good as invisible.

Jade had found it purely by chance, and seeing as the outside was still intact she had high hopes that the contents would be likewise.

Carefully, almost religiously, she retrieved her treasure, placing each item in the hazy circle of moonlight which descended through the ventilation hole.

The gun was there, together with five magazines of ammunition. Jade could tell that each of the metal rectangles had some bullets in it because she could see a gleaming cylinder through the small spy hole situated half way down the side.

After them came her collection of shiny stones and pebbles, the Lion Stone coming out last.

Looking at them, the young woman realised that a cross roads had been reached. She might never get the chance to return, for whatever reason.

Jade sat down on her haunches, rocking slowly in deep thought.

After several minutes she got up and wrapped half of the precious stones in a piece of kudu hide that was amongst the oldest in her collection. Constant use had softened it to such an extent that both sides felt just as smooth.

She placed the bundle at the very end of the long passage and then jammed a rock in front of it. Hopefully any intruder would think that the rock was the back of the hole and would leave it at that.

The Lion Stone, and a good number of its companions, would come with her, as would the gun. If nothing else, the weapon would serve to distance any would-be human aggressors. The fact that she didn't know how to operate it was beside the point. She put them all at the entrance to their home.

It was over half way through the night, but sleep had never been further away. Jade went out and sat on the balcony with the leopard.

There was no point in trying to track H in the dark. She could search for the spoor at first light. Besides, it was impossible for her to just up and leave. So she sat in the only place in the world where she felt secure and comfortable, and tried to get used to the idea of leaving it. Memories washed over her in their thousands, both good and bad, spinning round in her mind and then melting into the darkness. All the time she drank in the sounds, smells and sights around her, as if storing them up as an insurance policy against whatever was to come.

The first light of a crisp dawn came too quickly. It meant she had to act, but she was ready for the decision now. Jade stroked the head of Torn Ear who was dozing beside her and then went into the den to collect the few things she was going to take with her.

Looking round their home for the last time, she touched the smooth rock walls, running her fingertips tenderly along them and realising with a start that the small cave must hold untold memories for the leopard that she would never know about.

The agony and joy of birth. Excitement of new life. Small helpless crawling forms. Tumbling fights between sister and brothers. A safe haven from a new world outside, and a jackal who intruded. A mother and cubs who left and never returned.

By the time there was enough light to see by, Jade and Torn Ear were scouring the valley floor for tell tale signs. Incredibly, they found a set of prints in the sand almost immediately. There had been no attempt to cover or hide the spoor, or even use hard ground.

Jade followed the tracks for several hundred yards before she was satisfied that the trail was genuine and not just a decoy. Looked at carefully, the prints showed a harder impression on one side than the other, a clear sign of a damaged limb being favoured.

Back at the point where she had left Torn Ear, the solution came to her. H must have sacrificed stealth for speed.

There were no other tracks leading away from the bottom of the hidden path. they had examined every inch, their combined experience and different abilities failing to find anything. He must have gone this way.

Before leaving, Jade examined the gun. She might need its advantage in the future. She weighed the unfamiliar weapon in her hand. Shotguns she had handled before and fired - handguns never. Without touching the trigger itself, there were a limited number of buttons to push. One caused the magazine to eject itself half an inch or so, from which position Jade could pull it out entirely. She practised extracting and replacing the magazine. It made a satisfying click when thumped home into the butt of the gun using the heel of her hand.

As a next step, she removed the magazine so that the gun appeared to be empty. Then she aimed the weapon skywards, having judged that to be by far the safest direction, and squeezed the trigger. Predictably, nothing.

She brought her hand down, changed the position of the knurled safety catch at the back of the weapon and re-aimed.

The one remaining round in the breech rocketed into the heavens with a report that shocked a flock of white backed and griffon vultures into flight from nearby acacia trees. The power and ferocity of the recoil astonished Jade, who had barely managed to hang onto the weapon.

It was now definitely empty she decided and safe to explore intimately.

By a process of trial and error, and use of the magazine which she unloaded the remaining three rounds from first, Jade managed to gain a working knowledge of her new acquisition. Given time, and a supply of ammunition, she would undoubtedly have been able to perfect her aim as well.

She restricted herself instead to the three rounds, which she loaded back into the magazine.

*****

In the still, clear air of the early morning Kalahari, sound travels very easily indeed. Only over the surface of water would it have travelled any faster.

One lone shot, followed thirty minutes later by three more, carried very clearly to Harry de Beer, as he searched for a place to spend the heat of the day.

Self doubt reared its ugly head, as it had done many times since he had been able to free himself. He was the hunted party now.

Why hadn't he anti-tracked on the spoor ? Hell, he could do it standing on his head, and quickly too. He must have been cracked to assume it could buy him enough time.

The gun must have been there all the time. Why hadn't he been able to find it ? Then he could simply have waited and finished it once and for all. For God's sake, it's only a sodding girl and a big cat.

He swallowed the last mouthful of rotting, putrid tsama melon and forced himself into a walk again. Hiding from the sun could wait a couple of hours. He needed distance. The new muscles in his leg ached with fatigue from lack of exercise. Soon the stabbing pains of cramp would needle their way in. He would have to walk through the barrier of agony, again.

*****

Jade knew there was a good chance H had heard the shots, and in a perverse sort of way she wanted him to have done so. It told him the chase was on, and that she held most of the cards this time.

The woman and the leopard set off to follow the spoor, one on each side of the tracks. As she walked, Jade's feet broke the thin crust of already warm sand and felt the cooler layer immediately below.

Neither looked back at the familiar and comforting landmarks which were retreating into the distance. Life there was already a memory.

CHAPTER

EIGHT

A smoky yellow gold sunset brought an end to that first day of travel.

Sitting with her back to the warmth of a granite kopje Jade watched the remaining half dome of the sun sink slowly below the horizon, silhouetting two vultures perched on the branch of a leafless tree. They appeared like solid charcoal outlines when viewed against the wonderfully soft backdrop of diffuse colour.

The slightest sprinkling of sand grains showered gently onto her shoulders. Without looking up she flung her arms over her head as a mass of black fur and legs descended into her lap at speed.

The leopard rolled off Jade and, after a couple more somersaults, ended up on her back several yards away. Torn Ear bounced up immediately shaking her head to dislodge the sand from her ears. Mischief was on her mind and she surveyed the immediate surrounds for possibilities. If all else failed Torn Ear was sure that with enough goading she could persuade her companion into a good tussle.

A nocturnal flying insect made the mistake of coming too close to a cat in a playful mood, and was promptly swiped from the skies after a gigantic leap. The leap was fine, but landings were not too good tonight and Torn Ear soon had more sand to shake out.

Jade grinned broadly at the antics of her companion. She guessed that in such a mood Torn Ear might wander off into the gathering darkness to hunt, so she covered herself with a skin and settled down for the night, burrowing her legs into the warm sand. This technique of survival, learnt out of necessity, had now become a comforting habit when she slept under the canopy of stars.

Torn Ear watched the arrangements with disappointment. So she waited a while, letting her mood subside, until Jade was asleep. Then she painstakingly wriggled up alongside until both bodies were level.

An arm draped itself across the cat in an unconscious gesture. The leopard snuggled closer. She would not sleep, but would pass the night in alternate periods of pleasant dozing and watchfulness.

******

Darkness was the only friend of their quarry. As on his outward journey H travelled during the cool, sometimes frosty, night and rested in the heat of the day. The girl, he reasoned, would have to follow during daylight hours in order to be able to track, and would thus be slower. This gave him some small comfort, as long as he didn't examine his own logic too closely. She had shown remarkable abilities in the weeks he had been captive, so much so that he knew he often underestimated her.

The irony of his reversed direction of travel had not escaped him either. Hunter becomes hunted.

In the first few days he had pushed too hard at the wrong times, taking it relatively easy when he was rested and cool, and then panicking when dawn came and trying to make up more distance as the temperature rose, eventually forcing him to seek shelter.

Common sense finally dictated that he should travel fast and hard at night and rest all day. It may be frustrating but in the long run it was the only way he was going to win.

After the first unplanned day he anti-tracked on the spoor, bitterly regretting his decision not to do so from the outset. Wherever possible he used hard ground, avoiding the soft sand, which hung onto footprints like freshly fallen snow. Sometimes H followed well worn animal tracks, especially ones which had dried into a hard mud cake due to the recent rains. He walked in the prints themselves, taking care not to break any of the tiny fragile mud walls pushed up by the animal as it trod.

Areas of sparse grasses and vegetation were also avoided to a certain extent. If he had to pass through them he straightened any badly bent or flattened blades. He knew that most grasses would do this for themselves in about half an hour, but he couldn't afford the time to wait and be sure.

However, moonlight is not always adequate to anti-track by and every so often H missed tell tale signs. These were left like glaring beacons in his trail and completely negated the precious time wasted along the rest of the spoor.

He had only the vaguest of ideas what he would do at the end. The girl obviously could not be allowed to tell her story to the police in Windhoek, as was her stated intention. There was only one certain way of ensuring that. How and when were unknown, but H knew the moment would present itself. It had always done so in the past.

A familiar prickling pain danced around the new muscle in his thigh, bringing his wandering mind back to the present. It heralded cramp and fatigue, but as usual the big Afrikaaner ignored it until it actually began to seize and spasm.

H sat on a low stone and began to squeeze and pummel the muscle into action again. He would give it ten minutes rest and then continue, whether it was fixed or not. He figured the only way to get it fit was to use it, besides which there was no choice, he had to keep on the move. When it got bad again there would be another rest.

Without the constant sound of scuffling and crunching of detritus underfoot as he walked, the desert suddenly seemed eerily and painfully quiet. A low moon cast silvery shadows, making darkened corners pitch black and lighting other areas with a surrealist quality. For once, the Kalahari fauna of the night were quiet, making the silence vast and foreboding.

In such a situation even the sternest of souls might have been expected to experience the odd tremor of uncertainty and glance around from time to time, letting an imagination speculate as to the contents of these darkened corners in a hostile land.

Such thoughts never occurred to the animal instincts of the man seated on the low rock. The silence meant that he would hear any approaching creature and deal with it. The only things that were real were those he could see and touch, his mind had no capacity for useless imaginations.

H got up, shouldered the pack, and continued his journey with a short jog to wake the leg muscles up again.

******

Ever since they started out H had been following the same general direction. To start with they had checked his trail at every opportunity, looking for signs of change.

By now they had accepted that he simply intended to get to his goal by the quickest available route and they only checked for spoor markers once in a while. It meant their progress was much enhanced.

The pair ate up the miles with relish. Sometimes in the cool of early evening, when they felt particularly confident, they would settle into a gentle run and pound over the hard dry surface, leaping over small hollows and alerting all the animals around.

Even in the vast interior of the Kalahari it is not possible to travel continually without actually getting anywhere. Over the next couple of days Jade began to notice a very subtle change in the surroundings.

Sandy areas of dunes began to die out, being replaced by hard arid scrubland. As they continued, patches of grass developed in places. Not the hardy tussocks of desert grass that were to be found where they had come from, but thinner more tender plants, altogether greener and more luscious. Grass that looked civilised.

At first this new growth was very intermittent and sparse, but more appeared with every hour that passed. Of course it was all relative for nowhere in this African country would you find rolling fields and meadows, but there was a definite improvement. Jade felt a queasy sort of excitement building within her. It was like being afloat in a vast watercourse approaching Victoria Falls - she was being carried along with the tide of events in the general direction in which she was sure she wanted to go but there was a terrible barrier to get over first.

Jade upped the pace from now on. There was no way she could let H reach the edge of the desert before she got hold of him. Once he made it to a road he could hitch a lift if he was lucky, and then he was gone. Deep in her heart she knew she would never feel comfortable in her bed until he was behind bars.

My bed........how long is it since I had a bed with sheets and blankets........what is it like at the farm now......? She reached back into the depths and found that she couldn't conjure up a proper picture of the buildings and yards. She had no idea if Oupa was even alive. His malaria attacks must have got worse over these years. She hoped with all her strength that he would still be there to welcome her home. There was no doubt that it would come as a shock to him.

Torn Ear stopped dead in her tracks. Beside the leopard was a damp patch in one of the few partly sandy areas remaining. The earth was slightly discoloured, an indication Jade might very well have passed by. In this heat, damp sand does not stay damp long. Someone was here quite recently.

Jade dug gently at the site. The grains of sand felt cool. Beneath the surface were the skins of desert fruit, roughly buried, to prevent their chance discovery. The moisture in them had seeped out and given the game away.

She was ecstatic. She was certainly less than an hour behind him now, and none too soon, with the edge of the desert approaching rapidly.

Swiftly she glanced around to confirm her theory. Yes, there they were. Tiny little leaf stalks, betraying their underground cargo, which Jade had learned to recognise in her first days alone. H had made a hasty meal of some and buried the remains. A half hearted effort at concealment, probably because he was close to his goal and every second spent doing that was a second wasted.

Another ten minutes hard running and the pair came to a low ridge on the other side of which the land sloped gently away from them to a cool blue horizon. Dotted around were large green trees, the like of which she hadn't seen for years. Before the land mingled in a shimmering heat haze with the sky, she could just make out a crease in the landscape running horizontally across her field of vision. She stared at it, trying to focus on it, trying to work out what it was.

With a start Jade realised she was looking at a dirt track road, the most common sort, for only the main highways were metalled in this country. She had reached the threshold of the Kalahari Desert.

As she drank in the scene she made out two more features. On the far right as she looked, were a couple of large houses or barns, the smaller at right angles to the other. The track seemed to lead straight past them. That meant there would probably be people living there. People to be with and talk to. The excitement almost burst out of her like a balloon.

Swinging her sight left now, she could make out a tiny stick like figure. It bounced and swirled in the late afternoon heat, but not enough to disguise its identity, or its direction. It appeared to be heading for a shady clump of trees far away from the two buildings.

Jade checked the cover on her left. Plenty of spaced out trees and bushes here now. She could easily outflank H and confront him when he reached the clump of trees.

Twenty yards into her first sprint out to the left Jade's instincts told her something was badly wrong. She pulled up and the realisation hit her like a blow in the stomach, only hurting a thousand times more.

She was alone. The leopard was sitting exactly where she had been, on the ridge, staring after her. Torn Ear had made the decision which Jade knew she would eventually have to. The feline predator was on the edge of her world. She could go no further, no matter how strong the ties between the two companions.

Out there was a totally hostile environment for Torn Ear. It was dominated by the only creature she had real reason to fear, above any other.

Although the girl had been able to survive in the world of the leopard, the reverse could never apply, and they both knew it. It was only a matter of time before circumstances forced a split. Jade had to make her way in the civilised world again, although it would have been so easy to turn her back and retreat into the interior again.

Jade dropped her small bundle onto the sandveldt where she had stopped and raced back to the side of her companion.

Torn Ear sat bolt upright, tail curled round tightly bunched up paws, ears erect and alert. The young woman ran a hand lovingly over velvet fur on the leopard's head and then bent down to embrace and hug the friend with whom she had shared so many experiences and adventures.

There was so little time. She had to keep in touch with her quarry.

She felt her very existence was being ripped out from within her and the void was already aching and gnawing. A solitary drop of salty moisture was quickly engulfed by the dense forest of black hair into which it fell.

There was so much to say, and yet no need to say it. Jade knew she would come and find her friend again, and that was the only thing which made it possible for her to leave Torn Ear. The leopard knew it as well. At the moments of greatest stress, communication between the two of them was at its best.

Nevertheless, neither knew when that would be. A desert of loneliness stretched out before each of them in different directions.

A final hug and Jade was off and running, not trusting herself to stay any longer.

Quickly she picked her route through the arid tundra, darting from cover to cover, all the time outflanking H, whom she kept in sight.

The Boer was exhausted. She could see that from his stagger and indeed from the fact that he was finishing his travel in the heat of day. The lure of basic desires - clean water, wholesome food, cracking the top of an ice cold bottle of Castle's and a bed to sleep in again were so strong that for the sake of a few hours he had abandoned common sense for the second time and force marched during the day.

He had a definite limp as well. Although the injured leg appeared to be as strong as the other, there was a slight twist and shuffle as the foot hit the ground each time.

Several hundred yards to her right, H crossed the rutted dirt and stone track. Seeming to recognise the terrain, he straightened up and struck out with greater determination.

So intent was he in his purpose and so certain that he was safe, that he failed to notice Jade as she stood and watched him out in the open.

She was standing on the desert side of the track. Crossing it seemed to mark the transition from one part of her life to the next.

It was late afternoon and the sun was already lower in the clear blue sky. Long mellow rays stretched out from it like tangents to a circle, softening the landscape and lighting it with a gentle hue that hid the harshness.

Looking back to the ridge, Jade could still make out the shape and silhouette of the leopard. She was sitting in the same place. Squinting and concentrating, she thought she could even make out the split in the ear.

For a long minute Jade let the image of the jet black leopard burn itself into her memory. She never forgot the picture she saw there.

With an uncertain step the young woman crossed the two rutted tracks and looked again.

The picture was gone.

CHAPTER

NINE

H passed the clump of trees, which were his landmark, and then rounded a slight hillock to find that the Land Rover was gone.

He consoled himself with the fact that he had not really expected it to still be there anyway. You could start the thing with a rusty screwdriver in the ignition, and some time during the weeks, or was it months, that it had lain in the same spot a wandering soul must have decided to liberate it.

It was still a blow. A certain means of escape was gone, as was the water and food hidden in it. The thought of water jogged a scorched and weary memory, and the man with long matted hair and sunburnt body managed a weak grin. Slowly he looked around and found an area where the brave new blades of grass seemed thinner and paler.

Kneeling to the ground, his joints cracked and the dry sundrenched skin on his legs stretched and squealed at this unfamiliar movement. He didn't notice this new discomfort and started to dig at the hard earth with his bare hands.

After a while H searched around and found a chunky triangular stone which he grasped with both hands and smashed away the crust of surface dirt. He hadn't buried it deeply at all, so before long there was a triumphant cry as his searching fingers found the cord of a watertight canvas sack. He took hold of the material with both hands and stood up to his full height, bringing the bag out in a showering fountain of sand and earth.

With feverish movements he tugged at the knots, blessing his commonsense and foresight in burying supplies. Eventually the sack yielded and he plunged his hand inside.

His brain was instantly assailed with sensations from two parts of his body, and it didn't know which to give priority to. From his hand came the life saving message of water bottles, but from the bare skin at the back of his neck came a small, cold, circular sensation which hadn't been there a second before.

Holding the pistol to his neck, Jade was pleased that her grip didn't tremble in the slightest. She had outflanked him and made an approach with ease. Had he been fully alert and expecting her, she reckoned she could still have surprised him, such were her skills. However, she doubted whether the noise of charging bull elephants would have diverted him at that moment.

The experience of countless hunts had taught Jade to bide her time and strike when the prey is at its most vulnerable. She had learned the lesson well for she could have reached out and touched him at any time during the preceding five minutes, but had waited in patient silence until the moment presented itself.

A muscle twitched in the neck she was observing. His head moved almost imperceptibly to one side. He was still as dangerous as a gut shot buffalo.

" Rock forward, " she said to the kneeling man, " so that you are face down on the ground."

There was no response.

She pressed the barrel harder into the rubbery flesh. " Do it now."

Still no movement.

In one swift action Jade moved her aim six inches to the left, fired a shot, and returned the now hot and smoking barrel to the ring of whitened flesh that its pressure had left in his neck.

H flinched from the sudden unexpected explosion of sound and the line of powder burn which had stung his face.

In her moment of advantage Jade pushed H forward with her free hand. He toppled over, falling heavily. Before he was really aware of what was happening she sprang onto his back, dropping the gun, and pulled both arms together behind him. The handcuffs still dangled from one wrist for he had been unable to remove them entirely after his escape. Jade quickly worked the other loop so that it was open again and then fastened it firmly round his free wrist.

With him immobilised, she used her knife to rip a piece off his filthy shirt, twisted it into a thick long cord and then tied it as a gag around his head. Abhorring any further contact she jumped off and retrieved the gun.

Very pleased with her performance, and immensely relieved that she had recaptured him again, she flicked the safety catch on the pistol and replaced it in her bundle of belongings. The she dragged the canvas sack away a couple of yards to examine it.

The young woman grinned with delight when she felt the weight of the two metal flasks which she brought out. Right now, they were worth more than their weight in gold bullion.

Jade upended one flask and drank a long cool draught, purposely allowing it to overflow and dribble out of her mouth to each side. It was pure nectar, good clean water without any sand, sediment, or warm putrid matter which might or might not be dead. The taste of it brought her more firmly back into civilisation than any other one thing.

There was an element of spite to her actions, but as always, there was also a purpose. She needed a degree of cooperation out of him in the near future. He had felt the stick. Now it was carrot time.

Jade got up, shouldering the bag as she did.

" I'm going to those houses over there and you're coming with me. That is, you're coming with me if you want to live much longer. Don't get me wrong. I don't have to shoot you now, because as you can see, your hands are cuffed and I have the only water for miles around." She moved the flasks around in the bag so that the sound of water slopping inside could be clearly heard.

" You also appear to have something in your mouth, which could make life difficult. So, the choice is yours, and I reckon that you could just about make it through the night on your own, always presuming a rangy old Kalahari male didn't make a snack of you, all trussed up like this."

Jade waited a couple of minutes to watch his reactions. By the look of him, he could easily survive the night and the next day without water, but he thought he was at death's door.

Like a tired old camel , H struggled to his feet, both hands behind the back being a greater handicap than he had at first imagined.

Jade moved in behind him and without further command H started to walk to the buildings, which he recognised almost immediately.

******

At the junction of District Roads 3808 and 3809 in the area known as Hereroland stand two buildings. Even by the standards of Namibia two buildings do not warrant mention on the map as a *klein plekkie*, a very small place. So it has no name.

It is about eleven kilometres from Otjiyarwa and seventy kilometres from Otjinene. Both of these places have at least double the number of buildings, and get a name.

The larger of the two constructions is a long low barn-like affair with only the single storey. It is partitioned about a third of the way down by a thin wooden wall. The smaller part was originally meant to be a general store, serving the nearby community of this semi-desert outpost. The shelves are empty, riddled with woodworm and laden with the dust of many lifeless years.

The other part of this main building is home to two elderly residents, the only two. They spend their day on the wide verandah that runs the length of their home and is sheltered from the fierce sun by an equally wide overhanging roof from which dangles a faded metal sign bearing the logo of the Coca Cola company. It has rusted so much that the colours are barely distinguishable and it creaks and groans on its hinges when disturbed by the breeze.

The inhabitants are as old and weatherbeaten as the outpost itself.

A careful observer will find the key to their existence in the second building. It is a squat garage, made of brick and corrugated iron with double wooden doors at the front, secured together by a padlock.

On the left hand side of the garage, as you look at it, stands the only electric petrol pump in the entire district, provided many years ago courtesy of British Petroleum. However, it has long since ceased to function on its own, and anyone wanting to extract petrol from the small underground tank has to pump it by hand.

They are lucky to get a customer every week or ten days, and in consequence tend to remember each one.

They especially remember the Boer with his arrogant manners in his open topped Land Rover, who looked on and laughed while the old woman laboured over the pump.

The sound of a single shot roused the old man from a well worn wood and canvas rocking chair. His wife of more years than he cared to remember was inside the living area, preparing the meagre offering for their meal. In most other parts of the country, evening on the stoep would probably be accompanied by a sundowner of some description to help day slip into night. Neither cared to recall the last occasion that they had been able to do this.

Propped up against the sink for support, Alida painstakingly brought the meal towards completion, hindered by gnarled, arthritic fingers. It comforted her to hear the steady reassuring creaks and groans from her husband's chair out front. He was all right. He was all she had, and vice versa, since fate and National Service had taken both sons from them. Like most couples of their age, the companionship and love of the other was the most precious thing they had, and by virtue of that very passage of years it could not last forever. Silently, each dreaded that the other might die and leave him or her to carry the burden of grief and loneliness unassisted. It was the only subject they could not discuss, for fear of disturbing the bond that held them together. By simply bringing it into the open they might unleash the demon and it might happen.

Both wished with all their strength that events might somehow contrive to let them leave this world together.

The explosive sound and then naked silence from the verandah brought the old woman out of the house as fast as weary legs would carry her. She found Willem at the edge of the wooden boards, staring out down the rutted track. Alida joined him, nervously wiping her soiled hands on a crisply starched off-white apron.

For a long while there was nothing out of the ordinary to see at all. The familiar contours gazed back at them and there was an aching quiet.

Then, when they were about to give up, a figure materialised over a crest in the road. It slouched along and yet appeared defiant.

Alida soon recognised it as the big Afrikaaner and only just managed to stop herself from taking a retreating step behind her husband. She steeled herself with the grit that had seen her through life on the edge of the baking desert, and stood her ground.

Both of them then screwed up their eyes to try and make out the second figure. It moved about behind the larger one, keeping a constant distance, but often changing its position. The low sun made accurate viewing even more difficult.

The approaching couple were a completely unknown quantity to the old people, and in view of what they had already heard, and their isolated location, it might have been prudent for Willem to fetch an ancient shotgun from some dust laden rack as a precaution. He did not, for he possessed no weapon. Instead, he grasped the hand of his wife and they faced the challenge.

Not a word passed between any of them until Jade and H stood in front of the stoep, facing the owners and about ten inches below them.

" Goeienaand Meneer, Mevrou," began the young woman in halting and badly remembered Afrikaans. " I have travelled a long way and would like to rest." Jade silently thanked her foresight in gagging H, for she would be able to put her story to them without contradictions and accusations from him. She waited anxiously for an answer, while the pair of them were scrutinised.

Alida and Willem were having a hard time taking in the picture which confronted them, but their stony expressions betrayed none of it.

The girl was quite stunning. She had long unkempt blonde hair, bleached to whiteness, which was tied into a severe and rough ponytail which reached over half way down her back. She was simply clothed with two pieces of coarse material, the uppermost of which was only just managing to fulfill its function. On closer examination, the old man was a little astonished to find that they seemed to be cured animal skins. There was nothing on her feet.

Her body was covered with a deep mahogany sheen which left her looking lean and greyhound fit. It made a startling contrast with her hair. This was no two week holiday tan. This was constant life under an African sun, which would, in further years, turn the skin leathery and freckled. The colour shone through the layers of dust and dirt which had accumulated on this, her last journey.

Her face had fine, sharp features which seemed almost Egyptian in origin, due to the colour. Blue-green eyes sparkled from beneath whitened eyebrows as she looked from one to the other.

The old man looked down at what she was carrying. In her left hand Jade held a small bundle of skins, wrapped around her few possessions. In her right was the gun, pointed firmly at H. They turned their attention to him.

With both hands secured behind his back and a gag in his mouth there was no doubt as to who was in control. Despite their differing levels, he was still tall enough to look them both in the eye, which he aggressively did. His head and face were covered in an unkempt mat of hair which had acted as a magnet for all kinds of microscopic flotsam and jetsam of the desert. There was a glistening layer of sweat on his forehead which constantly overflowed down his face.

As the slight breeze changed direction the bodily stench of the man wafted across to the old people. It was practically physical in its strength, making them both feel quite ill after only a few seconds. The only sound to break an awkward silence was the hissing and rasping as H drew breath through his gagged mouth.

A tiny flying insect broke the deadlock, buzzing from one person to the next, looking for salt and sustenance. The sound it made was out of all proportion to its size.

It hovered for a moment too long by the old woman. Alida swiftly moved a practised hand and the noise ceased.

Jade wondered what she could do next to try and persuade them to accept her. The gun slipped a little in her hand due to the combined actions of perspiration and the smooth wooden butt. Suddenly it felt uncomfortable and unnecessary to have such an item brandished outside the home of this obviously peace loving couple. H was handcuffed, she reasoned to herself, what could he do ?

Slowly, she backed away from him, reversing with care until she was at the far end of the verandah. There she removed the magazine from the gun and racked the action to spit out the one remaining round, which she replaced in the magazine. Then she placed both items on the warm boards in front of her. Jade walked a few paces back and smiled, a little nervously.

The last of the old man's doubts crumbled like the walls of Jericho. He returned the smile and cleared his throat with embarrassment.

" Come inside. I think you have a story we should hear."

Jade smiled again, this time with relief and appreciation. Still standing behind H, she gestured at him with a nod of her head. The old man understood instantly and disappeared into the darkened interior of the building. He returned a minute later with a bunch of keys on a ring and led the two of them to the garage which he unlocked. H sat down without a murmur of protest.

The evening meal was vegetable soup, and a bowlful of the hot steaming broth was placed in front of a grateful traveller. Together with hunks of freshly baked brown bread and a mug of coffee, it was gorgeous. She had entirely forgotten the taste of bread, the crispy outside and warm moist dough. To save awkward requests, Alida carefully watched the level in Jade's bowl, refilling it whenever she was close to emptying it. The old couple went short themselves, but it was a long time since Alida had had anyone to care for and look after. Willem could see his wife getting into her stride again, fussing efficiently around and it pleased him.

When Jade finally pushed the bowl away and reluctantly refused more of the delicious soup, it was pitch dark outside. Hunger is the best sauce for food and for the first time in years Jade actually felt full.

Willem got up from the table and lit three gas lamps in the kitchen which spluttered into life and then illuminated the room with an effective, if shadowy, light. Then both he and his wife came back to the table to wait for the young woman to gain her confidence.

Jade got up and stood with her back to a wall. Leaning against it she could address the two of them without needing to look from one to the other all the time. She composed her thoughts carefully, for this story would be told many times in the future.

" My name is Jade Viljoen, " she began with a slight tremble in her voice. " I live on a farm owned by my grandfather, Tony van Niekerk. Every day I used to ride out to the edge of the desert - often to watch the sunrise. The colours are so beautiful and clear."

She left nothing out, telling everything in chronological order and very rarely needing to go back on herself. Reliving her life in the desert brought back memories and incidents that she had forgotten. She told of the harrowing first few days, the blessed honey bird that had saved her life, her gradual acclimatisation to her new home. With a lump in her throat she told the listeners of her friendship with the leopards. How they gradually banded together into a family and how they were destroyed.

A thoughtfully provided drink relieved her dry and aching throat at this point. Talking was still a new experience.

Jade explained how the partnership between the black leopard with the torn ear and herself had progressed. She told of the den, of the many hunts and experiences they had shared together. As she spoke, Jade realised that it all seemed a million years ago, on a different planet.

Several times during this session Jade turned to the window, gazing out into the inky blackness to hide the tears which welled up from time to time as she thought of the friend she had abandoned and cared for too deeply for words.

The story wound its way to a close with the arrival of H who was now held captive in the garage. With undisguised venom she gave graphic details, not bothering about her own personal embarrassment. The journey out of the Kalahari was the last stage and as she finished, her voice cracked with fatigue and emotion. The entire narrative took something over three hours to complete.

Jade excused herself, wished the old people goodnight, and went outside to check on H and find a place to sleep. The offer of a bed had been politely refused. There had been enough changes today already without messing her sleeping habits about. Besides which, she could no more imagine sleeping in a stuffy little room on a bouncy mattress than sleeping perched half-way up a flagpole.

She curled up under a tree a distance from the flickering lights of the house, and was deeply asleep before she knew it.

The night is always at its darkest just before the first rays of sunlight fight their way over the horizon. With no moon, and patchy cloud obscuring the pinpricks of starlight, this was a particularly murky night. Ideal cover for the silhouette which headed purposefully for the dwellings at the limit of her world.

Torn Ear gently nuzzled the neck of the sleeping Jade, whiskers tickling her bare skin. The leopard was nervous. It took all her courage to approach these strange and alien scents. She was out of her depth and knew it. Nevertheless, her friend was here so it must be safe.

Jade woke with a muted squeal of delight and hugged the velvet neck with all her strength, which was not inconsiderable. They were inseparable for several long minutes.

Finally she relinquished her grasp to look at the leopard. Torn Ear was clearly anxious and Jade knew what it had taken for her to come this far. Her ears were erect, eyes wide open and constantly looking around. She wouldn't sit still after Jade had let go of her, but paced around continually.

Jade tried her best to reassure and comfort the leopard but with no result. Torn Ear stayed long enough to convince herself that her human friend was alive and well, and then she went. Melting into the darkness as silently as she had arrived.

The young woman was ecstatic at the visit, and stared out into the night to try and get a last glimpse of the big cat. She was so happy that Torn Ear didn't think she had been abandoned that she nearly went in to tell the couple about it. Only two things stopped her doing that. Firstly it wasn't even light yet and they were probably asleep. Secondly, having a leopard pay a nocturnal visit to your house might not be everyone's idea of a favourite guest, no matter how friendly it was supposed to be. She kept her joy silent and waited impatiently for day to break.

Jade was right to assume that Alida and Willem were in bed. They were, but only just.

After she had left them, they stayed up nearly all night discussing the extraordinary event which had befallen them. They were responsible people, knowing that how they treated Jade and her situation now might have a pronounced effect on the way the rest of her life turned out.

She needed to be brought gently back into the world which she had left so abruptly. So many things had changed and there were so many things which she did not know.

So they drew up their strategies and planned their solutions. The role of instant foster parents was unusual though they soon warmed to the task, finding a caring interest, something which was lacking in their everyday hum-drum existence.

They finally retired, exhausted. It had to have been decided by morning however. The young woman would be impatient for progress. Out of her element she needed direction, and she needed it the very next day so that she could have confidence in them, and let them help her.

" Goeiemore, Juffrou Viljoen, " grinned Willem from the sunlit doorway. " Hoe gaan dit met jou ?" He had a cheeky twinkle in his eye, made all the more endearing by his advancing years.

" I am very well thank-you, " responded Jade. " Despite being civilised again." She replied in English, because although she could make out the gist of simple sentences in Afrikaans, to reply in that tongue was as yet beyond her. On the farm, it was all English and at school Afrikaans had come a poor second behind German and Latin.

The old couple spoke English and Afrikaans fluently.

The first task was to secure H properly in the garage. Jade covered him with the gun while Willem fastened one cuff to a metal stanchion. Then she removed the gag and made sure that it was not possible for him to escape the same way as before. The metal went straight into a block of concrete. They left him with food, water, a bucket and his thoughts.

Before padlocking the door, Willem searched meticulously through the shelves and lockers, removing from the years of accumulated debris anything which he could possibly use to aid an escape attempt. The they left him.

It was conference time again. The three of them were sitting around the kitchen table, as they had the previous evening, only this time it was a discussion and not a monologue.

" We have no telephone here, nor a transmitter," continued Alida. " The only way we have of keeping in contact with events elsewhere is by listening to what they tell us on our radio. " She indicated the modern Sony which Jade had already spotted, occupying a prime location on a shelf above the sink. Next to it was a simple cassette recorder, same vintage, and a box of Ever Ready's. They were of a different generation from the rest of the furniture and fittings which made up the large kitchen and living area.

" Every couple of weeks or so the Sergeant from Gobabis pays us a visit. If there is any mail he brings it with him, but we are right at the edge of his massive district so if there is anything else for him to do, we tend to get forgotten.

When he comes again you should hand the man over to him. Then you should go with him as well. It is the only form of transport out of here."

Jade nodded attentively as the old woman carried on. She could not help being impressed and slightly humbled by the commitment and thought which they had given their unexpected problem.

" Many things have happened since you went into the desert. Some have changed, others you never knew to start with. In the short time that is given to us, we would like to prepare you as much as we can. If that is what you want."

Jade stood up. " Thank you, " she said simply. " When do we start ?" Alida and Willem smiled as one.

The padlock was rusty and stiff. It took Jade several attempts to open it with the equally ancient key. She waited until her eyes had grown accustomed to the half light inside.

H was sitting propped up against a cupboard, and watched her silently with eyes of ice.

She strode up to him and placed a can of beer on the dusty floor.

" It's still cold, " she murmured, and left.

Schooling began at once. First thing in the morning Willem spent an hour or so teaching her Afrikaans, or rather brushing up on what she already knew and enriching her vocabulary. They would have tenuous conversations together and then practice reading and translating from old newspapers and books. It was certainly no easy ride, as she had half expected it might be.

Willem started each morning's session with a short exam and revision on the work they had done the previous day. His battle cry, uttered with the characteristic grin , was " Test Means Rest ! "

Jade took to secret studying in the evening to try and thwart this regular morning hurdle.

After a few days they decided to conduct all simple conversations in Afrikaans. It certainly concentrated the mind when you got no food if you couldn't remember the word for it.

Food itself was another tricky issue Jade discovered. She found she was unable to keep to regular mealtimes. Having been used to eating when she was hungry, or when food was available in abundance, she had no appetite when the couple ate and yet raided the larder during the early hours of the morning. Several times she guiltily made forays into the nearby scrubland to see if she could locate any of the beloved tsama melons. Her digestion however, welcomed solid cooked food back with open arms. She had no recurrence of the trouble in that department that she had encountered on first eating desert cuisine.

When her brain had been battered into submission by Willem, Jade was allowed some free time, but not too much. Then it was time to continue.

She was called into the kitchen and they all sat round the rough table to discuss some aspect of current affairs. Listening to their radio, their window on the world, the couple were up to date on most matters of importance.

Alida started Jade off with simple introductions to the system of administration and government in their country. How Namibia was in fact under the control of their neighbour, the Republic of South Africa, and the history of their current situation. How the South West Africa Peoples Organisation had been constantly campaigning for the country's independence since 1961 and the terror tactics which stood alongside its negotiators.

When she felt Jade had mastered the basic background they went deeper. Alida told her about UN Security Council Resolution 435 of 1978 which set out a framework for negotiation between all sides. That had been three years ago and they still appeared no nearer to a settlement. She left out the cruel blow which the conflict had dealt them personally, wiping out half the family.

Despite their years the couple had sharp agile minds and enjoyed their discussions. As soon as Jade had been given the relevant facts about an issue she was able to form an opinion and decide how she felt. If she disagreed with a point or felt strongly, she marshalled her ideas and evidence and went on the offensive. Occasionally her cut and thrust had the opposition diving for cover.

Once they had exhausted topics within their continent the discussions went world wide, with issues such as rising ocean levels, destruction of South

American rain forests and the plight of the Australian aborigine. Nothing was taboo.

Time flew by in these debating sessions, Jade finding herself eager for knowledge and the skill of how to use it. Quite unlike the old Jade in the schoolroom, she mused. *All I ever wanted was the freedom of the desert.....now I've had it and everything else seems to matter all of a sudden*

Quite often it would only be the setting sun which brought a close to their discussions. Then they felt exhausted, as if they had put the world to rights by themselves.

Evenings belonged to Jade. The second night she found buried treasure in the form of an easel, paper and pencils in a corner of the shop. They were caked in dust, unmoved or disturbed for years.

Jade hurried back to ask Alida if it was all right to take them out.

The old woman flushed heavily at the request and her hands trembled slightly at the sink. She was glad of the dusk which hid her. They had belonged to her eldest son, a present on his twelfth birthday, a memory from rosy days in a dim and distant past.. Many hours had been spent hunched over the framework, tongue hanging out in rapt concentration. The results were never going to hang alongside Van Gogh, but were precious to them.

" Yes of course you can, " Alida gathered herself together. " Do the thing good to be used again. It'll need a good clean and polish beforehand, mind you. There's an old cloth in the cupboard and I expect father can lay his hands on a tin of wax or something." Willem stirred uncomfortably on the verandah, wondering how the hell he was supposed to know where there might be one.

The easel was lovingly restored that evening. Jade cleaned it meticulously and Willem put a couple of drops of oil on the aching hinges. It was made of good quality hardwood and shone up nicely. A block of paper still stood beside it and after she had discarded the top three sheets, which had yellowed and curled up with age, the rest were quite usable.

Proudly she took it out onto the verandah and then sat in front of it for nearly an hour, waiting for inspiration. Nothing came and the paper was returned unsullied. The artist was returned disappointed. She consoled herself by listening to Bizet's Carmen, Willem's favourite, on the cassette recorder. She fiddled about with it, changing the batteries as the sound wobbled downhill, and an idea was born. Works well.......even comes with a microphone and stuff........might even do the trick.

H had his food delivered on a metal plate every evening together with a wooden fork, which was the least dangerous implement they could give him to eat it with. Jade regarded this as her task, to prevent him distressing the old couple, and to enable her to keep a regular check on him.

She set the stew down beside him. As she did so, her hair fell forward and the ends of it skimmed across his face. It left a fleeting aftershock of clean, close freshness.

Jade straightened up, allowing the tips of her fingers to trail faintly along his forearm. The she was out of the garage and the door was locked again.

The effects of adrenalin squeezed his heart tight, and there was the slightest undercurrent of an impossible thought.

Jade spent all her nights by the tree, under the stars. She found it hopeless to try and sleep inside. No matter how tired she was, slumber always eluded her.

Torn Ear came to see her every night, without fail. Each time she grew more confident, staying longer and seeming more relaxed. Jade loved the hours they spent together, even being tempted to accompany her on a hunt when the idea became apparent on one occasion. In the end she declined reluctantly, believing rightly that it might entice her back into the desert.

She also toyed with the idea of introducing the leopard to Alida and Willem. That idea died the death fairly quickly too. She wanted Torn Ear to regard every human, with the obvious exception, as the enemy. That was the only way to keep her at a safe distance from them. Hunters would value her as a trophy, poachers would take her fine velvet pelt to hang round some rich, powdered and probably wrinkled, neck. No, she must respect them with a fear of the unknown.

Days settled into a routine, of sorts, It was like a sort of half way house. She was back in the civilised world, but then again she wasn't. The spectre of the visit from the authorities faded into the middle distance, taking with it the trauma, excitement and desperate uncertainty which it would herald. Deep down inside she knew this was a false existence and would really rather have made the complete transition at one stroke. However, this is what there was and she would have to make do.

On one of her expeditions into the far flung reaches of the unexplored building, Jade discovered a large carton of paint tins. Not the sort she could use on the easel but the sort she could use on walls and ceilings. It was a modest repayment, but for the moment it was the only way she could think of to show her gratitude.

Convincing the occupants that a coat of paint was in order was easy. The colour was a different matter.

The carton had a variety of pigments but they were all stark and brash, from pure white through red, green, yellow and blue to matt black. To aid a decision, Jade put on a display of various mixes and painted pieces of card with each new colour so it could be held against the existing wall to see the effect.

The old couple were transformed into a pair of newly-weds, planning the decor of their first home. It took forever. In the end, they left the painted samples in each room, deciding to sleep on it and see what they felt like in the morning. They retired, talking ten to the dozen in excited voices.

Jade was exhausted. She knelt in the middle of the floor with debris strewn all around, as if she had sat on an exploding pile of rubbish and triggered it off.

Rather belatedly, she hoped she could remember what to mix with what to produce a particular shade. As an aide memoire she painted one brush stroke of each concoction on the wall - it was getting a new coat anyway - and scribbled the ingredients underneath.

Recovery was a young woman lying flat out on the still warm boards of the verandah.

The moon would be full again tonight, lighting up the heavens and earth with the help of the stars. Like the old days in the desert, Jade let herself be completely absorbed by the soothing light and unhurried movements in the sky. Time meant nothing. Her thoughts drifted into hazy oblivion until she was totally at ease.

She was held in that delicious space between alert consciousness and sleep, unknown nerve endings in the brain twinkling to keep her mind just receptive. Then she was with her friend, could see the leopard as if she were standing on the verandah. Torn Ear was satisfied, her belly comfortably full, and she was content.

As clear as day, a picture of the leopard appeared in Jade's mind. It was so close she could taste the familiar musky scent.

Moving slowly, so as not to disturb the image in her head, Jade retrieved the easel and set it up with her back to the moon, catching all the available light.

Shape and perspective flowed from her hand without a conscious thought. Drawing skills returned from the old life with a vengeance. She mixed colour and shade, and then added emotion and feeling. Hues were those which exactly matched the glorious variety displayed briefly in the Kalahari sunset. Like a master craftsman, she softly rubbed the crayon colours together where they needed it, creating to her own standards of perfection.

Only dawn brought the onset of intense fatigue. Jade rubbed tired eyes, giving herself purple mascara before she realised it. She lay down the worn crayon and closed the tin box that was its home, with a gentle click. Then she simply headed for the nearest shade, which happened to be directly under the verandah, and fell asleep.

Standing on the easel was a piece of cartridge paper with the portrait of a leopard on it. The cat was sitting bolt upright and was held by the golden rays of a setting sun. It was the picture Jade had thought was gone when she turned and looked from the other side of a desert track.

In the bottom right hand corner was a barely noticeable imperfection. The colour had been smudged by a single tear which had dried on the paper.

Boards creaked and crackled under measured steps. Willem looked up and down the verandah, rasping the back of his bony hand with an unshaven chin.

After an unusually long lie in, deliberating over painted squares of cardboard, the committee had reached a decision upon which they were unanimous. Now, where was the decorator ?

He had already looked around the tree where he knew she spent most of her nights. Then he had checked the bedrooms, just on the offchance that she was learning the ways of the world again. Nothing. Now he was a little concerned.

Willem walked down to the far end of the verandah just in time to miss Jade rolling out from underneath his very feet.

" Looking for anything in particular ? " she grinned. The old man twisted round on his heels.

" Only for a lazy...." he paused in mid sentence, thoughts cut off as he caught sight of the portrait. " This is marvellous. Did you.......of course you did. Where did you learn to do work like this ? "

" Nowhere, " replied a slightly embarrassed Jade, colouring beneath her tan. She hadn't intended the picture for show. Indeed she hadn't really looked at it properly, especially not in daylight. " I just felt like putting something down on paper. That was the first thing that came into my head."

Jade craned her neck over Willem's shoulder to get a better look. Even though she was the artist it took her breath away. There could have been a miniature Torn Ear sitting on the paper. It was the sort of picture that was so full of life that it could grab you as you walked past.

" Is that the leopard you told us about ? " Alida had joined them and was also admiring the work.

Jade nodded, stepping back to look from a different angle.

" I think you must love her a lot, " continued the canny old woman. " I do not think it is possible to make such a picture unless you have real feeling for what you are doing. "

Alida stopped her train of thought there. Both she and Willem had seen the pug marks around the tree and knew that Torn Ear was nearby. Notwithstanding natural fear of the species, they would have liked to see the leopard who had linked herself with Jade, but had no intention of forcing the issue. If it happened, then it happened. If not, well then that was the way it had to be.

Besides which, the presence of Torn Ear finally confirmed in their minds the validity of the events which had occurred in the desert.

Jade let out a self conscious yawn and groaned. She had had quite enough of being the centre of attention.

" Standing round here is not going to get the house painted. I think there is some work to be done. And, " she grinned, " if you two think you are going to sip cool drinks and watch me sweat, you've got another thing coming. I may be doing the painting but there are floors and walls to be washed and prepared, brushes to be cleaned and furniture to be moved. So let's get to it. "

The old couple pulled silent faces at Jade behind her back and then burst out laughing. She turned round in time to see Willem tugging a non existent forelock and smiling sweetly. She tossed her head back like a haughty film star and pranced inside.

*****

The bucket of filthy water was cold now. For nearly the first time in his life H had been glad to wash. The soap was hard as marble but had lathered eventually, eating its way into layers of grime. Then he had dried himself on the rough towel that Jade had provided, not at all easy with one limb cuffed to a pole.

Outside, Jade left him for about twenty minutes after the sounds of splashing had ceased. Then she pushed the creaking garage door open again. The padlock lay on the ground at her feet. In her hand was a different, much smaller, key.

H was lying down, as usual. He didn't speak when she entered, closing the door behind her so that only a narrow shaft of sunshine entered, giving a dim background light inside the building.

She sat beside him. He had taken his shirt off as far as the wrist of the cuffed hand so it hid the steel bracelet, showing how inactivity wastes muscle and encourages the belly to expand.

The young woman ran her fingertips along his upper arm, bringing body hair to attention and eyes to wide open.

" Tell me, " she whispered in a husky voice. " Did you like what you did in the storm ? Do you like to do it like that ? "

Jade moved her hand onto his chest, massaging gently and then letting it travel provocatively southwards. She could feel his heart pounding.

" Tell me, " she repeated, " tell me how you felt then. " The hand travelled further.

His mouth split in a sudden realisation, showing dirty yellow teeth. His breathing quickened, " Is that what you want me to do ? "

Jade made no reply, but got up and walked round to where the handcuff was attached to the stanchion. She knelt down, inserted the key and twisted until she felt the pressure release the cuff. She held the cuff in her hand and he watched as she started to pull it loose. Jade lowered her head, letting her hair fall forward over her face like a shield.

" You struggled so much, like a vixen on heat, " H started. " I had to hold you really tight. " The cuff continued its slow release. Not quick enough for Harry. Perhaps he had to go stronger.

" I never raped any girl as good as you before, you hated me so much. I like the fight. "

The reaction he got was certainly not what he had been led to expect. Jade spun the key out and clicked the cuff closed again round the solid metal. In a flash she jumped back out of reach and punched the air with a clenched fist.

" YES ! " she shouted with a savage joy. " Got you at last you bastard. Did you honestly imagine.........? " She laughed again out loud.

Then she ran to the door and flung it open. Outside stood the old couple.

Alida held the pistol firmly in both hands, pointing fair and square at the figure on the floor. " Just in case, " she said, " just in case. "

Beside her stood Willem. He held something of far greater use. A modern Sony cassette recorder with a remote microphone which had been placed in the open doorway, which Jade was now winding up round her wrist.

" Picks up sound really well. Carmen never sounded this good, " explained Willem in a matter of fact voice. " Tell you what, I'll give you a quick demonstration. " He rewound the tape and played it back.

" Rather good don't you think ? I'm sure I can think of some people who would love to get their hands on this "

The full implication of recent events dawned on H. Without a confession, detectives might have had a hard time making a rape charge stick in court. There was no physical evidence and certainly no witnesses. Only her word against his.

Now there was a taped confession and two witnesses to it. In a black fury he hurled the bucket at them through the open door. Jade dodged out of the way and it landed safely, spraying the contents over the cracked stones in the yard.

She leapt back and pulled the door shut, closing the padlock with a satisfyingly solid sound. From inside came a stream of shouted obscenities and threats.

Jade linked arms with both the old people and walked towards the shade of the house.

*****

Five days of back breaking labour with a brush was enough to test the hardiest of bodies. Jade sat against the rough trunk of her tree and massaged her aching neck. The ceilings were certainly the worst she thought, and she would have speckled hair for the rest of her life. Still, just the clearing up to do now, and then that was the end of it.

She stood up. Better get on with it. She patted the earth at the base of the tree. The pistol was better off under there. Wrapped in a strong paper bag, and then in a plastic one, it would survive. She knew Willem hated it, but they had both been shown how to use it and one day they might need it. It was madness to be out here on their own without one.

Jade started to walk back to the house. When she got to the garage she could see there was a vehicle parked in the yard.

It was a dusty little yellow truck. The cab was enclosed, but the sides consisted merely of thick wire mesh, with a solid door at the rear. On the roof was a single small blue light.

As she watched, a tall figure in blue fatigues got out.

CHAPTER

TEN

It had taken over a year to finally sort things out. Now she was standing on the threshold of the farm, wondering if she could bring herself to say goodbye to it, for she wanted an education and she wanted it somewhere different.

At long last Oupa was beginning to look like the grandfather she remembered. With the help of the tall Sergeant, Jade gently told him the whole story, easing him through the difficult and painful parts. She left nothing out. Better to get the entire mess out in the open to start with, rather than hit him with another revelation later on.

He had gone downhill fast in the years she had been away, the malaria feeding off his stress and worry. Rock bottom had been hit a long time ago but her return marked the start of the long climb back. He never once mentioned the circumstances of her departure - he was just happy, no, incredulous, to find she was alive and back. In the back of his mind lurked the spectre of guilt that it was his intransigence that had contributed to it in the first place. He couldn't believe the changes in his granddaughter though. She had left him a petulant, troublesome adolescent, and returned a young woman of steel with more life experience than anyone had a right to expect, or indeed should have to endure.

After that it was a long slow process to nurse both him and his farm back to health.

With no adequate leadership or control, the establishment had fallen to its knees. The animals were rangy and hardly cared for at all. Huge tracts of land were being left ungrazed because the hands couldn't be bothered to move the herds from one massive area to the next. There was no breeding programme and consequently no young stock, apart from a few unplanned occurrences. Many of the workers had simply left, walked off in typical African fashion with one sack, no cares and not worrying too much where the next meal was coming from or if they could carry over their pension contributions. Those that remained milked the place dry for their own benefit.

Jade went through the farm like a firework rocket out of control.

First she encountered the household staff. She fired three out of the remaining four immediately, for definite attitude problems, and promptly doubled the wages of the survivor. This made her " good boss lady " at once and as such she was apparently entitled to receive gossip and hearsay about the rest of the employees.

Carefully listening to the outpouring of rhetoric, Jade separated the wheat from the chaff, deciding as best she could what was malicious and what was truth. Armed with a little knowledge she ventured forth into the farm itself.

The first two stockmen she found were getting nicely drunk from a bottle without a label on it, whilst participating in a card game with a giggling young maid from the staff kitchens. Judging from the lack of clothing, she was losing.

Jade grabbed the bottle and flung it towards the far wall of the building. It smashed in an explosion of tiny fragments, leaving a dark liquid stain on the brickwork. Then she gave all three their marching orders. Such a forceful white woman was a real novelty, and when they weren't quite quick enough Jade surprised them further by performing the ceremony of the laying on of hands.

She soon found that the older ones were mostly glad to see order being restored. Many had lived and worked there for years. Even if they wanted to, there was nowhere else they could go.

When the purge was complete, Jade found she had about half the workforce left. She picked out two, those that appeared to command most respect amongst the others, and made them foremen. The she told them that they would be expected to work hard enough to make up for the loss of the others, and because of that they would receive those wages as well, as a bonus.

With that, she left them to it. For the time being she did not have the first idea how to run a farm and she had other things to worry about. As long as there were obvious improvements to be seen then she was happy.

Tony still suffered from bouts of malaria which had got worse during her long absence. The strain of coping with his granddaughter's disappearance and his abandonment of any form of medication hadn't helped the situation either.

After a couple of weeks Jade decided it would be safe enough to leave him for a day while she went into the capital, Windhoek, to, as she put it, " sort a couple of things out ".

The only vehicle left at the farm was an ancient old Toyota Landcruiser, veteran of many expeditions. Taking Molo as driver - he and Emmy had survived the purge - they rattled down the gravel road leading to the city.

Not counting time taken to fix the obligatory puncture the journey took about three hours. Jade left vehicle and driver at a garage on the edge of the city with instructions to wait for her there, and get the old tyre replaced. *Funny how things have changed between us....before, I used to have to do what he said.....now I've got to get used to telling him what to do......guess he thinks I'm all grown up now and taken Oupa's place. Suppose he's half right......and I never intend to grow up....* She walked the short distance into the centre, down Republiek and into Kaiser, the main street.

Nestling in a flat valley between the Auas and Eros mountains, Windhoek stands like a flower in bloom, sheltering in the corner of a rockery. It has a chequered history, and this is reflected in the colourful and almost continental atmosphere that assaults the unwary visitor, used as he is to endless rolling desert and bush land.

Old German colonial buildings stand alongside modern hotels and department stores. Down wide pavements, elegant white women rub shoulders with native Herero women, resplendent in their headgear and Victorian 'mission' dresses, their traditional garb.

The European types, whatever their exact origin, move at roughly double the speed of the other ethnic groups, always in a rush, dodging round the ambling tribeswomen and seeking refuge in expensive air conditioned stores. All ignore the crippled beggar sitting at the entrance to a shop, holding out the eternal bony hand.

Fierce sunlight bounces onto the paving slabs everywhere. Only those areas under the shady overhanging shopfronts are patronised by shoppers. The other side of the road is completely empty, baking the cars with their window blinds pulled down in a vain attempt to stay cool.

Jade sat, cross legged, on the thin patchy grass of Dr Verwoerd Park at the upper end of Kaiser Street. This modest area of green, in a sea of concrete, was amply supplied with trees for pleasant shade. In consequence, she could see four or five coloured men stretched out and fast asleep nearby. They were oblivious to the world and the world ignored them.

It was obviously a common practice, for as midday drew nearer more of the prime spots became occupied with slumbering forms. They had to fill their day with something - none of them would have jobs to go to that afternoon.

She considered her plan of action. The most important task came first, for if that failed, so would everything else. In the pocket of her new yellow shorts she fingered the pouch which contained the stones with fire inside them.

Jade got up and started down the main street, exploring all the bustling alleys which led off it.

The third shop looked like the best bet so far. The first two were wrong. They were shiny, plush and had very superior assistants who had invited her to take a seat by trays of jewellery.

This looked better. The nameplate said simply, " M.Herbert " and underneath it, " Gemstones ". It had one small front window with a couple of displays in it, and it was squashed between an Indian drapery establishment and an open fronted ice cream bar. She pushed the tired wooden door open.

It was dark and cool inside the shop. There was a glass counter at the far end, with a door to the right hand side of it. Perched on a stool behind the counter was a rather plump man who was examining something with the aid of an eyepiece. Without looking up he motioned her to sit. Jade looked round, saw no chair, and continued to stand.

" Terribly sorry, " he said, jamming onto his nose the pair of glasses that were hanging round his neck. " I was just in the middle of that one. Couldn't really stop or I'd lose the picture."

Max Herbert stepped down from the stool and repositioned the spectacles. He was a little man, somewhat past his prime. The shirt and tie were a bit shabby, the thin cardigan in need of replacement. There was no air conditioning in his shop, instead, a ceiling fan rotated lazily when it felt like it.

In front of him he saw a striking young woman, standing awkwardly like a guilty schoolgirl. Her skin was the colour of polished mahogany, but she had amazingly blonde hair which was long and brushed back in the simplest of styles. There was nothing on her feet. She returned his gaze, inch for inch.

" Well, " he continued, " what can I do for you ?" Beneath the acquired South African accent Jade detected a twinge of upper class British.

She walked up to the counter and placed a single stone onto the worn scratched glass. It was about middle of the range as far as size was concerned, she had ones smaller and ones bigger. Jade had chosen it deliberately because it was the one with the least colour. It was opaque and grey, and she considered it to be the least valuable. The others stayed firmly in their soft pouch, in her pocket, out of sight.

Max swallowed hard, as the spectre of temptation reared its ugly head again. Without needing to be told, he knew exactly what the situation was here. This woman had found a stone somewhere and now wanted to sell, under the counter as it were. That was why she had come to him. No other dealer round here would touch it, because as every merchant in this trade knows, all diamonds found in the country automatically belong to the state. They have to be surrendered immediately, there is no choice. Anyone found engaging in IDB, illicit diamond buying, faces tough penalties.

As always, there are two sides to a coin. Max knew several people in Jo'burg and Cape Town who looked forward to receiving small padded packages with 'South-West' postmarks once in a while. They never saw him and he had no idea who they were, but the money always appeared in his undeclared bank account.

The dealer walked quickly to the door, pulling the blind down and turning the cardboard sign round so that it read 'Closed / Gesluit'.

Then he trotted back to the counter, picked up the stone and disappeared into the back room. Jade waited.

" Come in, come in. Always nice to have an audience." The voice wafted back to her from the depths of a dimly lit room.

Max already had the stone mounted in a holder and was looking at it through a huge magnifying glass which he had swung round on its stand to get the best position. He ignored Jade as she clicked the door shut behind her.

This little back room was his own private world. Max Herbert was fascinated by diamonds, and always had been. Educated in England at a second rate public school, he had shown no aptitude for anything, causing his aged parents to despair as they pumped good money after bad into the establishment, term after term.

Tragically a car crash claimed both of them shortly before Max was due to leave and find a real job. As the only child, although now just an adult, he inherited their meagre savings and then sold the house.

That was enough to pay for the passage down to Cape Town where he took a lowly position with De Beers. Over the following years he moved from job to job, scrimping and saving, all the time learning about the love of his life.

Finally there was enough under the mattress to buy this lease in Windhoek. He would have preferred somewhere else, anywhere else, but it was better than nowhere.

That was twenty years ago, and he was still here. He was a canny buyer of stones, knowing most of everything there was to know about the lumps of carbon, but the big break had always eluded him.

Max shifted the thick magnifying lens a fraction and then increased the power of the light source. Every new stone was a thrill and a challenge, totally absorbing him for as long as it took to peer into its depths and get to know it intimately.

It was a good ten minutes before he spoke. " Low quality industrial grey. Not worth my while to take it off your hands. IDB and all that. Sorry. " Although buying illicit diamonds was indeed a crime, it was on the same moral level as defrauding a large bank. Nobody got hurt and nobody really lost anything, the only difficulty being if you were caught.

" I might be able to lay my hands on another, " said Jade, allowing a hint of certainty to creep into her voice. " Would that make it worth your while ?"

Max pulled a cord hanging from the ceiling and the room was flooded with light. He had fenced verbally with countless would-be sellers over the years and knew that Jade was bargaining from a position of strength.

" If it's the same as that one, then I need about twenty. How full are your pockets? "

Jade rummaged through the hidden pouch. She knew each one by touch, not needing to see the stone. She removed another. Almost the best, but not quite, and handed it to the still seated Max.

He held it up to the ceiling light, fully expecting a foggy brown interior. Instead, miniature shafts of rainbow fire fought with each other as the stone was twisted, Some appeared to launch themselves out of their cage at the observer, only to disappear as they reached the outermost layers of pure transparent carbon.

With an imperceptible tremble Max fitted it to the holder and plunged the room into semi-darkness again.

" It's a fancy " he said after a few minutes, but more to himself than Jade. " A fancy diamond has a distinct body colour, this one is violet. Red, blue and green are the rarest, with yellow, orange and your violet here, fairly common."

" Diamonds can vary from being colourless to black and all combinations in between, " he continued, engrossed in the exploration of the new world in his holder. Gone were the short staccato sentences, a relic of his sheltered upbringing, replaced by a monologue which the listener found fascinating.

" They can be transparent, translucent or opaque. Those used as gems are mostly transparent and colourless, but they are the rarest. Most gem diamonds are tinged with yellow somewhere. Ah, yes, here it is, " Max shifted position on his stool, " a faint ridge of yellow, practically invisible.

Most industrial diamonds, on the other hand, are grey or brown and are translucent or opaque. The better quality ones may grade imperceptibly into poor quality gems. "

Jade kept quiet during the pauses. She sensed that to interrupt or ask a question might bring him back into the present. There was some useful information being cast around here, especially considering she still had a pocketful of stones to rattle.

" The very high refractive power of a diamond gives it its extraordinary brilliance. A properly cut diamond will return a greater amount of light to the eye of the observer than will a gem of less refractive power, and will thus appear more brilliant.

The high dispersion gives diamonds their fire, which is caused by the separation of white light into the colours of the spectrum as it passes through the stone. "

The dealer stopped abruptly, pulled on the main light and leaned back in his chair, weighing up the considerations.

" I will take them both off your hands, " he said, scribbling with a pencil on a tear off pad in front of him.

Looking at the figure he had written, Jade thought it was a huge sum, having no idea what the cut stone would eventually fetch. Considering it, she had the overwhelming urge to accept the offer and run, get out with what she had and be done with it.

Common sense slowed her down. His offer was bound to be the very lowest he thought he could get away with.

She reached over, took the stub of pencil from the top of the pad where he had left it, crossed out his figures and inserted ones of her own, double the original value.

" Non negotiable. Or I'm going elsewhere with the rest. " She prodded the side of her pocket, making the contents jump around. Her insides had turned to jelly - *if this doesn't work then the farm's had it* - but the voice was steel.

Max looked at her closely. Not such a pushover, he thought. Still, even this price should leave him with a handsome profit once the credit transfer was made in Cape Town. Besides, unless those were lumps of quartz she was jangling, she had more to sell and he wanted to keep her sweet so she didn't feel the need to try any other dealer.

He unlocked a drawer of the desk he was sitting at, took out a bundle and started to peel notes off.

*****

A day's hard toil and a good deal of head scratching saw the brand new air conditioning unit fitted into the outside wall of Oupa's study. Within seconds of the noise settling to a gentle drone it was pumping icy blasts of air into the room. Outside, drops of expelled moisture fell onto the sandy ground, making a pitted damp patch.

A passing sand lizard cottoned on to this new feature of his territory and soon learned to catch some of the droplets in his upturned mouth before they hit the ground. He was often to be seen standing there, head skywards, like a worshipping member of the faithful before his idol.

Tony was over the moon. At last he had somewhere cool to retire to when the Kalahari heat and his illness got too much for him. The heat sometimes overpowered him like a physical force, pressing down on his chest as if trying to stop his breathing. In the new cool of his favourite room heat was banished, making him feel like a winner to start with.

Of course, it was all in the mind, but the mind is a powerful creature. Feeling good gave him an edge on the disease that periodically racked his body. Determination to control it returned, and he started to take the medication that Jade had obtained for him at the state hospital in Windhoek North.

The best medicine was the farm. He started to take an interest in it again, giving him purpose once more.

The wad of dog eared bank notes was soon gone. It had served to buy the unit, and to pay for several essential items round the farm, not least being the new wage bill which came in regular as clockwork, once a week. Jade reckoned she would have to make regular visits to M.Herbert Esq. until the farm started to pay for itself again.

On this score, at least, she had no worries for the time being. The stock of stones was more than ample and she was quite prepared to sacrifice them all in order to get things right here.

There were at least the same number again, in a cave, far away.

Weeks rolled by, and the girl from the desert gradually got used to life with people again. Well almost.

She still slept out in the open whenever she could, only using a bedroom when Oupa nagged so much that she had to give in. Even then she stretched out on the floor, leaving the bed well alone. There was no way she was going to sleep on that thing. It felt as if she were going to drown when her body sank into the mattress.

Sometimes Jade would drive far out along gravel tracks until she was completely alone, say on a ridge overlooking the boundaries of the Kalahari. Then she would spend the night dozing and staring deep into the heavens, letting her mind wander back to far off times. It was only then that she realised how much she missed the independence of survival, the beauty of the days, and the companionship of a leopard.

Occasionally during these nights she could feel Torn Ear close to her, although they might be separated by many miles. That comforted her immensely, for she knew then that her friend was well, and vice versa. Nevertheless it was a wrench to return to the farm.

Everyone usually turned out to watch the homecoming. She drove the battleship grey Mercedes 280 like Boadicea in her chariot. It was an open topped old warhorse, with tyres slightly wider than normal, and hugged the dirt tracks with a vengeance. Never encountering any other form of motorised transport in her travels, Jade drove with her foot flat down, jinking and swerving with acquired skill to avoid dunes and suchlike obstacles.

She delighted in sending up clouds of swirling sand from her tyres as she turned and braked. When the car finally came to a standstill in the big empty yard, she covered everything in a shower of sand, to much cheering from the assembled workforce. There would have been less chaos from the rotors of a landing helicopter.

Being of German origin, the car was naturally called 'The Hun' and used up two more diamonds in her collection.

Jade proudly showed it off to the tall Sergeant, Kris Alexander, who completely spoiled the occasion by mentioning the mere formality of a driving licence. Jade opened her mouth to protest her skill, and then shut it again without speaking when she remembered that the driving lessons given secretly to her by Molo might not cut too much ice.

So she swallowed her pride, took the minimum number of lessons and went legal. All to the disgust of The Hun, who never realised that so much time could be spent in the first three gears.

*****

The trial brought them all down to earth with a bump.

H looked thin and broken, sitting behind the bars of the dock with his uniformed escort. His head was close cropped again and the beard was gone. Even the pallor of his skin had turned to an ashen grey which looked ill and diseased. He stared at the ground between his feet the whole time.

Jade sat with Tony and their counsel in the front row, facing the judge. Every so often she stole a glance at the apparently defeated man, but try as she might, she could not squeeze an ounce of pity out of her soul for him.

At the request of counsel, Jade wore a pair of soft shoes while in the courtroom. These she removed the instant she was outside. She had also equipped herself with a small wardrobe of outfits which had interchangeable skirts and blouses, so that it appeared she wore a different ensemble every day.

Two days before the trial commenced Jade drove out to collect Willem and Alida from their home and brought them back to the farm. Kris went with her, primarily to go through their statements again with them while they were still in their own environment and relaxed. He also went through the line of cross examination they might expect from the defending counsel and briefed them on their responses.

The old couple hadn't left their home in years. Nevertheless, they shut the door firmly behind them and clambered into The Hun with only slight misgivings.

Alida clamped her little suitcase firmly onto her lap and shut her eyes tight. She refused to open them again until they were stationary in the yard at the farm.

Willem, on the other hand, opened his eyes quite soon after they got under way and kept them like that for the duration. Jade drove sedately, by her standards anyway, avoiding large potholes and thoughtfully slowing down for hairpin bends. She made a mental note to take Willem out on his own one day soon to show him exactly what this beast could do. She had a sneaking suspicion that he would enjoy himself immensely.

They now sat in the witnesses waiting room with Kris, outside the main court in Windhoek.

Jade spent the first day and a half in the witness box outlining the story of her time in the desert, in response to guiding questions put by her counsel. When she had completed her evidence, Tony was called to furnish the court with some details that she did not know, but the limelight belonged to Jade.

She soon had her entire audience enthralled, despite leaving out all the details of Torn Ear. She had no wish to test their powers of imagination by trying to get them to believe she had lived and hunted with a full grown leopard. It might very easily prejudice the rest of her evidence. In consequence, she hadn't even told her counsel about it.

Sitting in the body of the court was a young reporter for 'The Star', South Africa's largest daily newspaper. The lowliest of a small staff in the Windhoek office, he had the task of staking out the court and giving the results of any newsworthy trials. At best he might get a couple of lines at the bottom of a middle page, which would be attributed to 'a staff reporter' anyway.

He was doodling on a copy of yesterday's paper right now, making spiky little star patterns round the line of print on the front page which announced that the paper had been established in 1887.

To his credit, it was only ten minutes into Jade's evidence before he realised that here was something more than the average boring case. He flipped open the big chunky pad that went everywhere with him, and started to record verbatim the words of the startling young woman.

Day Two saw a healthy sprinkling of reporters in the court. They could spot a story as the vulture senses a kill.

On her way in that day, Jade had been accosted by a woman reporter with a microphone whose wire disappeared mysteriously into the depths of her clothing. She thrust the weapon under Jade's chin, demanding the answer to some spurious question. Tony pushed her aside, none too gently, and they took their seats.

By the time the court rose on that second day the woman had managed to acquire a television crew, and was eagerly waiting for Jade's departure. This was a good 'Robinson Crusoe' story, well worth fighting for.

It was a battle for them to reach The Hun, the two rather elderly court officials on duty at the doors being no match for a hardened film crew.

Kris was furious when he found out what had happened. He called his Captain to get permission to take a vehicle "off the road" to escort Jade and Tony from their hotel each morning and back again. There was no way even

The Hun could make the journey to Windhoek and back each day in a decent time from the farm.

The escort helped, but even then they had to go in and out via a back door, sneaking in as if they were the guilty parties.

Alida and Willem had the room alongside Jade and Tony. They had never experienced the luxury of a place like the Kalahari Sands Hotel. Cool marble floors, delicious air conditioning, sumptuous bedding and linens. Everything you could possibly want, simply by picking up the phone. The old couple were like school children on holiday. They took at least three baths a day in the huge sunken bath, becoming almost invisible in mountains of scented foam.

All their meals were sent up to the room, where they took most of them in bed, while flicking through TV channels on the remote control as if it was a game of space invaders.

When they tired of all this relaxing, they would race each other up and down in the double set of elevators. They were always very proper and sedate in reception, when getting in, but when the lift doors opened on the eighth floor they would crane their heads round and break into fits of giggling at the sight of the other doing the same thing.

On the fourth day, Alida and Willem were called to give their evidence.

Standing in the witness box Willem's hands started to tremble slightly. He took a firm hold on the bookstand in front of him and was quite relieved when the whole thing didn't start to wobble.

Prosecuting counsel was speaking to him now. The old man looked straight at him and tried to remember to address his replies to the jury, as he had been briefed.

His anxiety and trepidation were very soon banished in a gush of relief. The state appointed counsel for H rose, and after a brief consultation with his client, announced that his plea was being changed to one of guilty.

A ripple of hushed remarks broke out in the courtroom at this revelation, quickly silenced as the judge spoke.

" Let the record show that the defendant has changed his plea to guilty." He rearranged some unseen papers on his desk. " The defendant will stand. I intend to sentence you now." A small buzz of hushed voices ran round the court and pens could be heard scratching on cheap notepaper.

" Harry de Beer, " H looked sullenly down at the floor, like a wicked dog about to receive its beating, " you have now pleaded guilty to the rape and injury of a young woman. It is apparent that from the very outset of your mission into the desert your intention was to do just that. Lost in the middle of the harshest of environments, what she needed was help and assistance to survive,"

Jade permitted herself an inward smile. How little he knew, she needed nothing of the sort.

" instead she was assaulted in the cruellest of manners and it is my belief that you would have killed her, had she not been so able to defend herself."

Wonder why he never mentioned Torn Ear.........suppose he thought that the idea would make even him appear ridiculous and less believable........wonder where she is now.....right this second. Her mind bounced her hundreds of miles, just for an instant, and she smiled.

" Throughout this trial you have shown no remorse or regret, and indeed, evidence has shown that you promised to do the same again if you had the opportunity.

I intend to see to it that such a chance does not come your way for a long time. You will go to prison for fourteen years."

H looked up and stared slowly round the court, his facial expression betraying nothing. He fixed his glare on each in turn, on Alida, and Willem, and Tony and finally Jade.

" All of you who have need will remember me, " he spat out. The two warders grabbed his arms and pulled him round to face the door and concrete spiral staircase leading down.

" You will see me again," he screamed over his shoulder as he was pushed roughly through the open steel door, " you will see me again before I kill you."

The convict was hustled down the rough stairs, still struggling. As they spiralled down he would alternately catch the basic ironwork of the railings to his right, then smash into the untreated stonework to the other side on his rebound. By the time H was bundled into 'The Tank' as it was called, he had a collection of grazes and bruises on both arms and shoulders.

The old court only had one big detention room for all the prisoners due to be tried each day and today there was just the one occupant.

Cold damp stonework ate through his thin shirt as H sank into the darkened corner. It was completely silent, just a man and his thoughts, and a long straight road ahead.

Gradually rage subsided into fatigue and tolerance. There was no other way around it. Anger would make the time last longer and there was some time to get through. He had stared at this route before, but never with such a long stretch ahead of him.

H lifted a weary head from between his hands, raising it to look at the dim light cast down from the ceiling, the source shielded behind thick resistant glass.

" Revenge should be eaten cold, " hissed the man, staring upwards. With that he lifted both arms above his head and clenched his shoulder muscles until they shivered with pain and exhaustion. Then he let out a roar that penetrated the blocks of stone, making the warder look up from his paper outside, and sank back into the corner.

The stroke of a clerk's pen that afternoon decreed that prisoner de Beer H, Identiteitsnommer 66.3.16 would be transferred to Pretoria Central Prison, to serve his sentence under the care of the Republic of South Africa Prisons Service. The reason for the transfer was the seriousness of the crime and the lack of space any nearer.

All next day they travelled. Down highway B1 from Windhoek, through Mariental, Keetmanshoop and finally to the police station in Upington. The border of Namibia was marked only by a large white stone at the roadside which welcomed the traveller to South Africa. There were no other formalities and no barrier to halt in front of.

Sunlight streamed in the tiny barred window throughout the entire journey, but the man in the individual compartment in the cellular van slept, jammed against the door, arms folded.

Night was a hard iron bunk and a bowl of soup with some indeterminate bits floating in it.

H was woken from time to time in the darkness as hard pressed night duty officers wrestled with drunks in the charge room, eventually throwing them into the adjacent cell to sleep it off.

At dawn the next morning they set off again. This time two more of the cells in the van were occupied. H never saw the occupants, as he was hustled in first.

Again, hot sunshine filtered into his meagre space, bringing with it the aroma of melting road tar and dust. Again, the solid drone of the engine at a constant 70km per hour, propelling the van down an endlessly straight highway. There was nothing else to do but sleep, so he did.

Soon, traffic began to appear on the previously uncluttered road. The driver was even forced to stop behind a broken down cattle wagon because oncoming cars prevented him from overtaking straightaway. The truck was listing badly over to one side, appearing to have punctured both the tyres on one side of an axle at once. The driver was scurrying about, placing dead tree branches and vegetation for some distance behind the vehicle, the African Highway Code warning for a breakdown.

On they ploughed, through Klerksdorp and Potchefstroom, skirting the mass of Johannesburg and approaching Pretoria by mid-afternoon.

Then came Soetdoringstraat, a barrier lifted, and the prison van was in.

H woke to the clatter of a key in the lock behind his head. His muscles were stiff and aching from the cramped journey and his mind was sick with boredom and a strange fatigue from sleeping too much.

He was hustled out of the van by rough hands and into the initial reception pen. He had done it all before, so the big Afrikaaner just let himself be carried along by the tide.

Documented first, photographed and fingerprinted. Little scraps of cheap paper cleaning roll stuck to his fingers as he tried to remove the ink. The bottle of white cleansing lotion pointed out wordlessly by the warder had been empty.

As he rubbed, the fragile paper collapsed between his fingers. He let the remainder drop to the floor and forgot about the rest of the ink.

Next step was the humiliating strip search. Clothes taken from him, those that could be kept were put in a bag and sealed. He would see them again in fourteen years, the guard joked mercilessly. H stared at a spot on the far white wall, ignoring the jibe. If he didn't think about it, then it didn't exist.

Out of the compulsory showers and delousing, into a costume of coarse bleached calico. These were to be his clothes. They itched and the hard stabbing fibres were tearing at his skin already.

That was it. He was finished. In the soft plimsoles supplied, that were a size too small, H followed the warder through doors of metal bars and down endless corridors. Some gates opened by themselves, others needed a key to be selected from the huge master ring clipped onto a belt.

They stopped outside a cell with R58 stencilled on the door. The warder peered into the recessed spy hole and then swung the massive door back into the cell.

" Inside " he said simply, and when H wasn't quite quick enough, pushed him in and clanged the door shut behind. It locked automatically, the four inch steel bolt shooting firmly home.

The top bunk was occupied. It would be thought H. Second one in always gets underneath.

The figure rolled over to look at his new cell mate.

" Ugly looking bugger, ain't ya ? " it declared by way of welcome, " well I got what I want and it certainly ain't you, so get down there, keep your mouth shut and you may get through your time."

With that the form turned back to its original position and was snoring again within seconds.

For the first time since tasting life in custody again, H allowed himself a smile. It started slowly but soon spread to split his mouth into an evilly wide grin.

Quietly he took off the restricting shoes and placed them on the bottom bunk.

So, this was what he had to call home. Perhaps it might not be so bad after all.

CHAPTER

ELEVEN

The leopard knew that the girl would not be under the tree, but she went there nevertheless.

Torn Ear spent the night silently coming to terms with the fact that her friend had really gone now. She left before the first rays of dawn silhouetted the unfamiliar constructions which stood nearby.

This transition period had made it easier for them both, each learning that circumstances beyond their control made it necessary for them to part.

That didn't mean there was no pain.

Overhead a pygmy falcon swooped and dived, using the slight breeze and associated air currents to bolster his flight. Thermals would not develop for a couple of hours yet.

This most successful of the Kalahari birds of prey was looking for signs of its favourite meal, the sand lizard. Tiny bolt holes and the tell tale footprints in the sand were what he was after.

The bird peeled off to the right and then soared up again, showing off his white undercarriage which contrasted starkly with the slate grey and brown uppers.

Torn Ear watched the bird as he practised low level approaches, breaking off at the last minute before disaster.

A final pass, and the flying hunter was gone.

Torn Ear roused herself and continued her journey. For a couple of hours she padded through the scrubland and edges of the desert, picking her way between the spiky thorn bushes and tufts of dry grass.

As she got further into the interior she grew happier and easier with her surroundings. It had been a real mental effort to stay so close to human habitation to be with Jade. Were it not for the strong ties that existed between them she would not have had the motivation to do it. Now that Jade was gone, it was as if a piece of stretched elastic had been cut, catapulting her back into the world that was hers.

Surviving in the desert, without her companion, was something else entirely.

The leopard is by nature a solitary creature, coming together with a partner for the purpose of mating and then splitting up, usually at any rate.

The team of girl and leopard had learnt each others strengths and weaknesses, knew how to compensate for them and could trust the other fully. Together they were formidable, apart........apart was an unknown quantity.

Torn Ear found a mopane tree with a low slung branch that looked as if it could bear her weight. It did, without complaint. She draped herself over it, dangling all four huge paws in the unusual but very welcome breeze. She rested her head on the rough bark, letting eyelids droop over glittering alert eyes. Her ears remained erect, the wind slightly ruffling the soft jet black hair inside them. Pleasant it may be - safe enough to be complacent, it was never.

She yawned, arching her head back and letting her jaws split as wide as nature would allow. With an explosive grunt they shut again. She looked around, deciding it was in order to let half of her mind go into a light doze. Eyelids closed slowly.

When she woke the breeze had disappeared and it was time to find some better shade. The tree would do no longer. She rolled over in a well practised manoeuvre, landing firmly on her feet after the somersault.

As the day drew on she sensed that oestrus was with her once more. Her fur was exceptionally silky and there was a slight discharge. She had also lost her appetite.

In the past she had disguised her scent at these times by rolling in strong smelling plants and any other noxious substance which was to hand. This had resulted in temporary banning orders from the den, strictly enforced by Jade. However, it had kept any dangerous male interest at bay.

The increased demand for affection, which is also noticeable at these times, was adequately catered for by the presence of her friend. Now she was on her own, with a slight sense of loneliness. This was a completely alien feeling to the leopard, who had never really been alone in her life before.

There was a tiny rock crevice up ahead, with a thick bush overhanging the entrance. Torn Ear broke into a casual trot, eating up the ground with deceptively slow movements.

It was hot now. The sun had burnt through the thin streaks of white cloud that had been masking its power. The leopard could feel the rays begin to sear and scorch her black fur.

She reached the shelter. It was just big enough to accommodate her, and no more.

Quickly she explored it for tenants who might be persuaded to vacate. It was cool and dark inside.

Torn Ear put her head in, having first listened long and hard at the entrance. Leopards have fine hearing, with the ability to detect the precise origin of sound.

She waited several minutes for her eyes to become accustomed to the limited light before deciding that all was indeed safe. Then she withdrew her head, turned round and backed into the hole. That way she could see anything approaching her shelter and present it with a formidable array of teeth and claws.

A harsh guttural call brought the sleeping leopard instantly to full awareness. It was nearly dark outside.

Then silence. Nothing more. Torn Ear waited, fully alert.

" Grunt-ha ! grunt-ha ! " The harsh sawing call was repeated several times in quick succession. It was a rough coughing grunt, with air drawn in immediately after each call, giving a similar sound to that of sawing wood.

Despite never having heard it before, Torn Ear instinctively knew what it was. The resonating sound waves belonged to a male of the same species as herself. A male who was aware of her current female condition.

Fear and exhileration coursed along her veins side by side.

The leopard had boxed herself in. There was only one way out and in that direction was a creature she had never encountered before. Ears flattened against her broad head in the darkness and eyes closed to hunting slits. Paws tucked themselves under her bunched up body, quivering with tensed muscle power.

" Grunt-ha ! grunt-ha ! " The searcher had found his quarry. The sound was more determined and much, much closer.

The male found the bush overhanging the entrance. He gave excited little chuffling sounds and Torn Ear could hear panting as he scratched around, looking for the prize.

An amber and black head appeared in the space that was her only exit.

The jet black leopard propelled herself forward like a torpedo from its tube. Hissing and snarling in frightened fury, Torn Ear attacked the unknown face with devastating swipes from unleashed claws, backed up by opened jaws.

The male, alerted by a slight rush of air preceding the attack, missed the onslaught by the width of one of his whiskers. His own retreating momentum made him tumble backwards and collapse in an untidy heap.

Having failed to make contact, Torn Ear reversed back down into the cave as far as she could go. It went further than she had at first thought and soon her tail detected a change in temperature. Her hind quarters were now cooler than the rest of her. That could only mean one thing.

She kept on moving backwards, finding her body being directed upwards by a fallen sand dune which had caused the blockage at the rear of the cave. This had partially collapsed and given her an exit.

In seconds she was out and scrambling up the collapsed walls of sand to the top of the dune. All in reverse.

Not wanting to miss the advantage fate had given her, she set off immediately at a fast canter, little clouds of sand puffed up by her paws. This was done in near silence, so she escaped without alerting the male.

At the front, he sat down to consider the situation, letting instinct shape his intentions. If the female was not trapped, she would not have fought. Therefore if he sat here, she had to come out sooner or later. He waited.

Faced with the prospect of female company, however unwilling, time dragged by and his patience quickly wore thin.

The fully mature male leopard paraded up and down in front of the cave, giving what he hoped was a winning display of sight and sound. Impressive it certainly was, but the intended audience was putting yards between them every second of the performance.

Nevertheless, the display was not entirely wasted. A lone white backed vulture watched with interest from the lower branches of an acacia tree. He vacated his seat smartly when the irritated performer threatened to come and give him a personal show.

A thoroughly enraged and frustrated leopard returned from an unsuccessful attempt at vulture hunting to find no change in the courting situation.

His patience was at an end. This required another direct approach, with reverse pre-selected, just in case.

The moon was well and truly out by now, casting its pale light over the entire landscape. Every once in a while, when the male moved his head at a particular angle, rays of light caught his eyes and were reflected back out, making them glow.

As he agitatedly plucked up courage, the light caught his eyes for the briefest of moments, causing them to spark like matches flaring into life and then dying.

In the middle distance a lone jackal called out, pathetically howling into the night. There was no answer. Spark, the male, cocked an ear back to see if it warranted his attention. It didn't and the ear flipped forward again.

Enough was enough. He strode purposefully forward and then stopped short of the dark entrance to listen. No sound at all reached his ears, which he found curious. He should be able to hear breathing at least.

He risked a quick look in, half expecting a face full of claws. There was nothing.

Infuriated at having overlooked the possibility of a back door, he let out a disappointed grunt and sped round to see where Torn Ear had scrambled out. There was no way he could even think about getting into the cave itself.

Spark lay down on the half collapsed dune when he had fully examined the tracks in the sand. She would be well gone by now and, like most male hunting cats, he was too lazy to think about active pursuit over a long distance. The only sign of his disquiet was the ever mobile tail slashing from side to side, making a large half moon pattern from the millions of grains on which he lay. It would be a foolish member of the Kalahari fauna who came too close to this leopard right now.

In the sparsely populated desert this male had a home range of just over a hundred and twenty square kilometres. Within that range lived several females. They had all had cubs sired by him at some stage over the past few years. It was quite a novelty to discover a new addition to his flock, and despite the fact that he could soon find one of his regular harem to assuage his need, there was a certain something about this one, who had appeared to be completely black.

The tail moved faster. Spark looked round for something to vent his spleen on. Nothing moved. The rage would have to subside unaided, and that would take a long time.

Torn Ear moved on through the night. Knowing somehow that the male would leave her alone once she had escaped from the immediate vicinity, she kept her gait to a steady trot as soon as the danger zone was behind her, a lithe shadow moving silently through the whispering world of a moonlit desert.

Hunger pangs brought her to a stop in due course. She hadn't eaten properly for three days. The stinking remains of an old lion kill didn't really count, especially as she had spent most of the time driving off ever increasing numbers of vultures. They had eventually claimed the carcass as their own.

As sometimes happens, nature threw good fortune in her lap, and Torn Ear almost managed to miss it.

Lying by the side of the wildebeest trail she had been following, the leopard noticed fresh tracks which crossed her intended path and disappeared into scanty undergrowth on the other side. They were classic small antelope marks, in the shape of a split tear drop. These were quite long and thin, indicating a pocket-size, elegant creature.

Torn Ear backtracked some way and then started a flanking manoeuvre, all the time listening for movement or a twist of scent on still night air. Every few steps she stopped and cocked her head to one side, listening intently, like a bat eared fox in search of the tiny sounds that give away its equally tiny prey.

Dry leaves rustled, rubbing their parched bodies together, yet there was no breeze. At the same time a twig snapped, a noise like a pistol shot. Then absolute silence.

Torn Ear knew the signs. The silence meant that her quarry was aware of her presence and intentions. He had made a mistake and was hoping against hope that it had gone unnoticed. An unsuspecting animal grazing or foraging would have carried on munching and shuffling around.

Treading lightly and with infinite patience, the black leopard continued round, until by instinct she knew she was facing the animal from behind. Torn Ear was as good as invisible in the darkness.

A screech and howl broke the electric silence. It originated on the far side of the adult steenbok who stood petrified in the sparse undergrowth. He panicked, turned on his heels and bolted away from the disturbance, straight towards the waiting leopard.

Torn Ear had a few precious seconds to make her decision as the antelope came crashing through the vegetation.

She tensed, judged the distance and leapt for the reddish fawn throat just as it was upon her.

The steenbok never even saw the hunter. The strength of the impact broke his neck immediately, and death followed as the tangle of legs and bodies hit the ground.

With the ease made possible by immense strength and agility, Torn Ear dragged the warm body into the relative safety of a close tree. It was no effort at all to position the meal securely on a branch. She had successfully done the same with prey much larger and more cumbersome than this.

Now she could feed at leisure, dropping the less favoured parts of the anatomy to the couple of brown hyena who had already gathered at the base of the tree.

Occasionally one of the scavengers would try his hand at tree climbing and needed reminding whose meal this actually was. A ferocious snarl and a look at long gleaming teeth was quite sufficient for the purpose. Positioned as she was, the leopard could easily deal with any such attempt by a hyena.

Torn Ear stayed with the carcass until the relatively safety of dawn, when she softly jumped the fifteen feet or so to the sandy desert floor in one lithe movement. The hyena had long since departed, frustrated and bored.

She moved off leisurely to find shade. Water was also on the list, but not very high up at the moment as the body fluids of her prey had quenched the need for a while. It was going to be the usual scorching day.

*****

Following the rambling ways of the small Kalahari herds of springbok, zebra and wildebeest was the only fairly certain way of ensuring a food supply in this unreliable terrain.

Spark knew most of their regular, seasonal habits. He knew where they liked to rest, where they would drink if there was water and where they would go if there was none. He knew where they hid their new-born, and those he would leave alone, preferring the challenge and achievement of a stalk and kill.

Still feeling ruffled from the previous days' occurrences, he was now keeping pace with a mixed herd of springbok and wildebeest. They were spread out over a large area, searching the dried and parched ground for green stalks that might yield moisture and nutrients.

Unlike some others of his species, Spark disliked the mad hunt for food when hunger became too much. He preferred to keep his potential meals in the immediate vicinity and then pick one off when he needed to. It meant his movements were guided by them to a greater or lesser degree, but that in turn had its advantages. He was constantly learning their habits by being so close to them, which consequently meant he knew their weaknesses and that made them easier to capture.

Tonight he needed to make a kill. He would take an old one from the very edge of the herd, their usual location, trying not to disturb the others too much.

It was almost as if the elders positioned themselves in prime spots for him, protecting the younger and more healthy ones from his attentions.

The male leopard now sought shelter from the piercing rays which he knew would arrive. Above him the early morning sky was a crisp blue dome, the rising air as yet untainted by ethereal heat hazes. It was still cool enough for his breath to make little clouds of steamy water vapour as he exhaled.

Up ahead stood a lone granite kopje. With nothing else in sight it would have to do, although as the sun moved across the sky he would need to move round the rock to keep in the shade.

Spark trotted the few hundred yards to his shelter, passing within spitting distance of the grazing animals. They paid him scant attention, somehow knowing that for the moment they were safe, that the leopard was not interested in food.

The shade was perfect. During the night condensation had gathered on one side of the rock which jutted out by a couple of feet. The falling moisture darkened the sand below, making it especially damp and cool. Spark wriggled himself down onto this clammy bed, knowing he had the best site for miles around.

Not until late afternoon did the male leopard stir. Even then it was a most leisurely business, with much yawning and blinking of tired eyes.

Spark roused himself eventually and crawled out from under the kopje. Turning his thoughts to food he searched the landscape to relocate his four-legged meals.

The herd he was following had moved on but he could still see the back markers in the distance, heads down to the desert. The long dark tails of the wildebeest shimmered in the last of the hot air retained by the sandveldt.

The male worked out his line of approach, so as to keep down wind of them. It wouldn't take much to catch them up but this time he intended to stay out of their way.

Half an hour into his journey Spark caught the unmistakable aroma of hyena and then picked out the squat shape at the base of a lonely mopane tree. He hated and despised the creatures, but tinged his feelings with the slightest touch of respect as its powerful jaws could do him irreparable damage if they were to get hold of him in a fight.

Spark halted in his tracks. The hyena was desperately trying to climb the tree. An impossible task, as he just wasn't designed for it. However, it could only mean that there was food in the branches, food that could save the leopard an awful lot of work. As far as he could see, there was only one scavenger in attendance.

Spark looked around again, carefully, checking the horizons for approaching animals and listening to the sounds of the desert floating over the dunes. Nothing untoward.

The big male loped towards the tree at a pace slightly less than a canter, giving the hyena every chance to see his adversary and retreat.

Spark really wasn't paying attention to the situation, having already made up his mind that the hyena would scuttle off at the first sign of danger. Instead, he continued trying to get up into the tree, and then defied the leopard with a ferocious lunge and impotent snap of the vice like jaws.

The shocked leopard jumped back a pace, and then, angry with his own complacency, attacked with lashing front paws. His extended limbs kept the animals apart for the leopard's own safety.

The single hyena was gone within seconds.

Spark found treasure indeed on the branch above him. There was ample left on the bones to satisfy his hunger. He climbed swiftly into the tree and was straddling the kill when he noticed a pungent scent which made his heart contract suddenly and seem to miss its stride. The scent belonged to the female who had eluded him. This was her kill.

He looked down from the branch. All hunger had vanished. Standing some twenty yards away was the leopardess with the torn ear. She was standing stock still, as if frozen to the spot.

Torn Ear might just as well have been rooted to the earth. Her body was at its peak that night, demanding something that she didn't know existed, making urgent requests that she had no idea how to fulfill. She watched the male approach, her ears flattening back against the side of her head with apprehension. Yet she felt no desire to move, no sixth sense told her to run. Somehow there was no danger, just the unknown.

Spark moved ever closer, breathing rapidly with excitement as Torn Ear stood her ground.

His sex scent caught her nostrils and held them as its signals worked through to her subconscious. That particular smell of the male aroused an instinct that had been lain down by the breeding of countless generations before her. Suddenly she knew and the knowledge flooded through her body, and she was ready for him.

Spark was close to her now. He gently nuzzled her silky flank with the side of his face.

*****

Dawn broke. Still cloudy and overcast today, with the grey sky refusing, as yet, to give way to the sun.

Her neck was sore and stiff, the fur matted with a small amount of blood. At the height of her pain and ecstasy the male had bitten her on the back of the neck. She hadn't noticed it until this morning.

They had joined many times during the cool dark night, untroubled by any other creature, in the nest of sand hollowed out by their combined movements.

Torn Ear lay alone now, uncharacteristically docile and sedentary. She never saw the male leopard with the sparkle in his eyes again. But then the same instincts that had aroused her body had also told her this. It was simply the way things were.

*****

Over the next few weeks Torn Ear wandered into parts of the Kalahari she had never been to before. Not stopping long enough to establish a home range anywhere, she might stay for a week at the outside and then move on. The strange needs of her body had been satisfied for the time being, but she half expected the feelings to return after their usual gap. They never did.

Hunger guided the steps of the leopard back into her familiar territory, where game could be found at water holes. No ordinary hunger but a constant overpowering desire to eat. Thirst accompanied this increased gluttony. No longer were the body fluids of her prey enough. She drank actively from any available source, throwing herds of zebra into confusion as she knelt at the waters edge to lap the warm stagnant liquid.

Her body was in a state of turmoil and she didn't know why. Torn Ear found herself getting tired more easily and less able to tolerate the sun. The leopard sought out a suitable rocky crevice in which to spend the days, finding an ideal one with a small concealed entrance, opening into a snug but cool and dim area. She kept movements to a minimum, only going out to hunt and drink, and never during the day now.

It was not until the final three weeks that Torn Ear was able to discern what was due to happen. Leopards that have borne cubs previously can recognise the symptoms much earlier.

The realisation that her bodily changes were entirely natural settled the mother-to-be. The prospect of cubs gave her something to work for. She would have offspring to care for, train and educate in the ways of her world.

Her stomach moved within her, of its own accord. She looked down at it, just in time to see a flickering of the surface, like watching the spot where a fish has just dived underwater again. Nestling in the short fur, her nipples were already dark red and enlarged.

With every day she grew larger, her belly trying its hardest to reach the ground, which was passing so tantalisingly close below. It was as if the occupants were intent on making an early exit.

The extra weight and unwieldy shape made her usual style of hunting quite out of the question. She was reduced to scavenging, which thankfully, provided enough. Game was reasonably plentiful at the moment.

Torn Ear ate everything she came across that could remotely be described as food, for she knew that once she had given birth her fat stores would be used up as she nursed the infants, unable to leave them in the early stages.

The day grew closer and the hardship grew worse. Stifling heavy heat settled on the desert, which was multiplied two or three fold for the expecting leopard. She panted continuously, all day every day, trying desperately to lose heat to the already sodden atmosphere. Her condition forced her to stay in the den, when normally she would have sought out a high spot with at least the semblance of a breeze to ease things.

Trips out for food and water were abominations. She could hardly get herself out, let alone run after anything. It crossed her mind that she herself was vulnerable in such a state, but the risk had to be taken.

The final day was hell on earth. The heat stuck to her like an extra fur coat and she felt that her stomach would burst, such was the size and activity within her.

As the sun went down, and the temperature cooled slightly, the leopard felt a band of pain tighten in her gut and then subside. She waited, apprehensive.

It came again, harder and more aggressive. An involuntary whimper escaped. Then relief.

More pain. Her gut felt like it was being pulled out of her. Then nothing. The dancing lights in front of her eyes faded and waned into the distance. She was panting heavily.

Gaps between the bouts of agony got less and less. Soon there was no respite at all. One continuous long push and then gorgeous relief. There was a slithery form on the ground between her legs.

Torn Ear turned round to lick the specimen into life, washing the mucus and fluids from around its nose and mouth first. The miniature form responded with croaking and spluttering sounds.

She cleaned its body quickly and turned it over so that its feet now touched the ground, noting with satisfaction that he was complete in every respect. The first instinct of life took over and the tiny cub headed for his first meal, soft mouth and eager head probing for the source.

Slight contractions wrapped themselves round her gut again. Nothing like the previous ones though and after only a few minutes they expelled the afterbirth. She was to have a litter of one.

Torn Ear disposed of the redundant organ the only way she knew how, for the smell of it would surely bring unwelcome attention. Then she turned her attention back to the cub. He was about seven inches long with dark grey fur, already spotted with small rosettes like an adult. His eyes were still tightly closed, as if to say he'd already had enough shocks for one day and he had no intention of making matters worse by actually looking at this new world he'd been forced into. His paws and mouth were a dark red and he was suckling furiously. The belly would soon be as tight as a drum. Even at this earliest of ages his tail was continuously waving back and forth.

The adult curled round him, trying to make up for the lack of brothers and sisters.

A welcome breeze was funnelled into the den, along with the first signs of daylight. Delivery of the one precious bundle had taken all night.

*****

Eight days old now and his eyes were open. They had the bluey glaze that belongs to all very young cats.

Baby was hungry again. He hooked his tiny claws into his mother like crampons and started the climb back over to reach the food supply.

Little needles in her thick fur brought Torn Ear out of her pleasant doze. Food was now uppermost in her mind as well. During the time since the birth she had ventured out of the den once, always keeping the entrance in sight. She collected dead leaves and vegetation to make a rough sort of bed for Baby in the den. A litter of cubs wouldn't need this treatment as, rolled together in sleep, they made their own warmth and comfort.

Baby however, would only settle when nestled up to Torn Ear. As soon as she stirred and moved away, the change in temperature woke him up and he started to blunder around the den, making little calling sounds. Torn Ear needed to be able to leave him to go out and hunt. She needed to be able to do that very soon.

She gradually introduced Baby to the concept of his own warm corner in the den. He snuffled around in the leaves, brought his head up, and then sneezed once. The tiny explosion made him sit down suddenly on his fat little haunches, and he looked at his mother in surprise with his head cocked to one side.

Baby regained control and continued his investigation. Torn Ear watched and waited. Her trump card was hidden right at the back of the rustling heap.

She had found the body of a Namaqua rock mouse on her one and only foray. Amazingly, the skin was basically intact although the innards had been taken long ago. Torn Ear had cleaned it as best she could and placed it amongst the leaves. The idea was for Baby to be able to snuggle up against it, taking the place of other cubs, thus releasing Torn Ear.

The thing couldn't have been a more unqualified success. Baby took to it like a dog to a favourite bone. Firstly he dragged it out of the leaves to give it some close scrutiny, all done very laboriously and with lots of breaks.

When Torn Ear saw that he had nearly exhausted himself doing this, she slowly returned the pelt to the middle of the leaves. Not wanting to let his favourite toy disappear out of sight, Baby followed, stumbling over his outsize feet in the effort to keep up.

By the time the journey was completed, and both were reunited again, Baby only had the strength to collapse on it and fall asleep.

Torn Ear watched the little inert form. Strategy successful. She padded to the entrance, jumped up and out.

For an hour she kept a vigil from on top of a close rock. She was close enough to hear any cries from inside, yet far enough away so that any would-be predators might not immediately realise where the den was.

Far away in the distance a strange barking cry rang out. It was so faint that she had to strain her ears to hear it. Then it was gone. Torn Ear dismissed it, she still hadn't got used to all the sights and sounds of this new neighbourhood.

Long range hunting was out of the question now, the menu was limited to what could be found in the immediate vicinity of her new family. She survived on a diet of rodents, lizards and the odd rock hyrax. Occasionally she would eat sweet fruits that were to be found nearby. When this happened she took a piece back to the den and let Baby try it. The idea was to introduce him to the fact that there was more to food than mother's milk, but it would be many weeks before he was ready to eat solids instead of it. She lifted him out by the scruff of the neck to try these new delicacies in the open air.

Baby sniffed at the chunk of tsama melon, giving it scant attention. He was far more interested in the fascinating tufts of desert grasses and little piles of sand nearby. Without warning he launched an attack on the nearest one, making a dive for the stalks just above ground level. At least he liked to think of it as a dive, in reality it was closer to a waddle and a collapse.

Needless to say, the grass was equal to the assault, having the fearsome defence of filling the mouth of the pint sized attacker with sand. Baby withdrew rapidly to hide in his mother's flank.

Torn Ear replaced the defeated cub in the den. She was really quite satisfied with the small rocky cave, for, having a vertical entrance, there was no way Baby could get in or out on his own. However she knew that they would have to move on soon. The whereabouts of the young of any species quickly becomes known to predators in the area and then it would just be a matter of time before they made a move. Dim and foggy memories of a jackal in a much bigger den still hung at the back of her mind.

A stray tree mouse lingered for a second too long in the leopard's view. It would only be a mouthful, but a mouthful nevertheless.

Torn Ear made a standing jump, cutting off its escape route towards an acacia tree and the hole in the trunk that was safety.

She totally missed a repetition of the strange cries that had disturbed her earlier. They were closer now.

The mouthful jinked and swerved. The leopard countered the move, an instant behind. There was no match. She captured the meagre body between two massive front paws and dispatched it quickly.

Behind Torn Ear a large male baboon twisted a piece of bark from a low bush. The sudden noise of ripping and tearing made her spin round instantly, crouching into a defensive position.

The male examined the material in his hand carefully and then flicked it away with a flourish. He looked at the leopard, bared an extensive array of teeth and barked aggressively.

Torn Ear responded with a hissing display of her weaponry. She looked ferocious, but was frightened to the core. The animal was between her and the den.

The baboon jumped back a stride, slightly wary. He had encountered leopards before and disliked them. He reared up on his hind legs for a better view, and to increase the threat with his greater height.

Two larger males strutted into view, tails held high. They too began to bark and snarl, holding their ground.

Uncertain of her move, Torn Ear stayed put and let the situation develop. She hoped it was a baiting match, a mere show of force. She needed an ally, with sling and sharp stones.

The rest of the troop appeared. Long snouted heads showing now from behind every gap in the rocky slope.

Egged on by the barks and calls of companions, the three males developed courage. They made little attacking runs at the crouching leopard, breaking off just before they came within reach.

Torn Ear lashed out with claws at those who got too close, dark open mouth with jagged teeth promising instant death and destruction. The taunters were just nimble enough.

Several more jumped down from the spectators gallery. The odds were getting out of hand.

At this point the leopard would normally have made a tactical retreat, seeking refuge in a tree or simply beating a hasty retreat. This time she could not. An only cub meant she could not.

The line of would-be attackers increased, more coming down to join in the fun. They tried to get round the side of the leopard, forming a half circle of danger, wondering why she did not run. The odds were overwhelming now. The troop was a big one, over thirty, with at least half their number now facing the leopard.

Constantly they jibed and taunted, trying to goad her into action.

After several minutes there was a lull. A sudden silence in the commotion. And a frightened cub called to his mother.

The nearest baboon cocked its head to the sound, recognising it for what it was. It took a step for the den and Torn Ear launched herself forward, wild with anger and panic.

She burst through the line of creatures before they realised what was happening. Three strides later the baboon was lifeless on the ground, its throat ripped out.

The group fell on her as one, rushing to attack. Torn Ear felt the first teeth in her flank. She lunged at one, jumping on it and raking down with one long stroke of her back legs. Then she was out of the commotion.

In a mad rush the enraged troop descended on her again, forcing her back from the den. Torn Ear faced them once more. She leapt from one to another, in the classic leopard tactic when dealing with primates, disabling and tearing flesh as she went, but rarely staying with one long enough to be certain of its death.

Her progress was devastating, marked by agonised cries and mutilated bodies. Yet still there were more of them and still they attacked. Sheer weight of numbers bore down and exhaustion began to exact a toll on her.

She felt a sharp pain in her back. One was astride her and digging into her flesh with broad yellow fangs. Torn Ear rolled quickly and then recovered, dealing a final blow to this one with a fearsome slash from a hind leg as she got up.

Blood dripped into her eyes, clouding her vision for a moment. A shake of the head to try and clear it, but still it fell.

Torn Ear slowed a little, her energy drained. Her attackers sensed victory and pressed harder. Two were on her back now. Legs that could no longer hold the weight were trembling with fatigue. She crumpled to the ground.

In the grey mist of stinking, barking flesh that piled onto her, fate opened a cruel gap for the leopard in the seconds before she lost consciousness.

Through it she could see the apparent peace and tranquility that existed around the entrance to the den. In terrible slow motion she watched the nightmare, pinned helplessly to the ground by overpowering weight.

A thin furred arm snaked its way into the den from above, the owner squatting to one side of the hole. The limb withdrew suddenly, with a cry of pain. Then two more of the larger males climbed quickly down into the den.

She needed to see no more.

The gap closed, and very soon afterwards the world turned inky black and silent.

CHAPTER

TWELVE

The sun burnt fiercely on the back of his neck and it felt good. It was so long since his skin had tasted such power that he knew it would redden and itch like that of the insipid pale tourists that his country was so eager to encourage. It was still good. It was the pain of freedom.

A yellow van with wired windows sped towards H, horn sounding angrily. He stepped leisurely back onto the pavement just in time.

For the moment the South Africa Police held no fears for Prisoner 66.3.16. In one hand he grasped the drawstring of a small duffel bag, which contained the total of his worldly possessions. In the other was a form G371, a Vrylatingsertifikaat in the name of de Beer.H.

The release certificate was the document most dreamed about by all the inmates during their endless years of boredom and frustration. It meant official freedom. H threw his bag to the pavement, making a comfortable seat, and examined the crumpled rectangle of cheap paper. He was still within sight of the high walls of Pretoria Central Prison.

The only item on the certificate which did not have " Geen " or " No " scribbled roughly next to it was No.10(a). Under the heading " Gratifikasie vir behoeftiges / Gratuity for the needy " was shown the princely sum of one hundred Rand. It was the only money he had in the world, the crisp notes already burning a hole in his pocket. Looking at the bottom of the document he tried for a few minutes to decipher the scrawled signature which lay under the official stamp of the " Hoof van die Gevangenis / Head of the Prison ". Could have done a better job of the signature himself if he had had to, thought H. He had seen it often enough during the past four years.

The Boer folded the paper several times on itself and then placed it inside the meagre wad of notes in his pocket.

He got up, flung the bag over his shoulder and continued down the street. Following the age old custom of prisons all over the world, he had been released shortly after dawn and as a consequence the city was still half asleep with only a few people about.

Four years was a lot short of the original fourteen handed down by the judge in a Windhoek court.

Even now he didn't really understand why fate should have smiled so sweetly on him. Sure, it had all been explained to him by eager young South African lawyers - the forthcoming independence of Namibia, the change in laws, statute of limitations and so on. The bottom line apparently was that he was being used as a test case. Although he had pleaded guilty, his new squeaky clean lawyers said that his change of plea at trial was due to the fact that he thought his taped confession would have been held legal, and therefore damming. By pleading guilty, he had halted the evidence and saved the court from having to decide if the circumstances of the confession were admissible. Willem hadn't got as far as it in his evidence. Higher powers had decided in the meantime that that confession might be in doubt, so, as there were no witnesses or other material evidence, he was out. That was the long and the short of it.

Whatever, the fact was that the smart young men in their lightweight suits and BMW's with air conditioning had won the day. Not a pardon though, only a simple release. No statement to the effect that the authorities admitted a miscarriage of justice, just a G371.

Years of confinement had taken their toll on a physique that changed with its owner's lifestyle.

A thick mat of bristle like hair covered the bullet head and an impressive beard of the same material adorned most of his face, hiding a couple of additional knife wounds. He was thinner now, and there was very little fat. H had soon discovered that the prison gymnasium and weights room was out of bounds to all but a select few. These were the long term prisoners who had formed their own 'club' and defended it jealously and fiercely. Admittance was by invitation only, the main condition being a certain intimacy which made him want to retch and hit out at the same time.

H confined his attempts at keeping fit to the privacy of his own cell. He developed a series of exercises, including variations on the standard press up and sit up, and kept up a punishing regime for several hours each day. For cardiovascular fitness he would jog on the spot for up to forty minutes.

When this constant noise and activity caused his cell mate to complain, H tested out his strength in a most practical manner. This left him in solitary confinement as a punishment for something which was eventually written up by the authorities as "each prisoner equally to blame". The arrangement couldn't have been better.

Another new cell companion suffered the same fate, after which it was decided to leave H on his own. The staff recognised that although most prisoners preferred to have some sort of company, there was the odd one who just could not get on and needed no-one. While space permitted, they opted for the quiet life.

H turned the corner and the prison was out of sight behind him. Out of sight but not out of mind. He had to get rid of the release issue clothing, for it marked him as surely as a wildebeest with a broken leg in a herd watched by lion.

The first bus of the day pulled up beside him as he considered his next move. The further away he got from this place right now the better. H jumped on without bothering to look at the destination and picked a corner seat at the back as his own. The ancient transport pulled laboriously away, leaving a cloud of raw exhaust fumes in its wake which settled over a wide area.

By the time he reached the point where the bus would turn round and retrace its route, H had formulated his ideas.

The town of Bloemfontein in the Orange Free State was big enough to provide what he was looking for. After the three hour ride it was the middle of the morning and the place was bustling and vibrant. Anonymous in the crowd, H searched for the back street market to buy some cheap, secondhand clothes.

This done, he found a public telephone booth with an intact directory, and promptly mutilated it by tearing out a page which had the information he wanted.

Then a second purchase - a street guide to his new home. He knew what he wanted. A sleazy boxing and training gym for would-be future champions, where he could find employment as odd job man, trainer, sparring partner, whatever, as long as some sort of accommodation and payment came with it.

Of course, that was only for the short term, till he got on his feet again. Then he had a few visits to make, far away from here. Visits he had dreamed about for a very long time.

This one should do. Behind the station, in a quiet backwater where no-one came by chance.

In the absence of any sort of bell, H rattled the thin frosted door glass with his fist, hearing the noise echo inside the building.

Silence, and then the squeak of rubber shoe on wooden floor. The door opened three inches and a chain appeared at eye level, with an unshaven face behind it,

Just right thought H. Behind his back he crumpled up the torn out page in his hand and let it drop to the pavement.

*****

The only other traffic in sight on the dusty road was a utility wagon, quite similar to theirs, except a good deal older.

As it passed them, going in the opposite direction, the usual cloud of swirling debris descended. No problem for the occupants of the cab, but it put paid to the slim hopes that Jade had of arriving home in any sort of half decent state.

She was covered in sand, again. That made six full treatments and a couple of good attempts in the three hours since they left Windhoek. Jade was sitting in the open back of the Toyota truck, wedged into the far corner with outstretched legs. Mini sand dunes were starting to form between her two well travelled suitcases which were strapped down immediately behind the cab.

Jade shot another withering stare through the glass of the cab at the occupant of the left hand seat. It bounced off the back of his head and had no effect whatsoever. Still, even if he had turned to look it wouldn't have had any effect either. The owner of the backside that was parked on the seat was called Midget, and he was a very large opinionated Labrador of indeterminate fleshy colour. He was called Midget simply because he wasn't.

It was the same every time. Molo drove to Windhoek to pick her up from Eros Airport on the south edge of the city, and Midget always came with him.

Midget always sat beside the driver, it was his place. Just because Jade happened along once in a blue moon he saw no reason to allow himself to be relegated to the back.

After the first couple of holidays spent back in her home country Jade had given up and taken her place in the back. She had tried to persuade Molo to either leave the dog behind or drive out in The Hun, which Midget wouldn't travel in apparently. Water off a duck's back - here she was as usual.

Her only consolation, as the bumpy road tried to make her see lunch again, was that this would be the last time. She was home for good.

It was such a very long time since she had left the farm, Oupa, and her beloved desert with the closest companion of her life. Yet now it was all over and she was back. The years seemed to have vanished with the blink of an eye, a hollow and echoing memory that might never have actually happened.

The idea to finish, or was it to start, her education in Switzerland was entirely her own. She had to work hard to convince a protective grandfather to allow her out of his sight once more, but in the end he was quite enthusiastic.

Paying for the idea used up her last stone, the best, the Lion Stone. Max Herbert couldn't believe his luck when she presented it to him and neither could Jade when he actually offered her a decent price for it. She made him break with tradition and give her a guaranteed cheque which she could present to a bank in Switzerland when she arrived. The Swiss gnomes had a good reputation for guarding the secrets of their clients, and the rather dubious origin of the cheque would never be questioned.

Switzerland was another world. The first shock was seeing and touching snow for the first time, and the second was the temperature.

Jade had never really been cold before and the crisp lazy winds knifed through her clothes with ease. It was something she never got accustomed to, in all her time there. When others could manage with a thin polo neck sweater in the brisk winter sunshine, the girl from the Kalahari needed several layers before the shivering stopped.

Instinctively she knew she had made the right choice when she arrived at the school. The queasy ache of homesickness, uncertainty and guilt at leaving her only relative again retreated slowly from her mind.

The Institut Alpin Videmanette in Rougemont was a picture book setting. She had determined that if she was going to leave her place of beauty, she would go to one no less magnificent in its own right.

Rougemont was a picturesque Swiss village in the Vaud Alps, about 140 kilometres from Geneva. The four homely wooden chalets of the Institut nestled in the mountains, with wooded slopes and then towering snow capped peaks behind them. The air felt so clean and fresh it was almost like taking a shower each time you went outside.

Molo swerved the truck round a familiar bend. Not long now.

Physical activity on the curriculum had been a must for the girl who had thought nothing of running for miles in the killing heat of Africa. At 1,000 metres, the school was close to the ski runs of Gstaad and Chateau-d'Oex and quite naturally skiing featured highly.

Her stamina and fitness were beyond question but it did take her a while to get used to the idea of sliding around on this white stuff that she hadn't even seen before. Nevertheless within the first week she was executing quite adequate snowplough turns, and by the end of her first term she could keep up with the majority of her new friends, some of whom had learned to ski before they could walk properly.

Sometimes she wasn't exactly flavour of the month with the ski instructors though. As older men in the sole company of reasonably attractive young women, they liked to hold court and keep the limelight with tales of their prowess, detailing scrapes that " any lesser skiers wouldn't have made it out of ". When pressed by her classmates Jade could tell them stories of an alien world which fascinated the cosy little dining room into silence. Her matter of fact approach, coupled with a dash of inherent shyness and an unwillingness to embroider a tale for the sake of it made her company a sought after asset. Even the instructors gave way with good grace in the end. They could still knock her down an imaginary peg or two by making a crack about the African native who didn't know what a bed was and slept on the floor.

Jade never had got used to ordinary beds again, still preferring to wrestle blankets onto the polished wood floor and make her own sleeping arrangements there. The cleaners and domestic helps used to play merry hell with her.

She never mentioned the leopard with the torn ear. It would have seemed cheap and a betrayal somehow if she had done so.

Long letters in thick bold handwriting brought a breath of hot desert wind into the Swiss Alps. Oupa wrote regularly during the time that his granddaughter was away. Jade was glad he did, for she could tell from his scripts how things were faring back home. Not just what he told her, but how he wrote, and indeed the state of his handwriting itself.

Jade made a point of writing back equally regularly. She told him of her trials and tribulations, her domestic problems with Cordon Bleu cookery.........*can't get a decent wildebeest steak for love nor money......and they simply don't add gritty sand to anything.....*, the refusal of her tongue to master French pronunciation or indeed of her mind to remember it. Most of all she told him of the grandeur and splendid isolation of the high mountain peaks.

In a way, she wrote, they reminded her of the desert. As the heat cleansed there, so the bitter, dry cold kept the scenery pure and marvellously dramatic here. She told him of stupendous views from cable cars as they wafted their perilous way up between the peaks and of being on top of the world when you reached the summit. Of being able to look around yourself and see nothing that was higher.

Then there was the heart stopping thrill of launching yourself over the lip of a red run. Seeing the ski tips disappear forward over the edge and knowing that the only way of getting down in one piece was to follow them with courage grasped in both hands. Hesitate, and the snow knows it. It will down you without a second thought. To pull up in control at the bottom was achievement itself and the adrenalin high was more addictive than any drug. The first thing she wanted to do was go up and ski it again.

Both writer and recipient kept every piece of correspondence, each relishing the glimpse into another world and living another life by proxy, for a little while anyway.

The last end of term party was over and gone now.

Molo bounced the truck into the yard and Midget exited through the open window, now happy to welcome Jade back home.

Home, thought Jade. The place looks different each time I see it now.

" Oupa ! " she screamed delightedly as the old man descended the steps to greet her. His leathery face cracked into a grin the size of Fish River Canyon.

Despite advancing years he was just as strong as ever. Jade had to beat playfully on his back with clenched fists before he considered releasing his favourite girl from the bear hug which he had her in.

" Let me look at you," he said in the end, giving way to her pleas. " I don't know. I think I may have to sue this school of yours. I send away a granddaughter and I get a woman back in return."

" You call this a woman ? " Jade laughed and did a twirl, which brought a round of cheers from a few stockmen who had gathered to see her again. " I stand before you, exhausted, bedraggled and looking like a rock rabbit that's been buried in sand for the past six months, and you call that a woman ! "

" I'm parched, " the recently exhumed rabbit continued, " take me inside, buy me a beer and tell me all the gossip."

The grandfather gave his little grown up girl a hard disapproving stare.

" Well, all right, " she backtracked, " make it a jug of ice cold lemonade, some of cook's waffles, and we'll call it a deal."

Arm in arm, the pair went inside. Midget was running excitedly around their feet, slapping legs hard with his substantial tail whenever he could.

Molo watched them with the pride of an old tribal chief. Things would be better now because the boss man had his child back. The tall woman with the blue-green eyes and shock of blonde hair had always been a lucky mascot for this place.

Like many of the others, he remembered the day she first came back very clearly indeed. The medicine tasted bad but had done the trick. The farm was working well now. All the dead wood, in the shape of employees who didn't pull their weight, were long gone, dismissed and forgotten. They all knew what H had done, and his long overdue punishment, but it was never mentioned either in earnest or idle gossip.

A year ago the financial corner had been turned and they had entered the black, so to speak, for the first time. Molo was the only one of the twenty or so workers who understood anything about basic economics and the importance of making a profit, so Tony had taken him aside and painstakingly explained everything about the bookwork that was necessary.

All the profit that the bank would let them keep they literally ploughed back into the land and the stock. Yet there was still enough left over to give everyone a small bonus and buy a decent truck. The place even had an insurance policy now.

Molo lifted Jade's suitcases out of the decent truck and lugged them up the verandah stairs, into her old room. Even for his ample physique it was a struggle. It felt like she had brought back half the mountain as a souvenir.

Lying exhausted on a familiar floor at last, Jade realised how happy she was to be home.

Snatches of chatter floated in through the open window as the farm went about its business, and the pleasantly warm air was full of sounds she knew and loved. Late afternoon rays splashed soft orange light onto the far wall.

Above her head the ceiling fan rotated just fast enough to keep the room pleasant. As usual it clicked on every third full circle, something she had learned to ignore long ago, but now it was comforting and welcome.

Jade scrambled up and heaved one suitcase onto a protesting bed. She carefully opened a zippered pouch and took out a rolled up piece of thick paper. It was obviously well used because the edges were lovingly preserved with clear tape and each corner had several pin holes in it.

She pinned it to the wall, so that it was bathed in sunlight, and lay down again to admire it.

Her portrait of Torn Ear went everywhere with her and was always the first thing to be unpacked. Sooner or later, probably later, it would get properly framed but at the moment it was easier to transport the way it was. It had come back from Switzerland with her every time she visited home.

The door exploded back on its hinges, cracking the handle hard on the far wall. Midget bounced in, eager to renew his friendship with Jade, whom he had previously seen about twice a year. Finding her at ground level he jumped on top, punching the wind out of her and commenced a feverish attack with a huge pink tongue and cold wet nose.

Having heard Midget galloping down the corridor, Jade was half expecting the onslaught. The dog could open her door by hurling himself bodily at it, but only if he had got up enough speed first. This time he had been successful and Jade was suffering the consequences.

She wrestled with the dog for a while until he started losing the battle. Then he made a dash for the open door and was gone as quickly as he had arrived.

Jade grinned, a little wickedly. Midget had no idea what sort of animal she had learned to play rough with.

The contents of the suitcase beckoned to her with a funny sort of aroma. Wrinkling her nose in self disgust, Jade began to grade the laundry into piles labelled

' cleanish ', ' not so good ' and ' desperate '. She would do this lot herself. Molo's wife didn't deserve such a homecoming present. *What was her name again........oh yes......Emmy.*

*****

There was more than enough work to keep a young woman occupied at the farm these days.

First, and most important, she had to rescue The Hun from mothballs and get him back into working order with a service, oil change and so on. For this she surreptitiously enlisted the help of one of the stockmen who had plenty of garage experience.

Because it wasn't strictly part of his job she agreed to do his work, as best she could, while he worked on restoring her car.

As luck would have it, he was assigned to two days of simple animal counting, something he detested but which Jade wouldn't mind too much. It gave her an opportunity to get to know the hundreds of acres which now belonged to her family, and burnish her skin back to the colour it was used to being. A bargain was struck.

By the time two long days in the glorious open air had rolled by, she had her tan and her car back.

After that Jade settled down with her grandfather, learning what changes he had made, how the farm ran these days and generally easing herself back into the groove. It was a labour of love, for she adored working in the open.

Quite often she would go out for a day with one of the men, helping them work on the fencing or rounding up the stock. When they had got used to the novelty, they found she was quite capable and strong, and wasn't simply keeping tabs on them. Jade made sure she talked to them in Afrikaans, keeping her knowledge of the language up to date and fluent, after years of disuse.

A couple of months saw Jade totally back into the swing of things. Were it not for an address book stuffed with names of friends from all corners of the world, and several certificates of excellence in cuisine and skiing, she might never have left the place at all.

Once in a while she took a trip to Windhoek on her own, mainly to do some shopping, but also to check on the state of the finances and pay a visit to Max.

He was doing quite well for himself these days. He had bought the shop next door, knocked the wall down and extended into it. Despite his new found trickle of wealth, he still hadn't got the idea of how to smarten the shop up so that the rich old widows might stop and look in his window, instead of crossing the street to get away from the seedy atmosphere that exuded from it.

On one of these visits Jade spent the whole afternoon there, pointing out some basics in materials and design to him.

When the dreadful ordeal was over she even offered to come and do some of the work herself, but she could see in his troubled expression that he needed a little more time to consider this drastic upheaval.

Shutting the door behind her, she knew she had given him a sleepless night for sure.

In the rapidly gathering gloom she patted the warm brickwork of his shop and smiled to herself. He will come round soon, little shop, she thought. Then you will get all the customers you can handle.

She looked up at the sky. Almost night again. She had stayed longer than anticipated and now the whole journey back was going to be in darkness. Well, everything behind The Hun would be in darkness. Everything in front would be blinded by the powerful set of halogen racing lamps she had had fitted for just such an eventuality.

Max had his shop in one of the many small pedestrian alleyways that spawn off Kaiser Street. As Jade left, the cafe owner opposite was rearranging tables and chairs to entice the passing evening trade. He pushed one chair a bit too much and it toppled over, nearly felling a man walking past.

" Hey man. Watch what you're doing ", the prominent South African accent rang out. " Ought to knock your damn head off. "

Frozen to the spot by a terrible recognition, Jade watched from the shadows.

" Sorry, it was an accident. Can I get you something ? A beer on the house ?" The owner was fussing around, picking up the chair and dusting down an aggrieved party.

" Get off, you old woman, " the man spat out, pushing him away. " Wouldn't have your damn warm beer if you paid me." With that he strode off up the alley.

Jade didn't need to see the face. She knew the voice, she knew the walk, she could even smell the animal. It was H.

What the hell was he doing out of prison, she thought. It was unbelievable, but he must have escaped.

Keeping to the sides of buildings she followed him. *Have to see where he goes.......then get the police. Bastard. What's happened ?* All of a sudden she was breathing quickly, pulse racing. The main street was full of workers going home, crowding down the footways, wide though they were.

Jade had eyes for no-one but H. She followed at a fair distance, spotting dark corners and alleys all the time that she could dive into should he turn around unexpectedly. He didn't. Why should he ? He had no reason to expect that he would be followed.

Evil icicles of dread probed around at her thoughts. She remembered threats from the dock. Empty words that could now come terribly true.

He was heading up Kaiser, towards the City Hall. Then he was gone. Turned left down a small side road. Jade sprinted for the junction.

Holding the wall, she risked a lightening glance. Just in time to see him step into a boarding house and close the door.

Jade ran back to the main street, looking wildly around for what she wanted. A little way up to her left was the Kalahari Sands Hotel. She diced with traffic in the four lane highway and then ran full tilt for the luxurious entrance.

Nearly six o'clock meant nearly the end of the working day. The end of a twelve hour shift made necessary by sickness and a general unwillingness of the powers that be to employ more men.

Piet Coetzee shifted himself to a different position in the driving seat of Traffic Patrol vehicle Zulu 50. He watched the digital clock in the dashboard impatiently, above which was taped the call sign he had to use that day. Someone at Headquarters had a sense of humour he thought, that was for sure.

Windhoek that day warranted two high powered vehicles, purely traffic orientated. The rest of the calls were given to the little yellow vans.

Right now he was bored, hot and sticky, and his back ached from constant sitting. Piet let his gaze wander back to the traffic rushing through the wide junction they were watching.

" What you got on tonight ? " he said idly, without dropping his view from the fly splattered windscreen.

" Same as you I expect, " replied his colleague, not bothering to look up from the complicated pattern he was adorning the cover of their vehicle log book with. " Cold shower, cold beer, warm bed, with a bit of luck."

" Two out of three isn't bad, " agreed Piet, " wouldn't miss the shower or the booze. Too hot for anything else, so I'll just have to take the phone off the hook."

" Yeah, then you woke up. Tell you what, I'll start selling tickets for the queue and............"

" Any unit, vicinity of the centre can deal, " crackled the radio from in between the two seats. " See the female informant, Kalahari Sands Hotel on Kaiser. Alleges escaped convict under observation nearby. Any unit to deal. "

The sound of open carrier frequency filled the car. Nothing doing. After all, it was changeover time.

" Any unit read and deal my last, " pleaded the female operator. " Kalahari Sands Hotel on Kaiser."

Driver looked at operator. They both shrugged their shoulders. Piet reached for the handset while Alex flipped open the map.

" Zulu five zero, we'll take it if you've no-one else."

" Zulu five zero, thank you." Sounds of a computer keyboard being punched in the background, " show you assigned at one seven five three. "

" Route from here Alex, " Piet clipped the microphone back onto the side of the set, " only been on this sector a couple of days. " He turned the chunky rubber key in the ignition. Could do with a run to wake me up anyway, he thought.

The big three and a half litre V8 engine burbled reassuringly while Piet waited for his route. That was the way the traffic section worked, drivers could be moved around, but operators were supposed to stay on one area and get to know it.

" Got it. Right into Auas. "

The driver reached over and turned two switches. " Music and lights I think. Till we get close. " A tiny blue pinprick of light burned in the dashboard, a repeater, reminding the driver that his rotating roof lamps were on.

The big car forced its way into the junction, bringing everything to a confused halt. Piet eased it skillfully down the wrong side of the road, past the stationary queue of vehicles, like a hot knife through butter, then tramped hard on the accelerator pushing the nose of the powerful car high in the air, like a powerboat on the ocean swell.

" First right, Republic."

The wailing siren punched a hole in the traffic ahead, vehicles climbing onto the black and white painted kerbs to get away. The roof cluster shot out bolts of blue strobe light, while red and white beacons pulsed alternately, pushing their beams straight ahead. In the relatively low light of early evening the blue showed up to the crew, reflected on buildings they passed.

" Straight over the lights."

On the wrong side of the road again, into heavy rush hour traffic. Power steering slid the big car into gaps that appeared by magic. Alex changed the wail of the siren for a powerful yelp, which had a greater urgency about it.

" Right into Francois. Then left main junction into Kaiser."

Half way down Curt von Francois Street Piet turned the lights and siren off. The road was nice and empty anyway.

The traffic car eased to a halt a respectable distance from the plush entrance. No point alarming the American tourists with a show of force.

Driver and operator got out and walked purposefully into the Kalahari Sands. The aroma of burning brake pads lingered in their nostrils.

Inside it was deliciously cold. Both of them suddenly felt dirty and unkempt, shirts sticking to their bodies with sweat and nearly twelve hours stubble adorning their faces. They faced their audience of miraculously silent, immaculately turned out hotel residents for a full forty seconds before they turned and left, certain that no-one there was about to hand over an escaped felon.

Breathing the hot steamy air outside again was almost a relief. From across the main street of Windhoek came a piercing whistle. Piet looked for the source and saw nothing but a tall, stunning young woman with a shock of blonde hair waving frantically to them. No problem there, she could stop him for directions any day of the week. He dug his colleague in the ribs.

They dodged the traffic and walked briskly up the footway to Jade.

" You called us ? "

" Yes, he's in that little boarding house down there, " Jade leaned round the corner and pointed out the doorway. " Name of Harry de Beer. He got fourteen years for a rape four years ago, and I just saw him go in there. He must have got a key from somewhere because there's no way he should be out this early. "

" How come you know all this ? " Piet asked.

" I was the victim. "

That shut them up for a few seconds. Piet covered up a slight flush by peering round the corner as well.

" What's he look like ? " vouchsafed Alex

" About thirty five to forty, fairly tall with close cropped hair. When he went in he had a light blue windcheater on........"

" ....with a thin silvery stripe down both arms, right ? " cut in Alex.

Jade nodded.

" Well he's out again, heading down the alley away from us. Piet, get the car and block him off from the other end. I'll take him from this end when you're there. "

There was a squeal of tyres as Piet launched the car into traffic again, made all the more difficult by the fact that he couldn't use lights or horn for fear of alerting the quarry.

Thirty seconds later the vehicle pulled slowly across the end of the alley and stopped. H saw the door open and the driver get out, just as slowly and deliberately. Instantly he knew that he was the target, and that there would be another of them behind him. There was no way out. He had to front it, but what the hell had he done. Then he grinned ironically. With a past like his there would always be some skeleton in the closet.

" OK guys, " H called out. " I'm making it easy. Let's sort this out. " He put both hands high in the air and then leaned up against the wall, legs spread apart.

More suspicious of the innocent attitude, Piet drew his service revolver, covering the suspect whilst motioning Alex to go forward and search.

" Nothing, he's clean. " Alex straightened up and took two paces back from H, who lowered his arms slowly.

" Now, just what is this ? " H felt a bit more confident now. If they had anything more definite he would be head down in the back of the car by now. There was the gentle rasp of a weapon being slid back into a well worn leather holster.

" Someone told us you should still be serving time, a long time, Harry de Beer. We'd like to know what you're doing out and about. "

" So that's it. Maybe this will help clear things up. " He handed over the dog-eared release certificate and then looked past the officer to Jade. " Good evening, Mejuffrouw Viljoen. " He smiled at her like a rattlesnake just released from its cage.

" You're doing business with me here, boy. " Alex stepped back in front of H, pushing a night stick none too gently into his stomach. " Don't let's forget that. "

H's smile fell away like curtains from a window. He stared defiantly back, then remembered his position and reduced his glare to the dusty broken paving slabs on the ground.

Jade retreated into the shadows. She was getting apprehensive and a bit panicky. The man was so relaxed, so unafraid. He should have run, or fought, or something. A nasty thought occurred that perhaps he was on the right side of the law for once, and he had actually been released. If that was it, they'd have to let him go. With H free again, all her worst nightmares surfaced.

Piet stood up from inside the vehicle, clipping the radio handset back as he did so. He shrugged his shoulders at Alex. That said it all. Records confirmed his story. The man was in the clear.

Piet leaned against the car, stretching his stiff back, trying to make a current of air waft down inside a sweat sodden shirt. Least they weren't going to be late off now.

Alex handed the certificate to a grinning H.

" Thank you officer. May I continue my journey now ? "

The question went unanswered. Alex waited until H had walked out of the alley before turning to Jade.

" Sorry, everything looks in order. We've confirmed that he has been officially released, on probation mind you, but released nevertheless, and he has the certificate as proof of identity on him. Nothing we can do. Are you going to be all right ? "

" Yeah, sure. No problems. It's just that I can't believe he's free. " Jade ground to a halt. She was lost for words, aghast at the turn of events.

She leant against the wall, watched the patrol car pull away from the end of the alley.

It was ten minutes before the urgency of the situation hit her square on, like a good slap in the face.

She had to get back to the farm, to warn Oupa that H was out. They were all in danger now, if his threats could be relied on. Jade had no doubt whatsoever that the arrogant Boer could be relied on in that department.

Jade ran the one and a half miles to where she had left The Hun. Not for the first time she cursed the lack of a phone link to the farm.

The powerful engine sparked into life at the first touch of the key. Jade pressed the right hand pedal hard to the floor.

*****

H coasted in towards the farm, engine off and lights out. The place was in total darkness, as one might expect it to be at three o'clock in the morning.

An evil kind of warmth grew in his belly, a satisfaction at being able to fulfill ambitions he had harboured for long hard years. The dark balaclava helmet over his face hid a grin of forthcoming contentment.

He stopped the stolen station wagon on the handbrake, avoiding the red glow of brake lights. Keys were left in the ignition and the door wide open. If he needed to leave in a hurry the last thing he wanted to have to do was to hunt through pockets for keys.

From the safety of a dune at the side of the track he watched and waited. His original plan hadn't included a chance meeting with the girl that evening, nevertheless it was quite pleasant to watch her squirm. He found himself with some agreeable thoughts about how she had improved over the intervening years. Pity she was to die with the rest of them. But now they were warned and were bound to have posted a guard, or he didn't know her as well as he thought he did.

H waited twenty five minutes, with binoculars trained on the buildings that he once knew so well. The lens glass was shaded to avoid reflecting moonlight and giving him away.

A figure walked round the corner of a barn and into view. It was one of the newly recruited workers, well, new to H anyway. Hanging from one hand was a shotgun. He was carrying it broken, exposing both cartridges at the end of the barrel.

Good, he thought, a bit of sport before down to business. He waited until the guard went out of sight again and then ran silently forward, taking cover behind one of the first outhouses he came to.

The six hundred yard sprint hadn't even made him slightly out of breath. He had trained religiously at the boxing gym, suffering long punishing sessions. Now it was going to pay off.

The guard took another fifteen minutes to reappear. Ambling round in tired boredom, he now had a cigarette in his mouth. Every so often it glowed brightly as he inhaled.

He passed the outhouse, presenting H with his back view.

It was the easiest thing to do. Twisting the knife with one hand, holding the mouth with the other. No fun at all really. Nothing else stirred as he dragged the lifeless form back behind the building he had used as cover. H unloaded the shotgun, jammed it into the sand and threw the cartridges far away.

This was indeed the same guard that he had seen through the binoculars, but with uncharacteristic cautiousness H continued to watch the farm for a further fifteen minutes.

Satisfied at last that he was unobserved, H jogged back to the station wagon, returning shortly with two plastic containers which were filled with a slopping liquid.

Half of each container he poured liberally around the verandah and into the house through the letter box. Then he placed one at the door and the second by a ground floor window. That nutter in the army days said half a petrol bomb always went better than a full one. Just about to find out.

From within a dog barked once. The again, furiously loud this time.

He hurried round to the container by the window. Carefully he lit the soaked rag at its neck and then did the same with the one at the door. This one had a much shorter fuse and would ignite the petrol very soon. Taking his life in his hands, H paused to thrust a long flickering taper through the letter box before sprinting back to his transport.

As he ran, he was overtaken by two sounds. First the sound of shouting and the determined smashing of glass. Then a dull thud and whoosh as the first of his incendiary devices went off. Thirty seconds later the other detonated.

He turned to see the second huge ball of flame collapsing onto the side of the wooden building and sticking to it like a mass of flaming treacle. The yard and buildings were lit as if by a full moon, with shadows bouncing here and there as the flames took hold and licked skywards. Two stick like figures made pathetic attempts to douse the blaze with thrown buckets of water.

He jumped in through the open door of the vehicle and was gone, unnoticed.

*****

Tears of fury and grief coursed down her cheeks. They left tell tale lines in the dirt and soot that covered her face. She would have wiped them away, but her hands were too sore from pulling at scorched and burning wood.

She sat on the ground now, looking at the smouldering mess that was her home. Molo's arm was round her shoulder and she was glad of it. He was the nearest thing to a parent she had. Buried somewhere in the middle of the funeral pyre was her grandfather, suffocated in his sleep, in the bedroom that he always kept locked.

Buried also was the dog she never really got to know and who had saved her life with his barking at the smell of petrol. He had stayed at the locked door after Molo pulled Jade out of the inferno. As she fell on the sand outside, and was about to dash back in again, the roof collapsed burying the occupants, and any hopes of rescue.

There was a small explosion from within the wreckage. A fountain of sparks flew upwards and died in mid-air.

Within a scarred mind there was yet room for logic. Her train of thought led to H, led to threats in a courtroom, led further, to the next step. Alida and Willem.

She jumped up in abject terror.

" Molo, get a rifle and come with me........NOW ! " she shouted as the bewildered man stood and looked at her. " I'll explain in the car - now get on with it ! "

*****

Dawn was well under way by the time H arrived at the edge of the Kalahari. At an ancient garage which sold petrol from a hand pump.

As before, he coasted in without the engine on and walked the last hundred yards. The killer had removed his balaclava, for he wanted the occupants to know his identity.

From behind the house the sound of wood being chopped could clearly be heard.

H climbed the steps onto the verandah. Above, the rusty advertising sign announced his presence by groaning on its hinges, just as it had done for countless years, whenever the steps were climbed.

" About time too, old man, " came the mock scolding voice from within, " this stove won't light itself. "

No reply. Usually Willem managed some sarcastic comment in return.

" What's the matter ? Chopped out your tongue instead ? I should be so lucky ! "

Still nothing. Then sounds of continued activity from the axe outside.

Alida left her sink and the washing. Must be a customer.

Coming out onto the verandah she ran into H, towering above her.

She put her hand to her mouth and screamed once, then was silenced by the awful realisation. H smiled at the figure in front of him that couldn't run away.

The smile faded and he chopped at the frail neck with the edge of his hand. Hard, sudden and vicious. Alida crumpled to the weatherbeaten verandah in an untidy heap.

Harry de Beer moved the body with his booted foot. It rolled over and the head tilted back at an impossible angle to look at him with wide open eyes.

A sudden crash from behind made him start and twist quickly round.

At the foot of the wooden steps stood Alida's husband. Around his feet were strewn the pieces of chopped wood. As he fully took in the terrible scene the colour drained from his cheeks, and took with it his reason for being alive. He could see his woman was dead, he didn't need to go any closer. Indeed he started to back slowly away. Not out of fear of the assassin, but simply because distance might make it less real.

Then the old man seemed to wake from his unreal trance. Eyes swam back into focus. With all his might he flung the axe at H and, without seeing it hit the target, started to run back to where he had been working.

An attack was the last thing H expected and as a consequence he was slow to react. The sharp blade gave him a deep gash on the left forearm, and then the shaft pivoted upward to hit him across the jaw.

He staggered back, shaking his head to clear it. Blood welled up from the injury, quickly overflowing and splashing onto the parched wood below.

He bent down and ripped a length of material from the bottom of Alida's thin cotton dress. Then he wound it tightly round his arm and tied it harshly. Even as he finished, a pink seepage was visible through the makeshift dressing.

The pain made him angry, although he had been determined to be calm and enjoy his revenge. H stormed after the old man.

At the base of the tree Willem had found the plastic bag. His hands were crusted with dirt and there was blood on them from where he had ripped nails.

The weight of the gun felt strange, as if it were somehow unreal and dreamlike. He hadn't thought about it at all during the years since Jade had buried it there.

With slow detached movements, Willem prepared the weapon.

H appeared round the corner of the house, stopping in his tracks as he saw what the old man was doing.

Willem never saw H. His mind had one idea only and it was a final, all consuming concept.

Alida was dead and with her went his only lifelong companion. He had no wish to eke out the remainder of his days on his own, with only memories for company. To use the weapon on the killer of his wife never entered his head.

The metal was cold and lifeless on his lips, barrel trembling slightly. Dear God, he prayed it would work.

The explosion echoed through still air for eternal seconds. Then there was silence.

CHAPTER

THIRTEEN

They seemed so peaceful in death. Their still faces showed nothing but calm contentment.

Jade lifted the fragile body of Alida and placed it gently next to Willem, where he had fallen. He lay face upwards on the desert floor, for which Jade was thankful, as the front of his head looked completely normal.

Then she knelt at the feet of the couple and spoke softly for several minutes. Words which were for Willem and Alida alone.

Getting to her feet, she felt a familiar block of grief on her shoulders. It was a feeling she had hoped never to experience again. There were, however, no tears for the old couple that had eased her life back into the human world, for all her tears were already shed elsewhere.

Molo stood in the background, recognising that they were too late, by an hour at least, and that there was nothing he could do to help Jade right now.

The young woman trod wearily into the house. It looked so comforting and familiar. Everything was as it had been. She moved from room to room, touching and remembering. Even the smell was the same, evoking vivid and happy memories.

In part of the old store she found a knife in its leather sheath. Thoughtfully, Jade drew it out. It was wickedly sharp and the steel shone brightly as it caught rays of sunlight. She slipped it back in and then pushed holder and contents under the belt of her well worn canvas jeans.

Outside again, she held up the flat of her hand to keep the sunlight off, and walked to the track they had driven up on. Fresh tyre marks led away in the opposite direction. To her practised eye it was like reading a map.

There really was no choice. Everything she had grown to regard as her life was in tatters around her feet. She had been here before and let the civilised law exact its punishment. Now she would follow her heart instead of her head. It was a base emotion, pure revenge. Hatred began to burn inside, like a solid core.

Jade walked quickly back to Molo who was sitting cross-legged by the side of The Hun.

" I'm going after him. Stay here until the others arrive. Look after them, won't you ? " she said, indicating the bodies under the tree.

Molo nodded in silence. The little girl he had nurtured with Tony, eased into childhood and suffered into the teens, had grown up with a vengeance. It was perhaps not the wisest course of action, but it was what he had expected her to do. Etched onto his mind was the ruins of their home, comforted by the fact that Emmy had been pulled unscathed from the inferno, along with their unborn child. Jade had nothing again, so what was there for her to lose ?

He watched her pull away in the open topped Mercedes, looking carefully from side to side in case the tracks veered off anywhere.

Gradually the sound of the vehicle faded into the distance. The dust settled back onto the sandveldt and the heavy silence of heat descended once again.

Molo sighed, a long outpouring of emotion in one breath. He looked up at the sun, gauging how far the day had progressed by its height in the sky.

He covered the bodies carefully with a tarpaulin, weighted down at the sides with stones. Then he crawled into the cool dark space under the old wooden verandah, and stretched out to wait.

*****

Ahead of her on the little used track stood a station wagon. She guessed this must be his vehicle because the tyres looked big enough to have made the marks that she was following.

Jade pressed her brake pedal gently, bringing the big car to a halt, engine still ticking over.

There was no movement in the station wagon that she could see, unless he was lying down on the seats.

Jade inched The Hun slowly forward. She could hear grit and sand being crunched under the wide tyres.

Closer now. The drivers' door was not quite flush with the rest of the body panel, as if it had been closed in a hurry.

Jade got out, drawing the knife as a precaution. The old pistol was still beside Willem's body, but he might have another gun somewhere.

After five minutes of careful stalking she risked a look in the side window. Empty. Except for the key, which was in the ignition. She reached in and turned it. Immediately all the indicator dials registered some activity. All but the petrol gauge, which refused to move.

Looking around, she saw dried blood on the upholstery and some was splashed over the dashboard. Outside there were prints in the sand and more drops of blood.

Jade put the knife away and went back to The Hun. She took out a pair of skiing sunglasses, the type which fit snugly to the eyes and have an elasticated band which goes round the head as well, and a canteen of water which she clipped to her belt. There was nothing else of any use.

The knife was the most important thing now. She would put it to good use, for the footprints led straight back into the Kalahari. Strong emotive flashbacks reminded her of the last time she had set off into the desert, a headstrong teenager with no fear and the world to explore. Now she felt no joy at all at the prospect, just a dull cold anger and an overwhelming sadness.

The girl from the desert pulled the sunshields down and started to track.

*****

Deep in the scorched inhospitable wastes of the desert are areas rarely visited by man. In fact, rain falls on the sand more often than human feet.

The route of the black leopard skirted the worst of these areas, for even she was hard pressed to find sustenance there. Two days of relentless travel had shaken muscles into shape, using up reserves of energy provided by good hunting.

Years of survival in one of nature's harshest environments had left surprisingly few marks on Torn Ear. She was older now and wiser with it. Around her muzzle were the faintest hints of silver, but any creature would be a fool to mistake signs of maturity for those of weakness or inability. If anything, she was stronger and faster than in her younger days. Her whole body had thickened and bulked out, thoroughly occupying the massive frame.

Torn Ear weaved skillfully between two thorn bushes, refusing to alter pace for the obstacles.

Beneath silky fur, however, lay the evidence of injury and healing. Now the scars were hidden, but the memories were only masked. Six months of hiding in caves, trying to rebuild a shattered body when the only tools were time and patience, would always be with her.

Her stride broke into a flowing canter that ate mile after mile. The direction was constant, the end close now.

*****

Even after the first night, Jade found the spoor incredibly easy to follow.

H was travelling fast, at a punishing rate that he couldn't possibly hope to sustain, especially with the wound that he had. There was no attempt to disguise his tracks and every so often a spot of dried blood adorned the virginal sand beside the route.

Jade estimated that he was no more than a couple of hours ahead. She could have overtaken him if she had pushed hard, but then she would be tired and vulnerable so she was depending on his injury to slow him eventually, allowing her to catch up at her own pace.

Lying on the desert floor, waiting for the dawn to illuminate her path again, Jade watched harvester termites laboriously dragging minute pieces of vegetation into their underground nests. Their shiny black heads would glisten when the early morning rays struck them, but they were good protection, allowing the termites to forage all day.

Jade drained the last of the precious liquid from the small canteen and grinned ruefully to herself. She clipped the obsolete item back onto her belt.

Despite her mission, and the harrowing experiences of death, she felt a spark of happiness. It was due partly to being back in the desert again. She had forgotten how good the raw beauty and tremendous sense of independence made her feel.

But still there was something else that gnawed away at the edges of her mind. It was definitely something to be welcomed, however at the moment it defied identification.

All during that day she tried to work it out. Of course the harder she tried to think it through, the further away any result was. The annoying thing was that the feeling seemed to get stronger by the minute.

With her mind totally occupied, the day's travel slipped by, and it was still troubling her as she squeezed the gorgeous juice from chunks of tsama melon, late in the afternoon.

Long shimmering strips of orange light announced the end of day. As she watched the golden orb sinking towards the horizon, some benign cloud drifted across, breaking up the image and sending fantasies of soft multi-coloured patterns throughout the heavens. Every sunset was different but this one was superb. It quite literally took her breath away as she gazed on, feeling that it all belonged to her.

Another silhouette moved into her field of vision, blurred and unfocused as her eyes were relaxed and gazing out into eternity.

Something about the image triggered long overdue recognition. She jumped up and looked intently towards the silhouette. It was bounding towards her now, the dark shape of a large cat. As the silhouette got closer she could make out that one ear was split neatly down the middle.

Realisation exploded into Jade's mind, just about the same time as Torn Ear took a mighty, exuberant leap, and welcomed her friend back by knocking her over.

They were ecstatic at each others company again. Years apart simply melted away like a spring snow fall. It was as if they had never been apart.

They wrestled and played for an hour and then fell asleep, entwined and reunited. For Jade, the return of the leopard was the reappearance of the only constant factor in her life at the moment. It meant stability, friendship and protection. With it came her self confidence again, and more determination than ever to avenge loved ones and banish the sense of guilt she felt at being unable to protect them, despite knowing of the threat.

When the woman woke up, the leopard was waiting by her side. Torn Ear had spent the last half hour meticulously cleaning herself, twisting and contorting to reach those far off places, seldom seen but never forgotten.

Jade sat up, stretching and taking long deep breaths of the cool night air, savouring the luxuriant chill as she always used to do, and using the memory of it to sustain her through another baking day.

As soon as there was enough light to see by they followed the spoor again. Remembering their old techniques, the pair split, each tracking down a different side of the now sporadic prints and signs. In this way their overall speed could be increased without running the risk of missing a change in direction.

The concentration was total. After the first hour Torn Ear increased her pace to a light trot, seeming to recognise the urgency of the chase. Jade did likewise, but soon found that she was forced back to a walk for about half of the time. Years of comparatively light and intermittent exercise had got her body used to the easy life. Silently she cursed the chest pains and cramp that she had to ride out.

Despite that, their progress was markedly increased. At their feet, the spoor wavered and became more ragged and uncertain. For a while it would hold steady in one direction and then throw them into confusion for a minute or two by a complete reversal. That in itself was a good sign though, for the change was not in the manner of a cunning ploy to deceive followers, rather of a quarry lost, unsure and weakening. Along the trail there had been no signs that he had eaten or drunk. Jade guessed that he had been able to take a little water with him, but she had not seen discarded or buried evidence of meals. She forced herself to keep pace with the leopard now, running through the pain barrier.

Towards evening they halted for a short rest. Still breathing hard, Jade bent down to examine fresh blood spots on the now stony ground. She touched them gingerly as if expecting an electric shock. To her delight the surface lifted off on her finger, it was tacky. The discovery breathed new life into her muscles. She straightened up and continued the chase, ahead of Torn Ear this time.

The change from sand and scrub to a stony desert surface in this area stemmed back to movements in the earth's crust, countless thousands of years earlier. Grinding of huge surface plates had created a ravine a mile or so ahead of the pair. At the start the fissure had been massive, but the sides had gradually been forced together, making it deeper but not as wide. The upheaval had engulfed the natural sand and bush environment, replacing it with a rocky surface, which over the millennia had been weathered into sharp stones and pebbles. Some conquest of this unforgiving and barren landscape had been made by the occasional thorn bush and acacia tree, but for the most part it was flat and lifeless.

It was into this desolation that the spoor now led, although they needed to follow it no longer. For outlined on the horizon they could see a human form, bent over forwards, moving slowly.

As Jade got closer she could see he held his left arm close to his chest. Some primitive instinct made H stop at this point and look round. He saw her and knew he was almost caught.

He turned and started a stumbling run away again. Blood loss and lack of water had drained his strength right away. Within a handful of paces he tripped and fell, shooting stars and rockets flashing across his mind's eye as he struggled to hang onto consciousness. With a gigantic effort he got up and continued. H knew Jade's principles of law and justice, knew they were in tatters and knew he would not see another courtroom.

Not wanting to be conned into any false sense of security, the woman drew her blade and continued the pincer movement towards their target. The leopard was on the other arm of the trap, closing surely. They had done this so many times before. It was second nature.

Like an elongated triangle, the two base corners converged on the apex.

Jade was the only one he had seen. H ran, stumbled, fell, then looked back at his pursuer getting closer, and forced himself up only to stumble and fall again.

Beyond H the ground seemed to be darker and uncertain. At first Jade thought it was just a trick of the lengthening shadows but then she began to realise that there must be some sort of barrier or change in the terrain. Whatever it was, H was getting closer to it.

The triangle grew short and squat.

H found the edge. He found the end of his pathway. Beneath his feet loose stones dropped away into the abyss, kicked by his scrabbling limbs. He shrank back from the drop, not able to go back the way he had come and not able to go forward.

In desperation he turned to face his adversary, who was about fifty yards away now.

Jade couldn't see what was behind H. She only knew that he had decided to end the matter here and now. She took the knife with her left hand, wiped the sweat from the handle and returned it to her right, gripping it tightly. She still had no idea if he had a gun, but guessed she would find out soon enough.

She advanced slowly.

With his back to the ravine, H faced the threat to his right. He saw the blade. He saw the grim determination, her face white and pale as the adrenalin drained blood from it. Actual fear surfaced in him for the first time in many years.

A noise on his left. Movement. He risked a glance and saw nothing.

Then a rush of sound. A charging black mass filled his senses. Stones scattered in showers to either side of it. Gusts of angry ferocious noise assailed him a split second before the leopard came into focus. He measured his life expectancy as being the one half second it would take her to reach him.

Animal reflexes took over at the sight of rushing death. He jumped backwards inadvertently and his feet slithered over the edge.

H fell six feet before his flailing left arm caught a jutting out bush. He hung to that branch with all the strength that remained in his racked body. He tried to reach up with the other hand, the uninjured arm. To no avail.

The axe thrown by Willem, minutes before he died, had badly damaged a tendon.

The hand slipped and slid along the branch, unable to hold tight enough. Terror gripped the heart of the man, ice-cold fingers squeezing. He slipped further, stripping leaves from the bark.

There was no strength left in the arm. Pain circled it at the wound like a vice. He could no longer feel his hand as it slid further down. He could only look up and watch it. Abject fear of imminent death opened his bowels, in the ultimate expression of primitive alarm. The sensation brought H to the brink of awareness.

In a sudden rush, the hand lost its grip on life. For an instant it hung in the air, with a single leaf between the fingers.

H tumbled into the abyss of darkness, leaving a death scream hanging in the still, heavy air.

Far below out of sight, and long seconds later, a muffled sound drifted upwards. H had made his final journey.

EPILOGUE

Looking down from the top of the huge granite kopje, which it had taken the best part of ten minutes to climb, Jade could still see the set up of their camp, even though it must have been half a mile away.

They had decided to spend the night by the side of a gigantic whale of a rock. It was too big to be considered a kopje. One Land Rover was parked at one end, and the second, quite naturally, at the other. Most of the clients would sleep, carefully bagged up of course, under the shelter of the rock. The couple who refused point blank to risk opening their eyes during the night and see nothing but velvety sky and diamond pin pricks of stars, were as usual struggling with the intricacies of tent erection.

The little trailer, normally attached to Molo's vehicle, had been unhitched and dragged into the centre. As it contained the food and cooking utensils, it formed the focal point for most of the early evening activities. The crackling, spitting camp fire was the centrepiece for the nocturnal story telling and accompanying hilarity. At the moment they were warming up with a discussion on how to get butter out of the coolbox in the Land Rover, and onto a piece of bread before the heat turned it into a thin runny liquid which ended up as globules on the sand.

Knowing the bunch she had at the moment, the topics would turn considerably more basic as time and refreshment progressed.

Tomorrow they would all cram into one vehicle, poke heads and Pentax's out of the top, and go for a game drive, returning to the same camp.

When they got back, Molo would set them to work polishing lengths of thin wooden board with wax. They would use these for ' dune-boarding ' when they reached the huge coastal sand dunes in a few days time. This idea had been a great success on previous trips and was now a regular feature. Having laboriously climbed to the top of a mountainous dune, the intrepid client lay face down on the board and grasped the front corners of it. They then launched themselves down the slope and usually got tipped off at the bottom after an exhilerating ride. Those who felt the necessity to brake could do so by digging in with their toes as they went down, but most liked to experiment to see just how fast the boards could be made to travel.

All except Jade. After thirteen days of gruelling safari she felt she was entitled to a little time off. Molo would drive them around. Besides, who was going to stop her ? She did own the company.

On most of her trips in this area she managed to find time to be on her own in this, her most favourite of places. She also had a fair idea of who she might find here.

Jade slid down the kopje, landing skillfully and surprising herself by staying upright. In the gathering dusk, and the usual cacophony of sound from the night orchestra of creatures tuning up, the young woman walked deep into relatively unmapped areas of the Kalahari.

To cartographers it might indeed have been a challenge. The woman knew it intimately however. So did a leopard, to whom it was the home range.

Jade walked most of the night, stopping to rest only once, when the false dawn showed itself. The terrain was so familiar, and to her so welcoming, she always felt she was coming home.

Approaching a familiar land mark, she looked up the gentle rocky slope that lay to her left. Jade patted the trunk of the dead mopane tree there affectionately and waited, slightly nervously, for the inevitable.

This visit, Torn Ear chose to bowl her over from behind, charging her so that her legs collapsed from under her and she ended up astride the big leopard.

Jade lay on her back while Torn Ear nuzzled up against her. When the leopard looked like rolling over her for the third time, Jade sprang up. You could have too much of a good thing.

Torn Ear shook her head to get rid of some sand. Instead of coming forward to wrestle some more, as she usually did, the leopard started up the slight rocky incline with a clear indication that Jade should follow.

Curiosity was aroused. She followed close behind the swishing tail.

Torn Ear reached the top and then set off across the scrub. She didn't bother looking behind to see if her companion was there. She knew.

Jade kept up the pace that was set, although not without a certain amount of difficulty. With the vast distances involved in travelling safaris, most of her time was spent sitting still, behind the steering wheel.

Before the human was completely exhausted Torn Ear stopped at a large acacia tree. It had foliage on it and cast beautiful shade around its base. Jade felt no guilt whatsoever as she threw herself into it.

The seed that had eventually germinated into this tree of the desert had been blown to its resting place by a hot Kalahari wind, many years ago. Its growth had been shaped by the collection of rocks, against which it now grew. Time and climate had cracked and moved the stones, creating a secure, cool environment between them.

Jade looked at the leopard and then knew why she was proudly sitting by the entrance, sheltered from the sun.

Torn Ear dived into the unique cave and returned seconds later with a minute bundle of fur, held tenderly between the jaws that had dispatched so many victims.

She placed the bundle on the cool ground in front of Jade and went quickly back to the cave.

For a minute the bundle remained inert. Then it suddenly developed four limbs with huge paws and started to explore. Torn Ear returned with a second cub, who did likewise.

On the third, and final, trip the leopard placed another identical bundle in front of her. Well, identical in every respect except that where its siblings were dark grey and beginning to develop characteristic rosettes, this cub was jet black.

It rushed forward to investigate the intruder whose scent was totally alien, bit her swiftly on the finger and retreated before Jade had a chance to gasp with astonishment. Then she burst out laughing.

With permission of their mother, Jade stroked each cub gently, just once. This was her new family and she would guard them like a jealous godmother. Nobody knew the whereabouts of Torn Ear and that's the way it would stay.

Today she would stay with the leopard and cubs and get to know them. Tomorrow she would return to the occupation that allowed her to range over the Kalahari, showing off its wonders, and educating humans to respect it.

There were some places, however, where she would never take her safaris.

The home of the black leopard with the torn ear, and her family, was one of them.

AUTHORS NOTE

Sadly, Torn Ear and Jade are creations of my imagination. Their association and friendship are likewise, but I like to think it's vaguely believable, in a Rudyard Kipling manner.

The Kalahari is very real, as are the hardships, savagery, and intense beauty which I have tried to convey. The written word cannot do justice to some of the awe inspiring scenes which still exist in one of the last unspoiled areas of vastness.

Leopards exist in the desert and people can survive abandonment. I simply brought the two together.

The black leopard and the remarkable young woman have both survived, but Africa is a place of endless possibilities and they may yet follow the spoor again.

Charles Walker
2006

Lightning Source UK Ltd.
Milton Keynes UK
UKOW06f1811050216

267846UK00002B/157/P